ncompa

where water turns rock red

Book Three

What Authors and Reviewers are saying about the *Threads West* series:

"Just want say how much I like this story. Johannes is a rascal, and I love rascals! Epic storytelling, detail, and dialogue. Rascals! Passion! Action! Real! Keep writing the *Threads West* series!"

—Max McCoy
Author of the 4 Indiana Jones and 18 other novels, Screen Writer for Spielberg's Into the West, *Multiple National Award Winner, Professor of Creative Writing*

"Diverse characters...highly visual prose...a journey of gathering suspense...delicious and devastating results. Rosenthal delivers!"

—Josephine Ellershaw
#1 international bestselling author

"Reid Lance Rosenthal outdid himself with this novel. His settings and descriptions are stunning. I survived that snowstorm—felt the cold wet damp of the snow creep into the bones. The heat of the sun, warming a back, slashing through branches. The smell of a campfire, the tang of raw game, the stench of battle. I was there every step of the way. What a trek! The weaving of the stories together and apart flows easily, creating an incredible depth of experience for the reader... But it's Reid's people who just blew me away. (I hesitate to call them characters—that would insinuate that he made them up....) They are as real—if not more so—as most of the people I have ever met. I know Rebecca better than most people I have ever gone to school with. People I worked with for years have never solidified in my memory the way Sarah and Zeb have.... Maps of Fate flowed perfectly, without having to stop and think about where everyone was and when.... I love that—running into people I know.

I felt a surprising sense of appreciation for the diversity of the author's people and plots—every group—cultural, religious, racial. Following Eagle Talon's journey, Israel's escape, Black Feather's tragedy, as well as the Europeans, all of whom come from even more layers of origin, makes for a rich blend of experience, perspective, and understanding. Americans may have started out on a million different paths, but it's the strength, determination, and perseverance that all American ancestors had in common, regardless of where they came from and how, that created your purpose—a melting pot. There's a lot to be said for that. And Rosenthal says it beautifully."

—**Alexandra Brown**
www.RomanticShorts.com

"The book is riveting and the storyline captivating. I didn't want to put the book down once I was started. I have never read romance or western novels and I thought this read would be a stretch for me but as I got into the story I immediately became engaged and found myself immersed in each word as the tale, the characters and their lives unfolded."

—*Karen Mayfield, Msc.CC*
National bestselling author of Wake Up Women—
Be Happy, Healthy & Wealthy
and co-creator of the Wake Up Women book series.

Threads West
An American Saga

Uncompahgre

where water turns rock red

REID LANCE
ROSENTHAL

BOOK THREE

Third novel of the Maps of Fate Era 1854-1875
of the Threads West, An American Saga series

To Chris [signed inscription:] He third Happy
bet you can't need
just three!

ROCKIN' SR PUBLISHING
Cheyenne, Wyoming

To my mother June, who, among many gifts, passed on to me a love of, and talent for, writing. To my editor Page Lambert, who continues to remind me just how much I have to learn about the wonderful craft of prose. To Jordan Allhands, whose unsurpassed computer and Web design skills makes access to this series possible for so many. To Laura Kennedy, tireless publisher's assistant and master of all trades. To the characters—my friends and countrymen—who live in these pages. Finally, to America, her values, history, people and the mystical energy and magical empowerment that flow from her lands.

Also available on NOOK, Kindle, IBookstore and Kobobooks.com

Book Design by TLC Graphics, *www.tlcgraphics.com*
Cover by Tamara Dever; Interior by Erin Stark
Proofreading by: WordSharp.net

Photo credits:
Cover Painting by Nationally Acclaimed Artist Debbie Sampson
"Movin' 'em Out"
flag: ©iStockphoto.com/Blueberries
leather: ©iStockphoto.com/colevineyard
leather tooling: ©iStockphoto.com/belterz
scrolled leather: ©iStockphoto.com/billnoll
parchment paper: ©iStockphoto.com/ranplett
Kansas map: iStock: nicoolay

Indians: Flickr/Accession number: SIL7-58-08/Creator/Photographer: Edward S. Curtis
Woman's face: Bigstock, bigbang, 4243237

Printed in the United States of America

ISBN:978-09907003-1-9
Library of Congress Control Number: 2013918649

Uncompahgre
where water turns rock red
Book Three

TABLE OF CONTENTS

Threads West
An American Saga

Moccasin Tracks

Book Four

Preview

Uncompahgre

where water turns rock red

Book Three

This is the third novel of the *Maps of Fate* era,
(1854–1875) of the *Threads West,
An American Saga* series.

INTRODUCTION
to the *Maps of Fate* Era Novels
of the Series

THE YEAR IS 1854. AMERICA IS ON THE CUSP OF HER
great westward expansion and the threshold of reluctantly becoming a world power. The lure of the vast
territories and resources beyond the Mississippi
explodes the population of St. Louis, gateway to the
frontier, to almost one hundred thousand, an eight-fold
expansion from just a decade prior.

One thousand miles to the west lie the Rocky Mountains, the lawless, untamed spine of the continent. The
power of their jagged peaks beckons the vanguard of
generations—the souls of a few adventurous men and
women of many cultures and separate origins, to love
and struggle in the beautifully vibrant but unforgiving
landscape of the West. America's promise of land, freedom, self-determination and economic opportunity is now

known worldwide. Immigrants from many continents exchange the lives they know for the hope and romance of a country embarked on the course of greatness.

These immigrants drawn from the corners of the earth are unaware of the momentous changes that will shape the United States in the tumultuous years between 1854 and 1875, sweeping them into the vortexes of agony and ecstasy, victory and defeat, love lost and acquired.

The personal conflicts inherent to these brave, passion-filled characters—the point of the spear of the coming massive westward migration—are spurred by land, gold, the conquest of Mexican territory by the United States, railroads and telegraphs. Their relationships and ambitions are tempered by the fires of love and loss, hope and sorrow, life and death. Their personalities are shaped by dangerous journeys from far-off continents and then across a wild land to a wilderness where potential is the only known reality.

The epic saga of *Threads West* begins in 1854 with Book One. We meet the first of five richly textured, complex generations of unforgettable characters. The separate lives of these driven men and independent women are drawn to a common destiny that beckons seductively from the wild and remote flanks of the American West.

In Book Two, *Maps of Fate*, they are swept into the dangerous currents of the far-distant frontier by the mysterious rivers of fate, the power of the land and the American spirit. Secret maps, hidden ambitions, diverse cultural traditions and magnetic attractions inherent in lives forged by the fires of love and loss, hope and sorrow, life and death, shape their futures and the destinies of their lineage.

In Book Three, *Uncompahgre,* the time nears when the first of the next generation of *Threads West* characters will be born of the brave men and courageous women who have come so far and risked all. The men and women of the saga, having reached their initial destination: pre-Denver, Cherry Creek, are each faced with life-altering decisions. Some must decide to pursue or abandon torrid love affairs that have flowered on the dangerous journey from Europe and across America. Their lives shaken by events they could not foresee and converging with souls they could never imagine, they begin to build a nation that's essence is in transition. The life threads of characters of uncommon cultures and competing ambitions meld through fate and history. The Oglala Sioux family struggles to cope with the inevitable change casting shadows upon their lands, culture and sacred traditions. The elderly slave couple, and a renegade and his young, traumatized captive introduced in *Maps of Fate,* are bound ever more tightly to the arc of the story—their tragedy and triumph-filled tales weaving into the fabric of a collective destiny. Mormons stream west in the Great Exodus escaping persecution and searching for Zion. Driven north by the Texas Rangers, an outlaw vaquero with royal blood quests for a new sense of self and place. The black-hearted renegade is unknowingly catapulted by his tortured past into possible redemption. A young man, kidnapped in his Chinese homeland, is forced to labor on the railroad but his determination to escape remains undaunted.

In the fourth and fifth books of the *Threads West* novels (*Moccasin Tracks* and *Footsteps)*, the budding enmity between North and South flares into the winds of war, and the remote fringe of the frontier is destined to descend into virtual anarchy as most of the meager army troops are withdrawn to the east. On the Front Range of the Rockies, Cherry Creek will be renamed Denver as the city booms with the effect of gold discoveries in the Pikes Peak area and the Ouray, San Juan and Uncompahgre Mountain Ranges. The first newspapers in the West roll off the presses in Leavenworth and Lawrence, Kansas, and Platte Valley, Nebraska. The Sioux will grapple with the terrifying realization that they cannot compromise with the disdainful and greedy hairy-faced ones. A massive, unfeeling tide washes over their ancient traditions and lands essential to their existence.

A young man, kidnapped in his Chinese homeland, is forced to labor on the railroad but his determination to escape remains undaunted. The Mormon family begins to establish a dangerous but devout life in the Cache Valley, their thoughts drifting occasionally to those they have met in their travels West, unaware that twists of fate and the inexorable march of history hold future surprises. Chief Guera Murah dies, and the new chief of the Uncompahgre Ute, Ouray, though beset by his own personal tragedies, keeps solemn promises to the new settlers in the valley, despite enmity between the Sioux and the Ute, and growing evidence the words of many white eyes are far different than their deeds.

Momentous changes continue in Books Six, Seven, and Eight (*Blood at Glorietta Pass*, *The Bond*, and *Cache Valley*), igniting further greed and compassion, courage and treachery, rugged independence, torrid passions, and fierce loyalties. The Civil War erupts, and the fires of deadly tumult sweep west. A Confederate Army mustered in Texas is repulsed by the Denver Militia. The Mormon family contends with the demands of the church while creating a legacy in the Cache and Salt Lake Valleys, the fate of their lineage to be dramatically affected by those they have met long before. A tidal wave of hopeful souls, some displaced by the devastation of the Civil War, add to the torrent of humanity flowing west following the trail of the strong men and women of *Uncompahgre*. The meeting of the tracks of the Union Pacific Railroad from the east and Central Pacific from the west in 1869, underpin the rise of the robber barons, cattle empires and commerce, drawing hundreds of thousands to the Rockies and beyond.

The first *Threads West* generation born in the remote and sparsely settled west, and introduced in *Moccasin Tracks*, begins to mature and contend with this cauldron of events, their lives unsettled by personal tragedies, triumphs, love and loss. Colorado, Wyoming, Utah and Montana evolve into separate and distinct territories and then achieve statehood. Law and order struggles as outlaws linger on the outer edges and range wars erupt between the landowners and the landless, sheepherders, cattlemen and sodbusters. The clash of cultures, creeds and beliefs, and bitter rivalries over the control of scarce water resources, fuels further violence and cruelty.

Soon, railroads and telegraphs will pierce even this wild land. The broken treaties with Native Americans spread into bitter and contagious conflict throughout the West. The "resolution" of the "Indian problem" leaves families and hearts broken, a dark stain on the pages of American history, and the foreboding visions of the Sioux in Book Two, *Maps of Fate*, sadly fulfilled.

You will recognize the characters who live in these pages. These brave, passion-filled characters face conflicts exacerbated by a country in transition and the accelerating melting pot of diverse cultures that mark this magical moment in American history. They are the ancestors of your neighbors, your family, your co-workers, their lives the woven threads of men and women from different locations, conflicting values, disparate backgrounds, faiths and beliefs. Forged on the anvil of the land, they are bound by the commonality of the American spirit into the tapestry that is our nation.

These decades of *Maps of Fate* Era novels of the *Threads West, An American Saga* series become the crucible of the American Spirit, forever affecting the souls of generations, the building of the heart of the nation, destiny of a people and the relentless energy and beauty of the western landscape.

The adventure and romance of America, her people, her spirit, and the West.

Threads West, An American Saga. **This is *our* story.**

www.threadswestseries.com

An American Saga

THOUGHTS FROM REID ABOUT BOOK THREE

I AM OFTEN ASKED WHY I HAVE "TIGHTENED THE CINCH" on this immense story of America set in the West. True, I love to write, and yes, I am vested in these characters. Their personalities are compilations of people both you and I have met. Each carries a part of me. They are my friends.

I am infatuated with America's people—the hands, hearts, feelings, origins, personalities and spirit that built the United States, but my enthusiasm is also fueled by my love of country, and my bond with the land. I have always believed that a nation's essential elements are its people and its lands. It is the interaction with, and between, each that determines the direction and, eventually, the destination of society—its freedom, values and exceptional qualities. The trail behind leads to the path ahead.

I am delighted and humbled that this epic saga is being avidly devoured by readers from ages thirteen to ninety-six, with readership almost evenly split between male and female book lovers. I am told this is highly unusual. Perhaps it is due in part to the affinity readers develop for the unique, distinctive personalities of the men and women who live in these pages. Some brave, others cowardly, all independent, the vicious offset by the kind, conflicted yet resolute, laced with fears yet persevering. All are passionate, though the passions of some are infused with bitter thoughts and dark actions.

Perhaps many of you turn these pages because you feel as I do—the touchstones of the past are the guideposts to the future. *Uncompahgre-where water turns rock red,* is the continuation of this tale of America, her people and the West—new lineages join the many threads of uncommon cultures, differing origins and competing ambitions that entwine into the American spirit; lives and generations woven on the loom of history, propelled by fate and freedom to form the tapestry that becomes the whole cloth of the nation. It is uniquely American, this meld of the mosaic.

My life has been spent on the lands of the West. I am fortunate to have felt the ancient energies of sun-warmed canyons. My soul has heard the whispers of Spirit carried on mountain breezes that once caressed the leathery, bronzed skin of ancestors. Logs hewn by hands long before our time have shared their energy of history, hope and courage of years long past. I'm compelled and honored to tell this tale—driven to capture the visual and memorialize the singular passions of our individual paths merging to form the shared trail of our American spirit.

I am gratified your eyes see these words and your fingers touch and linger on these pages. I hope your American soul is as touched by the reading as mine was by the writing. Feel the spirit. Think of the history. Remember the struggles. Be proud—we are America and this is *our* story.

Thank you for reading *Uncompahgre,* Book Three of the *Threads West* series.

AUTHOR

An American Saga

Book One, *Threads West, An American Saga—*
The Vanguard of Generations:

MAJOR CHARACTERS

Inga Bjorne: There are few men who are not arrested by the intensity of Inga Bjorne's pale blue eyes. Tall, beautiful, curvy and athletic with long blonde hair, her life has been contentious. She suffered the painful loss of her Norwegian parents when she was eleven. That trauma was exacerbated by a lazy, alcoholic uncle who dragged her to New York. When she was thirteen, his final abuse afforded her the courage to escape from his perverse control. For seven years, she has done what she must to survive in the bustling diversity of squalor and luxury that characterized mid-1800s New York City. The timely application of her charm, looks and wit is finally about to land her a comfortable job with the mayor of New York, Ferdinando Wood, on his house staff at Gracie Mansion. Unknown to Inga, that stroke of fortune will tip the next domino in her life and will shake the foundation of her experiences and her caustic view of men.

Jacob O'Shanahan: Feisty, stocky, cunning and violent, Jacob grew up in the grimy streets of Dublin, Ireland, living hand to mouth, his focus only on the egocentric satisfaction of the day at hand and backroom poker, which is the mainstay of his livelihood. His quick temper and greed are about to thrust him over the precipice of a major life alteration. The coarse fabric of his existence intertwines with the threads of others in a quirk of unknown destiny that neither he nor they can contemplate or prevent.

Johannes Svenson: Both irreverent and charming, his military service in the Danish Heavy cavalry as a decorated officer instilled in him a quiet but mischievous worldly confidence. Tall, lean, blond, roguish, adventurous, restless, he and his Don Juan life are adrift. Johannes, in his search to find himself, is about to be swept by the mysterious rivers of destiny into the unknown currents of an unanticipated romance and a far distant frontier.

Rebecca Marx: A dark-haired beauty with ravenous eyes and a figure that turns heads, Rebecca is petulant, clever, demanding, spoiled and reluctant to give up her creature comforts and stature in English high society. Prior to her father's death, she shrewdly assisted him for years in the family trade. She finds the decline of the business her grandfather founded demeaning. Her last hope is a bequeathed, mysterious asset rumored to be of great value somewhere in rugged, unsettled land across the Atlantic thousands of miles to the west. She has only a map, her father's deathbed whispers and his bequeath of a mysterious Spanish land grant as guides. She leaves her mother Elizabeth, frail and elderly, to sail to America and the thread of another life begins to spool toward an unknown future.

Reuben Frank: Lives and helps operate the family cattle farm with his wise but ailing father, Ludwig, and brothers Erik, Helmon and Isaac. For twenty-one years, he has led a sheltered existence on the outskirts of the little town of Villmar, on the serpentine banks of the Lahn River in eastern Prussia. Though of medium build, his frame is toughened from working cattle and the farm. His agile mind, good business sense and quiet strength have not gone unnoticed by his father, whose health has been in decline since the death of Reuben's mother several years prior. Though the family has prospered, the expansion and perpetuation of their livestock operation is confined by lack of land and the rigid social structure of 1800s Europe. The heritage of Reuben's family and the future of their cattle business is about to be placed in his hands. His ability to rise to the enormous responsibly in an untamed land he has never seen is unknown, even to him.

Sarah Bonney: Youngest daughter of Richard and Nancy, Sarah is a curvy, petite young woman with lustrous blue eyes, flowing red hair and a determined dream. Following the death of her mother the Old World holds little promise. The glowing letters from her Aunt Stella in New York, an ambition and wonder that can be satiated only by exploration and a strange pull that flows from the unknown continent across the sea, is about to collide with the realities of life, and personalities more jaded, far more cunning and infinitely less innocent than hers. Sarah has made her choice, but will it prove to be the right one?

Zebarriah Taylor: Weathered, wiry and wily in the ways of the wilderness, this tall, thin loner seeks the solitude of quaking aspens, sun-drenched canyons, gurgles of rushing high country creeks and the still waters of beaver ponds that supply him with pelts for trade. Zeb is not much partial to people, intensely dislikes settlements and towns, and distrusts most who share his skin color. He is plagued by a tragic past—orphaned as a teenager by a renegade band led by the notorious vicious killer, Black Feather. Trying desperately to forget, he succumbs to the call of the West living for a time with an Oglala Sioux tribe learning the survival ways of the wild. His few friends are members of the Arapahoe and Shawnee tribes with whom he trades. Unknown to him, his tough and leathery path will inexplicably intersect with the life journeys of others, resulting in generational influences far more broad and long-term than his lone wolf nature can foresee.

BOOK ONE — SECONDARY CHARACTERS

Adam: Freed Aborigine slave, now voluntary servant with his wife and daughter to Rebecca and Elizabeth, Adam possesses a strange and powerful ability to sense the future, but how accurate will his predictions be?

Elizabeth and Aunt Stella: Rebecca's frail and failing mother, Elizabeth, distraught over the death of her husband, Henry, terrified by and opposed to Rebecca's journey to America to try to rescue the floundering family finances. Sarah's Aunt Stella, sister of Sarah's deceased mother,

Nancy, is plump, matronly, fussy and naïve. She has promised Sarah a job in her New York seamstress shop.

Emily, Nancy and Richard Bonney: Sarah's sister and beloved, deceased parents. Emily, the co-owner of their seamstress shop in Liverpool, is heartbroken and concerned with Sarah's departure for America.

Erik: Youngest of Reuben's three brothers and Reuben's closest sibling, he is emotional, a thinker and a student of music and the arts. Soft-spoken, slight of build, scholarly and thickly bespectacled, he is greatly influenced by their father, Ludwig, and his respect and admiration for Reuben.

Ludwig Frank: Patriarch of the Frank family and Reuben Frank's father. Deep-set brown eyes, hardworking, wise and devoutly Jewish, he built a highly respected cattle enterprise in eastern Prussia but is convinced America is the future.

Uncle Hermann: Reuben's uncle, Hermann left the farm and joined the Prussian army when he was twenty-two. After being wounded, decorated and discharged, he immigrated to America with his wife, corresponding with his brother Ludwig often—eventually hiring a scout to search and map the perfect location for a cattle ranch in the West. With wavy, salt and pepper grey hair, and of medium build, he struggles with a noticeable limp—a lingering badge of his former service. After his wife's death, he has lived alone outside of New York City with his servant, Mae, a kind, heavyset Negro woman.

An American Saga

THREADS WEST

Book Two, *Maps of Fate*—New Characters Weave Into This Story of *Us*:

MAJOR CHARACTERS

Black Feather: Bitter, aggressive killer with a band of like-minded followers and renegades, with a tall, angular frame, swart features and a thin white scar above his lips, his reddish bronzed features are framed by an explosion of long, dirty brown hair. Originally named Samuel Ray-sun Harrison, Black Feather grew up on the family farm. His father, Jonathan Harrison—white, older and lanky with graying hair—traded with the Osage Indians using milk, eggs and vegetables from his Missouri garden as barter. Black Feather's mother, Sun-ray, was a full-blood Osage, statuesque and beautiful. Her athletic body was proportioned perfectly with a thin waist flared to hips made for childbearing. Her perfect white teeth were always displayed in a broad and friendly smile that complimented her wide, acorn-brown eyes. Young Samuel loved her deeply. His parents were brutally killed by white men when he was twelve years old. Set on revenge, he tracked down the killers, taking two black feathers from their dying leader's hat and adorning his hair with those symbols of revenge from that moment forward. Haunted by a tortured past, he finds himself confused by the empathy he feels for the young, traumatized woman-child he captures.

Dorothy (Dot): Black Feather's fifteen-year-old woman-child captive taken from an ambushed wagon train. A thin, blonde girl, Dorothy is traumatized and muted by the stress of her abduction and the unexpected violence that has shattered her life. Whether she emerges from her emotional shell depends on circumstances neither she nor Black Feather can foresee.

Eagle Talon: A rising young brave, leader of the younger warriors of his small, adopted Oglala Sioux tribe. The only son of war chief, Two Bears of the Northern People, he marries the daughter of the shaman, Tracks on Rock, and moves to her clan's village as tradition demands. Eagle Talon is an expert hunter and intuitive statesman, but brash. Rigidly athletic, graceful and proud, he wears eight eagle feathers in his long black hair and an ornate shield painted with an eagle feather with a superimposed image of an eagle talon fastened high on one arm, its rounded top slightly higher than his shoulder. Is he wrong to ignore the premonitions permeating his soul?

Israel and Lucy Thomas: Married for twenty-four years, these elderly slaves have opposite but complimentary personalities. Israel's curly hair has turned salt and pepper. He wears thick, brass-framed spectacles. Taught to read by Mistress Tara, daughter of an Oklahoma plantation owner, he has studied the Constitution and

Declaration of Independence through smuggled newspapers. As he learns of the rapidly evolving dispute over slavery, he harbors the dream of escaping west to freedom via the Underground Railroad but first he must overcome Lucy's stubborn temerity and resistance to change. Her rounded figure and worn features also speak of advancing age. Her wide-set brown eyes and high cheekbones are framed by brittle, grey curls of hair escaping the edges of a tight wrapped bandana.

Mac (Macintyre): The short, wide-shouldered Irish wagon master. His full, light red beard and mop of dark red hair correctly foretell a joviality mixed with a quick temper and experienced, iron leadership.

Walks with Moon: Daughter of Tracks on Rock and wife to Eagle Talon, she and her husband share love and respect. Intuitive, passionate, protective and filled with a strong foreboding about the influx of white men into Sioux lands, she is now pregnant with their first child. One friend, Talks with Shadows, has shared a frightening vision—but will this turn out to be just another silly rambling?

BOOK TWO — SECONDARY CHARACTERS

Elijah and Saley: Kentucky pioneer family, consisting of husband Elijah, sallow-faced wife, Saley and four children. Their oldest son, thirteen-year-old Abraham is a crack shot and has been responsible for putting food on the table since the age of five. Two mules pull their modified prairie schooner westward. Along with Zebbariah

Taylor, Elijah and his son are key hunters for fresh meat for the wagon train.

Flying Arrow: War chief of the Oglala Sioux village. Elderly, grey haired, still broad-shouldered but having lost the sculptured muscle of youth, he carries a long, thick staff with a heavy wooden burl at its head that has counted many coup.

Joseph: Devout young Mormon, son of Charles and heir to a future designation as an Elder, this sincere and friendly man has an unusually long pointed nose and thin face. He, his equally religious wife and their toddler son are part of a Mormon wagon train on the Exodus along to Zion in Cache Valley, north of the Salt Lake basin.

Margaret and Harris Johnson: A kind looking couple with ruddy faces, thick set builds and a keen sense of American pride. Third generation Virginians, their lineage traces back to the 1600s. They proudly fly a several-foot-wide American flag, an old Betsy Ross banner sporting a circle of thirteen stars on a field of blue, from a knotty-barked pole lashed to the side of their wagon. Margaret is handy with a musket and a mother hen to their two children, Becky and Eleanor.

Pedro: Black Feather's right-hand man, he is the Mexican lieutenant of the outlaw outfit. Heavy-set, almost fat, with deep brown eyes and a round, mustached face missing two front teeth. His short, stocky body is perennially wrapped in a once colorful serape.

Snake: A seedy, snarling member of Black Feather's band, he deviously sows the seeds of insurrection. His thin, wiry frame is perpetually covered in a dirty, heavy cotton pullover shirt hanging uneven and tattered below the tops of his leather loincloth. A sweat-stained leather headband with a single row of beads above dark brown, almost black eyes, keeps his long unkempt strings of hair swept behind his shoulders.

Talks with Shadows, Pony Hoof, Deer Track: Young wives of the braves, the best friends of Walks with Moon.

Tex: A demented member of Black Feather's band but with more loyalty to Snake, he is stocky, bald, cruel and round-faced with a scar on his neck.

Tracks on Rock and wife, Tree Dove: Tracks on Rock is the wise, highly skilled medicine man of the Oglala Sioux. His wife Tree Dove, her handsome beauty marred by smallpox, is a strong soul who often gives him counsel.

Turtle Shield, Pointed Lance, Brave Pony, Three Knives and Three Cougars: The band of young braves of the Oglala, they are close friends with Eagle Talon.

May 27, 1855

$\mathscr{L}$OSS OF A BROTHER

"DON'T LIKE THIS AT ALL. NOPE, NOT LOOKING FORWARD to it. Not one bit, Buck."

The mustang's ears pricked at the sound of Zebbariah Taylor's raspy voice. The tobiano gelding snorted agreement. The mountain man, holding his reins in one hand and a lead rope in the other, twisted in the saddle and glanced behind him at Red, the wagon master's spirited sorrel mare.

The eastern front of the Rockies rose jagged in the early afternoon sun. Zeb slouched forward again and sighed, his eyes roving the horizon. Buck swiveled slightly back toward him, his sunlit head standing out in sharp contrast to the spring green of the grassy, rock-strewn slope. Patches of bitter brush and sage punctuated the soft plateaus as they descended toward the South Platte Valley. Miles out, the blemish of a small settlement was visible, flanked by clusters of distant tipis.

"What am I going to tell Mac's brother, Buck?"

Buck whinnied and shook his head slightly. Leaning forward, Zeb patted the gelding's neck. Behind him, Red answered the mustang's empathetic call.

Zeb nodded back at the mare. "Yep, I miss Mac too." He sighed again and straightened his tall, thin, buck-skin-clad frame in the saddle but he couldn't quite free his shoulders of their droop. One hand absently stroked his mustache where the tip hung between his lips and the dark grey tinged stubble of his jaw.

The well-muscled horses picked their way steadily toward the Cherry Creek settlement. Lulled by the sway of the mustang, Zeb's mind drifted between scattered images of time spent with Mac over the years.

Their meetings were few, Zeb's trapping cabins being hundreds of miles southwest in the mountains, far from the tiny but growing settlement of Cherry Creek. The mercantile was the primary buyer of Zeb's furs and he and Mac soon became close friends.

Mac and his brother Randy had been fresh from Ireland in the early 1840s, searching for adventure, opportunity and a place where being Catholic didn't matter. They began as traders and teamsters. Then ten years back, they started the ramshackle *Gart's Trading Company and Mercantile*. Randy handled the store and local trade with Indians and whites. Mac guided wagon trains of settlers west, building a reputation as a jovial but no-nonsense, quick-tempered wagon master. On his return trips to St. Louis to organize the next band of westward pioneers, his wagons were always loaded with leather, pelts and occasionally, salted buffalo meat, all of which were in ever-increasing demand as St. Louis expanded eight-fold to one hundred thousand people in the late 1840s and 1850s.

A yellow jacket hovered around Zeb's face and he slapped at it with an absent wave of his long, callused fingers. The insect's annoying drone broke his reminiscence and dredged up the shock and anger he felt when, two weeks before, he had discovered Mac's short, extremely powerful, broad-shouldered form crumpled, one leg bent haphazardly under the other, his bloody hand still clutched around the shaft of an arrow protruding from his wool shirt. The coagulated dull red-brown of blood and death contrasted oddly with his bright red hair and long beard.

Zeb shook his head slowly. *Bad enough if it would've been Pawnee...but by the hand of that sneaky bastard, Jacob.* He paused and looked up at the sky. "You didn't deserve that Mac, my friend; you surely didn't." Behind him, Red whinnied again and Buck shook his head, the leather of the hackamore squeaking slightly in the spring heat of the afternoon.

"Buck, I suppose we'll tell Randy straight out. No other way to do it."

With an effort, Zeb tried to turn his thoughts in a different direction, toward Sarah and her bright blue eyes. His mind's eye drank in the petite, shallow curves of her trembling slender figure, the freckles across the bridge of her nose and her lips—not too full—perfectly shaped. His memory drifted to the creamy smooth of her skin and her small well-formed breasts, exposed when, at her frantic, almost hysterical insistence and in spite of his embarrassment, he had cut the bloodstained chemise away from her skin. That had been just a few weeks ago, on Two Otters Creek.

Zeb felt the heat rise in his cheeks and knew it wasn't the sun. He half grinned to himself. The soft curls of her red hair had faded to burnished auburn and had grown longer over more than two months on the trail. The prairie schooners had ventured a thousand miles from St. Louis, triumphantly, yet tragically. They had arrived just hours before and the wagons were circled behind him now on the high ground, five miles northeast of Cherry Creek.

"She seemed to like them high-top moccasins I made for her, don't ya think, Buck?" The mustang rolled his eyes and Zeb laughed. "Jealous are ya?" Zeb's mind wandered back to the first time he had seen her, small, huddled and defensive, her face white and pinched, sitting as far as she could from the stocky towheaded man on the wagon seat as he drove their team onto the barge on the east side of the Mississippi. Zeb's mules had also sensed the dark energy between the two as Sarah's wagon had passed them, nervously shifting their weight from left to right.

The scene unfolded in his mind vividly: the upstream breeze rustling, the sparkles of the Mississippi current in sun-reflected bursts, the lap of the water against the thick planks of the barge's hull as it made sluggish progress toward the west bank, the murmur of current, the hollering of men, bleats of oxen and nickers of horses floating in the light wind. Then there was the altercation, shouts, the meaty hands of the towhead closing around Sarah's delicate neck, her lips parted, gasping for air as her thickset companion pinned the back of her head against the tailgate of their wagon. Zeb could almost feel the texture of the brown canvas jacket under his fingertips as he reached out with one long, lanky arm, his fingers jabbing the man's broad bulky shoulders.

"Stay out of my business, coonskin," the man had spat. Zeb remembered the feel of the handle of his fourteen-inch blade as he slid it from his back scabbard and the venomous look in the man's eyes as they faced off. *Should have kilt you right then, you dirty bastard...and Mac would likely still be alive.*

Sarah had been trembling then too, as he led her back to Buck and the mules. Her eyes had traced the twin, long, purple scars that ran their way unevenly from below his ears to his chin and then his hands were on her shoulders, steadying her as she retched uncontrollably over the side of the barge.

He smiled as he recalled Buck's nuzzle to the back of his head as he watched the unintentional, provocative sway of her hips as she made her way back to the wagon and her glowering traveling companion. The mustang had cocked his head to the side, his big brown eyes staring directly into Zeb's. "What the hell you lookin' at, Buck?" he'd said. "If I want to say more than five words to a woman once every ten years, that's my business." He smiled now, thinking about his one-sided conversation with the horse.

A jackrabbit exploded from behind a sage bush causing Buck to tense up momentarily. "Think I should make my move too, eh, Buck? I'm twice her age, ya know. She can't be much more than eighteen and she's a lady—this ain't like you and me." The mustang snorted again. "All this solves nothing," he sighed. "Right now, we gotta deal with Randy. Never had to tell a white man he don't have a brother no more."

***

AN HOUR LATER, ZEB REINED THE HORSES IN FRONT OF a partial brick, two-story building. The sign, though newly painted just the year before, had already begun to fade from the high altitude sun. *Gart's Trading Company and Mercantile.* The main building was attached to the original low, rambling, wooden buildings that seemed in danger of collapse. Several large, ingeniously rigged, heavy canvas tents contained piles of pelts. He swung one long leg over Buck's head and dropped to the makeshift street, dusty with the unhurried bustle of carriages, wagons, horses and people. An air of subdued excitement and energy, which Zeb had never been partial to, buzzed up and down the block-long settlement. *Like too many squirrels in a tree.* He carefully grasped the stock of the 10-gauge shotgun Mac had purchased in St. Louis. The 1855, state-of-the-art Colt five-shot cylinder was wrapped in leather. He withdrew it slowly, cautious not to scratch either it, or his own .52 caliber Enfield, which also rested in the lowest tier of the double-belly scabbard, below his .52 caliber Sharps rifle.

He stood for a moment, thinking and then walked reluctantly into the mercantile. A long counter stretched on one side of the store. Its display case held .36, .44 and .45 caliber Colt Navy, Dragoon, Army and London revolvers. Brand-new Sharps, Springfield and Enfield rifles and muskets were displayed on pegs in the wall. There were cases of powder, trays of cartridges for breechloaders like his, containers of muskets and bullets and rows of tools and sundries.

Two harried clerks tried their best to accommodate a queue of customers. At the opposite end of the counter, a broad-shouldered, red-haired man with a beard barked out orders in a loud, Irish brogue. It was Randy's usual position in the store. Randy and Mac weren't twins; Mac was a year older but there was no mistaking them as brothers. Built the same—short, wide and powerful—they had identical accents and startlingly similar mannerisms.

Zeb began to move toward the counter. Randy's eyes caught his above the sunbonnet of the woman he was assisting. A wide grin creased his face but faded immediately at Zeb's somber stare, replaced by a look of earnest questioning. The woman was talking animatedly to him but he ignored her and leaned backward to peer out the wavy, blown glass windowpanes into the street-side window. Zeb knew he could see Buck and Red and the two panniers behind Mac's empty saddle, bulging with Mac's belongings.

"Thomas, would you help this lady please?" The young clerk's head snapped up from the invoice he was writing, his eyebrows arched. Randy came around the counter with tentative steps absent his usual jovial bounce. He reached out his hand and shook Zeb's firmly, his eyes peering intently into the mountain man's. There was a long moment of silence.

"Dead or hurt?"

"Dead."

Randy's shoulders sagged and under his beard, Zeb could see his cheek muscles quiver. He held up Mac's shotgun. "He was mighty proud of this. I have his Muskatoon Smoothbore out there on Red, too."

Randy's voice was quiet. "I thought the wagon train was a little overdue. I expected you midmonth."

"The rivers back in Missouri were up from the early melt off the Ozarks. Got held up for several days crossing the Gasconade. We took that southern leg to avoid the Missouri-Kansas border towns and cut northwest across a corner of Kansas. Mac was concerned about the ruckus between the pro-slave outfits and the free-staters. Bushwhackers and red shirts, he called them. He didn't wanna have nothin' to do with them. Then we got hit with a hell of a blizzard. That slowed us up several days gettin' to the main Mormon trail and Fort Kearney. But worst was a big fracas on Two Otters Creek. Fifty or more Pawnee warriors came down on us like the wrath of hell. No time to even circle up."

Zeb realized he was talking fast, too fast and too much. It was nerves but he couldn't stop running on. Randy listened, shoulders still sagging.

"We weren't doing none too well either, 'til a small band of Sioux hit the Pawnee from the other side.

Damnedest thing I ever saw. Seems they were from the Oglala tribe up on the Powder. I wintered with 'em when I was just a pup on my way west. We lost nine folks...." His mind flashed back to Johannes' shoulders hunched over the tall, slender form of Inga, her blue eyes staring skyward without sight from between Nordic blonde curls. He pushed away the memory. "Several more got hurt. Three died of cholera just north of here, a day's ride. Burned the wagons with 'em in it."

Deep pain clouded Randy's pale blue eyes. "And Mac?" he whispered.

Zeb wrestled with how much to tell him. *Either just mention the arrow or the whole story?*

"His arm got pretty tore up in the fight. He lost a lot of blood." Anger boiled in Zeb's chest, tinged with regret and guilt. He took a deep breath.

"That was how he got killed?" Randy's eyes narrowed.

Zeb thought for a moment. *He deserves to know.* "There was a rogue son of a bitch on the wagon train. A woman beater, rapist, cardsharp and, I suspect, murderer before. I had several chances to kill him and I should've. He and Mac got into it early on. First night, in fact. Mac taught him some respect with the bullwhip but he was cunning and smart. While we were preoccupied after the ambush, he must have sneaked down to Mac's wagon. With the blood loss, I 'spect Mac couldn't hold him off. He killed your brother with an arrow. Stabbed him in the chest. There was a struggle but Mac lost. The bastard tried to cover his tracks to make it look like the Indians done it."

Randy's cheeks flushed, his eyes narrowed dangerously and his jaw tightened. "Where is the son of a bitch? That judge up at Fort Laramie is too far. We can have our own trial. I'll string him up myself."

Zeb shook his head slowly. "No need, Randy." He reached out his hand and squeezed the thick upper arm of his longtime friend. "His name was Jacob O'Shanahan." Randy blinked. Zeb nodded, "Yep, Irish too. He's dead."

Randy turned to look back out onto the side street where the horses stood. His gaze landed on Mac's empty saddle; then he turned back toward Zeb. "Well, I hope he suffered. How did he get kilt?"

Zeb's mind flashed back to the small boot prints of Rebecca and moccasin prints of Sarah along Badger Creek, and the thick form of Jacob lying face down in bloody, matted grass by the creek. Each of the countless stab wounds to the Irishman's back had turned the canvas of his jacket a mottled, dark, brown-red. There was a frightened look on the two women's faces when they emerged from the woods where they had been hiding. He had kept the arrow that killed Mac as evidence, determined to bring Jacob to justice somehow. He plunged the broken half of the very same arrow into the dead man's back and then rolled the corpse over, brushing out his tracks and those of the women. He scalped the Irishman to make it look real and tossed the piece of flesh and dirty blond hair into the creek. He remembered Sarah and Rebecca's eyes as the three of them swore a pact never to tell, just before he let them loose in the woods upstream of Jacob's body, near the wagon train.

He looked back into Randy's eyes. "Pawnee—an arrow in the back, but they played with him with their knives and scalped him."

Randy nodded. "That's no pleasure to me but then again, I guess they saved me the trouble." He sat down heavily on a powder keg. The wooden slats groaned with his weight. He raised his fingers to his forehead and rubbed his hands up and down his face and then he looked back up at Zeb, his eyes misted. "I will never have another brother. Besides that, don't know how to replace him. Got to run this place, Zeb. We was partners since I was twelve. Things worked good with him handling the wagon trains from St. Louis, then the freight back east and me here at the store. What am I going to do?" Randy looked down at his feet and shook his head slowly.

Zeb stood, silent. He desperately wanted to walk out of the store, mount Buck and get right back up to the wagons and Sarah. "Don't rightly know, Randy." The mountain man reached out a tentative hand toward Randy's shoulder but then withdrew it.

Randy looked up at him again, "What about you, Zeb? You know the way. Folks listen to ya. I've seen it. You take the wagons back and forth. Way better money than hauling pelts in those damn mountains and worrying about whether you will keep your hair or get mauled by some riled up bear. You keep goin' and you'll have claw marks down your other cheek, too."

Absently, Zeb ran his fingers down the two purple scars that stretched from just under his right ear almost to his chin. He shook his head. "Grateful for the offer

Randy, but my heart's up there in them mountains and I made a commitment to some folks way back in St. Louis to help them get across. And..." he fell silent, "... I may have met someone."

Randy's head jerked up, a smile momentarily cutting through his grief. "Met someone? You? I'll be damned." He chuckled humorlessly. "What's Buck say to this?"

Zeb smiled, held out his hand and Randy rose and shook it. "I know bringing me the news and Mac's stuff didn't bring you no pleasure. Thanks."

Zeb nodded his head once, turned to go and then turned back. "Your supply wagons are up with the train. John got his leg shot up in another little run-in we had with some renegades. We left him in Fort Kearney to mend. I 'spect he will be along later this summer."

"Charlie?"

"Dead. The Pawnee."

Randy shook his head.

"I'll get the supply wagons down to ya in the next day or two. Most likely'll be several folks down from the train on their way south to get cattle. One is named Reuben—dark-haired, young, on the quiet side, about six foot. Not big, but powerful. Rides a tall palomino. His sidekick is Johannes—Danish accent, very tall, blond, soldier-type. You'll recognize the army in him right off. He lost his woman up there on Two Otters Creek. Reuben was Mac's assistant...and friend. Mac was teachin' him. The survivors voted him head honcho after Mac was kilt. Did a good job of bringin' the wagons in. Smart as a whip and tough. Has a pearl-handled Colt

Navy he carries low on the right hip. One of them holsters you don't see much of. They need a couple of good hands. If you know of any, give them their names."

Randy's eyes widened. "A pearl-handled Colt? You said you had a run-in with renegades. Is this the kid that shot six of 'em out of the saddle in less than half a minute?"

"You heard about that already?"

"Hell, the whole territory has heard about it. We heard from some army when they came through, headed south to powwow with the Ute. And they heard from some Mormon wagons coming through Fort Laramie headed toward Salt Lake—which reminds me, I got some letters for your folks that got dropped off a few weeks ago by the stage out of Fort Laramie. They had heard about it from someone along the trail, too. Is it true?"

Zeb nodded slowly. "Yep, it's true. In all, we took eight out of that bunch. Must've been thirty to start with. It was Black Feather's band, Randy."

The bearded man's shoulders jerked, "You mean that scarred scum that burned out your family's farm back there in Missouri when you were a tyke?"

"Yep."

Randy looked at him closely. "He still alive?"

Zeb felt his lips purse tightly. "He is."

Randy shook his head, "Let me fetch them letters for you." He turned and walked heavily into a back room. Zeb stood, slowly stroking one side of his mustache.

Randy's hand shook slightly as he sorted each envelope, handing some to Zeb. "You got a Rebecca Marx on your train?"

"Sure do. She's Reuben's woman." Zeb chuckled, "Though neither of 'em will admit it. A real lady, from London, temperamental but a spine of steel and the best damn female shot I've ever seen."

"Well, there's two letters to her from England and another here for Reuben. I think it's from Prussia, if I can read it right. A long damn way for letters to travel."

"Well, maybe that's because it's a long damn way."

Randy wiped his eyes with the back of his sleeve, bit his lip and handed the stack of envelopes to Zeb. "Here, I can't focus too good. Check them over and make sure they are all in your bunch."

Zeb sifted through the letters, mouthing the names as he carefully and slowly read them. He handed two back to Randy. "That gal and feller is dead. Cholera."

"I'll make sure they get returned with a note," said Randy, placing them gently on the counter.

"One more thing, Randy, if you wouldn't mind doing me a favor?"

"Sure, Zeb."

"You know Mac was awful attached to that mare. Feisty, obstinate, damn sorrel. Never saw that horse take a likin' to anyone other than Mac—and this Rebecca woman. She and that horse get along well—same personalities. I offered the horse to her cause I figured Mac would've done the same. But she thinks she might be going back to England. So—I'd consider it a personal favor if you give that horse to her if she decides to stay and says she wants it. She was good friends with Mac and I'm sure he would've had it that way, too."

"I'll do that, Zeb."

Zeb strode from the store into the bright sunlight. He slowly untied Buck from the hitching post and, arrested by an unexpected vision of Sarah's smile, paused with one toe of his high-top moccasins in the stirrup and one hand on the saddle horn. *There's been enough death.*

He swung into the saddle, "Let's get back to the wagons, Buck. I think I'm going to take me a walk. You're gonna have to amuse yourself for a spell." Buck craned his neck back toward him, then pointed his muzzle forward and shook it impatiently against the reins, stepping into a trot.

May 27, 1855

*G*IRL TALK

SEVEN MILES NORTHEAST OF WHERE ZEB WAS GIVING
Randy the painful news of Mac's death, Sarah stood on
the rough ground of a small rise, surveying the circle of
prairie schooners and Conestogas that lay fifty feet east
of her. Their once bright, canvas tops were muted and
streaked with the rigors of a thousand miles of weather,
river crossings, sun and dust. Many had bullet holes or
patches where arrows from that horrible day back on
Two Otters Creek had torn the rigging. The customary
small, cautious evening cook fires had been replaced by
several large fires, thigh-high flames licking the cool
clear air, clusters of pioneers excited to finally have
arrived at Cherry Creek, trading stories, sharing plans,
reviewing goals and saying goodbyes.

Sarah snuggled into her shawl, then laid a blanket on
the ground and sat down, curling her legs under her
until she was comfortable. She hadn't wanted to be part
of the jubilant crowd. She had had little time to herself
since leaving Liverpool and had much to think about. *I*

am not the same woman who had eagerly embarked the *SS Edinburgh* in Portsmouth Harbor five months ago. The surety of continuing her English seamstress career with her Aunt Stella in New York had evaporated and her dream of opening her own shop had—at the very least— been postponed. She had made new, close and unexpected friends during the journey west and, sadly, had lost some of them.

Below her stretched the broad basin of the South Platte, low-lying folds of lands that seemed to stretch and roll forever. The fires and occasional oil lamps of the several hundred residents of Cherry Creek shined far away, lonely flickers of light in a land of creeping shadows, their luminescence, like the faintest stars, daring the approaching night. *I have lost my innocence...and carry his spawn in my belly. Conceived not of love but rape.* At the thought, anger rose from her womb and her teeth bit into her lower lip. Tears came to her eyes and the expanse before her blurred. She blinked them away and looked to the west. The sun hung suspended behind dark, silhouetted mountains, the thin layers of softly glowing clouds laced with silver and bold strokes of fiery orange-red. Underlying them, a deepening purple sifted down from the highest peaks and curled around the foothills, spreading like a fog of color across the rolling plains. *This land, the people; I had no idea how it would call to me.* Transfixed by the sheer power of the scene, Sarah felt tiny and insignificant yet empowered at the same time. *So many choices.*

Her attention was diverted by three ground squirrels, a mother and two babies, thirty feet in front of her. Sarah cocked her head to the side and smiled. "Cute," she said aloud. The mother studied her two young kits, wiggling her nose with an apparent air of bored detachment.

She watched as the two young squirrels wrestled playfully. Suddenly, one turned and antagonistically knocked the other over, biting it. The injured sibling squealed and the mother chattered angrily. Sarah felt a sharp twinge in her belly. She held her hand to her rounding stomach, trying to soothe the pain. The squirrels ran down the rise, disappearing in the grass, the smaller of the two kits limping where the other had bitten it.

As she watched the animals disappear, she saw Rebecca walking toward her from the wagons. The petite, curvy brunette—though not swathed in London's finest that she loved so much—was clothed in a loose-fitting, light, riding dress, the high quality, pleated wool skirt clinging to the curve of her hips. A deep blue cotton shirt peeked above the cardigan top of an expensive grey knit woolen sweater, the ends of her dark brown, almost black hair falling over her shoulders. That she remained the best-dressed woman on the wagon train was unquestionable. "Sarah, may I join you?" she asked, her smile somewhat obscuring the angry red, unhealed scar over her upper right lip.

Sarah patted the blanket beside her and Rebecca gathered up her riding dress and sat down heavily, slightly off balance, almost rolling backward.

"That was graceful, milady Marx."

Rebecca laughed. "Wasn't it?"

Rebecca looked out over the landscape, breathed in deeply, held it and then slowly exhaled. Sarah studied her profile, high cheekbones, evocative curve of nose and almost perfect lips. Rebecca had also embarked on the *Edinburgh* at Portsmouth but they had not begun as friends. Their competitive interest in Reuben—Rebecca aloof and sarcastic and Sarah unimpressed with Rebecca's overdone high society demeanor—had fueled their immediate abrasion. They had sniped at one another throughout the five-week voyage, even during immigration at Castle Garden before they had gone their separate ways—neither of them anticipating how the threads of their lives were destined to interweave again.

The two women sat silently side by side, watching the shadows elongate as the high peaks absorbed the sinking sun, one bright, yellow bit at a time. "It truly is magnificent," Rebecca said, an unmistakable note of wonder in her voice. Sarah said nothing. The moment spoke for itself. She drew the shawl up over her shoulders, the temperature dropping in concert with the disappearing sun. The painful twinge in her stomach seemed to be gone.

"Sarah," Rebecca was looking at her with earnest, wide eyes, "Can you remember England?"

"Sometimes it's difficult," she admitted. "I have flashes at times. The inside of our sewing shop, the jostle of shoulders when I walked to the market but it wasn't long after we left St. Louis that I could not even remember the smell."

Rebecca nodded. "I can't recall the color of the front door to our London home—not even the color of the marble steps or how many up to the landing."

"And the sound. You know, Rebecca, that constant noise that you only notice when you don't hear it?"

"There was a night on the wagons," said Rebecca, staring at the last remnants of sun, "that I sat on the banks of the Missouri and realized what was important only months ago was fuzzy, dreamlike—somehow, it seemed like forever. London is like a book I read long, long ago. Not the place where I used to live."

"I know, Rebecca, I know. My anticipation of America was the hustle, bustle and throngs of New York, working in my Aunt Stella's shop, saving money to open my own. I really had no idea—"

"—that this," Rebecca swept her arm grandly, "could exist."

Sarah turned to her, surprised at how effortlessly Rebecca had finished her thought. She put her arm around the brunette's shoulders. Rebecca did the same and they leaned their heads together.

"It changes you somehow," whispered Rebecca.

Sarah nodded, feeling Rebecca's hair brush her cheek as she moved her head. "Perhaps more than change, it *alters* you—as if you've stepped into a bright sunny room with no walls and you can't go back." She paused for a moment. "Have you decided, Rebecca?"

Rebecca sighed. "There is so much to consider. For some reason, I expected Cherry Creek to be *more* than it is...."

Sarah started to laugh, pointing at the sparse cluster of lights all but swallowed in the massive descending blackness. She flourished her hand with an exaggerated grandeur. "Imagine, a great city!"

Rebecca chortled. "Reuben let me look through Mac's telescope this afternoon when he and I rode. I couldn't hold it very still but I got the impression that it is one dusty street and part of another, all less than a block long. I'm not even sure there is a solicitor there. I've no idea how I am going to conduct business or get my family's land sold...if that's my ultimate decision." After several seconds of silence, she added, "It seems I have come a great distance, yet not arrived."

"I know. I shared your anticipation of Cherry Creek but there seems to be but a few buildings. It's more an Indian village," Sarah sighed. "I had no idea. I'm not even sure there's a place to set up a sewing shop—or that there would be any customers. Maybe they are all like Zeb and they do their own sewing."

That thought made them both laugh. "I'm sure there arc still plenty like me down there who wouldn't know," Rebecca said, "and who don't want to learn which end of the needle to use."

Sarah's head jerked with a thought. *The maps.* Jacob's stolen gold map was now in the secret compartment at the bottom of her carry bag, along with her money. "Rebecca, did you get the opportunity to ask Reuben about the map?"

"No, he's been too preoccupied with the excitement of getting to Cherry Creek. And he has said some odd things. I think he knows good and well that Jacob did not die by the Pawnee."

Sarah was startled. "Reuben's very much in love with you. You know that, Rebecca, don't you? And...and...you told Inga and me that you had..." Sarah carefully considered her words, "...you had *been* with him."

Rebecca shook her head, "It does not matter. I know he cares for me...." Her voice trailed off and she looked up into the sky. "And our passion is...is far more intense than even my wildest wonderings before I gave him my virginity but I'm not sure that it is love. In the end, Sarah, we all have our own paths."

Sarah fell silent, thinking about Rebecca's words. The chatter from the large campfires drifted in the breeze. Below the small hill where they sat, the dim form of a horse and rider moved across the land toward them.

"It's Zeb," Sarah smiled. The mountain man dismounted where the ground squirrels had been, his buckskin-clad leggings blending with the color of the grasses as if he had grown from the land. He walked up the shallow rise toward them, Buck close behind.

"Hello, Zeb," said Rebecca.

"Rebecca. Miss Sarah. Purty night."

"I'm surprised to see you back, Zeb. For some reason I thought you'd stay in town, perhaps with Mac's brother, Randy." Sarah could see Zeb's head shake against the light of the first stars. His hands moved in the fading light, the skin backlit when the fires behind them occasionally flared, their greedy flames feeding on yet unburned buffalo chips. Sarah realized he was rolling a cigarette.

"How did Randy take the news of poor Mac?" asked Rebecca softly.

"Good as can be expected." Zeb shook his head, "but it ain't sumthin' I want to ever do again."

"Oh, almost forgot," Zeb said, reaching into his fringed jacket, his hand fumbling underneath the leather. He drew out three envelopes. "Seems to be mail for you, Rebecca. Got some for Reuben and a few of the others, too. I'll go over and pass 'em out. There was one for Thelma and the Doc," he said in a low tone. "Randy will return them with a note."

He handed Rebecca two envelopes. "And this one," he flapped it back and forth, "is for Reuben. I can give it to him or you can; makes no never mind to me."

"How did these letters get here before us, Zeb?"

"Stage has been running between Laramie and Independence since 1850. Occasionally, the army drops down this way from Laramie and when they do, they bring whatever's up there that belongs to fellas down in Cherry Creek."

He started to lift the cigarette to his mouth, then, sensing Sarah's disappointment, added, "Sorry, Sarah, that's all there was. I'm gonna go hand out these others. Would you walk with me?"

"How could any woman refuse such a gallant, well-mannered request?" Sarah answered in a teasing voice. "I would be delighted to."

Zeb stretched out his hand. Sarah took it and he pulled her to her feet. "I'll be excited to hear what's in your letters, Rebecca," she said as they turned to go. "I hope it's news from home."

Rebecca stood at the rear of the wagon, the two letters clutched in one hand, Sarah's blanket tucked under one arm, her other hand lowering the ladder. She paused for a moment, watching the petite redhead in a traveling dress and the tall, lanky mountain man, his fringed leather etched by the brightness of the fire as he stood passing out the letters. "That would be perfect," she murmured to herself.

May 27, 1855

ENTLE SURPRISE

ZEB AND SARAH WALKED SIDE-BY-SIDE TOWARD THE
bonfires. Zeb stepped over the wagon tongue and held
out his hand. *Such a nice man.* Sarah took it and he
patiently helped her over.

The letters were quickly distributed, Zeb calling out
"Mail!" and then the addressees' names, struggling with
the occasional pronunciation. The lucky pioneer generally ran to him, grabbing the envelope from his
outstretched hand, turning immediately away and fumbling to open it with a muttered, "Thanks, Zeb."

Sarah caught a glimpse of Rebecca, about to climb in
their wagon, but pausing for a moment to look over
toward the fire.

Several of the people around one fire tried to engage
Zeb in conversation but he would have none of it. "Got
things I got to take care of. We'll talk in the morning
before you pull out."

The chore dispatched, they walked toward the far side of the circled wagons. Then she saw Johannes. His lithe six-foot-six form and blond hair, reddish in the firelight beneath the light colored, flat-brimmed cowboy hat was unmistakable. He was striding rapidly toward them leading his bay, Bente. "Sarah! Zeb!" he called out in a thick Danish accent, "I'm headed out, over the east ridge we crossed this afternoon. Got a night guard out in every direction, although we will rotate twice, instead of once, tonight. Tomorrow's a big day and the men need time to get organized." He smiled. "All are excited, as well they should be. I don't want to keep anybody from their families too long tonight."

"What about you? Want me to spell ya later?" Zeb asked.

"No; I appreciate the offer, Zeb." Johannes looked up at the sky to the east. "I will enjoy the night out there. Would you tell Reuben where I am and about the guard rotation for the night?"

"Sure thing," Zeb answered.

Johannes' eyes drifted down to Sarah. "I went through Inga's things," he said to her, pausing to take a deep breath. She noted a tremor in his voice as he spoke again. "Rebecca helped but it was mostly me." He took another deep breath. "She doesn't think any of her clothes will fit either of you. Inga was too tall."

She could tell this was difficult for Johannes. He dropped his head, a catch in his breath. "But I know you and she were particularly close. There is one thing I found that I am sure she would like you to have." He raised his eyes to her, turned, walked around the horse and fumbled with the saddlebag. He reached in and pulled out something. Leaning on his horse, she heard him clear his throat. A few moments passed before Johannes walked back to them.

Inga's silver brush shone and reflected in the firelight in his outstretched hand. Sarah took it slowly, reaching out and resting her fingers on his arm. "Johannes...I..."

He didn't let her finish. "That was the only thing she had from the old country. She treasured it, as you know. She said it reminded her of her parents before their death when she was young and the fjord where she grew up. I'm sure she'd want those happy memories to flow through to you."

Before Sarah could say anything, Johannes nodded to Zeb. "Tell Reuben, would you?" Then he abruptly turned, leading Bente away from the wagons and toward the east. Zeb and Sarah watched them both disappear from the firelight.

Sarah looked down at the brush and turned it in her hands, remembering. The fire sheen on the silver metal blurred. "Oh..." she said softly.

Zeb put his hand on her shoulder. "Let's go," he said quietly, leading her away. They stepped outside the curved line of rigs, the frontiersman's right hand holding the .52 caliber Sharps, his left arm hanging loosely in the darkness next to her. In a few paces, he stopped and turned. "We can walk around the wagons or we can walk out to that little rise yonder," he pointed south to a raised portion of the shelf slightly more than one hundred yards from where they camped. "Your druthers, Sarah."

"Let's go up there, Zeb. I just have to make sure I don't trip and fall in the dark with this dress."

To her surprise, he took her hand. "I won't let you fall, Sarah," he said, shortening his steps. Her hand seemed lost in his warm, protective grip. She liked the rough and gentle feel of his touch. They reached the elevated area and stood silently, a vast blanket of stars over their heads twinkling with hope and promise. The mountain man did not take his hand from hers and she realized she was glad, feeling perhaps more found than lost.

"Always was partial to the sky," said Zeb quietly, looking up. "Tells you there's more."

She squeezed his hand, her fingers barely wrapping around the edges of his palm. "Me too, Zeb. On both those thoughts."

Far in the distance, she heard a long, lonely howl, shortly afterward answered by another from a different position but close to the first.

She squeezed his hand again and looked up at the dark, rugged form outlined by stars. He turned toward her slowly, then seemed to hesitate. She took her hand from his, turned into him and wrapped her fingers into the folds of soft leather below the rawhide ties at his throat.

"Thank you, Zebarriah Taylor. You have been so very kind, looking out for me and trying to protect me from Jacob...." She could feel his eyes on her face even through the darkness. He wrapped his arm around her back, below her shoulders and bent down slowly, his kiss tentative as he drew her to him, his embrace firm yet not insistent.

Her surprise at the kiss quickly evolved from questioning to responsive, as she felt the pressure of his lips on hers. She tightened her grip on his leather shirt. The tickle of his mustache was pleasant and his lips were warm, respectful and gentle—particularly gentle.

He lifted his face from hers slowly and straightened up. Sarah dropped her arms, wrapped them around his waist and hugged him. She felt him wince and realized his ribs, broken in hand-to-hand combat at Two Otters Creek, were still sore. "Sorry," she whispered, the side of her face pressed against the bottom of his chest. Neither said a word. In the distance, the wolves again sang their calls to one another under the faint glow of a silver moon.

Sarah trembled slightly. "They won't bother us, Sarah. It's just the male and the female talking to one another." He paused, looked up at the sky and then down to her, clearing his throat. "They mate for life, ya know."

With her head still pressed to his shirt, Sarah could feel the rumble in his chest. "I'd never let you fall, Sarah, in the darkness or otherwise. The kid neither." Her eyes fluttered open; she jerked and began to pull away but he held her to him, his grip tender but strong.

"Yep, I know. You bein' sick and all. Knew for sure that day in the wagon, back there on Two Otters Creek when...when I helped you with your clothes."

Sarah relaxed into him and quietly began to cry. *My first real kiss and he knows, but can I ever trust a man again?*

May 27, 1855

*P*ULL BACK

REBECCA TURNED AWAY FROM THE FIRE, CLIMBED THE
ladder swiftly, lit the second oil lamp and found a comfortable perch on her bedroll. One envelope had the
return address of their solicitor in London. It was
addressed to her in formal, stilted letters:

> *To: Lady Rebecca Marx*
> *Care of General Delivery, Cherry Creek Post Office*
> *Kansas Territory*
> *United States of America*

Below that, "*Hold For Recipient.*"

Her eyes lingered for a moment on the words, "*United
States of America.*"

She put that letter in her lap and picked up the second, her hands trembling slightly. It was addressed in
her mother's ornate scroll—formal but warm—each letter with its own delicate curve. The address was the same
as the solicitor's correspondence, except after the words,
"*Hold For Recipient,*" were the words, "*My Daughter.*"

She held the envelope up to the light, turning it to try to see the postmark date, well-worn after months en route. *February 27, 1855.* Her hand fell to her lap. *I was on the Edinburgh, just before New York.* Then Reuben's green eyes floated through her mind and she corrected herself. *We were on the Edinburgh....*

She held up the other letter. Its postmark was two weeks after her mother's. She held one in each hand, balancing them. "Which of you should I open first?" she asked them, and this time it was a vision of her mother's stooped diminutive figure, grey hair, face and kind smile that floated through her mind. Her fingers shook as she carefully peeled back the envelope flap, which had been secured with three small pressed wax seals embossed with the family coat of arms. She could picture her mother's frail hand as she pressed down on the wax with the stamp months ago, five thousand miles away. She pulled the two-page letter from the envelope. It was on the heavy, scalloped stationery her mother preferred, scribed with her Mum's favorite feather fountain pen.

My Dearest Daughter,

You've been gone only weeks but I miss you as much as I miss your father, my dear Henry. I've always been proud of you. You have great courage and your father's quick wit and strength. While I wish you were here, home with me, Adam, Sally and Eve—who miss you too—I realize our unfortunate predicament has left you no choice but to make this dangerous and difficult journey. It is, perhaps, the most brave I have ever seen you. Wherever this letter may find you, far from these shores, I hope that you are well.

Adam has tried to tell me, very gently, that you will not return. I pretend to ignore him but in my heart, I know he may be right. Henry always said Adam saw the future clearly. I am old. Perhaps I should have departed this earth with or shortly after my dear husband but God has seen fit to keep me breathing. I feel, Rebecca, I may not last through the year. Adam feels it too. I can tell by how he looks at me and the gentleness with which he and his family treat and care for me. I write you this letter not to worry you, nor to beseech you to return quickly. Quite the contrary, I may not be here when you get back, if you come back. As my life draws to a close, yours spreads out before you. Do what you must. Follow your heart.

The words blurred as tears came to her eyes. She folded the letter, saving the rest for later. Her elbows resting on her knees, her hands over her eyes, she hunched over and sobbed softly. Time passed. She got up and refilled one of the oil lamps that was flickering, wiped the tears from below her eyes and took a deep, shaking breath.

She picked up the letter from the solicitor. It was written on plain, white paper. Smooth linen without personality. *Just like him,* she thought, as she began to read.

Dear milady Marx,

I write to advise you of the passing of your mother, Elizabeth Marx on March 18, 1855.

The letter slipped from Rebccca's hand, her breath wrenched from her and she groaned, her anguish melting into the coarse canvas of the wagon cover. *The very day the wagon train headed west from the Mississippi.* She swallowed hard, rubbed her eyes and bent over to pick up the letter again.

We shall handle your affairs as you instructed. You have been bequeathed the estate in substantial entirety, some small items being left to your servants, Adam, Sally and Eve, no known last names.

There are questions on the disposition or maintenance of your home and, regrettably, on the significant remaining outstanding debts of Sir Henry Marx's trading business.

We write further to inform you of an Offer to Purchase this office has received on your behalf for all lands to which you now travel, located in the southwestern part of the Kansas Territory, United States of America, consisting, more or less, of twenty-five hundred deeded acres pursuant to Land Grant by King Ferdinand of Spain, 1847, location 107° 41' East and South of the Uncompahgre River, Kansas Territory, United States. The offer is for two hundred and forty seven pounds per acre or one hundred thousand pounds to be paid in cash upon the transfer of a deed. We understand this offer to be generous. We urge you to return to England with all due haste to handle these important affairs as soon as possible. This letter will...

The letter went on for several paragraphs but her vision blurred. Suddenly exhausted, too tired to read another word, too overwhelmed, she put the solicitor's letter back in the envelope and folded both letters in the blankets she used as a pillow. She untied her high leather riding boots, pushed them off with her feet and lay down, drawing the other blanket over her head. *"Mother,"* she whispered, *"Reuben."*

REUBEN RODE INTO THE DUSK IN SEARCH OF SOLITUDE. He needed time to think about the push over the mountains and who might accompany him. The questions appeared more formidable than he had imagined. He grimaced to himself. The palomino moved surefooted in the moonlight, which cast a silver net across the land. Three large fires marked the wagon train, a half a mile out.

Reuben reviewed his mental list aloud while he rode. "Have to talk to Johannes, Zeb and Rebecca." He sighed. "And many goodbyes left to be said—the Johnsons are headed south toward an area they call Pikes Peak, the Kentuckians are headed due west of Cherry Creek and others in many directions."

He leaned forward and patted the palomino's neck. "You don't have much to say Lahn, and damn few answers but I appreciate you listening." The big horse's muzzle seemed to nod up and down and he blew softly through his nose.

Reuben shook his head. "The longest most difficult journey lies ahead of us, Lahn. Do you think we can find several hundred good head of cattle within a weeks' ride of camp?" He clicked off the tasks that would be required. "Cattle. Hire three good men. Get supplies. Purchase additional wagon to haul building supplies. Perhaps a third wagon for provisions. Teams for the wagons." The list seemed endless and Lahn still seemed to have no answers.

Reuben fell silent. The scout hired by his father and uncle indicated on the map he drew that it would be a two or three-week journey to the Red Mountains and the valley of the Uncompahgre River, where he recommended the ranch be established. The scout had written the same words repeatedly in different areas on the map. *Rugged. Steep. Uninhabited. Ute Indians. Some Navajo.* According to the scout's letters, the first snows could blanket the Uncompahgre by early September in some years. *Would there be enough time to put up a decent shelter? If not, then what?* The scout had written about winter temperatures well below zero and snows over ten feet. *Will I need to acquire title or legal claim to the land before building?*

He patted his coat pocket and ran his fingers down the lower seam, pressing against the heavy wool fold until he could feel the six small stones. *Ludwig's diamonds, the family trust.* The image of his father's wise face, pinched with pain, intense green eyes staring into his own across the dining room table of the family farmhouse in Prussia was etched in his mind. He and his brothers, Isaac, Helmon and Erik, completely silent and still, had waited for the patriarch to speak to them over the unrolled parchment map he had just shared and his father's words, "Reuben, pack light—just one duffel, the map case and one small trunk. I have sent money in advance to Uncle Hermann in New York. In addition, your work coat is back from our friend Marvin, the tailor. There are six diamonds sewn into the hem. The monies you may use as you see fit to buy equipment and supplies and to hire the men that you may need.... The diamonds, however, are to be used for one thing only— to buy our land. They are to be used for nothing else." Reuben sighed. *Almost there, father. Almost there.*

Completely distracted, Reuben rode back into the firelight of the wagons and without realizing it, up to their prairie schooner—and Rebecca. "Like a magnet," he chuckled to himself.

He tied Lahn onto the rear wheel with two quick loops. The oil lamps glowed inside the canvas. He knocked on the tailgate. "Rebecca? Sarah?" There was no answer. The flap was carelessly tied as if someone had been in a rush. He opened the tailgate, slid down the ladder and climbed in, intent on getting out his maps, studying them and then going over to where others were still gathered by the fires. As the elected wagon master after Mac's death, he needed to ask which wagons would be departing, when and where they were bound.

The blankets on Rebecca's bedroll stirred. So intent had he been in his plans, he had not noticed her slight figure, sunk in layers of bedroll laid out over the flour sacks, almost empty from the journey. He sat beside her and peeled the blanket from over her head. Her appearance startled him, even in the dim light. She had been crying and she was awake.

"What's wrong? Is everybody okay?" A single tear slowly rolled from the corner of her eye, down the side of her nose.

He reached out, wiped her face gently with his thumb and then leaned down and lightly kissed the partially healed scar above her lip. "Would you like to take a walk? Or head over to the fires? We were going to talk anyway and I'm not a bad listener." Again, she shook her head slightly. "You are feeling okay, right?" She nodded.

He stood up. "Reuben," she said, "wait. There was mail for you in Cherry Creek at the mercantile. Zeb brought it up." She stuck one hand out from under the blanket and pointed, "The envelope is on top of your map case in the forward corner of the wagon."

Reuben took an eager step forward, then stopped and turned to her. "Did you get mail?"

"Reuben, if you don't mind, I really don't feel like talking, but, there's a problem in England."

That hollow, uncertain feeling gnawed at him again. He looked at her, swallowed, turned and made a long reach for the letter on the map case. He paused at the tailgate. "Rebecca, I'm here if you want to talk. Do you want me to stay?"

"No, Reuben. Thank you."

He stood for a moment longer, jumped to the ground, closed the tailgate and tied the bottom of the canvas. He desperately wanted to read his letter. A quick glance told him Erik, his younger brother, had written it. The first word from Prussia in five months deserved attention, which would be difficult to give if he headed over to the fires.

A voice called out, "Reuben!"

Zeb and Sarah approached, one of Sarah's arms wound around his, her opposite hand fixed on his arm above the elbow and her head leaning into his upper arm. Reuben grinned. *About damn time.* Sarah smiled up at him as they grew near, her face more relaxed than he had seen it since their first meeting on the *Edinburgh*. Zeb's expression was, as always, inscrutable but Reuben thought there was a slightly different look in his deep-set eyes.

"Johannes wanted me to tell ya he's out on the ridge east of here for the night. The night guards are getting switched out twice tonight, so the menfolk will have more time with their families."

"Thanks, Zeb."

"Sarah, there is something not right with Rebecca— I think it was the mail that came in for her today."

"You received a letter too, Reuben."

"I know—I am looking for some light to read by. But I think Rebecca received some bad news from England. She wouldn't talk to me about it."

He looked down at the ground for a moment, fighting the tightening in his throat. "And she didn't want me to stay, but I think someone needs to be with her."

"I'll stay with her, Reuben," Sarah said, touching him lightly on the forearm. "Don't worry. Do what you need to do and if you need a private place to read your letter, use my wagon. There's an oil lamp."

She smiled up at Zeb, her face soft and radiant. "Thank you, Zeb. I'll think about that question."

"My pleasure, Sarah."

She lifted up the hem of her dress and walked quickly toward the wagon.

Zeb and Reuben exchanged a long look. "I think you ought to mosey on out and talk with Johannes. He seems a might down in the mouth to me."

"I'll do that Zeb, as soon as I read this letter."

"I'm gonna head down and camp maybe a third of the way toward those Arapaho tipis north of Cherry Creek. I probably know some of 'em. I'll head into their camp in the morning. Be back about midday and you can tell me what the plans are."

Reuben nodded and turned to go.

"One more thing, son."

Impatient to read the letter from Erik, Reuben spun around. "Yes?"

Zeb held his eyes. "I ain't never lied to you and I never will. But I didn't tell ya everything back there in St. Louis when you asked me to guide you...." Zeb cleared his throat.

"Oh?"

"I'm a mite more than a little familiar with that country you're headed to. My trapping cabins are on the sides of them mountains, the Red Mountains."

Reuben stood, absorbing the information. Zeb continued. "Know the country like the back of my hand. I know exactly where that ranch land is laid out on them maps of yours and Rebecca's gold map, too. Same place. Fact is, there's some mistakes in 'em. I aim to help you get set up. It'll still be a strange, wild land to you, but through me, you won't be a stranger. We have all been headed to the same Red Mountains, Las Montanas Rojas de la Uncompahgre, since the git go."

Reuben began to say something but Zeb had already turned and was walking away, outside the circle of wagons.

Reuben let his arm drop and shook his head. He hustled to Sarah's wagon. Not bothering with the ladder, he vaulted up on the tailgate of the makeshift old farm wagon, stumbling in the dark, looking for the lamp, burning his fingers with a match. He got the lamp lit and looked around the interior. Sarah had thrown all of Jacob's belongings, except his pistol and two marked decks of cards, into a heap and burned them two days before. She had found his hidden second pair of boots. After examining them, Zeb confirmed he was Mac's murderer. Sarah burned them, too. She had moved her belongings back in to make more room in the prairie schooner where she was spending the nights and days with Rebecca.

The wagon still held some of Jacob's malevolent energy. "We ought to burn you, too," he said aloud to the canvas. He thought about reading the letter elsewhere but this first news, this first touch from his family back in Prussia, could not be delayed. It was addressed to:

Herr Reuben Frank
Cherry Creek
Kansas Territory
United States of America

Standing, he roughly tore open the envelope. The letter was only two paragraphs long:

March 10, 1855

Dear Reuben,

I write to tell you that Father has died.

Still holding the letter with both hands, Reuben sat down on a crate, the letter on his knees, his legs shaking. He took a deep breath and blinked his eyes.

The rest of us are fine. Not yet knowing the town near the new farm, I hope this address is correct.

Reuben sighed. *Erik, you have no idea. There are no towns.* He continued reading.

The farm is prospering. The cattle have had good weight gain with the early spring. Helmon and Isaac are the same; obstinate, overbearing and resistant to new ideas. They will never change. There's talk of war with Denmark. The Jews, as usual, are being blamed for the unrest by those who need to do so.

Helmon said to tell you hello. Isaac is still angry at you. I'm thinking seriously about coming to America. Helmon and Isaac will never leave the farm. I have been reading everything I can on the United States and missing you. I believe Father was right that night in the kitchen when he selected you to go. You are the right choice. I keep hearing his words, "America is the future. Where there is land, there is opportunity." I will write you again soon.

Love,

Your Brother, Erik

· 41 ·

Reuben looked at the date. Erik must have posted it soon after he and Johannes had arrived in St. Louis, maybe while they were still on the train between New York and Missouri. He folded the letter carefully, shoved it deep in his pants pocket and blew out the lamp. Jumping down from the wagon, he secured the tailgate and walked toward Lahn, a picture of his father's strong green eyes in his mind.

May 27, 1855

A WORD TO THE WISE

THE MUFFLED, SLIDING SOUND OF LAHN'S HOOVES MOVing through grass and the occasional sharp, metallic tick of his shoes hitting rock cut through the still, chilled night air.

"Mississippi," came a voice out of the darkness.

"It's me, Reuben."

Johannes rode up to him, smoothly slipping his Sharps .52 caliber carbine into a cradled position in one arm.

"You're still using that password Mac gave us? Are you coming in tonight?"

"No, Reuben. As Zeb would say, this suits me just fine."

Bente and Lahn were standing side-by-side, their noses pointed at the Rockies, a looming, forbidding mass of jagged dark silhouettes rising without texture in the night, blotting out a third of the western sky.

Johannes turned his head in the darkness, looking at the mountains. "It is an enormous, dangerous, wild, exciting, spectacular country, Reuben. Coming all this way we had the support and company of other wagons, more than a hundred brave, strong men and women. From here on, it's just us. I have a feeling this next leg over that country up there is going to make what we've done thus far feel like a close column drill on a parade ground."

"I suspect so," said Reuben.

"I'll be direct, Johannes. Are you going to help with the push over the mountains and establishing the ranch down in the Uncompahgre?"

There was a long silence. "When Johannes Svenson makes a promise, Reuben, he keeps it. That's why I don't make many." He laughed in a sad, self-deprecating sort of way. "That, unfortunately, includes some promises I should have made."

"And then?" asked Reuben quietly.

"And then, Reuben, my friend, I'm going to be what I am. A cavalry officer, as I was in Denmark. Knew it all along, I suppose, but facing off with that renegade band, the battle on Two Otters Creek, my talk with that Captain Henderson when we met up with the cavalry patrol from Fort Laramie—it's all a message, a reminder that we are all what we are. There's no changing it." He sighed. "And, with Inga gone, no reason to."

"Got a letter from Prussia today. I just learned my father died in March. He chose me for this, you know. Even though he is...was...thousands of miles away, I had his support." Reuben felt his throat constricting again.

"We're all going to die, Reuben. It is the inescapable circle. That's why it is so important to live when you can," Johannes paused, "And you still have his support."

Johannes' words struck a chord. Reuben's eyes widened. "Have you asked her?"

Reuben's mind snapped back from where it had been, somewhere on the other side of those mountains. "Asked who?" And, as he said the words, he realized what Johannes meant.

"That's what I like about you Prussians. A quick wit." The two men laughed.

"So? Did you?" Johannes' tone was serious and Reuben could feel his friend's intent stare through the darkness.

"I thought about it, but when I inquire if she's going back to England, she avoids answering. I tried to bring it up twice in the last two days. Each time, something interfered and I have this feeling that she's glad she didn't have to answer."

"Remember back there, that morning at Two Otters Creek?" Johannes voice cracked. "I told Inga we would talk that night."

Reuben nodded, silent. *All too well.*

"Are you in love with her?"

"Yes."

"Then, my friend, a word to the wise. You need to tell her. Moments don't come often, Reuben. It is the one thing I have learned since first looking in Inga's eyes, back there on the train to St. Louis." He sighed and looked up at the sky. "Don't let a moment slip by, Reuben. You might not have it again."

Johannes reached a long arm over and slapped him on the back. "The worst she can say is, 'No.'"

May 27, 1855

*T*ORRID CONFUSION

REUBEN URGED LAHN INTO A GENTLE LOPE DIRECTLY toward the campfires, the landscape soft, silver and shimmering in the lunar light. The grievous news of his father's sudden death and Johannes' adamant advice to live his life heightened his determination. *Father, how did you ask Mother?* "Rebecca, I love you and I think you love me. It would be a good life if we married."

"That's not too damn romantic, is it?" Lahn snorted. "Rebecca, I'm in love with you. Marry me." Lahn snorted again.

"Rebecca, we've had our disagreements. I learned tonight my father has passed away. It was a shock. But it reminded me of the shortness of life and the importance of family and love. And, somehow, from the first time I saw you on the *Edinburgh,* I knew I'd be honored to have you as my wife." Reuben sighed. "That's a bit better don't you think, Lahn? I ought to get down on one knee. Father told us he did that with Mother." Reuben felt a stab of loss as he recalled his mother smiling as

Ludwig told the story to his sons. Erik had been her favorite. *It would be nice if he came to America.* Reuben shook his head at the night. *No—he is too young. Helmon and Isaac will not allow it.*

Reuben's jumbled thoughts returned to Rebecca and he stiffened. *And flowers. Got to have some flowers.* Reuben jerked back on the reins. "Easy boy, easy. I'm sorry. I wasn't thinking, or maybe thinking too hard."

Dismounting from the palomino, he led the horse, bent over, his eyes searching the moonlit ground. He cut the leafy silver tops of several sage plants with his knife, cursing when he stumbled over a rock. He cut several stems of early black-eyed Susans, one of them with petals partially displayed, the others just buds. His eyes were arrested by several shoots of delicate, purple-blue-petaled blossoms. He quickly gathered a handful, then paused and looked up into the stars. "It is unlikely Father, that I shall ever be back to place flowers on your grave. So know I pick these not only for the woman I hope to marry but for you, too." He wiped his eyes with the back of his wrists, then spent a moment arranging the stems. He held the wild bouquet out at arm's-length against the starlight, critically surveying his handiwork. "It'll have to do." Carefully holding the flowers, he mounted.

He skirted the outside of the circled wagons, determined not to be distracted by the pioneers gathered around the fires. He rode directly toward the soft amber glow of their wagon's oil lamps, sliding off the saddle when he reached the rig, holding the flowers to one side. He hurriedly tied off Lahn on the customary rear wagon wheel. He thought he heard the murmur of Sarah's and Rebecca's voices as he rode up but the wagon was suddenly silent.

He knocked tentatively on the tailgate. "Is that you, Reuben?" Sarah asked.

"Yes."

He could hear the women whispering. His eyes rose to the sky. *I need your help, Father.* He shifted impatiently from one foot to the other, wiping the dust off the top of each boot on the calf of his britches. He waited a moment and cleared his throat. "May I come in?"

Sarah unwrapped the ties from the rear of the canvas top, her figure appearing silhouetted by the oil lamp.

Though her face was in shadow, Reuben thought her smile held an air of apprehension. "Please do, Reuben," she answered.

He opened the tailgate and Sarah lowered the ladder, then walked over to Rebecca and put her arm around the brunette, who was sitting up on her bedroll, the soft folds of a grey, brushed wool blanket drawn around her shoulders and snugged to her neck. Her face was puffy, her red eyes fixed on Reuben's. Her gaze dropped to the flowers and a slight hint of a sad smile played on her lips. Ludwig's face flashed across his mind. *What has upset her?*

"I'm not interrupting?" The two women looked at one another, something in their shared glance completely female and alien.

Rebecca moved her eyes from Sarah and stared at him. Reuben couldn't be sure but the only time he had seen that look in her eyes was back on Badger Creek, the evening they stole away to passionately cleanse one another of the horror of the Pawnee attack.

There was a silence and then Sarah rose. "Perhaps the two of you need some time. I will stay in my wagon tonight."

Leaning down, Sarah squeezed Rebecca's hand and kissed her on the forehead. "If you need me, you know where I'll be, Rebecca. I'm so sorry. It will be okay." Rebecca looked up at Sarah and nodded. Sarah swept past Reuben with a pained expression, then laid her hand gently against his arm. She began to say something but then shook her head and clambered down the ladder.

"WHAT WAS SHE 'SO SORRY' ABOUT?" REUBEN'S GAZE returned to Rebecca only to find her still staring at him in the same odd way. He could feel a trickle of sweat running down his sides under his armpits. He cleared his throat, "Rebecca...ah...I..." He thought of his father and suddenly the timing seemed all wrong. *This is a bad idea.* Rebecca continued to look at him, unblinking, silent, her eyes misty.

Reuben felt his shoulders drop and began to lower the wildflowers he held above his waist and slightly extended. *They don't look so good in the light.*

"Perhaps tomorrow would be a better time to talk." Reuben began to turn toward the open rear of the wagon.

"Wait, Reuben." Rebecca rose and walked to him, reaching for the bouquet. She raised the sage and flowers to her nose and inhaled. "I am really beginning to love the smell of sage," she said softly as she raised her eyes to his. She took a half step forward and wrapped her arms around him. There was a tremor in her embrace. "Hold me," she murmured in a half sob into his chest.

Does she know about my father? How could she?

Reuben obliged, lowering his lips and kissing the top of her head. Rebecca's arms tightened and he began to repeat the gesture but she raised her head and intercepted his kiss with her own—just a brush of parted lips at first, then an increased pressure tinged with passion. She carefully laid the bouquet down on the flat surface of a cartridge box. "Tie off the canvas, Reuben. Shut the tailgate."

Reuben felt his eyes widen at the command in her voice. He shut the rigging and closed the tailgate. When he rose and turned, Rebecca was standing just inches away, her brown eyes wide, teary, looking up into his, full of sorrow and something else Reuben couldn't quite fathom. She slowly let the blanket fall from her shoulders. She wore nothing but a sheer silk chemise, almost transparent, every curve of her lithe young body glowing in the low light, the pink of her nipples erect, clearly visible and straining against filmy material.

Despite his surprise, Reuben could hear the sudden rush of blood in his ears. It became a roar when she reached out one small, delicate hand and firmly cupped the rapidly increasing thickness below his belt.

"Rebecca, I..."

His voice was stilled as she raised her other hand to his mouth, touching his lips with the tips of her fingers.

"Don't talk, Reuben. Not a word." Her fingers tugged at his belt and fumbled with the buttons of his breeches.

He stepped back, gently pushing her hands away.

She froze.

Her lower lips trembling, she lowered her hands. "I realize I must look a sight, Reuben."

Reuben sighed. "No, Rebecca, you are beautiful, as always." He paused. "My father died."

Her hand flew to her mouth. "Oh..." She sat down heavily on the bedroll and bent her head "Oh..." Her shoulders began to shake.

A vision of Johannes carrying the limp, bloody body of Inga through the smoke from the wagons, a shovel dangling from one hand, his shoulders hunched, flashed before Reuben's eyes. He sat down slowly on the blankets next to Rebecca and pulled her toward him. She buried her face in the crook of his shoulder and through his open jacket clenched his shirt with one hand. He stroked her hair quietly. She sobbed softly again. "My mother died, Reuben, on the very day the wagon train left St. Louis."

Reuben's hands, by their own volition, stopped their motion as he struggled to comprehend this torrent of conflicting passion and emotion. "I'm so sorry, Rebecca," he whispered into her hair. "Neither of us has had good news from across the ocean tonight. A part of each of our hearts is gone."

She shook her head into his jacket, dropped her hand to his knee and slowly traced his inner thigh, hesitating just below the "V" in his pants. She pulled her head back and stared into his eyes. "I need you Reuben." Her voice cracked. "We need each other."

Reuben felt lost, swimming in the sea of their combined grief, pulled by the tide of his love and awash in a sudden wave of desire for her. He nodded almost imperceptibly at the question in her eyes.

This time, her fingers were gentle as they worked at the constraints of his belt. Reuben shed his jacket, then reached down to help her. His trousers open, she reached in and held him firmly, her small fingers not quite encircling his girth. Her eyes, still tear-filled, never left his, the sheen of the dimming oil lamps accentuating the slight, moist part of her lips. She rose, blew out the oil lamp and then standing in front of him, pushed him down on the blankets. Grabbing one of his boots, then the other, she slid them off and then stripped his trousers and long johns from his lower body. Her curves were backlit by the campfires of the circled train, filtering through the wagon top. Reuben's mind was racing, his body alive with surprise and passion, his thoughts numbed by their combined loss. He realized he was painfully rigid, the insistent throbbing in his loins rhythmic with the rapid beat of his heart.

Rebecca hurriedly drew the chemise over her head and Reuben's eyes traveled the length of her now naked body. She bent over and kissed him, a demanding, hard kiss, her teeth gently nipping his lower lip as her hands tore at the buttons of his shirt. He began to sit up but she forced him back onto the bedroll, her knees straddling his hips. She took one of his hands and placed it against the darker patch at the apex of her inner thighs. Instinctively, Reuben's fingers probed the wet silken flesh that seemed to pulse beneath his finger. *Wet, very, very wet.* She reached down, held him firmly and began to lower herself, his tip spreading her tight velvet, her breath coming in gasps, tears falling on his chest. Reuben's hips began to buck uncontrollably. Pulling her face down to his, he kissed her, then lowered his lips and nuzzled her neck. He felt her shiver.

She sank slowly down onto him, raising herself just slightly, then began her descent again, desperation in her movements. She groaned and fell forward onto him, her lips moving frantically against his chest, the wetness of her flowing down his entire length still only half buried in her. He reached out calloused hands, caressing her sides, found the inviting curve of her hips and drew her down on him, widening his legs, spreading her inner thighs, tilting her pelvis and then he thrust, then again. He could feel the depths of her yield to him. Rebecca collapsed, moaning in his ear in a frenzied exhale of moist, warm breath. He felt her spasm around him and she groaned. Then they were locked together, inseparable in shared desperation, her hips meeting his every upward motion.

Her small frame shuddered and she raised herself partially, her hands pressing into his shoulders and began to slide her pelvis roughly against his, back and forth, her back arched, quivering uncontrollably. "Reuben, Reuben, Reuben." Her voice was a breathless whisper. She collapsed on him again, shuddering involuntarily, instinctively clamping herself tightly to the base of him, her inner contractions causing him to groan. He wrapped his arms around her back and pressed her roughly against him. His hips drove upward in one last, strong push, feeling the center of his soul, the essence of his being; empty deep, deep in her belly. Rebecca gasped, spasming yet again. Reuben felt as if every inch of their flesh pulsed in unison at the epicenter of the earthquake that her core had become.

"Oh my God," she whispered, "Oh my God." She began to cry soft, muffled sobs into his neck, her body trembling with aftershocks.

Still locked together, Reuben rolled her gently to her side and began to withdraw but she tightened her legs around his buttocks. "No, Reuben, no. Stay there please. Stay there, Reuben." He relaxed, one open palm gently on her hair, the fingertips of the other hand lightly moving up and down the hollow of her spine.

Rebecca drew back her head and through the darkness, he could feel the intensity of her gaze.

"Such an unbearable loss," she said in a muffled quiet voice, "for both of us. Perhaps they are together somewhere. Perhaps they will meet," Reuben's throat constricted and he nodded his head. They lay in silence for minutes, Reuben listening to her breathing, trying to reconcile their physicality with the dark news they had each received. He could feel himself softening. Rebecca shifted her position to keep hold of him, pressing the heat of her pelvis tightly to his and sighing. A few long moments passed.

"Rebecca, I came to tell you, tell you about my father and..."

Rebecca covered his mouth with hers, then drew back, her forefinger pressed against her own lips. "This is not the time to talk," she whispered. "Reuben, thank you for the flowers. I did notice right away." she giggled sadly, "though it was not my focus."

He thought hard. *Should I say nothing? This is not the right time. Perhaps maybe wait until morning...?*

As if reading his thoughts, Rebecca gently disengaged from him, her hand delicately stroking his muscular pectorals and wandering down his belly, closing lightly around him. She leaned down, licking his tip and then kissed it softly. Reuben jerked in shock.

Rebecca brought her face back to his. "I like the way we taste." She pressed her lips to his, then drew back. "Reuben, I hope you don't mind but I really want to be alone for the rest of the night. I have much to think about. Very different paths to take perhaps. Very different pulls...and responsibilities."

Reuben was stunned. "But, Rebecca—"

"Thank you, Reuben," she interrupted him. "I knew you'd understand." Her voice sounded exhausted.

Reuben blinked into the darkness, his mind reeling. Without a word, he rose and dressed. He began to say something but Rebecca was breathing rhythmically, already asleep. He slowly and tenderly covered her with a blanket, stood looking at her for moment and then walked to the back of the wagon, reclosing the canvas and tailgate after he clambered out. He walked over to

Lahn, feeling both drained and satiated, shaking his head, completely suspended in a numb emotional void. He paused. Lifting his fingers to his nose, he breathed in the smell of her. The horse turned his face toward him and nuzzled his shoulder. "No, I didn't ask."

Reuben removed the saddle from the palomino and shoved it carefully under the wagon bed, untied his bedroll and spread it. Lost in thought, he absently took off his boots, stripped off his britches and rolled them up, wadding them on the saddle to complete the pillow. He lay down on the bedroll and pulled the loose side of the blanket over him. The roaring flames of the campfires had died to embers. Reuben stared at the underside of the wagon, thinking about the small, beautiful brunette above him in deep, troubled slumber.

REUBEN AWOKE WITH A START. THOUGH THEY WERE trying to be quiet, to not awaken other wagons that would be pulling out later that day or in the days following, several of the families of the wagon train were already hard at work. Abraham—limping from the Pawnee bullet he had taken at Two Otters Creek—his father, Elijah and their Kentucky family, Margaret and Harris Johnson, their two little towheaded girls and several other wagons were hitching their teams of horses and oxen to their Conestogas and prairie schooners, planning an early start. *No way to be silent about hitching up teams, especially when you have young'uns.*

Reuben shifted his head slightly on the saddle and watched across the circle of rigs as the various families struggled with their sometimes reluctant teams and stiff harnesses, trying to control the children who evidently had caught the contagion of excitement from their parents.

He felt a sudden pang. *Father died.* Somehow, the scene of the busy pioneer families comforted him.

"Becky, Eleanor—come here this instant," Margaret hissed. "You hush up now. Not everybody's leaving today. Some folks are still trying to get some sleep. Sit down here by the breakfast fire."

Reuben chuckled wistfully into the blanket. For some reason, watching the two youngsters prompted his eyes to shift up to the floor of their prairie schooner. Above those floorboards were cargo, trunks, supplies...and Rebecca. Closing his eyes, he could almost feel the perfect press of her breasts against his chest, the quivering length of her body, her nails digging into the back of his shoulders as he pumped his soul deeply into her.

Shaking his head, still lost in the scene, he began to throw the bedroll from his body and he realized he was rigid. He chuckled. *Best to wait a few minutes. Can't go around saying my goodbyes like this.*

There was a creak above the weathered underbelly of the rig. From the sounds of it, Rebecca had risen and taken a few steps in the tiny space not covered with gear and supplies.

Reuben waited impatiently for his body to relax. Sarah was walking from her wagon toward theirs. The tailgate opened and Rebecca slipped the ladder to the ground.

Reuben threw the covers off, rolling out from under the wagon bed. He had started to button his pants when he looked up to see Rebecca staring below his waist and he followed her gaze to the definite bulge in his pants. He looked up and she caught his eye. Her eyes were puffy and red but a slight smile played around her lips and there was a strange energy in her stare. Reuben felt himself blush.

"Are you okay?"

She stretched stiffly, "I am fine, Reuben."

Reuben began to speak but Rebecca cut him off. "One of the letters..." Rebecca took a deep ratcheted breath, "was from her. She seemed to know she did not have long. The other was from our solicitor. It appears someone has made an offer on our land in the Red Mountains."

Stunned, Reuben tried to make sense of what he had just heard. He walked toward her and wrapped his arms around her. She did not resist but neither did she press back.

Sarah cleared her throat. She had stopped ten feet from them. "Good morning, Rebecca, good morning, Reuben." Reuben thought he detected surprise in her face when her eyes shifted to his bedroll under the wagon. Reuben noticed her usual traveling dress and petticoats had been replaced by a dull red wool riding skirt and heavy cotton blouse. He recognized the skirt as one of Rebecca's.

"I'm not interrupting?"

Rebecca pulled away from Reuben, one finger wiping a welling of tears. She took a deep breath, "No, not at all, Sarah." Rebecca turned back to Reuben, looking at him for a long moment. "Let's talk this evening. Sarah and I have decided to ride into town later today."

"Yes, we want to see the sights." Sarah offered with a smile, followed by a look, almost apologetic, toward Rebecca.

"That might be a very short trip," commented Reuben.

"I wish I had told Zeb to leave Red here," said Rebecca pensively and then quickly added, "for a little while." She looked around. "I think we shall ride Sonny and Sterling. I think Sonny is gentle enough for Sarah."

Reuben, surprised, looked at Sarah, "I didn't know you rode."

Sarah smiled, "I don't but Rebecca's going to teach me."

Reuben nodded. "Yes, I would agree, Rebecca, Sonny is the horse for Sarah. He won't cover a lot of ground quickly but that's probably a good thing, considering she's a beginner."

"Well, if you'll excuse us, Reuben, we are going over to say goodbye to the Johnsons and the others." Rebecca's voice trailed off as she glanced across the circled wagons. "It seems as if they are close to being ready to pull out."

"I plan to do that myself, ladies but I have a few quick chores to attend to first." He stared hard at Rebecca who seemed to be making a point of not looking back at him. "I think Johannes and I will be going into Cherry Creek also. Need to check on supplies, see what folks down there know about the availability and location of cattle south of here. And I want to meet Randy and offer my condolences."

Rebecca finally returned his gaze. "Then we each have our plans."

Reuben nodded. "Perhaps we will run into you on your return or perhaps we'll see you in town."

Rebecca broke her eye contact. "Sarah, let's go over to the Johnson's first. It looks like they are furthest along in their preparations. I need a hug from those two cute little girls."

"Me too, Rebecca. Let's go."

Fighting a feeling of helplessness, Reuben watched the two women move across the camp. *Shit.* Stooping down, he retrieved his saddle from beneath the wagon and whistled for Lahn. The big palomino had slipped Reuben's hurriedly tied hitch of the night before, and was grazing the now thoroughly cropped grasses a hundred feet from the wagon.

7

May 28, 1855

I DON'T PUSH

"You want it snug but not too tight." Rebecca straightened up from fastening the cinch under the grey mare. "Sarah, run your fingers between the cinch and the horse's belly. You should be able to feel both but shouldn't have to squeeze it in there."

The redhead bent over and tentatively stuck her hand out, glancing nervously at Rebecca and the horse.

"I think I've adjusted the stirrups for you. They should be about this same length as mine. When you step up, lead with your left foot and put just the toe of your boot in the stirrup. If something goes wrong you will be able to get off in a hurry," Rebecca laughed, "or at least not be dragged."

Sarah's eyes widened and Rebecca laughed again. Then suddenly, tears began to well. She wiped her eyes and shook her head.

"I'm so sorry about your mother, Rebecca," Sarah said.

"Thank you," she said. "Yet, sometimes the only thing one can do is focus on the present and that's what I must do." She shuddered and let out a deep sigh. "So, after your toe is in the stirrup," Rebecca demonstrated, "hold the reins in your left hand—don't ever let go of those reins—put your left hand up on the saddle horn like this and then swing your right leg over the back of the horse and settle into the saddle like this. Put your other foot in the stirrup so that your weight is on the balls of your feet." Rebecca looked down at Sarah. Her friend's eyes were wide and her lips a thin, nervous line. "Oh, don't worry about it, Sarah. The last thing your old gelding wants to do is move faster than a slow walk. You'll be fine."

A THIN FILM OF DUST COVERED EVERYTHING IN CHERRY Creek like a gritty blanket. The air seemed filled with a slightly opaque, light brown cloud that gradually dissipated as it rose higher from the hooves of horses, the roll of wagon wheels and the scuff of boots. Rebecca felt as though she was a figure in a lithograph.

Sarah, her voice plaintive, asked, "Are my thighs and knees supposed to ache like this?"

"As a matter of fact they are dear Sarah," Rebecca chuckled. "When you dismount and walk you'll find that your behind will feel a bit sore too."

Rebecca looked around, soaking in the feel of the tiny settlement. "There's not much to it, is there, Sarah?"

The redhead's expression was pensive. Sarah looked slowly and followed Rebecca's eyes down one side of the street toward several Indians whose finely colored mustangs were piled high with pelts. "I think Zeb said they were Arapaho."

From the second-story window of one of the few buildings made of wood rather than canvas, a bareshouldered woman, her auburn hair piled in tight curls and her lips red with thick lipstick, leaned from an open window. She caught Rebecca's eyes, gave a disdainful shake of her head and drew back into the window, shutting it hard.

Rebecca pointed, "That combination of old tents and wooden buildings attached to that newer partial brick one must be the mercantile."

Rebecca dug her heels into Sterling. "Come on, Sarah."

Sarah kicked back clumsily into the rear haunches of her horse. The gelding stood still. She did it again, harder, almost falling from the saddle, when Sunny took a half jump forward and then stopped again. "Rebecca, Rebecca come back. The animal won't move."

Rebecca reined in, wheeled her horse and trotted back to Sarah circling the rear of the old gelding. As she did so, she reached out and slapped his rump. Sunny lurched forward, almost tumbling Sarah over the back of the saddle.

From across the street there was rough laughter. Rebecca saw the red creeping into Sarah's cheeks and quickly appraised the four men leaning against the log uprights of the porch overhang of a rickety storefront. They grinned lewdly back at her. Rebecca could feel a clench steal into her jaw. Two of the men were heavyset, one was quite tall and very thin, the other was medium build and powerful. *A bit like Reuben.* Her baleful look seemed only to add to their merriment. "Did you see that cute thing almost topple off that horse, Andy?"

"Sure did. She would've landed straight on her back too," the tallest of the quartet chuckled. "That woulda made it easy."

They were all dressed in dirty, torn cotton shirts of varying faded colors. The rest of their clothing looked like it had long ago outlived its originally planned lifespan. Rebecca noticed that one wore a gun belt and the other three had pistols tucked in their belts. The attention of the man with the medium build—unlike his three companions—was not fixated on Sarah but rather directed at her. Rebecca reined in on one side of Sarah and in a smooth motion drew the .52 caliber Sharps rifle given to her by her father years before. She laid it across the saddle, thumb on the hammer and one delicate, thin finger stretched out across the trigger guard, the muzzle pointed at the four men.

"Lookee now, would ya? One of them fine lassies has a gun."

The heaviest of the four spit a gob of brown saliva into the dust, wiped his stubbled lips with the back of his hand and thrust out his hips, "I got me a gun too." Except for the man with the medium build, the group broke into gales of laughter. He simply stared at her, his eyes unabashedly scanning her profile, then again, a slight smirk on his lips.

Without taking her eyes from the men, Rebecca said in a low voice, "For God's sakes, Sarah, stay in the saddle and follow me."

Once in front of Gart's, they reined in. Rebecca sprang lightly from the saddle and watched, amused, as Sarah gingerly swung her leg backward over the top of the horse and eased herself to the street with unsure, wobbly motions.

"This is how you tie them off on a hitching post, Sarah." She wrapped the reins around the crossbar twice, slid the end of the leathers back under the wraps and pulled. "Try it, Sarah."

Sarah wrapped the reins, then hesitated, throwing a questioning stare at Rebecca.

"You bring the ends underneath the loops, then pull."

Following instructions, Sarah completed the tie-off and straightened up with a satisfied air. Rebecca laughed. "Let's go shopping!"

Sarah giggled, "Yes, let's do."

There was something very pleasant in the odor of the mercantile—a mixture of licorice from big glass jars, freshly oiled leather, gunpowder and seasoned wood. Rebecca had smelled this somewhere before. She felt her brow furrow as she tried to remember and then she drew a deep breath. *Father's ships.* She was aware Sarah was staring at her, "What is it, Rebecca?"

"Memories."

Rebecca blinked rapidly to clear the sudden blur in her eyes and looked around until her eyes spotted a short, powerful man with red hair. She shifted the

Sharps to her other arm careful to keep the muzzle pointed at the floor and nodded to Sarah. "That must be Randy."

Rebecca was aware that the store had grown quiet and the two clerks had stopped writing. The customers at the counter turned around and several other roughly dressed but not unfriendly looking men in the store had stopped what they were doing, one of them with his arm frozen in half-reach for something on the shelves.

"It doesn't seem like they see ladies in here often," whispered Sarah.

"Apparently." Rebecca squared her shoulders, lifted her nose slightly in the air and with Sarah close behind, walked toward Randy feeling the half-dozen sets of eyes following every move.

Randy was seated in a high-backed chair carefully counting musket balls, which he was moving from one tray to another. His head jerked up as if he was suddenly aware of the silence that had descended on the store.

His eyes caught Rebecca's, the initial look of surprise quickly yielding to wrinkles under his eyes as a smile spread under his beard. He rose, leaned over the counter and stuck out his hand. "You must be that dark-haired woman who has a fancy for Mac's horse."

Rebecca tried to mask her surprise, "Yes, yes, I suppose that would be me."

The smile under Randy's beard widened and he raised his eyes over Rebecca's head to Sarah. "It ain't often we have two women as pretty as you in the store at one time." A deep laugh rumbled from his belly that reminded Rebecca of Mac. "Fact is, it ain't often we have any women in the store." Randy glanced around at his clerks and customers. "You got invoices to write. The rest of you got stuff to buy. So let's get to it," he bellowed. Still leaning over the counter, he swung his massive hand toward Sarah. "And, your name, ma'am?"

Rebecca was sure Randy already knew Sarah's name.

"Sarah Bonney." Randy's quick nod affirmed Rebecca's hunch. "A friend of Zeb's?"

Without turning around, Rebecca knew by the twinkle in his eye that Sarah had just turned scarlet.

"That's quite the rifle you have there, Miss Rebecca." Randy's eyes had fallen to the Sharps cradled in her arm.

"Your brother used to call me Miss Rebecca," she said softly. His eyes snapped up to hers. He blinked several times quickly, his cheek muscles tightening over the curl of his beard. "Is that so?"

Rebecca noticed his hands had clenched into fists on the countertop. She gently laid one of hers across his knuckles. "I'm very, very sorry Randy. Mac was a good man who was my friend. He protected Sarah and me and the others on the train more than once."

Randy blinked twice again, his eyes slightly filmy, and cleared his throat. "Thank you very much for saying that. Guess I thought we were immortal. It wasn't something I expected." Randy cleared his throat again. "What may I do for you ladies?"

"We need to pick up soap and just a few other items, Randy. We can find them."

"I'll have none of that. No friends of Mac have to wander around these aisles searching for things that I can find for them."

Their supplies gathered, Randy led them back up to the front of the store and began to write out the receipts. He looked up mid-sentence. "Who did you ride out here with?"

"Just the two of us—and this," Rebecca patted the rifle.

Randy's eyebrows rose quickly, then sank into a frown. "That's not all too wise, Miss Rebecca." He straightened up, looking harder at her. "There's Indians out there that ain't friendly like these Arapaho. And there's some whites who are even meaner. That Bummer Gang has been pretty busy. A hardscrabble bunch of sneaky thieves—maybe worse. You women need to be cautious and keep your wits about you. You should never come back down to town alone."

"We will be careful, Randy." Rebecca patted the Sharps again.

His eyes narrowed. He looked like he was about to say something but he just nodded. "If ya wanna take Red back up there with you, you're more than welcome to ride her. She will just get fat and lazy down here. If that horse ain't bein' worked, she gets in all sorts of mischief."

Rebecca smiled. "That is very nice Randy and a good idea. I'll take good care of her until I make a decision on exactly what I am going to do. Is there a solicitor in town?"

Randy looked at her blankly. "Solicitor?"

"I think you call them attorneys."

He shook his head. "No. The law is the army passing through once in a while and the circuit judge out of Fort Laramie, though he ain't here 'cept every four to six months. We ain't likely to see him between December and early March."

Sarah spoke up, "Randy, does anyone do sewing in town? I am a seamstress."

"I would imagine you could get yourself a pretty good trade mending britches and jackets and such. Not much of those goods get out this way yet and folks have to make clothes last."

Rebecca pushed the small wooden crate full of soap and sundries that she and Sarah purchased back at the thickset Irishman. "Would you mind looking after this for a while? Sarah and I would like to take a stroll through town."

Randy's belly rumbled with a low laugh. "Won't be a long walk, Miss Rebecca." His eyes flickered between the two women. "Heard a few of that Bummer Gang is in town."

"We shall be fine, Randy." Rebecca turned and she and Sarah swept out the door. Sarah walking automatically over to the hitching post.

"No, Sarah. Let's walk. It won't take long. There are just a few other stores here. I would like to see what they have. We can talk to some more people about your sewing and maybe somebody will know where there is a solicitor."

The two women walked slowly, peering into the windows and open flaps of large wall tents where grizzled merchants were selling goods, tack, elixirs and knives.

Colorful residents mingled with others just traveling through or coming into town to trade, drop-off pelts and pick up supplies.

Suddenly, Rebecca was shoved roughly from behind. As she tried to regain her balance, the rifle was ripped from her arm. The heavier man of the foursome, a long scar over one eye, leered at her with an almost toothless grin. His hand gripped Sarah's upper arm, completely encircling it. Directly in front of Rebecca, holding her Sharps and pretending to look it over, was the smaller of the four men. He ran his fingertips down the length of the rifle's stock with an exaggerated, suggestive stroke, raising his eyes in a bold stare at Rebecca, the same sarcastic smirk curling his lips, a look of confidence and control in his eyes.

"That's my rifle." Rebecca drew herself to full height. "Return it immediately and tell your friend to take his hand off her." Clenching her hands to mask the trembling in her fingers, she felt her cheeks redden. "Right now. This is not something gentlemen would do."

The smaller man holding her rifle had pale blue eyes. *Like those shepherd dogs from Australia*, she thought. His gaze swept up and down her body and his tongue darted over his upper lip. "I don't never remember claimin' to be no gentleman." His hand darted out and grabbed Rebecca's forearm. She tried to twist away but his grip was like a vice. "What say you and that pretty little red-haired thing go for a ride with us? There's some nice country around here we could show you."

Crude laughter erupted from the four men. The taller, heavier outlaw flashed a hungry half-smile down at Sarah, then shifted his gaze to Rebecca. "Folks around here know us as the Bummer Gang. Don't suppose you two are known around here, though, being new to town and all."

Rebecca steeled her voice, the anger rising in her chest. "Take your hands off both of us," she said, reaching out for the Sharps, "and return my rifle."

"Lady, I ain't taking no guff off you or no one else. We're going for a ride."

Sarah tried to pull away but her attention shifted as a cold, level voice came from the street. The outlaws stiffened and froze.

"It would be a good idea if you do what the lady says."

Rebecca's heart leapt at the sound of Reuben's voice cutting through the dusty glare of the sunlit street. Reuben stood on the other side of the railing of the wood walkway, his legs slightly spread, shoulders loose, hands dangling at his hips, his right hand just inches from the pearl-handled Navy Colt that hung angled and low on his hip. Next to him, Johannes sidestepped away, his Sharps carbine perched on one forearm, muzzle raised, one finger on the trigger.

"Floyd? Floyd?" The heavy man nervously addressed Rebecca's captor as he stepped to the side and squared off facing Johannes.

Floyd snickered and his eyes dropped to Reuben's Colt. "Fancy pistol," he said in an acid voice.

Fighting against the weakness in her knees, Rebecca looked over at Sarah. Her eyes were wide and her lower lip trembled. One of the two stocky members of the quartet separated himself from the others, his older Enfield musket at the ready.

A twisted smile spread across Floyd's face. "I think I heard 'bout you. You just coming off that wagon train northeast of here?" The man's eyes slipped again to Reuben's Colt.

Reuben's voice was level, emotionless. "Don't matter. Let her go. Same with the redhead."

It happened quickly. Sarah, emboldened and quick to take advantage, brought the heel of her boot down hard on the instep of the outlaw holding her. The man yelped in pain and hunched over, releasing his grip. Sarah turned and bolted down the wooden walkway. A look of rage flooded Floyd's face. He shoved Rebecca roughly and she stumbled, watching the event unfold as she fell heavily to the walkway. The outlaw's eyes slid rapidly back to Reuben, his hand moving swiftly to the handle of his pistol, his face twisted and his eyes narrowed to slits.

Rebecca hit the weathered wood hard. The impact jerked her head back. She heard a shot and half raised herself frantically trying to see. Floyd was holding his hand, blood spilling from a hole just below his wrist. He staggered back a few feet to one of the uprights support-ing the covered walkway and leaned heavily against it. Reuben stood lazily, his Navy Colt in one hand, gunpow-der smoke still rising several feet above the muzzle. One of the other men moved and Rebecca heard the distinctive hammer-click of Johannes' Sharps, which he had raised to his shoulder. Reuben swung his pistol. The heavy man with the Enfield took a step back and dropped the musket, raising his hands. The tall outlaw froze, one hand clenched around the handle of his still holstered pistol. He straightened up slowly, moving his hand carefully away from the sidearm and raised his hands to his shoulders, palm out.

Reuben's attention shifted to Rebecca. "Are you all right?"

She struggled slowly to her feet, her legs wobbly, "I'm fine, Reuben."

Floyd's hand was steadily dripping blood on his boot. A mean look simmered under his paled complexion and a snarl laced with pain curled his lips. "Reuben, huh? I will remember that name."

Reuben's eyes shifted back to Floyd. "The last name is Frank." Reuben gestured with the muzzle of the Colt. "It's time for you to leave. Drop your gun belts."

"We won't do no such thing," spat Floyd.

Reuben's jaw clenched. He grimly cocked the hammer of the Colt. "I don't push, mister. You got exactly two seconds."

The four men exchanged nervous glances, their eyes shifting between themselves and Johannes, standing rock steady with his Sharps just twenty feet away and coming to rest on Reuben's Colt. The stocky man who had dropped the Enfield fumbled with his belt, his lead quickly followed by the tall outlaw, whose hands were shaking. Floyd, his face etched with hatred, shrugged; his uninjured hand struggling with the buckle of his cartridge belt. "You ain't heard the last of this," he said through gritted teeth as his pistol hit the wood with a thud.

Rebecca had been so transfixed that she had not realized that all activity in the street had come to a halt. Men crouched down between barrels, pistols drawn. Several peered over the top or from the sides of wagons with rifles. A hundred feet away stood Randy, Mac's shotgun in his arms. Down the dirt street in the opposite direction, another man on horseback had his rifle out. Behind him was a young woman. The attention of Cherry Creek was riveted on the scene.

"I think I have," said Reuben quietly, "but if not, you know my name."

Muttering, the men moved away, backing up at first then turning and walking hurriedly to the other side of the short street and toward the perimeter of the buildings and canvas tents a hundred yards away.

Reuben holstered the Colt. Johannes eased back the hammer of his Sharps and lowered it. Sarah, who had ducked into a doorway, emerged and ran to Rebecca.

Reuben stood at the street edge of the walkway looking up into Rebecca's eyes. "Better pick up your rifle," he said softly.

Rebecca fought to control her trembling. "Reuben, you could have—"

He cut her off. "I wasn't. Could've don't count. Johannes and I have some supplies to pick up. I want to meet Randy and talk to some other people in town. If you and Sarah will wait, we can ride back together."

Rebecca felt a rush of surprised anger but couldn't quite place why. She threw back her shoulders and raised her chin, "We're going to head back now. We'll manage."

Reuben's lips compressed. "Suit yourself." His attention turned to Sarah, "You still have that Derringer on you?"

Sarah nodded, her eyes still wide and her fair complexion colorless.

Reuben's gaze returned to Rebecca, "Make a straight line back to the wagons. Don't detour. Keep your eyes open and those weapons handy. We'll follow along the same route shortly." Reuben gave Rebecca a long look and then, turning, his face impassive, nodded to Johannes.

Johannes' eyes flashed to Rebecca and then Sarah. He shook his head disapprovingly and then took two long steps until he was at Reuben's side. The two men started toward the mercantile and Randy, who had lowered his shotgun and stood waiting for them outside the store entrance.

May 28, 1855

ℒONGHORNS

JOHANNES LIKED THE FEEL AND SMELL OF THE MERCAN-
tile. Randy, the powerfully built, red-bearded man who
had stood at the ready with Mac's shotgun just minutes
before, strode up to Reuben and him, his hand extended,
a smile on his face, "Those Bummers have had a face-
down comin' for quite a spell. It was a pleasure to watch."

"We appreciate you backing us up," said Reuben,
shaking his hand warmly.

"No bother. No bother at all." Still smiling broadly
but with searching eyes, Randy turned to Johannes. He
stuck out his powerful paw again and Johannes shook it,
liking the feel of firm and steady strength in the other
man's grasp.

Randy's eyebrows furrowed, he blinked and his lips
tightened behind the curls of his mustache. "Sounds like
we both had a bad day at Two Otters Creek." Johannes
felt a sudden burning sear his eyes and involuntarily
swallowed. "Yes, we did, Randy."

Mutual understanding and compassion flowed between them. Their handshake had not broken. The broad-shouldered man turned and spoke to Reuben, "Zeb tells me you're planning to move on?"

Reuben nodded. "We're headed to the Uncompahgre. Going to establish a ranch down there for my family back in Prussia."

Randy shook his head, "To hell you ride. Matter fact, wouldn't be surprised if they didn't give that name to a town down that way sometime. A ranch? Getting cows out of there to a market might be tricky, though it is a good time to raise meat. If things blow up over the slavery thing back east, there's gonna be several armies that need lots of beef. Where exactly ya headed in the Uncompahgre? That's mighty big country."

Johannes noticed Reuben's expression became more attentive and the young Prussian chuckled, "Yep, one thing we need for a ranch is cattle. We're headed to the Red Mountains."

"Las Montanas de Rojas?" Randy's eyebrows arched. "Me and Mac spent a summer down there with Zeb years back." He swallowed and fell silent. Johannes had a feeling Randy had not finished the story.

Reuben waited expectantly too, but Randy appeared lost in thought. Reuben threw a quick look at Johannes. "You know where we can find some?"

"Huh? Oh." A slow grin spread across Randy's face. "Man by the name of William Bent started Bent's Fort and another, Fort St. Vrain. He had to rebuild Bents a few years ago. Both are established trading posts, and have outfitted maybe thousands, but they are too far east from where you need to head to. What most don't know is they also brought about two thousand head of them Texas Longhorns up through the Panhandle some years back. Most of those cows are on ranches toward Santa Fe, south of San Luis and Pueblo, which are just a few buildings each—maybe ten to fifteen folks." He laughed. "Not like this big city," he brandished a thick hand toward the window. His face grew serious. "Most of them people at El Pueblo got massacred by Ute and Apache at Christmas." He shook his head and sighed. "Anyways, ain't been down there for years, but I understand the herds have grown to a goodly number and there's been a new army fort built north of there a few years back, Fort Massachusetts. Lord knows how it got that name. A couple of them ranchers, a few days' ride south and east of there, Dawson and Christiansen, sometimes drive cattle east. Meat for them city folks back there and some for the army."

Johannes moved over to the counter. Leaning against the top with one elbow and settling his hip against the edge, he listened closely.

"I've heard those longhorns are a hardy breed," said Reuben.

"Hardy and ornery. They were originally called Criollo or 'cattle of the country.' Bred up with the Spanish Andalusia cattle that came from Spain in the early 1500s, I hear. Started with six heifers and one bull, if you can imagine. By 1540, there were thousands. Then that Coronado fella lost about five hundred in Texas in a storm sometime in the mid-1500s. When them Texans ran the Mexicans out in 1845 or so, there was tens of thousands of them wild critters. They started experimenting, breeding the Spanish wild blood with English cattle, which some say drifted over from Louisiana. I've heard those cows are about three parts wild and two parts European. Shortens up the time it takes to get them to full weight. Used to be six years, now I guess it's around four. I heard tell of two-year-old steers almost one thousand pounds—pretty hides too. Seems like most of 'em are all big spots of color."

Johannes watched Reuben's face. His younger friend was fixed on Randy's every word. *That brain of yours is going to spin outta your head, Prussia, if it was going any faster.*

"I'd say chances are good one of them two outfits will sell some," Randy continued. "They are about five or six days' ride south but still north of the New Mexico Territory." Randy paused, "but trailing cattle and wagons to the Uncompahgre from that far south ain't none too safe. You know how far that is? Some say the Uncompahgre ain't even in the Kansas Territory anymore but in the Utah Territory. That southern route is the northern range of Comanche and Navajo, too. And those Southern Ute and Jicarilla Apache down that way ain't all too partial to white men either."

Randy swiveled his eyes from Reuben to Johannes, then back again.

Wants to make sure we are listening, Johannes thought.

"Ask Zeb, he knows the way but might not be a bad idea for you to trail north around the southern edge of the San Isabel after you get your cows and meet your wagons at Fort Massachusetts. They can head south from here, then west over La Veta Pass into the San Luis Valley. The fort sits north of the west side of the pass. Save ya lots of miles going all the way north to the South Platte, and Kenosha Pass can be tough on wagons. Matter of fact, you would still find snowdrifts going that way and that's Southern Ute hunting lands and they don't like sharing."

"Any supplies you don't get here you can outfit out of Fort Massachusetts. Then over Wolf Creek Pass and then you got some choices. Zeb likely knows some short-cuts. Them San Juan Mountains are quite a sight."

He looked hard at the two of them, "There's one or two other big passes, too. After about mid-September you ain't getting back this way 'til May or June. Winter stays a long, long time up there. Them Red Mountains are a hell of pass. Ends on the west side on the Uncompahgre River up over the headwaters. Big gorge and full of hot springs the Ute are partial to. That's the hunting grounds of one of the more or less friendly Ute tribes, headed by a Chief named Guera Murah. He's Jicarilla Apache. Married a Tabequache Ute woman who died after their second son was born. One of their boys, Ouray, carries a lot of weight with the tribe. The Tabequache's winter camp usually sits on the Uncompahgre River upstream of the Gunnison River. Ain't much in the way of settlers, though. There's suppose to be a building or two on the upper Animus and one over on the San Miguel River. Let me show you." Randy turned abruptly, grabbed a piece of paper and began shaving a pencil.

Johannes' eye was caught by a faded poster with the rough drawing of a young woman, *maybe a girl*, tacked to the wall at the end of the counter: MISSING—DOROTHY ANNE

EBERLYN—Age 14. Family Murdered In The Poudre, March, 1855. Kinfolk In Independence, Missouri WILL PAY $100.00 REWARD For Information.

"It's okay, Randy," Reuben said, "What you said bears out the map and the recommendations of the scout my father and uncle hired. He didn't have the names of those passes, though the map shows that upper Uncompahgre hot spring area and a building on the Animas."

At the young Prussian's words, Johannes turned his stare back to Reuben. *Let him draw the map, Reuben— not going to hurt anything and we might learn something.*

Randy, surprised, looked at Reuben, then shrugged and set down the pencil. "Well, there are damn few white men. I haven't heard of no one trying to establish a big ranch over in that country, though rumor is that summer grass grows high as your waist. If you can figure out how to feed them though the winter, you might put a lot of pounds on them during the good weather."

Johannes detected a slight change in Randy's tone. There was more doubt and warning than promise in his voice. Johannes looked down at his boots and for a fleeting moment regretted the promise he had made to Reuben.

Randy's eyes flickered to Johannes. "I see you been studying that poster of that poor Eberlyn girl."

Johannes nodded, glancing at the poster again.

"What about hands?" Randy asked Reuben sharply, then, before the young man could answer, questioned Johannes, "You going with them?"

Johannes nodded, "I am."

Randy reached under the counter pulling out a duplicate of the poster on the wall. He extended his arm over the counter, stretching the paper toward Johannes. "The Army figures it was the Black Feather bunch." His gaze shifted momentarily to Reuben's Colt. "You boys have met them bloodthirsty bastards. Here—take it. Ya never know; though, she's likely dead or far worse."

Johannes took the poster, studying it briefly again, *very young*, then folded the heavy paper, shoving it in his jacket pocket.

Refocusing his attention, Randy glanced at Reuben sharply, "Any womenfolk traveling with you?"

Reuben pursed his lips, hesitating. "That's not been decided yet."

Randy smiled softly and cleared his throat. "Told that dark-haired girl she's welcome to take Red back up to the wagons with her 'til she figures out what she's going to do." Randy's eyes closely studied Reuben's expression as he delivered the offer.

Reuben shrugged, his face impassive, "That's her decision."

Randy chuckled again. "I figured she wasn't one to take to a bit. She clearly has her own mind."

Reuben's facial muscles tightened. "Yes, she does," he said, tossing Johannes a quick look.

Randy shook his head. "If you have some ladies traveling with you then you have someone to cook and tend camp. That'll be nice after pushing cows through rough country all day and keeping your eyes peeled for Injuns. How many critters you plan to start off with?"

"Three hundred cows and twelve bulls if we can find them," answered Reuben.

Randy whistled. "I don't know if those spreads will part with that many. Guess you're serious. You're gonna need two, maybe three, more men. Them longhorns is good beef but they are an edgy breed and tougher than nails. You could do with fewer hands in the flats but up in that timber and canyon country, keeping that herd intact, gathering up strays and just having enough guns to defend an outfit that's going to be spread out a half mile, is going to be a task."

Reuben nodded. "Any idea where we might find those men?" he pressed.

"Reuben, you got a good base. You and him," he gestured at Johannes, "and Zeb makes me think you're well down that road."

Reuben laughed. "Yep, well Zeb hates the thought of cattle. Had to promise him he wouldn't have to spend a minute with them."

Johannes straightened up. "And I'm no expert on cattle, either."

Randy scratched the back of his neck. "Might be one man in town. Don't know him all too well but I heard he's been on a cattle drive or two from New Mexico." Lowering his voice, Randy confided, "name's Philippe Reyes. He's first generation Mexican. Parents were French and Spanish. He's quiet, tough, keeps to himself. I hear tell his family was wealthy, with a huge estancia down south of the border. Got in some trouble and they disowned him. Started rustling back and forth across the border and had to come north when the Texas law got onto him. Right now, he's just doing some odds and ends and trading. Lives in the tipi of a widowed Arapaho woman. It's kind of set off from the rest. The tribe was none too pleased with her taking up with a white man." Randy chuckled and corrected himself, "I mean a someone who's not an Indian."

Randy rubbed thick fingers up into his beard. "There's also a place about five miles southwest of here on Bear Creek. Family of seven—daughter and four sons. I think two of the boys are in their mid teens. I've never figured how they make it with one hundred and sixty acres and unreliable seasonal water from that creek. Whenever they come in here for supplies, they watch their pocketbook mighty close and try to barter whatever they can. Them boys might be lookin' for something and their folks might be happy to have two less mouths to feed. Their name is Sampson. The two older boys are Jonathan and Michael. I ain't certain but I think Michael is sixteen. He's a year older than Jonathan. Ain't the sharpest pencils but they seem to have grit."

Too young, Johannes thought.

Reuben's head bobbed. "Much obliged."

Randy cast a sharp look at the young Prussian, "Mac used that phrase a lot," he said softly.

"That's where I got it. And your brother taught me way more than that, Randy. He was a good man."

Randy cleared his throat, the corners of his lips twitching, one large hand again absently stroking the red curls of his beard, "That's a wild place you are going to. The Utes are not partial to squatters."

Johannes knew Reuben would react to that suggestion and smiled inwardly when Reuben stiffened.

"We are not squatters. I intend to pay for the land."

Randy looked at him for a long moment. "Aim to pay? Who? The government? Ain't no government there. Some other person if you can find someone who claims they own something? That land is forever. If I was you, I'd get some papers somehow so it was legal in white man's terms but I'd sure as hell make friends with them Utes. They don't give a damn about deeds and you want to keep your scalp and your place from being burned out."

"Thank you—"

Randy cut Reuben off. "Do what you please. There ain't no give in that kind of place, son. In addition to Injuns and no law, from what I hear, winter over in that country is tough."

Reuben glanced quickly at Johannes, then back to Randy. "When does winter usually set in up there?"

Randy's broad shoulders rose in a shrug. "Don't rightly know. You know, Zeb has trapped that area for years. In fact, his cabins are in them Red Mountains, though they will be several thousand feet above where you'll likely homestead. Altitude makes a big difference."

Johannes felt his eyebrows rise at the revelation of Zeb's past trapping in the same specific mountains where they were headed. He felt even more surprise that Reuben was apparently already aware. Johannes forced the thought from his mind and listened carefully.

"Your best bet for that herd will likely be Bill Dawson. Maybe four or five days ride south without pushing your horses too hard. I ain't never heard nothing bad about his outfit but if you buy from the other place, the Christiansen spread, you better have yourself a counting rope."

Randy threw a piercing look at Reuben, "You gonna leave those two women alone while you go out for cattle?"

Reuben's jaw set. "They can handle themselves pretty well; Zeb will be staying and there will be several wagons that aren't pulling out just yet."

There was a long silence. Randy stared out the wavy, mullioned glass into the sunlit street, his eyes unseeing. Johannes saw his shoulder sag as he slowly returned his stare to Reuben. "If that woman wants the mare, she can have her. Mac most likely would have wanted it that way."

Reuben extended his hand and Randy clasped it for an extended period of time, his blue eyes misty but blazing. "I appreciate all you did for Mac," his voice cracked. "You did a mighty fine job getting them wagons through and taking charge after that bastard killed my brother. Hold on a minute."

Randy walked down the counter to where the Colt 10-gage shotgun rested on the wooden top of the display case. He picked it up, hefted it, then walked back to Reuben.

Reuben shook his head. "That's mighty nice of you, Randy but I will most likely never need or use a shotgun."

Mac thrust the weapon at Reuben. "Take it. You were obviously a good friend of Mac's." He swept a muscled arm at the walls, "and I ain't got no shortage of guns here. I'm sure he would want you to have it," he said gruffly. Then he smiled and added, "And if you keep on making enemies like today, you're gonna need it. Here's that ammunition. You boys get what else you need and then come see me at the front counter and we'll get squared up."

CHAPTER
9

May 28, 1855

THE MULE

THREE HUNDRED FIFTY MILES NORTHEAST OF THE FACE-
off between Reuben, Johannes and the Bummer Gang,
Israel led the old, grey, stocky mule deeper into the
shade of the leafing cottonwoods along the creek they
had been following southwest. Sunlight, warm with the
coming summer, seeped through the passages in the
trees, its bright rays dissipated by unfurling leaves and
muted by the dark, course bark of the riparian forest.
He paused before leaving the tree line they had been
skirting, carefully searching the nearby creek bottom for
any danger, now and again casting quick glances over
both shoulders and behind the mule.

"Let me help you down off that mule, wife."

"You are gonna have to, Israel, I think my bottom
might be glued to this critter. I'm not sure what's worse,
walking or riding." Hunching over the forequarters of
the mule, Lucy reached down and rubbed her swollen
left knee, barely visible below the hem of her skirt.

Israel chuckled and looked up at the plump, rounded figure of his wife. There was a definite expression of discomfort on her full, round and high-cheeked face. Thin trickles of sweat seeped from the graying strands of wiry black hair pressed against her forehead by a blue print bandanna. She looked tired.

"Traveling all night is tiring and having to stay off the main trails makes it all the more tough," Israel commiserated softly. Gazing upward toward the sun, he raised one dark-skinned hand to his head shielding his eyes. "I reckon it's late morning, maybe noon. Why don't we hole up here 'til evening and then get on the trail again?"

Lucy groaned. At the sound, the mule turned its light grey, almost white muzzle back toward his rider, one ear forward, one ear back and blew through his lips.

"See, Sally don't want to be moving around in the dark either."

Israel pursed his lips. "I'd rather be walking in the daylight myself—a lot less stumbling. But we ain't safe yet, Lucy. From everything I've read and what folks in the stations along the Underground Railway been sayin', we ain't safe 'til we reach them Rockies and even then we will have to be careful. I don't think we'll breathe easy 'til we cross over them mountains and reach the west side. You heard what that farmer, Charles, told us at the last stop."

Lucy shook her head, heavy cheeks wobbling. She sighed. "I know you're right Israel. Everybody been telling us that, and Mr. Charles was real clear on his advice. And thank you again Lord, for Mr. Charles. He was a godsend."

Israel reached up and grunted, his thin frame and stooped shoulders straining with the effort of assisting Lucy as she leaned off the mule and half fell into his outstretched arms. Her legs almost buckled as he lowered her to the ground and steadied her.

"You all right?"

Reaching down, she rubbed her knees. "My knees are mighty sore, Israel but I suppose that riding is better than walking."

"It is far better than walking woman—and that will be double when we start going over those mountains. I'll help you over to that big tree but first why don't you walk around just a little bit and get that riding stiff out of your legs. Let me get us something to eat."

Lucy nodded, hobbled a few steps, paused, then took a few more ginger shuffles. Israel walked to the rear of the mule and began undoing the rawhide ties on the flaps of the makeshift leather saddlebags.

Lucy stopped, swaying lightly. Craning her face toward Israel, she commented, "That was pretty smart making them carrying cases, Israel."

Israel nodded, his fingers fumbling with the rawhide ties. "I'm sure glad we had enough leather from the cowhide left over after I got through fixin' Charles' saddles."

"He will be mighty pleased with what you did for his tack, Israel. It looked almost new. I am sure he won't mind none you took a few scraps of leather. Besides, you left a dime and that note."

"I'm not sure he can read my chicken scratch. Miss Tara sure enough taught me to read on the sly but we never could sneak enough time together for me to learn to write proper."

Israel pulled out several hard tack biscuits and unwrapped a chunk of cheese from the wax paper and cooling, damp cloth it was bundled in. Leaning down, he checked the makeshift cinch he had fashioned to keep the saddlebags in place just fore of Sally's rear haunches. It was snug but not tight. "Holdin' up real good but when they get wet that cinch is gonna stretch out a bit. Keep your eyes peeled when we get into rain, Lucy."

With a firm grip on Lucy's arm, he helped her over to the trunk of a particularly large, gnarled cottonwood. She eased herself to the ground with another groan and he handed her a biscuit and some cheese.

She was lifting the hard tack to her lips when, laughing, her hand suddenly dropped to her lap.

Israel looked at her, puzzled. "What's so all fired funny, woman?"

"You know Israel, here we are, two old runaway Nigga slaves in the middle of nowhere heading across a continent to some place we seen once on a map at that nice old white lady's house in Topeka and we can't hardly pronounce the name of where we're going. We are plumb crazy."

Israel felt his eyes narrow. "Ex-slaves, Lucy. We is ex-slaves." He took a deep breath and smiled. "*Un-com-pah-gre,*" he said, slowly mouthing the word in an attempt to pronounce it correctly. He chuckled, "and of the twenty-four years you been married to this scrawny, salt and pepper man, you just now figurin' out we're crazy?"

"Yeah, that's the name. It's no matter anyways; it's hundreds of miles away or more, neither of us rightly know. We been chased by dogs, had bushwhackers hunting us through bleeding Kansas with torches and thick rope that they sure wasn't going to use to tie our hands. We've had sheriff's deputies poking and prodding grain bins we been hiding in, near choking to death trying to breathe through cane break stems. We was hidin' in trash heaps back there in Holten, slept with rats and frozen ourselves half to death in snowstorms. That frostbite in my toe still ain't right. Except when you snare a rabbit or can catch some fish with them fishhooks you brought or them folks at the stations along the Underground Railway were kind enough to part with some vittles, we been mostly starvin'." She looked down at herself and chuckled without humor, "You'd think I would have turned back into a skinny woman."

Laughing, Israel knelt down and kissed her on the forehead. "I think you're just the right size, Lucy. I stayed married to you for all these years. Don't know what else I can do to convince your pretty self—even if you do still taste like grain dust."

"And what would you expect, husband? That oat grain in that bin you stuck us in came up six inches or a foot over our heads." Lucy shuddered. "I never want to do that again. How long you figure we was buried in there?"

"I don't know. Maybe an hour, maybe more."

"Well, it felt like a lifetime." Her features softened and she smiled lovingly up at him. "I woulda never made it if you wasn't holdin' my hand."

Rubbing long thin fingers over the knuckles of his right hand, Israel smiled. "I think you popped two of my joints; you were squeezing so hard."

Lucy's expression grew serious, her lower lip began trembling and she blinked rapidly. "Israel, do you think we will make it?"

"I suspect we will, wife, but that's in God Almighty's hands. If we don't, it won't be for lack of trying. I told you this before but I'd rather die a free man on the run than a slave saying *yes massuh and no massuh* back in the Oklahoma country."

Lucy nodded slowly, doubt etched in the press of her lips. "Miss Tara always called it Oklahoma, Israel." She paused. "How much further we got to go, you think?"

"You ask me that every day." Israel started to laugh. "I don't rightly know but I guarantee we are one day closer. Now eat that biscuit and cheese. I figure we got enough food, if we're careful, for a little more than a week. Maybe we'll take a full day off our travels, catch some fish and smoke 'em."

Lucy looked at him hopefully. "Can we have a fire now? It's chilly here in the shade and I sure miss that old 1735 Castrol stew stove we had in that hovel on the plantation. Say what you will Israel but we had a roof, we were warm and mostly dry, unless it rained real heavy."

Israel felt an angry constriction begin to well in his chest. He took a deep breath and shook his head, "But none of it was ours and we weren't free. We been traveling for two months. I had my very first job for pay fixin' them saddles in return for Sally the mule, here. We got ourselves leather saddlebags, fish hooks, snares, guttapercha parkas and clothes—and we still got nine dollars and ten cents left of the nine dollars and seventy-five cents we started with." He paused, feeling better after voicing their blessings, then added, "We're getting' to be downright rich."

He grinned and looked up. The blue of the sky highlighted the greening of the early summer leaves. He took another deep breath and the tightness left his chest. "And we got nobody to tell us what to do. In my book, that counts way more than a stove or roof."

"You still got that paper, Israel—you know, that New York whatever paper with that Constitution printed out in it?"

"I do, Lucy. It's wrapped in them gutta-perchas in the saddlebags."

"Read me some of that Constitution. I like it when you read me parts of that. Reminds me of when Mistress Tara was first teaching you how to read and you'd practice by reading to me from the Bible."

Chewing on the biscuit, Lucy's gaze wandered out through the trunks of the cottonwoods toward the great open spaces of the western edge of the Nebraska Territories. She froze and stopped chewing. The anxiety in her voice was palpable as she whispered, "What's that, Israel? Who are those people?"

Israel pivoted and crouched down, peering through the tree trunks. Perhaps a quarter of a mile from the creek was a long line of horsemen, riderless horses— some pulling travois—and many people on foot. Israel couldn't be sure but a number of them appeared to be women and children.

"Can't be certain at this distance but I think it's Indians."

Lucy's eyes widened, her dark brown irises swimming in a pool of white, "Indians?" She whispered, "What kind? Are they friendly? What will they do if they catches us?"

Without taking his eyes off the roughly organized column moving east, Israel shook his head. "I don't know much about Indians, just what I've heard and read a bit. I think they are like any people anywhere. There's some good, some bad. Looks to me like this might be an entire village moving." Israel reached over and pulled on the halter rope, bringing the mule closer. "You be quiet now, Sally."

Glancing behind him through the trees up and down the creek, he said in hushed tones, "One thing I have read is they are awful good at living in the wild and great warriors, some tribes better than others. I would think they would have some scouts...."

They both froze at the distant downstream snap of a branch and the muted whinny of a horse just audible above the gurgle of the creek. Sally's ears, usually one back, one forward, pricked to attention, her eyes fastened downstream. She blew softly through her nose.

"Hush now, mule," hissed Israel. "Sure wish I had me a gun. That's the next thing we are going to get, Lucy. It's downright crazy be out here without a weapon.

Besides that, I could hunt. Most likely bring in more meat than them snares we've been setting when we stop."

Another branch snapped, this time closer. The muscles in the mule's neck tightened and Lucy grabbed Israel's hand, squeezing it hard.

May 28, 1855

THREE HUNDRED FORTY MILES, SOUTHWEST OF THE
meanders of Mink Creek, the wagons formed a circle in
the gentle ridges above Cherry Creek. Walks with Moon
stretched under the buffalo robe, lingering in that state
of sleep just before waking. She reached one delicate
bronze hand down to rest on the rounding of her belly,
while extending the other to touch Eagle Talon. Moving
in their annual search for tatanka, the tribe had pitched
their tipis in the rolling, elevated bench above Mink
Creek two hundred fifty miles southeast from their winter camp along the south fork of the Powder River.

Her eyes bolted open when her fingertips failed to
find his warmth and she realized he was no longer under
the robes with her. Her surprise cleared her mind of
slumber and the unsettling events of the previous evening
flooded her memory. She sat up suddenly, clenching the
edge of the robe high to her chest to keep the morning
chill from her square, delicate, brown shoulders. The sky
beyond the smoke hole at the top of the tipi was still pre-

dawn. The hide walls of the tipi glowed softly from the last embers of the night fire, silhouetting her husband's naked figure as he squatted, facing away from her.

Eagle Talon's powerful back rose angular from his muscular buttocks. The ebb and flow of the embers lit the space between his long black braids and the taper of his neck where it met his shoulders, accentuating the rippled definition of strength in his arms.

She watched him poke and prod at the coals in the fire ring, throwing his prodding stick into the ring with a sigh, shaking his head and whispering to himself. A small flicker of flame sprang from one end of the piece of unburned wood, adding a tremble of light to the interior of the tipi. His shadow danced on the wall.

Eagle Talon's mutterings evoked images of the strange glow in Talks with Shadows' eyes the previous evening as, seemingly possessed, she shared a vision with Walks with Moon and Deer Track. She spoke in an eerie monotone voice not her own, her pronouncements accentuated by the wild dance of flames inside the lodge she shared with her husband, Turtle Shield. Like Eagle Talon, he was a young and ascending warrior, though more introverted and less brash.

Yesterday had started well. *How quickly things can change,* mused Walks with Moon. Three Cougars, returning early from his advanced scouting position, had led The People to a large herd of tatanka, almost thirty arrow flights wide and more than three times that long. The sun had not fully risen when the herd of their brothers stampeded to the northwest leaving behind sixteen carcasses felled by arrows and lances. She had spent most of the day in happy chatter with the other women of the tribe gutting, skinning and cutting meat to smoke and salt.

Deer Track was perhaps Walks with Moon's closest friend and wife of Pointed Lance, another of the band of five close warrior friends of Eagle Talon. Unable to endure the suspense alone, she had come, wringing her hands, to the tipi of Walks with Moon. The two women had then nervously walked to the lodge of Talks with Shadows, where the three of them had shared the evening anxiously awaiting the return of their husbands from more than one-half moon as the far forward eyes and ears of The People. The forward scouts traveled several suns ahead of the tribe as the village migrated slowly eastward in the annual life and death search for tatanka. Rumors had swirled around the camp all day, some bits and pieces flavored with wild exaggeration as could be expected in the gossip between lodges. Soldiers, a hairy-faced-one, the Pawnee, a battle, many coup—but much of the talk was apprehensive whispers over the council's displeasure and conjecture at what had transpired between her husband, his small band of warrior friends and others from a distant village.

The chiefs and elders took the rare step of setting up the council lodge, an act rarely undertaken when they were on the move, accentuating the grave worry of Deer Track, Walks with Moon and Talks with Shadows. The three friends soothed each other as the tense drama unfolded during the late day and into the evening.

It was then that Talks with Shadows had had her vision. At first, Walks with Moon and Deer Track were startled, sure that it was a joke, just another one of Talks with Shadows' many bizarre and usually incorrect prognostications. But their friend continued to speak in a strange, flat singsong voice not her own, her eyes wide, unseeing and reflecting eerily from the fire. Her hypnotic intonations seemed different to Walks with Moon, far more powerful than the norm.

A hollow feeling of foreboding gripped Walks with Moon as she stared at the squatting form of her husband and remembered more. The words of Talks with Shadows echoed in her mind: *Counted many coup... How does the baby in your belly grow? Does he feel strong? The men have brought shame upon themselves. The Council will decree it will be so for one moon.... Eagle Talon has bonded with a hairy-faced-one, whose woman reminds him of his love for you.... Your son will come to know them.... The future of The People is not bright.*

Walks with Moon swallowed and shook her head. "Eagle Talon," she called out softly.

Her husband neither acknowledged her voice nor turned his face to her. Instead, he added several small sticks to the fire and blew gently on the heat of the faded coals, finally coaxing the fuel reluctantly into flame and brightening the lodge.

She raised her voice, "Husband?"

Eagle Talon rotated slightly on the balls of his feet, turning his gaze partially over his shoulder in her direction.

She studied him carefully across the length of buffalo hide that separated them. She had tried to comfort him the previous evening by coquettishly inviting him under the robes with her when he finally returned from the unfortunate meeting with the Council. In uncharacteristic fashion, he had gently shunned her suggestion of lovemaking, a want and passion they frequently shared—sometimes to the point of being the subject of gossip, particularly between the older women in the tribe. Walks with Moon was convinced they were jealous.

He had silently lain down beside her, facing away. Pressing her breasts into his back and softly kissing the base of his neck, she had delicately probed for information, the feeling of unease in her belly growing at his terse and unknowing confirmation of Talks with Shadows' visions before he drifted toward a morose sleep. "I ruined the shirt you spent so much time on this winter, though it did help save Brave Pony's life.... We trailed the Pawnee and attacked as they charged the white wagons.... I counted five coup. We avoided a small group of soldiers... but the most memorable event was—please don't think me crazy, wife—I met our spirit brother and sister.... They are hairy-faced-ones. The woman's name is Ray-becka and her man is Roo-bin. They remind me of us—very much in love...but now I have been shamed...."

She had lain awake long after Eagle Talon had fallen into deep and heavy breathing. The sounds of the burrow owl outside the tipi, *co-huu, co-huu* and the sharp yelps and howls of the coyotes feasting and fighting over the tatanka carcasses strewn in the great grassy bowl below their camp, had at once both relaxed and unsettled her. The dark, melancholy energy of the night permeated her senses as she finally drifted off to a troubled sleep.

She forced herself back to the present. Eagle Talon was obviously distraught over events and preoccupied with trying to understand their meaning and ramifications. *Should I tell Eagle Talon of Talks with Shadows' vision and if so, how much?* She decided instead to learn more than a few short details he had briefly shared— especially about Roo-bin and Ray-bec-ka. Walks with Moon knew many important events had transpired in the sixteen suns since Eagle Talon and the other braves had left their lodges as directed by the Council.

She took a deep breath to slow her racing pulse. Clasping her hands to hide the nervous tremble of her fingers, she smiled, "Tell me, husband. Tell me everything."

Eagle Talon regarded his wife for a long minute. Her wide, questioning eyes, set above high, bronzed cheekbones, were the golden brown of a young beaver pelt. He saw the flicker of worry in them as his gaze traveled slowly down the taper of her throat to the straight, feminine shoulders that descended to where her smooth flesh disappeared at the edge of the robe she clutched, the hide not fully concealing the swell of her petite but shapely breasts. His gaze traveled down the dark brown hair of the tatanka hide to where he knew their child grew in the protruding rise of her belly, framed by the deep evocative curves of her hips.

Despite his dark mood, he smiled back at her. "I suppose our unborn wants to hear the story of my disgrace, also?"

She giggled. "But of course our son wants to hear all the tales about his brave father and leader of the young warriors."

Eagle Talon grunted, threw the one remaining stick in his hand into the fire ring and turned fully back to his wife. "We hope for a son, Walks with Moon but this is the first time you've said 'our son' with certainty. Do you know something I do not?"

Walks with Moon cast her eyes down for a brief instant, her lips lightly compressed, one cheek quivering. Her gaze returned to his. "No, husband. I just think it will be a son because I believe Spirit will bless us with a son—but any child is a blessing from Wakan Tanka."

Eagle Talon regarded his wife in silence. *There's something she is not telling me.* He decided not to press the matter. "It was a long and busy half moon. I and Brave Pony trailed the Pawnee warrior band. At various times, there were at least forty, sometimes up to sixty braves. A large war party. Three Cougars, Turtle Shield, Pointed Lance and Three Knives were a half sun's ride from us and from each other, searching for tatanka and any alert to possible dangers." He chuckled. "Those Pawnee have the eyesight of old women. They never spotted us. Twice we had to double-back to avoid Army patrols. One group of cavalry was perhaps twenty soldiers, the other was larger, perhaps forty. I assume they came from the white man's fort they call Kar-ney, a five or six-sun ride when we encountered them."

"And the soldiers?" asked Walks with Moon.

"They were well-armed. All had muskets. Their leaders had pistols and sabers." A thought struck him, *like the tall blond warrior on the wagon train*! "Many of the soldiers did not sit their horses well. Bareback, they would fall off. They had flags and rode in lines of twos...." He shook his head disgustedly, "very foolish, bunching up like that. The biggest thing that struck me, wife, was that unlike Indians, even the Pawnee, they did not seem to be of the land, they seemed to be merely on it."

"And after you evaded the soldiers?" pressed Walks with Moon.

"Brave Pony and I decided we knew where the Pawnee were headed. We took a shortcut trail through rolling hills that Tracks on Rock showed me many winters ago but we did not know that we would run into a wagon train." He shook his head. "It was foolish perhaps but we were very curious. We've had few opportunities to study white eyes closely without them knowing it. We hobbled the ponies in a draw perhaps twenty arrow flights from the wagons, which for some reason had stopped between mid-sun and dusk. Spirit told me to focus on one man in particular. He is slightly taller than me but we are built in similar manner. He wore a big brown hat...."

"Cowboy hat, that's what Tracks on Rock calls them."

"Yes. He had a better rifle than the soldiers had. His pistol had a white handle like the pearls in river mollusks. He rode out from the wagon with a dark-haired white woman shaped much like you." He paused, admiring the glow of his wife's skin in the light of the small morning fire. "They both rode well and unlike the soldiers, guided their horses across the land toward a small creek as if they knew each curve, each tree.... I could feel it. We could see them dismount but it was a very long distance...." He grinned at her.

Walks with Moon's eyes flickered downward and she blushed. "You think they—"

Eagle Talon nodded. "When they rode their horses back, they were close together, holding hands. Brave Pony and I had crept through the grasses to some low-lying brush less than half an arrow flight from their wagon. When they dismounted, he looked in our direction. I think he sensed our eyes on them. Then they spoke and he put his arms round her and kissed her deeply."

He stared at his wife. She looked transfixed by the story, her tongue involuntarily wetting her lips. Eagle Talon continued, "A long, great kiss. It reminded me of us." He cleared his throat. "And Spirit spoke to me. I heard it clearly."

Walks with Moon's eyes widened. "What did Spirit tell you?"

"*Friend, strength, honor.*" Eagle Talon paused. "I knew at that moment that the hairy-faced-one and I would bond, that we were somehow brothers and shared some future destiny. And I think, wife, that you will bond with his woman."

"Oh!" Walks with Moon raised one hand to her lips and stared at him.

Eagle Talon stopped talking and looked at her closely. *That's an odd reaction, as if to something else other than my words.*

"There's nothing to be frightened of," he added hastily. "It was either the next sun or the sun thereafter that the Pawnee cut the track of the white wagons. They doubled back and began to shadow the white eyes through the shallow roll of the hills. They were undetected, though the wagon chief had scouts out in all direction from their wagons. One scout, as skilled as any of The People, knew we were there—a trapper, tall, dressed in buckskin, a raccoon cap, two rifles and two pistols, riding a clever, brown spotted horse that would make any warrior proud."

Eagle Talon traced lines in the dirt floor of the lodge with a stick as he spoke, as if sketching each thought. "I had sent up smoke to summon Pointed Lance, Three Knives and Turtle Shield. The sun following, they arrived. If the Pawnee attacked the wagons, we did not plan to interfere. On the third sunrise the wagons crossed that swift creek Tracks on Rock says has more otters than any other. When a wagon broke down in the water, the Pawnee ambushed and killed a white scout, striking without noise."

"Not the one with the raccoon cap?"

Eagle Talon shook his head. "No, no. No Pawnee will kill that man. But something alerted the trapper that morning. He galloped toward the wagons from a great distance shooting a pistol in the air to warn the other hairy-faced ones and then the Pawnee attacked."

He looked up at his wife. She was riveted to his words.

"Many Pawnee scalps hang from my lance. This you know. But I thought of the women and children in the wagons—and of the hairy-faced-one and his woman." He shook his head and sighed. "It was decided that we would help the hairy-faced-ones. And now, I carry the weight of that decision to disobey the Council."

"The battle went well?"

"Yes, Spirit rode with us. I counted five coups and Three Knives counted four. The hairy-faced-ones also killed many Pawnee. One man in particular, with golden hair like the rising sun, very, very tall, probably killed seven or eight that I saw, by himself." Eagle Talon looked at her. "Five of them died by his saber, like an army sword." He grinned. "I hope they all don't fight like that."

"Why would you say something like that?" Walks with Moon interrupted in hurried, anxious voice. "Do you plan to fight them?"

Eagle Talon looked at his wife, surprised. "No! We should all be able to live in peace. There is much land. It is ours. But if they respect it we can let them use it." He paused. "And, if they abuse our generosity we will fight and we will win."

Walks with Moon relaxed. "After the battle, the Pawnee retreated. Brave Pony was severely wounded. We rode out of the smoke and dust of the fight and up to the wagons. Through the trapper, I spoke directly with the hairy-faced-one that Spirit had guided me to—Roo-bin. I saw his woman Ray-bec-ka kill at least one Pawnee with a rifle. She seemed wounded or stunned but brave and beautiful like you. In speaking with Roo-bin, I knew that everything Spirit told me was true. He knew it too. And I learned something very interesting....," Eagle Talon paused, waiting for his words to sink in. He smiled when Walks with Moon took the bait.

"What? What did you learn? Tell me!" she exclaimed, her voice rising.

"You know the trapper, the man wearing the raccoon cap."

"I do? How could that be so? That's impossible."

"Do you remember the stories you told me, of how when you were a little girl of just a few winters, a white man stayed and traveled with The People for a winter? How he became friends with Tracks on Rock and Flying Arrow? How you said they taught him how to hunt, trap, track and survive?"

Walks with Moon's eyes widened, her mouth dropped opened and one hand flew to her lips. "Oh! They called him Zeb-Riah. I used to tickle his wrist. He was very kind."

"Yes, it is the same man. He remembered you and Tracks on Rock and your mother, Tree Dove and her sway with your father and the Council."

Eagle Talon let out a deep guttural laugh. "He was just as surprised as you! But now the news is not so happy. We found water and saved Brave Pony's life, which is why that beautiful shirt you made me is missing a sleeve. When we approached the camp as the sun set, the last of the women were just leaving their day's work fleshing out the bodies of our buffalo brothers down in the basin. Three Cougars galloped up to us, very nervous, telling us they had set up the Council lodge and Flying Arrow wished to see us. We left Brave Pony at his tipi. Then, with a dark cloud hanging over us, we went to the Council gathering.

"The Council was angry. Flying Arrow was disappointed that we disobeyed his orders and became embroiled in a fight not of our own, leaving The People without eyes in front of the trail."

Eagle Talon hung his head. "Now I and my friends that I talked into the misadventure are shamed for a moon. We can talk to no one, even each other and no one will talk with us. We can only hunt alone. We can do nothing for the tribe unless asked." He looked up and held her eyes, "And I have shamed you too, wife."

"Yes, husband, you have."

Her tense but calm, non-accusing tone unsettled Eagle Talon.

His surprise and hurt must have flashed across his face, because Walks with Moon's lips quivered and tears welled in her eyes.

"You misunderstand me, husband. I meant we are together in this. I am your wife. I carry your child. I am proud of you..." she lowered her voice to a whisper, "... and I think the Council has made an error."

"I am sorry," he said softly and stood, silent.

"Do you feel better having shared that with your wife?"

"I do feel lighter. The weight is partially off my soul. Thank you for listening. I think I shall walk and watch the sunrise."

Without another word, Eagle Talon tied on his loin cloth, wrapped a buffalo robe around his shoulders, untied the tipi flap and stepped out into pre-dawn chill.

OUTSIDE THE TIPI, HE WALKED FIFTY PACES, STOPPED and fixed his eyes on the yellow glow and waves of rose hue spreading from behind the green-gold waves of land, but the dawn did not afford him its usual comfort.

Should I tell her the rest? Though Council members would not even look in their direction as they left the lodge, Flying Arrow had come to him out of the dark before he returned to her and told him he wanted to speak of the hairy-faced ones, Roo-bin and his woman, Ray-bek-ca. He was very curious. He'd told no one else yet about the raccoon cap. He felt his jaw muscles tighten. *And I shall inform Flying Arrow when he chooses to talk with me.*

The sun rose with the smile of a new day but its warmth did little to chase the chill from Eagle Talon's heart.

The camp was fully awake and the shadows had lost their length when he returned to the tipi.

Inside, the lodge fire burned brightly. He let the robe drop from his shoulders, tied the flap and turned to his wife. He was surprised to see her still lying under the tatanka hide. Walks with Moon flashed a wide smile. Her eyelids lowered and lips pursed seductively, she threw the robe back from herself, revealing the splendor of her lithe, trim body. She raised one hand, crooked her forefinger and wagged it, inviting him back to the buffalo robe.

Eagle Talon lost himself in the comfort of her touch, her passion drawing the worry from his mind, her tenderness like a salve to his heart.

———

EAGLE TALON KISSED HER EARS AND PRESSED HIS LIPS to the rapid pulse of her neck. With Walks with Moon's inner thighs wrapped tightly around his hips, he could still feel her spasms of culmination contracting, then relaxing around him.

She half-sighed, half-murmured, "I missed you, husband. I was upset that you left before breakfast."

"Since I am in shame for the next moon we shall have plenty of time to make up for the nights we were not together but now I must rise again. Speaking with my friends is forbidden but perhaps if I walked by their lodges I can get a sense of what is going on. And we will need one more buffalo besides the one that Soaring Eagle kindly killed for us while I was away. Now I must hunt alone—" he sighed heavily, "which is much more difficult. When I do kill one of our brothers I will come and get you and then together we can gather the fat, skin, cut and prepare the meat."

He felt her lips smile against his shoulder at his words. Walks with Moon reluctantly relaxed the wrap of her arms around his neck and slid her legs slowly from around his middle. "I am also busy today. I must help the women finish collecting fat and we must begin the process of tanning hides. Most of our meat is already salted or the smoking started but I must wrap it."

Eagle Talon kissed her again and then gently disengaged his body from hers and rose. He stood and looked down at himself, breathed in deeply and smiled. "I love the smell of us."

"You remind me of the wapiti," she teased, "snorting and tossing your antlers. So proud of yourself." Then she reached down and touched herself, lifting her fingers to her nostrils. "But I will be thinking of you, too, my husband, when I am with the women, wrapping that meat."

EAGLE TALON LED ONE OF HIS PONIES BETWEEN THE tipis of the camp, trying hard to appear nonchalant as people glanced at him and then looked hurriedly away without a sound. He was surprised to hear Flying Arrow call out as he passed the old chief's lodge.

"Eagle Talon, come into my tipi." Flying Arrow's voice was brusque and curt. Eagle Talon grimaced. *This would obviously not be a social visit.*

Eagle Talon grabbed his pony's nose and squeezed gently, his command to stay. He lifted the partially open flap of the tipi and took one step forward, standing silent.

The tall, frail thin frame of Flying Arrow, still with an aura of power but without the musculature of youth, sat cross-legged in front of a small, low-burning fire. His famous staff that had counted so many coup, his shield, antler breastplate, lance and bow, rested within close reach. He raised his head—his wide nose and weathered face, framed by long grey hair that fell from high cheek-bones toward thin lips pressed grimly together.

"I do not call you at this time to talk of the hairy-faced-ones. Nor that Spirit has perhaps spoken to you of them. Instead, I find myself in an awkward position. Ten of our warriors are out on the trail ahead of The People as our eyes and ears. Unlike you, I hope they will not be distracted. We find ourselves shorthanded for near guard scouts. We'll be breaking camp as soon as the women finish their work sometime after mid-sun. I wish you to stay in the tree line of the creek."

He paused, his eyes narrow and his voice harsh, "You are to leave each morning before dark and return only after the sun sinks. No one else will know this. Today, you will ride behind us until you are hidden by the high ridge to the rear. When you are out of sight, go to the creek. You are to report only to me and only in the event of danger. You will follow my instructions exactly, no deviation for any reason. Do you understand me?"

Eagle Talon's tongue pressed thickly against the roof of his mouth, dry and mute. He tried to swallow but could only nod.

"Say it," said Flying Arrow sharply.

"Yes, I have taken your words to heart." *I would not like to think of what will happen if I disobey these instructions.*

Flying Arrow nodded his head sharply just once, then waved his hand dismissively. "Why do you stand there? Go."

May 28, 1855

RED & BLACK

IT WAS MID-SUN AS EAGLE TALON RODE SLOWLY TO THE edge of the creek. The rush of water was only as wide as the length of his lance but flowed with late spring strength. The current glistened and sparkled in the glow of the day. There was a cautionary hiss to the whisper of the stream as it caressed the dirt and stone edges of the streambed on its forever journey to points unknown.

Eagle Talon and the spirited red, brown and white mustang he rode wove warily back and forth between willows and cottonwoods along the bank. Kisses of warmth on Eagle Talon's bare upper torso from rays of the sun alternated with quick, brief stints of chill as shafts of sunlight streamed through alleys in the trees, then transitioned to shadows on the sunless side of the cottonwoods. The slight breeze stirred the old growth grass of the previous winter and rippled the early summer leaves. The mustang's head suddenly rose. His neck tensed, nostrils flared and his ears flicked forward. He peered intently upstream into the timber.

Eagle Talon stopped the horse and listened carefully, his eyes searching every shadow—nothing. He thought he heard a sigh as if from the heavy exhale of an animal. Adrenaline coursed through his fingertips. Deftly, quietly, he slid the bow from where it hung diagonally across his shoulders and withdrew an arrow from the quiver on his back, notching it carefully and then resting the bow against his left leg. His left forefinger held the arrow in place where his left hand clenched the bow's rawhide grip. His eyes probed carefully once more and then he gently dug his heels into the mustang.

The pony had taken less than fifty steps when Eagle Talon again stopped the horse. He heard something else—an almost imperceptible sigh, out of place in the air currents among the cottonwoods. The mustang's ears remain pricked, his eyes fastened on some point still upstream and slightly off the creek to their left. Eagle Talon raised the bow to the ready, its long alder body held with an almost rigid left arm diagonally across his chest. He slipped his fore and second fingers over the arrow notch just behind the fletching of duck feathers.

The mustang took two more careful steps. Suddenly, Eagle Talon caught a movement from the left corner of his eyes. His pulse raced. The battle with the Pawnee was still fresh in his memory and he was high strung by the events of the last two suns. He brought the bow to full draw instinctively, without thought, sighting down the arrow shaft. At the end of the length of the arrow, over the shape of the triangular flint arrowhead, was the forequarters of a mule. Below the animal, two people huddled against a tree. One of them, a man, was seemingly shielding the body of the other. His dark face looked directly at Eagle Talon and the pony. One hand was stretched out in front of him, pointing at the warrior and his horse.

12

May 28, 1855

ERIK

FAR TO THE EAST FROM WHERE EAGLE TALON WAS
deciding whether or not to release his arrow, across a
body of water greater than Eagle Talon could imagine,
Erik drummed his long, uncommonly delicate fingers
against the rough planks of the kitchen table. He pushed
back his thick, black spectacles until they were firmly
over the bridge of his nose, close enough to his eyes that
when he blinked his long eyelashes touched the glass.
He looked down at the half-written letter. *How do I properly phrase this?*

He leaded over the water basin, peering out the wide,
multi-paned kitchen window framed by dark oak slab
cabinets. The glass faced east toward the farm's main
fields and the church spires of the little village of Villmar, two miles down the dirt thoroughfare from the
farm gate. The languid waters of the Lahn River drifted
lazily past the great white barn. The fields were separated by fences and hedgerows, the cultivated land
between those barriers green with late May growth. The

grass and row crops near the river where his brothers could get water to the land in the ditches his grandfather had dug were green and almost ankle-high. Two solid, heavily muscled Belgian draft horses were hitched to a plow between the house and the barn. From the corrals drifted the smell of manure and the bawling of sixty weaned calves. In a pen on the other side of the two-track farm road, their mothers bellowed equally anguished protests. *They will find tomorrow far more upsetting.* Tomorrow, they would be branded and castrated. Neighbors from up and down the dirt thoroughfare that led from Villmar past a number of farms like theirs would be on hand to help, as would Rabbi Bernhard Frank. He would bestow blessings on each procedure and calf, an all-important step to being able to market the meat or live animals, as kosher.

Sighing, Erik's eyes traveled the length of the kitchen countertops. Large bowls heaped high with potatoes that needed skinning and boiling, three huge jars of jam he had canned himself and ten loaves of rye bread purchased just hours before at Goldberg's kosher bakery in the village. Since their mother's death in 1852 and their father Ludwig's failing health shortly thereafter, it had somehow fallen to him, the youngest, smallest and most frail of four brothers, to keep the house clean, do most town errands and prepare virtually every meal.

Putting together a huge noon lunch for the twenty or more neighbors expected for the celebration of calves was one of his biggest annual challenges and an occasion he usually found himself looking forward to. It gave him the opportunity to play his violin and harp for others during lunch and later when the work with the cattle was complete, for those neighbors who would invariably linger until dark, delighted to have an excuse to gossip, complain and get slightly intoxicated, sipping another of Erik's creations, apple-cherry wine. Sometimes too, a neighbor would bring along one of their pretty daughters, though Erik found himself too shy to ever muster a hello and his two oldest siblings, Helmon and Isaac, thought him too effeminate to interest the girls.

His enthusiasm was absent this year though. Outside the window, the fields turned bright emerald in ripples of moving sunlight and then transformed instantaneously to a dull, dark green as clouds skittered across the sun's face. *A living mosaic.* He returned his eyes to the half-finished letter:

May 28, 1855

Dear Reuben,

I trust by now you have received my letter about Father's death. I'm sorry we are not together to console each other. I wrote you immediately after he passed, and honestly, was not disposed to speak in detail. Father went downhill quickly after you left for America. Beginning three or four weeks after I brought you to Bremen in the wagon to board the Edinburgh, he began to ask me to check for mail every day. He never saw the short note that you sent from St. Louis on March 17th saying all was well and that the next day the group of wagons you had associated with were leav-

ing for Cherry Creek. The letter did not get here until May 2nd.

We received an earlier letter from Uncle Hermann in New York. He said you looked well and were eager to get west to the lands mapped out by the scout he and Father had hired. The third map, the one the scout told Uncle Hermann was a map of where the scout had heard there might be gold in the mountains to where you are headed, never did arrive. The scout's brother, Mickey, was supposed to deliver it to Uncle Hermann. It remains a mystery. Perhaps in your travels you have learned something.

Uncle Hermann also said you were with a tall, lanky Scandinavian man who Uncle Hermann was certain had military experience and with whom he felt quite comfortable. He wrote briefly of the weapons he had suggested you purchase and of your delight when he gave you Father's gift, the .52 caliber Sharps rifle, with the special distance sights—I think they call them Enfield ladder sights. I look forward to understanding more about these weapons, holding one in my hands and learning how to use it.

Erik stared at the paper, his eyes moving to the corner by the kitchen door to their old Blunderbuss hammer pull shotgun. Its nicked and scarred walnut stock and darkly blued, almost black, flare barrel melted into the dark color of the wood wall where it rested, butt down, the tip of its wide muzzle obscured by the hems of their field coats on the coat rack just inside the door. His eyes traveled back to the letter. He dipped the quill in the ink and continued writing, the pen making a scratching sound on the heavy linen paper—the very last sheets of his mother's store of good stationery.

We have no such weapons here as you know. Only the military is well armed. I fear one day our country will learn the folly of that.

I write you, brother, not knowing when or where this letter will reach you. We are so far apart. Father said it was at least 5000 miles, perhaps more, from this kitchen table to your destination in the Kansas Territories but I have made an important decision.

Erik put down the quill. *A critical dangling thought awaiting finality.* Forcing his eyes from the incomplete letter, he drummed his fingers again on the tabletop. Through the window, he could see his brother Helmon and the eldest, Isaac, standing by the plow gesturing at it and then leaning toward each from their waists, pointing fingers and waving their arms in the air. Helmon's large, slightly overweight frame was particularly agitated. Isaac, almost a head taller than Helmon and built like an ox, seemed—as usual—to be getting the best of whatever argument had erupted between them this particular day.

Erik took off his glasses and rubbed his eyes wearily. *This bickering, constant fighting and continual test of dominance is so tiring.* Closing his eyes for a long minute, he thought and then gazed slowly around the kitchen. Although a year prior, the scene was suddenly alive in his memory; everyone had gathered for the evening meal.

"Helmon," he had said to his brother, "you have been sitting there for half an hour, I told you I would call when supper was ready. The least you could do is help set the table."

Helmon had risen and fumbled around the kitchen in his usual oafish but well-intentioned way. He put out the dishes and silverware. The uneven placement of the silverware bothered Erik but he said nothing. Erik could hear his own voice calling out, "Supper's ready!"

Isaac had come stomping in, his frame almost filling the doorway. "If you were a woman, I'd marry you." His florid face broke into a nasty grin. To a casual observer, his words would have been humorous but Erik felt the underlying barb and it hurt. He quickly busied himself putting the boiled potatoes in a serving bowl. When their father's health began to deteriorate, as the senior and most belligerent sibling of the four, Isaac had taken it upon himself to act as the head of the household, although the beefy man would often reluctantly defer to Reuben's careful reasoning. Isaac was a good farmer though and made the land prosper.

Reuben had been his usual supportive self. Erik was far closer to Reuben than his other brothers were. "It does look good, Erik," Reuben had complimented him as he placed the platters of kosher sausage and boiled potatoes on the table. Reuben's praises took the sting out of Isaac's needling. Erik had pointed out the jam, knowing that Reuben loved jam with his rye bread, he remembered Reuben's smile as if it was yesterday. "My favorite."

The brothers had taken seats but waited respectfully for Ludwig. His slow but steady footsteps as he made his way in the kitchen indicated both his frailty and his strength. They bowed their heads as their father said the Hebrew blessing over the food. As tradition demanded, he was served first and then, jostling each other, the four brothers filled their plates. The scratch of utensils on plates was the only sound for several minutes.

As they were finishing the meal, Helmon and Isaac, always competitive, teased each other about which girl in the village was the prettiest and who, of the two of them, she favored.

"Saw you walking with Hilda the other day, Helmon. She's a fine figure of a girl," Isaac had teased as he sat back wiping his mouth with his sleeve.

Helmon had been chewing a huge mouthful of food. Although his response was mostly indecipherable, his tone of voice was not. All of them had laughed.

Squeaking their chairs back, the brothers began to rise from the table for evening chores but waving a gnarled hand, Ludwig motioned them to stay seated.

His memory paused. Erik's eyes drifted over to the head of the table to the larger chair with the high, ornately scrolled backrest of gleaming, waxed black cherry wood. His father had sat in it for every meal from the time Erik could remember to the day before he died. *I miss you father.* He took a deep breath and, annoyed, swiped with his fingertips at the wetness he felt on his cheek below the corner of one eye.

His father had asked him to clear the plates. The old man winced as he reached behind him and placed an old, worn but sturdy brown leather map case on the barren surface of the table. The brothers exchanged expectant looks.

He could still hear his father's strong but calm voice and see the steady, commanding sparkle in his green eyes. *The same as Reuben's, even down to the green turning grey when angry.*

"As you know," his father had begun, "we are unable to expand our land here in Prussia. The gentiles, though friendly, would rather not sell to Jews. Uncle Hermann in New York and I have written back and forth for years. There's trouble brewing in America between those who want to keep slavery and those who do not. The government wants to ensure federal power and settle the western parts of the country."

Erik could feel the rapid pounding of his heart as his father fell silent, his eyes moving brightly but slowly around the table. "From what Hermann has written to me and from what I've read in the newspapers, the western part of America is inhospitable, almost lawless but there is land and where there is land, there is opportunity."

His hands shaking slightly, he spread the maps he had slipped from the old leather case across the table. He asked Helmon and Erik to hold the corners down. He traced the maps with a crooked, still calloused forefinger, demonstrating the route from Villmar to Bremen, then across the Atlantic on the steamship *SS Edinburgh*, landing in New York at a place called Castle Garden.

His finger paused as he looked at Reuben, and then resumed its movement on the rough textured paper west to St. Louis and then west again from there through an area the map indicated was completely unsettled, to a place called Cherry Creek. Then even further west across what the map indicated was a large mountain range. Erik had not been sure but the final destination seemed to be mountains in an area of the United States designated as the Kansas Territory. The mountains were located above a valley the map called 'Uncompahgre.'

He remembered as his father's eyes traveled around the table again, apprising each brother but Erik. The patriarch's gaze finally came to rest on Reuben, a look of combined pride, love and worry showing in the elderly wrinkles of his face, its features suddenly stern.

"Reuben, I have booked your passage on the *SS Edinburgh*. The ship will be launched later this year. Its new condition should make the voyage more comfortable. It leaves Bremen in the evening, on January 16, a little over eight months from now. It makes port for a short time in Portsmouth, steams to Liverpool, and then continues to New York. January 16 is a Sunday. You will need to be on the road before daylight that day. I do not wish you to travel on the Sabbath. Erik will take you in and bring the wagon back."

Ludwig continued with instructions to pack light. He informed Reuben that he had sent money in advance to Uncle Hermann to use to buy equipment, supplies and hire men who Reuben might need.

Erik would never forget the intensity of his father's eyes as they bore into those of his favorite brother at the end of those instructions, "Your work coat is back from our friend Marvin, the tailor. I have hung it in the front closet. There are six diamonds sewn into the hem. The monies you may use as you see fit to buy equipment and supplies and to hire the men that you may need. The diamonds, however, are to be used for only one thing— to buy our land. They are to be used for nothing else."

Reuben had looked flushed, surprised and nervous. His eyes were twice as wide as normal. The two older brothers sat, stunned. Slamming one meaty hand on the table, Isaac began to make a scene but ceased immediately after a sharp, stern reprimand from Ludwig. Erik remembered the sinking feeling in his own stomach. *My favorite brother leaving, I may never see him again.* He remembered looking at Isaac and Helmon, trying to imagine what life would be with them without Reuben's buffering support. He heard himself laugh aloud in the empty kitchen. *I was exactly right to be concerned.*

He shook his head to clear the memory, wiped the quill on the blotter, dipped it in the ink well and staring down at the paper, continued to write:

I've decided I am coming to America to be with you. I've been reading up on the United States. I think Father was right when he talked about America being the future. But of one thing I am certain—I have no future here, at least, no truly happy future. The farm prospers. Persecution has not increased but neither has it diminished. I know you will put this letter down at this point, look into space and think, 'but Erik, what about your music?'"

Pausing, Erik absentmindedly cleaned the quill on the blotter again. Through the window, his two brothers were still in animated discussion with their faces now only a foot apart. Erik inked the quill,

I'm sure there's music in America too, but more important to me than my music, is me. Helmon has not been kind and Isaac has been...

Erik's eyes flicked up to the window as he searched for the right word,

...unkind. My work is not appreciated. My music is not respected. With Father and Mother gone and you in America, I've had to spend more time on the farm and less time in school. I really don't think that Isaac considers me a man. I know they both think I'm too soft or too much like a girl, as Isaac likes to say but I know I'm a man. I think America might be the best place to demonstrate that.

Erik pinched his lower lip between his upper and lower teeth and carefully read the last paragraph. *It is the truth. I will leave it.*

By coincidence I will also be sailing on the Edinburgh and departing from Bremen. The ship sails on a Sunday again, which is good. I've made arrangements with a friend of mine at school to bring me there. I'm quite sure Helmon and Isaac would refuse. I have not told

them yet and do not look forward to it. But they must have some notice because they will have to find someone to do the work they do not think I do. Uncle Hermann knows my travel plans. I went through Father's things and have the directions I need to get to Uncle's house when I arrive in New York. I'm sure he will give me instructions from there on how to find you.

I so look forward to seeing you Reuben, and helping you establish the ranch, as Uncle Hermann wrote to me a farm is called in the West. It should be a grand adventure. You haven't gone off and got married, have you? Gretchen still asks about you. Don't worry, I never did tell her that was me in the tree watching the two of you at that picnic.

Erik chuckled to himself as he wrote the last line, imagining Reuben's smile as he read the words.

The Edinburgh sails on June 17th. It is expected in New York on July 25th. Uncle Hermann says it will take a week to reach St. Louis by train and then six weeks to two months to get to Cherry Creek. He was unsure of how long the journey from Cherry Creek would take or what travel arrangements are available to the Uncompahgre. It's a strange name but I like it. Uncle Hermann says it is American Indian for "where water turns rock red." How odd. I look forward to seeing why the Indians gave it such a name.

Love,

Your Younger Brother, Erik

The light slanting in the windows was at the odd angles of late afternoon, its beams across the kitchen dissected by the shadows of the mullion that separated the blown glass panes through which it streamed. The patterned sunlight fell directly on Ludwig's chair, imparting a cheerful gleam to the antique wood, the grains in the cherry reddish amber and dark brown.

Looking fondly at the chair for a moment longer, Erik carefully folded the letter and slipped it in the envelope, sealing it with wax in three places. He smiled at the chair, still radiant with the fading light from the window. *You approve, don't you Father?*

"Reuben and I will make you proud, Father. We will establish a great ranch. I know you will be watching and I will prove to you I am a man."

May 29, 1855

PHILIPPE REYES

REUBEN STRAIGHTENED UP FROM TIGHTENING THE CINCH under Lahn's belly and turned to Zeb. A thin rim of bright yellow from the rising sun pierced the pale, blue, dawn sky above the higher ground east of the wagons. Johannes was already mounted and he was checking the load in his Sharps .52 carbine. Buck and Lahn quietly nickered to one another and brushed their nuzzles together.

Zeb half-smiled, "Appears our horses get along."

Reuben chuckled, "Like masters, like horses. I think the best plan, Zeb, is we will meet you at Fort Massachusetts. Randy seemed to think that would save coming back all this way and that route might be a little bit easier with the cattle and wagons than going over Kenosha Pass."

The weathered leather that passed for skin around Zeb's eyes crinkled, "Randy said? If his feet ever left that damn store, he might know." Zeb smiled. "Just so happens in this case he is mostly right. It's gonna take us a good six or seven days to get to the San Luis with these wagons. When do you expect you might be there with the cattle?"

"Well, first we have to find cattle, then we have to talk somebody into selling some. And until we talk to that Mexican vaquero Randy suggested and that ranch family with the two older sons, we don't even know how many hands we'll have." Reuben paused, glanced at the wagon where Rebecca and Sarah slept and turned back to Zeb, "You going to be okay alone?"

"Ain't going to be quite alone. The McKinley wagon is going part of the way and they ain't in no rush to hurry down. Their course is set for somewhere around that Pike's Peak country. That gets us about halfway," he paused and looked at Reuben, "and I suspect Sarah and Rebecca will be driving their wagons."

Reuben was silent for a moment. He glanced again at the wagon where the women were still asleep. "Sarah, maybe—but we both know that..." he grinned at Zeb and was sure he saw the slightest uncharacteristic blush color the mountain man's tanned cheeks, "...but I'm not at all sure about Rebecca."

"You gonna say goodbye?" asked Zeb quietly.

"Already did. Last night. She told me she would either be with you or she wouldn't." Reuben swallowed trying to ignore the empty feeling in his gut.

Zeb was silent. Reuben looked at him for a moment, "If she decides to go back to England, I think you ought to burn that wagon of Jacobs. It has a bad feel. Sarah can drive the prairie schooner."

Zeb shook his head, "No sense burnin' a good wagon. I got a couple of Ute friends. One has strong medicine, a great *puwa*. I think I can trade him some pelts for him to cleanse the wagon of Jacob's energy."

Reuben knew the doubt showed in his face and Zeb saw it.

"Don't be doubtin' the power of Spirit," Zeb said seriously, his eyes boring into Reuben's. "You felt it yourself—when you met Eagle Talon back there at Two Otters Creek."

A vision of the Sioux warrior, statuesque on his painted mustang, like an apparition in the lingering smoke and dust of battle, his war shield with an eagle's talon high on his extended arm, his hand palm out, coursed through Reuben's memory. He was the obvious leader of the four warriors behind him, one slumping in the saddle. "Roo-bin, Ray-bec-ka," the brave had said while Zeb interpreted.

Reuben nodded his head slowly.

Zeb watched him. "Figured you'd remember. It might be good to have a second wagon for supplies. Cases of nails, some mortar mix, tools, wire for fence," Zeb smiled. "Maybe even get some of them windows. I reckon we can pack 'em so they don't break. I hauled one up to the cabins ten or so years ago. Only lost one pane. Besides, I can tie them mules off behind it. The extra horses will be behind the prairie schooner."

Zeb reached out a long arm and squeezed Reuben's shoulder. His grin grew wider, "I think Rebecca's gonna require you build her a house. She sure as hell ain't going all that way to live in a wagon."

Reuben took a deep breath and exhaled slowly. "Time tells all tales. Why don't you plan on being down at Fort Massachusetts, let's say, twelve days from today. We might be a day or two behind you. It will be a lot easier holding the wagons in one place than those cows, if we are lucky enough to get any."

Zeb nodded and waved to Johannes. "See you on the other side of La Veta Pass. Watch your top knot."

Reuben's eyes must have widened because Zeb chuckled. "Your scalp, Reuben, your scalp." Still chuckling, the tall trapper turned away and led Buck toward the McKinley Conestoga on the other side of the now diminished circle of wagons.

Reuben walked Lahn over to Johannes and Bente and mounted. "Let's see if we can't go hire cattle-rustling Philippe."

Johannes grinned widely and shook his head. "Crazy Prussian," Reuben heard him mutter.

———————

THE ARAPAHO VILLAGE WAS UPSTREAM OF THE CONFLU-ence of Cherry Creek and the South Platte. The sun had fully risen and the sky pulsed brilliant blue, Lahn and Bente picked their way slowly down the steep, greening sides of an old river meander, which curved toward a cluster of almost one hundred tipis, smoke curling in thin streams from their smoke holes, a number of smaller tipis surrounding one much larger lodge in the center of the camp. One tipi was pitched a good two hundred yards downstream of the rest of the village.

Reuben glanced quickly at the sun.

"Nine o'clock, maybe," offered Johannes.

Reuben nodded and pointed at the tipi on its own, "Based on what Randy said, that must be it." In front of the tipi, they could see a man's shirtless figure sitting on a stump in front of a crackling fire.

"Well, let's go. Never met a rustler before," said Johannes, dryly.

———

PHILIPPE REYES LEANED TOWARD THE FIRE, HIS ELBOWS on his knees, his bare shoulders warming in the morning sun. He spit on the honing stone, turned over the long thin blade of his knife and began sharpening its opposite edge.

With lowered head, he watched the two riders approaching. One was medium build, square shouldered and moving easily with the big palomino underneath him. The other was tall, very tall, with longer blond hair. Something in his posture screamed military—or maybe law. Without moving other than the slightest turn of his head, Philippe said in a low voice directed back at the tipi, "Woman, bring one of my pistols and the Smoothbore. *Pronto.*"

From inside the leather walls came a whiney, plaintive response, "Get them yourself, you lazy dog."

Philippe felt the muscles in his jaw clench. *Worthless squaw.* "Goose Feather, there's two riders coming in. Might be law. Bring the weapons, *ahora mismo!*"

The tipi flap snapped back and the round, pudgy, deep copper face of Goose Feather, her jet-black hair hanging in greasy strings around her shoulders, poked partially into the sun. The squints of her eyes took in the riders. Muttering to herself she ducked back into their tipi, emerging seconds later with one of his onyx-handled .36 caliber Colt Navy pistols, it's silver barrel flashing in the morning light and his .45 caliber Smooth-bore Musketoon.

Philippe stood slowly, wanting to appear nonchalant. He turned and watched Goose Feather waddling the last few feet toward him, her shoulders swinging back and forth with each step. Dirt-smudged grease stained the leather, which clung tightly to her ample form, the sagging layers of flesh squeezed into the doeskin imparting skin-filled folds to the material. *She puts on any more weight and she will have to add leather to that dress.*

Philippe took the pistol. He shoved it into his belt, positioning it perfectly for a quick right-handed draw. He didn't have to check the load in the Musketoon—he routinely checked it several times a day and each night before he crawled under the robes with Goose Feather, invariably turning his back to her and pretending he was asleep when she tried to fondle him. He held the rifle loosely in his left hand.

The riders reined up ten feet from him. The smaller, younger of the two, dark brown curly hair underneath a dark brown cowboy hat that looked more new than old, crossed his forearms on the saddle horn and leaned forward. Philippe's eyes fell to the pearl-handled Navy Colt in the holster, low on his hip.

When his gaze returned to the young man's face there was a smile in the green eyes that returned his look. "I'm Reuben Frank. This is Johannes Svenson. No need to be jumpy...." Reuben paused, "We're not the law."

Philippe shifted his eyes to Johannes who was watching him intently. The tall blond man nodded.

Philippe felt himself relax. Reuben's eyes flickered over his shoulder and he knew Goose Feather's heavily jowled face was staring out the flap of the tipi to which she had retreated. Johannes' eyes were fixed on the long scar that ran from his beltline across his well-defined abdominal muscles and up the front side of his chest almost to his sternum. He grinned at the tall blond. "A minor dispute over *una muchacha muy bonita.*"

Johannes broke into a laugh. "Who got the girl?"

Philippe pretended to look affronted, "Why, *Señor* Johannes, I did, of course. Would the two of you like to join me for some café? It will not take long and you can tell me why you honor me with your visit."

Reuben dismounted and walked within a few feet of Philippe, his gaze steady. "Thank you but we have a long ways to go and we are short on time. I have two simple, direct questions for you. First off, we were told you know cattle. Is that true?"

I like his direct approach. Philippe smiled, watching Reuben closely, "Well, *compadre*, judging by you telling me you are not the law, I believe you are aware that I have experience with cattle."

The young man grinned. "And the second question is, I'm headed over to the Uncompahgre with Johannes. There might be a few others—ladies—joining us and the mountain man, Zebarriah Taylor, is our guide. He will be helping out some too. We are headed south to get cattle. I intend to establish a ranch. We could use a good hand. Interested?"

Philippe's eyes flickered momentarily upward. *Gracias Dios.* He returned his gaze to Reuben, "and the pay?"

"Ten dollars per month, plus room and board." Reuben chuckled, "when we get a roof up, that is."

"And how long do I have to get ready?"

"About five minutes."

Philippe smiled, "You drive a hard bargain, *Señor* Reuben. But it just so happens I am currently unemployed." He paused and laughed. "And I am already packed."

Goose Feather had now lumbered fully from the tipi. She stood behind and slightly to the side of Philippe and Reuben. Her features were flushed and the usual squint of her eyes were narrowed to slits by the lowered hard lines of her eyebrows. Her great bosoms rose and fell rapidly. In one hand, she held a bloody half-fleshed beaver pelt and in the other a six-inch curved skinning blade Philippe had given her in return for staying in her tipi. She pointed angrily with the knife and shrilled in Arapaho.

Johannes put his hand over his mouth trying to stifle a laugh and Reuben took a half step back, his eyes widening.

Philippe turned to her, "Shut up, squaw." His voice was grim. Without warning, his long left arm extended and in a blur, his thin strong fingers grabbed the hilt of the knife from her. He turned and threw it out into the sage.

Turning back to Reuben, he stuck out his hand, "You have a deal, *Señor* Reuben." The clasp of the younger man was warm, strong and sure and Reuben's eyes never left his. "And know this *Señor* Reuben; Philippe Reyes will ride for the brand, always, unless I tell you in advance otherwise."

Reuben nodded.

Turning, Philippe raised a hand, inserting his pinky and forefinger into his mouth. He blew a piercing whistle toward the line of river cottonwoods fifty yards away. A sleek, muscled black gelding appeared from the trees at a gallop.

Philippe flashed a wide smile at Reuben. "Diablo is very fast."

"Really?" There was a good-humored doubt in Reuben's tone.

Philippe winked at him. "There are many who could attest to his speed. Sometime I shall tell you."

Philippe shot a look at Goose Feather whose lower jaw was trembling, a look of hurt permeating the anger in her eyes. He said nothing, instead ducking into the tipi to gather his bedroll, clothes and the second of his brace of black-handled Navy Colts.

May 29, 1855

$\mathcal{N}$OW THERE WERE FOUR

"THAT IS SOME HORSE YOU HAVE THERE, PHILIPPE," said Johannes, the appreciation in his voice evident.

Philippe's teeth flashed white in a wide, proud smile. "I bred him myself. Diablo is an overo-mustang cross. The long legs of a racing horse and the stamina and smarts of a wild pony. I am convinced Diablo is faster than any horse in the territories." He laughed, a deep baritone laugh that boomed out to the cottonwoods, startling several wrens from their perches. All three horses pricked their ears. "Indeed this gelding has outrun the best the Texas Rangers could muster on many occasions."

Philippe turned to Reuben. "Where are we headed *Señor* Reuben? I don't think three of us are enough to handle three hundred longhorns. I am very familiar with the breed," Philippe flashed another smile.

"Zeb thinks his mustang Buck is the fastest horse in the territories," quipped Reuben. He grinned at Philippe. "Maybe the two of you will have to race. Johannes and I can make wagers. We are headed out to the Sampson

Place. It's more or less on the way, just a few miles west of the Platte on Bear Creek. Randy told us they have two sons. Same time he was kind enough to tell us about you. Perhaps one or both may want to join us."

The three men rode in silence punctuated by the occasional sharing of small talk about weather, cattle and horses. *Just getting the gauge of each other,* Reuben knew.

Reuben noticed Philippe wore his twin Colt Navy .36 caliber pistols tucked crosswise in his belt. The brace of Colts had black agate or maybe onyx handles—Reuben couldn't be sure—but they were the opposite color of his own pearl-handled grip. Reuben noticed numerous faint scratches on the silver barrels where they protruded below the leather of his belt. *He has slid them out from behind that belt far more than once,* Reuben thought.

It was sometime in early afternoon, shortly after fording the strong currents of the South Platte when Johannes raised himself in the saddle and pointed, "That must be the place."

Reuben slipped Mac's telescope from his pocket and extended the brass, "Doesn't look like much."

As they rode toward the distant buildings, the disrepair of the small ranch was obvious. The loafing shed leaned at a crazy angle without bracing. Trash and debris were scattered along the two-track into the ranch house. The house was dilapidated, unpainted and several windows were missing panes. Two older horses listlessly trotted toward them. They weren't starving but the ribs showed through their hide. Several more were fenced next to a small barn missing a portion of its roof.

Reuben's trained eye immediately picked out about fifty acres of land that had been farmed in the past and grown some type of crop. The tract was laid out along the creek and obviously watered from that source by ditches that looked clogged with debris and old growth.

He turned to Johannes, "Didn't Randy mention that creek doesn't run all year?"

"So?"

"Well, right now the water is up due to spring runoff. This is the time to take water out of the creek and get it on your cropland but it doesn't look like they've even plowed that acreage. It hasn't been seeded and they don't have water going."

Out of the corner of his eye, Reuben caught a quick glance from Philippe and a nod of agreement.

They reined in front of the house. Broken planks pockmarked what had once been a veranda. Their splintered edges tipped toward the ground under the stoop. The left-hand riser on the stairs up to the porch had settled, canting the stair treads at an angle. The remnants of a broken chair cluttered one corner.

"Hello?" called out Reuben.

There was no response and no one came to the door. Reuben was sure he heard some type of movement inside. He was just swinging his leg over the saddle to dismount, when the door was flung open with a loud creak and a bang.

A large slovenly man, unshaven, potbellied, his eyes noticeably bloodshot even at a distance of thirty feet, swayed in the doorway holding a double-barreled shotgun. "Waddaya want?" His words were slurred. Reuben was aware Philippe's right hand was slowly moving up his leg toward his pistol. Johannes' eyes were on Reuben with a 'What now?' look.

"You can lower that shotgun. Randy from the mercantile sent us out here."

"I told that red-bearded bastard I would pay next month." The barrel of the shotgun raised slightly.

Reuben thought quickly. "No, it's not about money. I'm Reuben Frank; this is Johannes Svenson and Philippe Reyes. We're starting a ranch and heading south to pick up some cattle. Randy said you had two sons out here who knew their way around cows. We want to see if they were interested in signing up."

The man belched loudly, then wiped his mouth with the back of his forearm. Slowly lowering the shotgun, he asked, "Is it a paying job?"

Reuben saw Philippe's hand relax and slide back down his leg to rest on his thigh. "Of course. Eight dollars per month and room and board once we get a bunkhouse up. Are you Mr. Sampson?"

The man lowered the shotgun to the floor unsteadily and leaned against the doorway. "Yep. You must be talking 'bout my boys, Jonathan and Michael." He belched again. "Come on in. Meet the boys and the wife. I think we got some coffee. I could use some."

Johannes, Reuben and Philippe began to dismount.

"Not you, Mexican," came the surly voice from the doorway.

Philippe froze, his right leg parallel down Diablo's spine, in the process of dismounting. The lines of his face hardened.

"Either we all come in, Mr. Sampson or none of us do." Reuben felt, rather than saw, Philippe's surprised, appreciative look. "I suppose we can trail those cattle with three hands. Thank you for your time." Reuben made a show of beginning to remount.

"Hold on. Hold on. I guess it won't do no harm to have one of *them*..." he spit the word, "...in the kitchen one time." Sampson called back over his shoulder. "Get some coffee out for these boys. Two cups..." he paused, "I mean three." His eyes shifted nervously to Reuben and then turning, he waved his hand for them to come in.

Reuben was appalled at the interior of the hovel the Sampson family called home. He followed Johannes' stare upward toward the roof. Blue sky poured through the cracks of half-rotten planking in at least a dozen places. *Colder than Hell in the winter and wetter than Hades when it rains.*

One little girl with curly, dirty brown hair was fixated on her barren plate and two slightly older boys stared at them from smudged faces with rapidly blinking eyes from the large, stained rickety table. Two older teenaged boys—one frail and thin, the other large and heavyset sat in the furthest chairs.

The father stood, swaying slightly, behind the two older boys. "This here's Jonathan. He's fifteen but not too handy. This here's Michael. This boy knows cattle. He can wrestle a steer to the ground by his lonesome."

Mr. Sampson slapped a beefy hand on the thick, sloped shoulders of the large youth. The boy's oval face drained of color. His eyes were wide and frightened.

"We're having a late breakfast. If we'd known, we woulda set out more food."

Reuben could see the filthy surface of the wood stove from where he stood. Two large iron skillets that appeared not to have been cleaned for years sat on the stovetop. Eight small biscuits were lost in the black expanse of one cast iron pan, sizzling in the other were eight strips of bacon, also appearing lonely in the wide bottom of the cast iron. Reuben's eyes roved the interior. He could not see any significant food stores.

"Pa? Pa?" Michael stammered in a low voice.

"Shut up boy, your Pa is making a deal for you." Turning, he bellowed, "Where is that damn coffee?"

A small, frail shell of a woman with hair like her daughters looked anxiously over her shoulder. There was a purple bruise on her cheekbone. "It's comin'. It's comin'," she said anxiously.

"Actually, Mr. Sampson, I don't drink coffee."

"Neither do I, *señorita*." Philippe removed his hat, bowed and swept the sombrero toward the floor. "No need to prepare a cup for me but thank you."

Johannes threw a glance at Reuben, "I drink coffee but I must have had three pots this morning, so you can count me out too."

Reuben was sure Sampson's wife's shoulders sagged with relief and she leaned on the counter for support, her back still to them.

Sampson slid his eyes to each of the three men. "Okay, no coffee. Makes no never mind to me. So, I think you should take both these boys. Make 'em into men and pay them a wage."

He looked down at his two sons, "And you remember to send them wages back to your Ma and Pa. We kept you alive, fed and kept a roof over your head all these years. It's the least you can do."

He took a few weaving steps toward one of the two cabinets above the makeshift kitchen counter, opened one, took out a bottle one third full of an amber liquid and tipping his head back, gulped a large swallow. His face contorted. Smacking his lips, he swiped his mouth with his shirtsleeve and then replaced the bottle in the cupboard. He cleared his throat. "So, will they do?"

Reuben turned his attention to the younger of the two brothers. He was small with wire-rimmed glasses and an unkempt towhead mop that had not been cut or trimmed for some time. His thin face and frail-looking frame reminded him of Erik. "How old are you, Jonathan?"

Jonathan cast a frightened glance at his father. "Damn near sixteen," Mr. Sampson rasped loudly, "and old for his age."

Reuben shifted his gaze to Michael. The big, heavy youth's mouth was agape. His eyes were darting wildly from his father to Reuben.

"How old are you, Michael?" Reuben asked gently.

Sampson cuffed the boy across his head and Michael cringed. "Well, answer the man. These people are real-life cattlemen. They ain't got heaps of time."

"Six...six...sixteen," Michael stammered. Reuben, Johannes and Philippe exchanged glances.

Reuben's first inclination was to leave but he kept his silence and studied Michael. *Maybe I can save this boy's life and besides, we need the extra pair of hands.*

"Well, Mr. Sampson, I'm sure Jonathan here is a good hand but he's a little too young for what we'll be doing; however, we might be needing help in the future. Michael, though, will do fine. I think he'll make a good cattleman." A slight hint of a shy smile flitted across Michael's face at the praise but it disappeared immediately and he looked apprehensively at his father. The two sisters and two younger boys sat at the table looking down at their empty plates. They had not said a word and had barely raised their eyes, even to see who had entered the house.

"Michael, gather up your gear. You have a horse don't you?"

Mr. Sampson stuck out his chest belligerently. "What kinda outfit do you run, Mr. Franklin or whatever your name is? Never heard of a cattle ranch that didn't have horses for their hands."

"He can have my horse," Michael's mother had turned from the stove, her hands nervously wringing her apron. Ignoring her glowering husband, she continued in a fast, tremulous voice, "Michael you go get Sam now. He'll do you good and I never ride anymore anyway. Go on now son; don't keep these men waiting." She cast fearful eyes at her husband who frowned menacingly back at her from over Michael's head.

SEVERAL HUNDRED YARDS FROM THE RANCH HOUSE, Michael craned back around in the saddle. Reuben followed his gaze. The slight figure of his mother was waving from the porch. Raising one arm, he clumsily returned the goodbye, then faced forward looking down at the back of his old gelding's neck. He raised his hand and swiped his cheeks with his fingertips.

Philippe noticed the youth's tears also. His face softened. "Muchacho, let's ride a bit ahead of these tenderfeet and see if we can keep them out of trouble." His eyes briefly met Reuben's and Reuben winked at him.

"O...O...Okay," replied Michael, surprise in his voice.

Reuben watched them lope ahead and turned to Johannes. "Why don't we just work our way down this west side of the river?" Johannes nodded agreement.

May 29, 1855

*H*EADIN' SOUTH

AN HOUR PASSED. FAR TO THE SOUTHWEST ROSE A HIGH pyramid-shaped mountain glowing white on its sharp crown. *Must be Pikes Peak.* In front of them, one hundred yards farther down the trail, rode Philippe, his slender frame form-fitted to his beautifully engraved saddle replete with silver conchos that accentuated Diablo's sleek and powerful movements. Philippe's broad shoulders were shaded by a wide-brimmed black hat with a tall round crown. His black wool jacket tapered from the shoulders to the narrow waist at his belt as if tailored. His chaps were darker than Reuben's or Johannes,' with rounded edges and heavier, shorter fringe. *Drier climate down south.*

A half-horse length behind Philippe rode Michael. The big youth sat his saddle comfortably, his sloping shoulders hunched slightly over his heavy torso, his upper body rolling with the gait of his older sorrel horse. He wore a dirty, brown wool vest over a grey wool shirt.

He had a .44 Colt Army revolver tucked in his pants. *Too far towards the hip,* Reuben observed, *in no position to be played quickly.*

His thoughts were interrupted by Johannes' question.

"So, did you sleep under or in the wagon last night?"

Reuben felt his jaw set. He nudged Lahn slightly forward of Bente, swiveling his eyes away from the bright May sun to the east, to the country west of them.

Undulating foothills swept down from forested mountains. Beyond the foothills loomed the sharp spines of snow-covered peaks.

He turned to Johannes, "You know the answer to that. You saw me getting out of the bedroll this morning, bumping my head for the thousandth time on those damn struts underneath Rebecca's wagon bed."

"Yes, I suppose I did," Johannes chuckled.

Leaning down, Johannes adjusted the lariat hanging from the side strap of the saddle. He jiggled the stock of his Sharps 1852 slanting breech carbine to make sure the scabbard was on securely. The curved hilt and hand guard of his saber and the tip of the saber scabbard, stuck out on either side of the bedroll lashed behind his saddle.

Hoping to steer the subject away from Rebecca, Reuben craned his head toward Johannes. "You think four is enough?"

"I guess we will find out. And I will remind you, my Prussian friend, it's really three and a half. I told you way back on the train when you first raised this crazy idea of me accompanying you out here," he grinned and winked at Reuben, "that this son of a Viking knows nothing about cattle." He laughed, "And, I'm not all too sure I want to learn."

They rode in silence for several minutes, listening to the soft plod of their horses' hooves on the sandy clay soil and the occasional muted roar of the high spring flow of the South Platte a quarter mile east. The pace of the river's flow would slow by the time it reached its confluence of the North Platte, two hundred miles southeast of where they rode. High overhead, enormous flocks of Canadian geese periodically pierced the cloudless blue sky in huge V-shaped patterns. Even at that distance, their high guttural honks and calls echoed off the soft folds of the country.

At one point, the birds were so raucous that Reuben lifted his cowboy hat and, shielding his eyes from the sun, looked up admiringly at their formations. "Mac said that when geese fly north you can count it as a sure sign that summer is close behind." Aware of Johannes' stare, he adjusted the hat back on his wavy brown hair and turned to his tall blond friend.

Johannes normally prided himself on things being kept in military order, asking Inga to trim his hair at least once a week but he had not cared for it at all since her death. His hair sprang from beneath his grey-brown campaign hat, gathered in waves around his ears and ended in almost full ringlet curls that now brushed his shoulders. *He does look a lot like a Norseman.*

"Any decisions?" Johannes' voice was nonchalant.

"On what?" Reuben realized he had snapped back at the question more harshly than intended. Johannes' blue eyes, bright and piercing even in the shade of his wide-brimmed hat, were steady and concerned.

"You're trying to avoid an inevitable discussion, my friend. Did you talk to Rebecca?"

Annoyed, Reuben slapped his hand to his chaps where they covered his thigh. The sudden sound startled Lahn and the palomino took an extra dancing half-step, then settled back down.

"You seem mighty worried about me and Rebecca. It will be what it will be."

"Frankly, I've grown to like her. But I'm not as much interested in Rebecca, as I am concerned about you."

Reuben glanced quickly at his friend, immediately regretting his quick temper. The question made him face the anxiety he felt at the uncertainty of he and Rebecca's future. He took a deep breath and exhaled slowly. "Matter of fact, we did talk. For about three hours after you and I got back to the wagons. She has me quite confused, Johannes. You have far more experience with women than I do. I swear, sometimes I think we're making progress in the discussion and then thirty seconds later she's back on the same point she was stuck on ten minutes before."

He shook his head. "I love her and I'm fairly certain she loves me. When we get along, it's almost as if we can read each other's minds. And when we are..." Reuben looked down, embarrassed, "...together..." He sighed and felt the heat in his cheeks. "While I don't have near the experiences of some people I know," he half grinned at Johannes, "all that seems completely satisfying for both of us."

"So, when you can't be sure where she stands, you feel frustrated and exasperated. And when you're getting along, everything else in the world plays second fiddle?"

Reuben nodded, "That sums it up well."

"The problem, my friend, is that you do not love Rebecca...." Johannes held up his hand as Reuben started to retort. "You're *in love* with her." Johannes laughed. "Loving someone and being *in love* are very different. *In love* is the most blissfully confusing state of mind in which a man can find himself." He looked sharply at Reuben. "Are you two reaching a resolution on anything?"

Reuben leaned forward and wiped the top of his saddle horn vigorously with his thumb, "Only that she will make up her mind one way or the other whether she is staying in the Cherry Creek area until she gets her land sold or coming over to the Uncompahgre with us."

"You mean with *you*."

"Yes, with me, or going back to England. She explained some things about her father's trading company and related outstanding debts she had not shared before. In addition to cleaning that up, she's concerned about their aborigine servants, their house in London and, of course, all the family possessions. I got the impression she didn't really trust the solicitor who handles the family affairs. If I distill what she said, her family seems to have some type of financial problems right now—which is why she wants to sell the land that her father bequeathed her out here. But they still have quite a bit of assets, both sentimental and valuable back in England. We talked about a fourth possibility—she goes back to England and then returns. Problem is; I think if she does that she will never return."

"What did she say to that idea?"

"She didn't. She just did her famous foot stamp, jutted her pretty little chin out with fire blazing from those big brown eyes the way she does and told me I was selfish to be burdening her with so much to think about at a time she had so much to think about." Reuben shook his head and chortled without mirth. "What were those words you used? Exasperating? Frustrating? Yep."

Johannes' blond eyebrows scrunched in a puzzled look. "But if we are meeting Zeb and Sarah south of here at Fort Massachusetts with the cattle and then heading west to the Uncompahgre, we won't get back to within one hundred and fifty miles of Cherry Creek. How is she going to tell you what she decided?"

"I asked her the same thing. She shrugged and said she would either be with Sarah and Zeb or she wouldn't."

The lengthy ensuing silence that followed was broken when Johannes muttered, "Interesting."

"What's interesting?"

"The completely opposite riding styles between Michael and Philippe. That ranch youngster looks like he was poured into the saddle. Each step the horse takes his body is like gelatin, moving, absorbing. Philippe on the other hand, rides with such a stiff back posture it is as if somebody lashed two metal bars to his back. He looks just as comfortable though and at home in the saddle as the kid. My company of heavy cavalry once took on a like-sized unit of Royal Spanish Cavalry—some said it was a detachment from King Ferdinand's personal guard. They rode like Philippe does, stiff and statuesque but they surprised us. Some of the best riders and most versatile cavalry we ever fought."

Reuben waited but Johannes offered no more of the story.

"Well, don't leave me hanging. You're picking up bad traits from Rebecca. Who won?"

Johannes looked slyly sideways at him. "Captain Johannes Svenson of the heavy cavalry of the Danish crown never lost an encounter, Reuben." Then he grimaced and a look of pain swept briefly across his face, "Except with his own pride."

Johannes lowered his voice slightly, "What did you make of that whole situation at the tipi when you rode up, introduced yourself and less than a minute later asked Philippe if he wanted to ride with us?"

Reuben thought for a minute. "I liked him immediately but I sense he has a dangerous streak."

Johannes nodded.

"I think he is one of those men who is either your friend or your enemy. There's no in between for him," Reuben continued.

"I agree with your assessment. But didn't you think the interaction between he and his Arapaho woman was a bit strange?"

Reuben laughed. "Not at all that strange. He was happy for the excuse to ride out but she was not pleased."

"I thought for a few minutes she was going to come after you with that knife she was using to skin that beaver," Johannes chortled, "either that or she was going to use it on Philippe for not displaying any reluctance to leave her company."

"Well, I think leaving had been on his mind long before we rode up. Either that or he's one of the most organized men in the Rockies or it's just his habit to have things packed in advance, in case he has to move quickly. At any rate, based on what Randy said and our discussion there at the tipi, he knows his way around cattle...."

"Well, at the least he knows about rustling them," observed Johannes dryly.

"Everybody makes mistakes." Reuben did not miss the sharp sideways glance Johannes threw at him. *That didn't come out right at all*, Reuben chastised himself. "I have the feeling he knows how to handle those twin Navy Colts, too."

Johannes was quiet for a moment. "I think there's more to his story than we know, Reuben. The way he rides, I would say he's definitely Spanish trained, perhaps even in Europe but certainly by Europeans. And his features are..." Johannes searched for the word, "... aristocratic."

It was Reuben's turn to nod assent. "I noticed that too—his polite mannerisms, but I don't think Philippe Reyes bows to anyone."

"And what do you think about the boy?"

"He's not a boy—he's sixteen. I think we were damn lucky, in the space of two hours ride, barely going out of our way from the direction we were headed anyway, to come up with two hands who know cattle."

"I don't know, Reuben." There was a note of doubt in Johannes' tone. "Michael is awful young—in many ways. It's not just years that make the difference, you know."

"Yes, he is but I didn't sense anything bad about him. He's deathly quiet, maybe even to the point of shy. There's not much in his handshake and that stutter..." Reuben shook his head, "but then again how could you have self-confidence growing up in that situation?"

"They were dirt poor for sure."

"Yes, they all but pushed him out the door, though I think his mother did it out of love. We'll see how he bears up in the coming days. Sometimes someone like that just needs a chance. You and I and maybe Philippe, who knows, can spend some time with him. I think if we get him comfortable, teach him to think for himself and build up a little of his confidence, he could turn out to be a good hand. He'll certainly be loyal—he has no place to go. I'm not too sure his family would take him back in."

"No," said Johannes dryly, "with him gone they can each have a biscuit and a quarter in the mornings."

"Well, I'm sure that he'll miss them just because it's his family and that's all he knows. He certainly hasn't had any examples set." Ludwig's green eyes flashed through his mind. *Thank you, Father.*

"What's that?" Johannes suddenly pointed off toward the tree line of South Platte. Ahead of them, Philippe and Michael had reined in their horses.

Reuben reached into his jacket pocket and pulled out Mac's brass telescope. "Dammit Lahn, hold still." He extended the tube. "It's a band of Arapahos, maybe twenty braves and about the same number of women and children. Four or five travois. A small village on the move, I suppose."

Johannes relaxed and pushed the Sharps carbine back in the scabbard from its half-withdrawn position. "Guess I'm just a little jumpy after Two Otters Creek."

Up ahead of them Philippe dismounted and, after a moment, Michael also swung down off his saddle.

"What are they stopping for?" He and Johannes exchanged glances, dug their heels into their horses and broke into easy lopes that closed the distance in seconds.

PHILIPPE REYES KNELT DOWN WITH ONE LEG, CAREFUL not to put his knee into a prickly pear. He quickly began gathering rocks within easy reach. He had about finished a small circular fire pit, when Johannes and Reuben rode up. Michael, who had been watching him build the fire pit without a word or any offer of help, took a half step back from the approaching riders.

Philippe paused and perched one long arm over his raised knee. He nodded to Johannes and smiled at Reuben. He had liked Reuben from the moment the young Prussian had ridden up to the tipi, dismounted and firmly shook his hand while looking him in the eye. *A firm handshake and direct eye contact is the mark of honor and a gentleman*, his father's oft-repeated words bubbled up in his memory.

His initial sense of the young man was confirmed by Reuben's refusal to tolerate the surly prejudice of Michael's *Padre*.

Reuben leaned down from the palomino, his forearms crossed on the saddle horn. "Why are you stopping? Anything wrong?"

Philippe felt a chuckle rise from his chest, "No *Señor* Reuben. It is my custom to stop around midday to brew café."

Philippe rose, sauntered over to Diablo and unbuckled one flap of the saddlebag.

"I like that buckle idea," called out Johannes. "Easier and saves time when you want to get in and out to get something. Where did you get it?"

Without turning around, Philippe responded, "My father imported a number of them from Spain."

Philippe didn't catch the look Reuben and Johannes exchanged. His groping hand found what he was looking for and turning, he triumphantly held up a small sack of Arbuckle's coffee. "Amigos, you're right in time for the best cup of café this side of that range of mountains," he swept his arm expansively down the vista of the Rockies.

Reuben laughed and dismounted. "We've been going since sunup and a short break for the best *kafee* this side of the Rockies ought not to do any harm."

Smiling, Philippe poured water from his waterskin into a small pot and efficiently built a fire with sagebrush, which reduced to coals quickly. He placed two flat-sided rocks inside the fire ring on either side of the coal bed he gathered into a smoldering heap. Placing the pot on the rocks, he grinned at Reuben and Johannes. "Keeps soot off the bottom. I hate soot in my saddlebags."

Michael was shifting from one foot to the other, looking very uncomfortable. Philippe stared at him. *Poor timid mouse of a soul.* "What is the matter, Michael?"

"I...I have to...to...to...to pee."

Surprised, Philippe looked quickly at Reuben and Johannes. They too, appeared astounded, "Well, what are you waiting for, *muchacho*? We are all men here. You don't have to ask permission."

"Thank...thank you," blurted Michael. "I...I will go over to...to those rocks."

"You are a grown man, *muchacho*. You can go wherever you wish—except in my café." He heard Reuben and Johannes chuckle behind him. Watching Michael lumber toward the rocks, Philippe shook his head and turned back to the fire, deftly sprinkling coffee grounds into the boiling water, occasionally stirring the pot with the stem of a bitterbrush he had cut with the twelve-inch knife that hung from a black leather scabbard off his hip. The boil subsided as the sage coals quickly died.

With one finger over the spout, he poured in small trickles of cold water from the water pouch, beginning at the outside of the pot and working his way to the center in a spiral. "The cold water settles the grounds. The trick is just the right amount of water so as not to dilute the richness of the café."

Reaching for the handle of the pot with his left hand, he glanced up, enjoying the looks on Reuben and Johannes' face. "We will give it just a minute to settle. You might want to get your—"

His sentence was interrupted by a loud cry. Michael, fifty feet away, was buttoning up his britches, his thick shoulders less than a foot from several jumbled rocks that formed an outcropping almost neck high. On top of the rock coiled a large diamondback rattlesnake, disturbed from basking in the warmth of the late spring sun. It was rattling, coiled and ready to strike. Instinctively, Philippe drew one of the Colts from his crouched position with his right hand and without thinking, fired, the muzzle blast sending a shockwave into the top of his thigh and the under part of his left upper arm below and above the barrel of the pistol. His shot seemed to blend with an echo report so close together as to have been one. The snake's head flew off in a spray of red and scales, its long muscular body writhing on top of the sunlit, blood-sprayed rock. Michael stumbled backward, his face ashen, his breeches still partly undone.

Philippe looked down curiously at his pistol, turning it over in his hand. *How could it have possibly fired twice?* He looked up in time to see Reuben spin his Colt and slap it back into the low-slung holster.

"I'd say we both hit him about the same place," observed Reuben with no emotion.

Philippe tilted his head down, the wide brim of his sombrero masking his astonishment and smiled down at his own Colt. He stood, spun the cylinder, slipped a cartridge back in the empty magazine and then smoothly shoved the Colt back into the same position behind his belt.

His eyes met Reuben's and they held each other's gaze for a long moment. "*Señor* Reuben, that was very fast."

The young Prussian pushed his hat back on his forehead. "Actually, Philippe, you had the much more difficult shot. Very impressive." The two men nodded at each other, an understanding passing between them.

"Now, amigos, how about that café? Bring those cups over here." Philippe turned and called out to Michael who was still standing where he had stumbled back from the rocks, one hand on his forehead. "*Muchacho*, the snake is dead. Time for café. And finish buttoning those breeches." He, Reuben and Johannes broke into laughter.

May 29, 1855

RENAISSANCE OF THE SOUL

ONE HUNDRED SEVEN MILES NORTH OF THE WRITHING, decapitated remains of the rattlesnake, Black Feather picked a small stone from the base of the sage where he squatted and tossed it lazily at Pedro's corpse, aiming for the bullet hole in his forehead, which still seeped blood from where he'd shot him two days before. *Told ya a hundred times it was a bad idea to challenge me.* The pebble hit Pedro in the nose, scattering the swarming flies, and careened to the side rolling down the shallow bank to the canyon floor.

Without shifting his position, he turned his gaze to Dot's pale face. Her head rested against the blue wool of his jacket wadded into a makeshift pillow between her head and the rock against which she partially reclined. The young woman's parted lips were still slightly blue, her eyelids changing shape as her eyes moved rapidly beneath them in unconscious delirium.

Black Feather let his stare travel slowly down the thin

taper of her neck, her small breasts and the slight flare of her hips showing promise of the woman she would be in several years. Reaching over, he gently turned her calf where he had sliced her wool pants, examining the chunk of skin and muscle he had cut out with his blade to stop the spread of the rattlesnake's deadly venom, the deep red excavation encircling what had been twin puncture wounds. The clean edges of the incision were partially coagulated, filmed with a clear ooze. There was little puss. Nodding his head approvingly, Black Feather reached up to her thigh loosening the bandanna and stick tourniquet one-half turn. His eyes shifted back to the pale, porcelain face framed by blonde hair. Her lips were moving slightly and she groaned.

"You are gonna be fine," Black Feather said quietly, the soft compassion in his voice surprising him.

Raising his eyes, he scanned the shallow walls of the box canyon. The red rock outcroppings forming the eastern rim were now glowing in the sinking sun. His gaze drifted coldly and without emotion back to Pedro's awkwardly sprawled body. Shaking his head, he looked down at his own sinewy, bronzed forearms resting on his thighs. *I kill my right hand man I have ridden with for years and feel nothing. Yet I feel a sense of relief and protection for a scrawny, half-grown white woman who's been my captive for just several months. Strange.*

"Boss! Boss!"

Black Feather lifted his head toward Johnson and the thirteen remaining members of his renegade band. Some were standing by their horses; others were sitting on rocks.

One, Bama, sprawled on his back, ankles crossed, hands clasped on his belly above his brace of old powder and ball pistols, his sombrero pulled low over his face, sleeping.

My band cut by almost two-thirds in under a month. Eight kilt in seconds and that son-of-a-bitch Snake lighting out day before yesterday with eight following. And Pedro. Pressing his lips together, Black Feather picked up another stone and hurled it at Pedro's skull. *It all started with that dark haired kid's pearl-handled Colt. I should've known what he was up to when he got off that horse.* Black Feather shook his head disgustedly remembering the repeated bark of the young man's six-gun, bodies of various members of his band crumpling in their saddles or falling sprawled from their horses. *That's when it began, the distrust and discontent.* Extending a long arm, he again gently twisted Dot's calf to examine the cutaway flesh where the rattlesnake bite had been. Satisfied, he loosened the tourniquet another quarter-turn. Brooding, he recalled the day when he had plundered her family's wagon just miles from where they now camped. A shadow flitted across her form continuing like a dark ghost over the sage. The first of the turkey vultures had appeared yesterday. Now they had been joined by others flying circles high above them, their wings black against the deep blue sky high above Pedro's body.

That dispute with Snake was bound to come. We're both evil, but he is without a soul. And Tex? Crazy. A lunatic. His head bobbed slightly. *It's for the best. Better thirteen good men I can trust...* Squinting toward the remaining members of his band he corrected himself. *...partially* *trust—than thirty, half who would gladly slit my throat and far worse for her.* He again moistened his bandanna with whiskey, pressing it gently against the edge of her wound, slowly wiping the girl's calf where her skin was discolored a reddish purple above and below the wound.

"I'm sorry, Dot. Your leg will never be beautiful again, but in time the muscle will heal. You should be able to walk with only a slight limp." Reaching out, he gently brushed back her hair where it had fallen over her eyes and forehead. His touch evoked a slight whimper, and her eyes darted from side-to-side under almost translucent lids. The feel of her skin under his calloused fingertips again brought back the day he had abducted her—her screams, her mother clutching at her throat as she was thrown backward over the wagon seat into the canvass covered bed by the force of Snake's bullet, the wide petrified eyes of her father, suddenly lifeless when he had shot him with his Smoothbore .45 caliber from just feet away, blowing off the top of his head in a spray of blood and brain matter.

"Boss!"

With a start, Black Feather realized he had not responded to Johnson. The lanky Texan had been with him almost as long as Pedro had. Through seniority, he was now the new second in command.

"You want us to bury the Mexican? He is starting to stink."

"No, we will leave some food for the buzzards."

Johnson walked toward him. "You ain't got much shut-eye the last day or two. How's the girl doing?"

"She will be fine. That whiskey came in handy—I will make sure you are amply repaid the next time we take wagons or a homestead."

"Well, Boss, I'm not sure we have enough men left to rob too much from too many. We're gonna have to watch for singles or maybe a stagecoach."

Black Feather nodded. His new lieutenant was right. "Johnson, we're going to have to stay until the mornin'. The girl will not be fit to ride until then. I wanna good scab over that cut before her legs are hanging down over the edge of a saddle bouncing on a horse."

"We could put together a travois," suggested the Texan.

Black Feather rose. "We could, but by the time we put one together sturdy enough to survive being dragged in this rocky country, it'll be nightfall anyway."

Johnson nodded. "Suppose so...."

"We've been holed up here too long. Get Bama and Chief up on top of those canyon walls with Tom. Tell 'em to keep a sharp lookout. We will have to stay without fire. After all this commotion there ain't enough of us left to take on a cavalry patrol."

"Where we plannin' to head to tomorrow, boss?"

"I think we will head north of Horsetooth Rock. We'll stay in the creek bottoms between the hogbacks and then make our way up the Cache La Poudre River. We'll camp one night a few miles up into the canyon. The day after, if we push the horses, we ought to make it to above the Narrows. We'll camp above them where the valley widens out. It's a good defensible position. We can see anybody coming down from Cameron Pass and one or two men could hold off an army where the canyon is narrow behind us. We'll rest up there a spell, kill some deer or an elk and get back our strength."

Johnson sighed. "The men could use a break. We ain't had nothing but bad luck since we tried takin' that wagon train and that kid with the pearl-handled Colt. Shit— weren't figurin' on anything like him." Then the tall man smiled. "Ain't been over there in years, but I heard tell there's a couple of isolated homesteads over on the North Platte and the Michigan in that Northpark country on the other side of the pass. Maybe we can pick one of them off."

Black Feather nodded, careful not to agree. "Where did that lizard, Snake, say he was takin' that crazy bunch of loons?"

"The Uncompahgre. It's a valley far south of here. Many ranges bigger than the Rawah but almost unsettled. Ain't no wagon trains. He'll find the pickin's slim."

"Didn't he spout off somethin' about gold?"

"Only a rumor. Some say there's no gold down there. Others say there's a few prospectors that dug some up. But it is big, wild country."

Black Feather swept his arm out toward the undulations of the Great Plains stretching endlessly eastward from the mouth of the canyon. "Yep, I have heard something about it. Even bigger than this, they say. Fewer folks and much more rugged." His lips curled into a sneer. "Like you said, it will be slim pickin's for Snake."

Johnson nodded grimly, "Maybe Snake will chance into that young son-of-a-bitch and his pearl-handled Colt."

Clearing his throat of phlegm, Black Feather spit onto the ground between his legs. "Don't know about Snake, but I'll wager we'll meet up with that Colt again."

May 29, 1855

SNAKE

TWENTY-TWO MILES SOUTH OF DOT'S DELIRIOUS STRUG-
gle against the effects of the venom, the Big Thompson
River cascaded from its canyon mouth, spilling between
rocks, frothing and filled with frigid debris from the
spring thaw unwarmed by the afternoon sun. Beyond
the canyon, it slowed to a more placid, meandering
flow between eroded banks. Still murky from the
upstream turbulence, it continued its journey toward
the South Platte.

Snake stood and stepped away from the naked, mid-
dle-aged woman curled in a fetal position at his feet, her
body lying amidst the ripped remnants of what had been
her clothing, her skin pale in the glare of the sun.

Raising his leather loincloth to button his dirty breeches,
his thin lips twisted in a mean, satisfied smile. He turned
to the eight men circled around them and nodded, his
meaning clear.

Tex started to step forward, his round face contorted
in a demonic smile, the discolored scar on his neck puls-

ing. He drew his lips back, revealing only a few yellowed, blackish teeth, a gaping hole between them. He pushed his tongue between the toothless gap, drew his knife and peered hungrily down at the sobbing woman.

"Put that knife away, Tex. You can have your fun later, after the others, like you did with that banker's wife back in Nebraska."

The Texan nodded, light reflecting from his hairless skull, his eyes fixed on the bruised, terrified female form lying on the ground. Several of the men chuckled nervously. Snake noticed their eyes, fixed on the Texan's blade. *No doubt, remembering.* Snake apprized what had, earlier that day, suddenly become his own band of thieving outlaws.

"Could I go next, Meeestir Snake?" Morales was the smallest of the men who had joined with Snake in the split from Black Feather's band. The young Mexican, his eyes darting back and forth from the woman to Snake, was already unbuckling the worn, brown leather belt that held up the filthy canvas pants he had sewn from the top of one of the wagons they had plundered the year before.

"Please, please, good Lord Jesus Christ, have mercy, please," she moaned in broken, panicked wheezes.

"Morales, help the poor woman out." The group cast approving looks at Snake and broke into gales of laughter.

An hour passed. The sun was now well behind the foothills at the mouth of the canyon and the current of the Big Thompson swirled a filthy pink with the fading day's light. Snake rifled the clothes of the woman's dead husband, rolling the heavy man's corpse from side-to-side in the buggy seat where he had been shot to get access to his pockets. There were only a few small coins. An old sorrel mare stood wide-eyed and trembling in the traces of the buggy.

A cottonwood twig snapped behind him and he whirled. *Crazy Tex.*

"Snake?" the stocky man drawled, his eyes asking the question.

Snake smiled. "Just make sure when you're done she can't talk to no one about nothin' ever."

Tex wheeled, half running back toward the cluster of men fifty yards back from the river, pulling his knife from its sheath.

"Morales, Beanpole, come on over here. Let's torch this buggy." The two men broke off from the group, moving obediently in his direction. At six foot six, Beanpole was the tallest of the band, his sloped shoulders always hunched forward as if in a perpetual state of apology. The two men sauntered up. Beanpole grinned. "You're right, Snake. That damn captive girl Black Feather had was bad luck. This is the first bunch we've knocked off in more than a month."

"It's a start. Musta been on their way to neighbors for something. Sure didn't have enough money to be making a supply run and no extra clothes with them. Beanpole, why don't you—" his command was interrupted by a piercing scream from the woman. Snake looked up to see the rest of the men scatter and Garcia, a pudgy dark-skinned Mexican, bent over retching.

Morales turned pale and swallowed.

"Beanpole," Snake said, turning back toward the buggy, "slit that old mare's throat."

"Kill the horse, Patrone?"

"Yes," snapped Snake, "damn thing is old and half-starved. Won't do nothing but slow us down or wander off to some neighbor by happenchance and get people riled up and looking for these two before they have to."

"But," protested Beanpole, "what about the fire? The smoke?"

"Let it burn for a few minutes, enough to take out anything that might be a sign leading to us. Then push the damn thing into the river." Snake laughed. "Or hell, let the mare drag it down there and then kill her. We'll be on our way shortly, riding all night. I want to get down to that Uncompahgre country, and I wanna be there by late June. Find some folks with gold. These two-bit outfits 'round here ain't gonna have no money, and we ain't got enough men anyways. If we ride most of the dark, we'll be long gone by the time these folks is missed."

Morales and Beanpole exchanged looks. Beanpole shrugged and drew his knife.

"Let's get saddled up, boys," Snake called out.

Turning his head into the chill dusk breeze that boiled over the rocky ridge, he smiled to the southwest. *We're gonna have some good fun down there, along with gold. Them pilgrims can dig it and we can take it.*

May 29, 1855

$\mathcal{T}$HE OFFERINGS

EAGLE TALON'S MIND RACED, YET THE MUSTANG BENEATH him stood motionless. His shoulder trembled against the tension of the drawn bowstring but the shaft and arrowhead pointed at the two people huddled at the base of the tree remained steady. *They have no weapons*, he realized, *and they are neither Indian nor hairy-faced-ones*.

He eased back on the draw of the bowstring but kept the arrow nocked, moving his ankles almost imperceptibly along the flanks of the mustang. The horse responded, stepping toward the two huddled figures. Only two lance lengths away now, Eagle Talon could see more clearly. *Old man. Old woman. Old mule*. He relaxed the slight pull he had maintained on the bowstring, halting the mustang with equal pressure from his knees. The man's slender arm stretched protectively around the woman, his dark, thin body shielding her darker, thickset one. He lowered his arm and with some effort rose. The woman reached up, grabbing the worn sleeve of the man's jacket, pulling on it.

Eagle Talon stared, fascinated. Her skin was like the smudge of charcoal on the white bark of an aspen. The old man bent his graying head toward the woman. The tone of his voice seemed reassuring, much like Eagle Talon might speak softly to Walks with Moon. Then the man turned and faced Eagle Talon, looking up into his eyes. Only the length of a single lance separated them now.

The man spoke, his tone nervous yet friendly, but Eagle Talon could not understand his words. Perhaps it was the same language the hairy-faced-ones in the wagon train spoke but with a strange inflection. Remaining silent, Eagle Talon studied the pair.

The thin man seemed in good enough shape for his age, though his clothing showed signs of long travel. The heavy woman held a pudgy hand rolled in a tight fist and pressed to her lips, shaking. Large, dark brown eyes peered over her clenched fingers into Eagle Talon's. He dropped his own gaze when he realized he was staring back, embarrassed by this breech of etiquette.

The old man spoke again, pointing to the woman, then to himself and then in the direction of where the sun sets. The mule regarded him quizzically, one ear forward, one ear back, grey muzzle extended, sniffing toward the mustang.

Gesturing to Eagle Talon to wait, the man extended a finger at the mule, then walked over and opened one of leather pouches straddling the animal's haunches, reaching far into the saddlebag to find what he was looking for. *Only meager rations left*, thought Eagle Talon.

Withdrawing a small square of white shiny paper, the man pulled back the corners and held it toward Eagle Talon. Lifting his hand higher, the man waved his finger from the food to Eagle Talon, then back, the old woman looking on anxiously.

Lifting one leg over the mustang's head, Eagle Talon slid fluidly off the pony. The old man took a step backward. Eagle Talon reached into his own parfleche, withdrawing two small wrapped chunks of pemmican Walks with Moon had given him that morning. Turning, he took a step toward the man, who again stepped backward, lowering his own offering. Eagle Talon stopped and, unwrapping the pemmican, took a bite, chewing and swallowing, smacking his lips. He waved to the man to put away his food, and then raised his hand, offering him the pemmican. The dark-skinned couple exchanged surprised glances and the woman dropped her fist to her lap, her fingers opening and relaxing. Pointing at the pemmican, Eagle Talon walked slowly to the man, extending his arm.

With some hesitation, the old man reached out and took the offered food, saying something. Eagle Talon did not understand the words, but the tone of his voice was grateful.

Eagle Talon nodded, turned and walked the few paces back to his pony, his left hand reaching up to grab the horse's mane, his body concurrently springing up and over the horse's back in a half side somersault. Slinging the bow across his shoulders, he raised his hand, fingers to the sky, palm toward the dark-skinned couple. The man and woman exchanged wide-eyed glances again.

Then, tentatively, the old dark one raised his hand, palm out to Eagle Talon.

"*Toksa, kola,*" Eagle Talon said firmly. Without further words, and without looking back, he wheeled the mustang and rode slowly into the shadows of the alders toward the creek.

June 4, 1855

EPIPHANY

"HAVE YOU DECIDED?" AN ANXIOUS LOOK TURNED THE corners of Sarah's eyes.

Rebecca didn't answer. Her gaze traveled between the few remaining wagons. Aside from their own, there remained only Sarah and Jacob's makeshift, converted freight wagon, the Solomen family's prairie schooner, the Livingston rig with its lingering aura of grief over the loss of a father and husband at Two Otters Creek, and the McClintock family's Conestoga, worn from its long journey from Pennsylvania. The McClintock's were Mennonites, all of them thin, the man and woman of medium height with worn features from years of laboring on their small farm. The children were older, though not yet in their teens, quiet and well-mannered like their parents. *Perhaps the least obtrusive travelers in the entire wagon train.* Paul McClintock had been ridiculed by some of the men, and had been the subject of hushed whispers between the women on the train after the fight at Two Otters Creek. Refusing to bear arms, he had not participated in the battle. But even as the fighting was still raging, he was first to aid the wounded. *No doubt, he saved several lives at the risk of his own.*

Rebecca stared at their wagon, remembering Paul hunched over a wounded Pawnee, the immobile, bleeding brave's dark eyes regarding him with suspicion and hate. As attentive to the Indian as he was to the men and women of the train, Paul had just finished dressing the gaping wound in the warrior's chest when he was shoved roughly aside by two other men from the train. Rising, he tried to intervene, but it was too late. Both men fired several shots into the helpless form of the Indian. When the other men left, Paul stood over the brave's corpse, tears streaming down his cheeks. Compassionately folding the dead man's arms over his chest and closing his still wide-open eyes, Paul had walked slowly and sorrowfully back to his wagon.

Her eyes traveled to the other two wagons remaining, the wide gaps between the rigs a reminder of departed friends bound for wild, unsettled destinations whose names she had never heard and did not recognize. *I miss the Johnson family—Margaret, Harris, and those two cute little girls.*

Before being knocked almost unconscious by a stocky Pawnee warrior's shield, Rebecca had glanced up while reloading the Sharps and seen Harris' heavy frame struggling with an Indian trying to steal their heirloom American flag, which had flown from the front of their wagon all the way west from the Mississippi. He had proudly told her on several occasions his grandfather carried the flag with thirteen stars circled on a blue field in the Revolutionary War. The flag had again gone into battle with Johnson's father in the War of 1812. *So different are these people from the effete, well-dressed snobs of London, but so tough-minded, resolute and fearless despite their fears.* Rebecca shook her head and grinned ruefully. *No wonder my England was twice defeated by these men and women.*

"Does that mean you're not coming with us?" Sarah's voice cut into her reverie. "You're going back to England?" She looked up into her friend's wide, searching eyes.

A painful queasiness shot through her stomach as it had around the same mid-morning time the last several days. *The pemmican must be going bad—or perhaps the biscuits or bacon have some mold. I shall have to check.*

"I have not decided, Sarah. I must decide what to do with father's land. As strong as the forces that entice me to stay are—Reuben, this country...," she swept her arm out at the mountains, "... and these people...," she nodded at the remaining wagons, "there are other considerations, which compel me to return to England. Mother's estate must be settled, and my father's remaining debts repaid. Adam, Eve and Sally, our Aborigine servants, will be quite lost with all this. They began as slaves, but my dear father gave them their freedom many years ago and they stayed with us voluntarily." She sighed. "They will have no idea of what to do. They became my friends. Adam, the father, seems to have an ability to foretell the future, or at least my father thought so." Sarah stared, listening attentively.

Rebecca paused, remembering the morning she had left their stately townhouse. The ornate black carriage with door ajar held open by the smartly uniformed driver, frail and aged mother Elizabeth sobbing at the head of the marble steps in the doorway, and the tears and somber expressions on Sally and Eve's faces. And yes, the wise, aging, brown eyes of Adam looking unblinking, deeply into hers as he spoke. "It will be a different life, Mistress, but you shall prosper."

She had stared at him, taking a half step backward, unsure whether his English—more than she had heard him speak at one time in fifteen years—or his words surprised her more. "Adam, I am impressed by your English. And thank you for your good wishes, but I shall return before winter."

Adam's brooding eyes had again penetrated hers with a look of sad wisdom. "The power of the land and the man will hold you," he had said quietly.

Another wave of mild nausea brought Rebecca back to the present moment.

"What is it Rebecca?" Sarah asked. "You look pale."

"Oh, it's nothing. I was just remembering something back in London." She paused and waved one hand at the wagons. "And thinking about these amazing people we journeyed with over the last two and one half months now scattered to places with strange names, building their lives, and following their dreams. Quite impressive, very different from what I have known and considered normal before coming to America."

Sarah was silent but her eyes were piercing as she looked at Rebecca. Her eyelids narrowed almost imperceptibly and she nodded slightly as if she suddenly understood something.

"You look as if struck by an epiphany, Sarah. What is it?"

"I was...," Sarah's gaze suddenly focused over and beyond Rebecca's shoulder. The brunette turned. It was Zeb approaching them, leading Buck.

"Good morning, Rebecca," he said cheerfully. His tone softened and there was a slight tinge of color under the leathery tan of his cheeks, "Good morning, Sarah."

Sarah stood beaming, reaching out a delicate hand to his forearm. "Good morning, Zeb. I thought about you last night guarding us out there all alone with Buck."

Looking momentarily embarrassed, he patted her hand. "Weren't no bother." He cleared his throat. "The McClintocks tell me they're pulling out today, heading north to the Big Thompson country. Got a sister up there with a small homestead. The Solomens are joining a small wagon train forming up in town, then heading up Clear Creek and over the pass to the Blue River Valley. Good land, good water that way."

His eyes shifted to Rebecca. "Are you all right, Rebecca? You're looking a mite clammy."

"I'm fine Zeb. Thank you for asking. I've been a bit under the weather the past several mornings—slightly nauseous and a tad of a cold sweat. I think it is something to do with our dinners. I am carefully going to check the pemmican and the last of the hardtack roles and bacon today. Have either of you been nauseous?"

Zeb and Sarah exchanged quick glances, then Sarah turned back to Rebecca again, her look sharp and probing. "I have not."

"Not me, neither. I think the food is just fine." Zeb chuckled. "First time I ever had two women cookin' and fussin' over me at one time. Feel a might spoilt."

Both women laughed and the paint horse tossed his head.

"The Livingston widow and her young-uns are goin' partway with us as I told ya. I'm gonna have them pull their wagon in close to ours. Sarah, perhaps you could drive Jacob's old rig over closer, too. No sense being too spread out here. It's just been me and John Solomen standing guard since Paul won't fight, and now it'll just be me."

"I'll take my turn at guard duty," said Rebecca firmly.

Zeb regarded her for a long moment. "No, Rebecca you won't. But I thank you for offering." He caught the narrowing of her eyes and added hastily, "I told Reuben I'd look after you, and you wandering around in the pitch black in the middle of nowhere doesn't quite fit that bill." He smiled. "Even though you are mighty handy with a rifle."

"Zeb, Rebecca and I were just discussing whether she's going back to England or staying here."

Zeb's lips pursed. "Well, I know what my choice would be, but I understand you got to make your own decision."

He looked pensively west toward the mountains, the massive wall of earth towering above the plains, their jagged peaks crowned by bright white snowcaps shimmering in the morning sun. "You ladies can start making preparations. Reuben wants to meet up on the twelfth. I figure about six days' travel in these rigs. We will plan on leaving early on the morning of the fifth. That'll give us an extra day just in case we hit weather or have a breakdown. I aim to head down to town to get our supplies lined up. Later on, we can all go down in Jacob's old rig and load up. It was built to haul freight; no reason it shouldn't serve its purpose."

He fell silent for a long moment, then cleared his throat. "Rebecca, if you decide you're staying in Cherry Creek or heading back across the sea, we'll drop you off in town. I'm sure Randy can wrangle you a place to stay until his supply train heads east." Zeb's voice dropped and he swallowed, "Or when he finds a replacement for his brother. There will likely be a cavalry patrol that would be delighted to have the company of a lady back up to Fort Laramie. You can certainly catch a wagon or coach headed east from there." He looked at her closely, opened his mouth to say something more, then stopped. Without another word, the mountain man turned, clicked softly at Buck and led the paint off in the direction of the McClintock's wagon.

Sarah sat down next to Rebecca on one of the empty storage kegs they had pulled out of the wagon. She threw several pieces of twisted, thick sage roots into the fire and then, reaching out her hand, setting it lightly on Rebecca's thigh. "How many days have you been feeling nauseous?"

Rebecca blinked, surprised at the intensity in Sarah's voice. "Why...well...it began the morning before yesterday. Quite uncomfortable and yesterday I actually vomited. Though I don't feel quite that queasy now. I'm sure it is just something in the food that is not agreeing with me or perhaps I'm catching a cold."

There was a long silence.

"What is it Sarah? You look possessed."

Sarah wet her lips, a pink hue stealing up her light-skinned cheekbones beneath her freckles. She leaned forward, speaking in a low conspiratorial tone. "You said that there's a clammy sweat that comes with this upset stomach?"

Rebecca nodded. *What is she driving at?*

"Rebecca, if you pardon me for asking—are your bosoms tender?"

Rebecca started, leaning back in surprise at the question. "Yes, I have noticed some tenderness. But that comes periodically as we both know...." She paused. "Oh, I see. You're thinking it's the monthly curse coming on."

Sarah blinked, shaking her head. "No, I'm not. When did you last have your time of the month?"

What strange questions. "Let me think—perhaps two weeks ago. Right around the time that Army patrol visited us prior to the wagon train taking that cut off from the Platte."

Sarah leaned forward farther, darting furtive glances left and right. Whispering, she asked, "Were you *with* Reuben before he and Johannes left?"

Rebecca felt a hot rush of color flood her cheeks as she remembered Reuben's muscular form beneath her, and the desperate, rhythmic movement of her pelvis against the base of his manhood embedded thick and deep within her the night they had learned of their parent's death.

Sarah, watching her closely, pressed her lips together and nodded. "You have been." She leaned back with a deep sigh, one hand unconsciously drifting to her belly where the rounding was becoming more pronounced. She blinked rapidly, silent.

Rebecca tried to keep the impatience from her voice. *Strange questions.* "Why do you ask?"

Turning, Sarah slowly stretched out her hands, taking one of Rebecca's between them and squeezed. Her eyes were wide and compassionate. "Do you love Reuben?"

Rebecca felt her annoyance rising at this series of inquiries. "I am close to Reuben—but love? I have given it no thought, Sarah. And it really is quite irrelevant in any event."

"Rebecca...it is very relevant," said the redhead in a low, measured tone.

"Really, Sarah. You are being silly. How does it possibly matter?"

Sarah inhaled deeply, held her breath and then exhaled her words, "Because I believe you are pregnant. I believe you are carrying Reuben's child."

June 4, 1855

THE OUTFIT

BLUE EYES BRIGHT WITH LIFE BUT GUARDED FROM EXPErience held Reuben's gaze from across the round, ornate but well-worn oak table in the kitchen of the Dawson ranch house. Silver-white hair draped Dawson's broad and still powerful shoulders. His eyes, slightly squinted by habit against the sun, were set wide within the frame of his darkly tanned, weathered and wrinkled face.

Logs crackled in the Oberlin stove by the entry and steam curled from two large mugs of coffee, one in front of each man. The thick log walls of the kitchen were squared, separated by thickly applied lines of white-grey chink. The corner logs fit snugly with little gap despite the imprecision of hand tools. The window openings were painstakingly squared, surrounding multi-paned windows, their wavy, blown glass dissected by mullions. Carefully made cabinets, each with a large brass pull, separated an icebox, ornate six-burner wood cook stove and a large water basin perched beneath a water keg, its faucet fed by gravity. Reuben could feel the tense stare at the back of his head from Johannes standing by the stove near the entry door. Outside, he could hear the muffled sounds of Philippe talking with young Michael though he could not make out the words.

Dawson watched Reuben's eyes roam the room. "Spent more damn time on this part than the rest of the house combined. Gotta keep the Missus happy. Hard enough to find womenfolk who would live in the middle of nowhere to begin with." A hint of a smile played on Dawson's lips and his eyes twinkled. "You got yourself a woman, Mr. Frank?"

Reuben forced a chuckle, "I'm not too sure."

Laughing, Dawson slapped the table with one meaty hand and the coffee cups bounced, a small spill splattering over the edges of Reuben's coffee. "Ain't that the truth. Let me tell you, young man, we're never sure, and they always are. She already has it all figured out whether she's your woman or not. You don't have no say."

Reuben looked down at his mug. "That's true enough. I figured out some months back I have no say." Picking up the mug, he took a sip, then placed the drink slowly and deliberately back on the table and held Dawson's eyes. "I really need three hundred head and I can't do with less than ten bulls with that many cows. Twelve or thirteen would be better."

Dawson leaned back in his chair, the arched oak legs creaking with his weight. Reaching out a thick forearm, his hand enveloped his coffee mug and took a deep swig, his eyes boring into Reuben's over the lip of the cup. "I told you, young fella, I can't spare that many cows. Just bought out a neighbor to the south, and I need to stock that land. Grass ain't worth a damn if nothing's eatin' it."

Reuben took another sip and let the silence build. The tick tock of the grandfather clock in the living room beyond the kitchen seemed unnaturally loud, echoing off the log walls. "I have much the same problem, Mr. Dawson. But mine is compounded. I have to push these critters over the Divide and into the Uncompahgre. Finding more cows will be near impossible over in that country," Reuben paused, "I think we're agreed on five dollars a head and nine for the bulls. Did I understand that correctly?"

Dawson shook his head slowly. You got five dollars for the cows. Right young man? Assuming it's just two hundred head. But nine dollars on the bulls was your number. I want fifteen." His eyes were unflinching. "Been building this herd for almost twenty years and them bulls is a perfect mix of European and native. Great birth weights and hardly ever lose a calf. Put on pounds faster than just about anyone else's in these parts."

Looking down at his coffee cup, he turned it round and round several times on the table with massive thumbs and forefingers. He peered at Reuben sharply. "If I was to part with two hundred and fifty cows I'd have to have five fifty for each. That's how much more work it will be for me to stock up, or raise more heifers from the next calf crop, or head down south and find critters to buy."

"Would Mr. Christiansen sell you some?"

Dawson's eyes narrowed and he visibly flushed. "I don't abide by folks who steal other people's grass, then try and feed me guff 'bout some type of accident. I wouldn't buy cattle from him if his was the only cows between here and China."

Reuben nodded, focusing on his coffee to hide his surprise. He, Johannes, and Philippe had all been impressed with the Christiansen family the day before. *Their manners and friendly natures.* Unfortunately, they had just signed a contract with drovers to push most of their herd east to Kansas. The Army was the buyer.

Reuben let his eyes wander around the kitchen again. One of the open shelves held several fine whiskey bottles and brightly polished heavy shot glasses. *Like Ludwig used for Schnapps.* A scene from long before— his father, smiling, holding up a shot glass in the Villmar Pub pointing at the neighbor's prize bull out in the street, flashed across his mind.

Trying not to smile, he gazed lazily at Dawson, "Is there anything I can do to convince you to sell me three hundred cows at five and ten bulls at ten dollars each?"

Dawson wagged his head slowly. "Can't think of anything Mr. Frank. You want those two hundred head or not?"

Reuben pointed at the neatly stacked shot glasses on the far shelf. "If I eat one of those shot glasses, would you sell me three hundred cows at five dollars per head and twelve bulls at nine dollars per head?" *I hope I am not pushing too far.*

Dawson sat back in his chair, his eyes widening. "Eat one of them shot glasses?" He turned around regarding them, and then swiveled slowly back to Reuben. "You understand each one of them weighs five or six ounces. Them is all Belgian glass."

The same as in the pub. Reuben nodded. The floor creaked back by the door as Johannes shifted his weight.

Dawson leaned forward, both muscled forearms on the table flanking his mug. "Tell you what, Mr. Frank, you eat one of them shot glasses and I'll sell you three hundred head at five dollars each, and twelve bulls for nine dollars per bull, but if you don't, then you buy two hundred head at seven dollars each and five bulls for twenty each."

Reuben nodded. "I'll need five things before I agree."

"And what would they be?"

I need a hammer, a raw slab of sirloin steak two or so inches thick, about eight inches by four inches or as close to that as you can get, a slab of butter, a heavy napkin or cloth, and a big pitcher of water, if you wouldn't mind."

Laughing uproariously Dawson slapped the table sending the coffee mugs several inches into the air. "By God, you're serious. I got them things and you're welcome to 'em and whatever else you think you might need."

Dawson yelled back into the house, "Mama, you better come out and see this. If you wouldn't mind, fetch me that hammer off the tool crate back there in the mud room and one of your fine, white, cotton napkins. Tell Josie to cut a big slab of sirloin off that steer we butchered day before yesterday and bring it in here."

Leaning back in his chair, Dawson folded his arms across his chest, his mouth curled in a half smile. "How you wanna choose that glass you're going to..." he coughed trying to hide a laugh, "...cat, Mr. Frank?"

"I'll let you choose one of them out of the three stacks on the shelf."

Dawson's wife bustled into the kitchen the thick cloth in one hand and heavy hammer in the other, her looks clouded with the same weathered appearance as her husband. Her eyes kind, but past their beauty, darted curiously from Reuben to Dawson.

Dawson didn't introduce her. "This young man and I have a slight wager, Mama. Has to do with buying cattle." He stood up, the chair squeaking behind him as he slid it out, and lumbered over to the shelf. Picking up each of the glasses in the three stacks, he studied them carefully, then chose one that Reuben was sure had a thicker bottom than the others. He brought it back to the table and, reaching out one long arm, slapped it with a sharp thud next to Reuben's coffee. "Mama, give Mr. Frank that hammer and napkin." Turning his head he bellowed over his shoulder, "Josie, you killin' that steer all over again? Bring that steak."

A young man of around twelve came rushing into the room, one hand holding a thick piece of beef still dripping blood, a butcher's knife in the other.

Must be the youngest, Reuben thought.

"Mama, get some of that butter from the icebox." Dawson turned back to Reuben. "I think that's all you asked for, ain't it?" Reuben nodded, "Except for the water. I noticed a flat stone out there by the front steps. Would you mind if I ate the glass out there?"

Dawson stared back at him incredulously, "Hell, you can eat it up on the roof of the barn for all I care. I just want to see you do it."

Reuben rose from the table. "Josie, my name is Reuben Frank." He lifted his eyes to Dawson's wife and nodded, "Would you mind bringing that steak out behind me. My hands are full." As he walked toward the kitchen door he caught a worried, puzzled frown from Johannes. The tall blond shook his head. *He thinks I'm crazy.* Reuben grinned at him.

Outside the sun was well past noon, the late spring slant of light lengthening shadows of the cottonwoods around the house. Philippe and Michael walked over, the vaquero carefully studying each person's face as they came out of the house, his eyes shifting continuously between the glass, butter, hammer, napkin and Reuben.

Reuben sat cross-legged in front of the big flat stone by the walkway. Brushing away some dirt off the rock, he laid out the napkin centering the shot glass in the heavy, white fabric, and then the steak. Wrapping the glass tightly in the napkin, he twisted and held the loose end in his left hand. With his right, he raised the hammer and began to methodically pound the bulging cloth. He could feel the stares but focused on the task at hand—reducing the heavy glass to powder.

When he was satisfied, he carefully opened the napkin and using the claw end of the hammer sorted the finely pulverized glass to make certain there were no large, sharp shards left. He looked up, "All there, Mr. Dawson?"

Dawson nodded, a concerned look in his eyes. *He's figuring it out.*

Slowly Reuben sprinkled the powdered glass down the center of the steak. "Could I have the butcher knife, please, Josie?" The boy glanced quickly at his father, then handed the knife over handle first. Reuben cut a very thick slice of butter, smoothing it over the powder until the pulverized glass was virtually invisible under the fatty spread. Folding the steak over the butter and glass he raised the meat to his mouth and took a deep bite, chewing carefully and swallowed, following the procedure with a large gulp of water from the pitcher, not bothering with the cup Mrs. Dawson had brought out. He took another bite, chewing slowly and swallowing.

"I'll be damned and go to hell," Reuben heard Dawson mutter almost under his breath.

Five more careful bites, extended chewing, and virtually the whole tumbler of water until nothing was left.

Reuben leaned over the rock and spat, making sure there was no blood, then stood.

"I'll be damned and go to hell." This time Dawson said the words loudly, his voice almost booming and tinged with surprise and respect. "Now I have seen everything. Going to use that trick myself sometime. Where'd you learn that?"

Reuben burped, and cast a quick look at Mrs. Dawson. "Excuse me, ma'am." Turning back to the rancher, he smiled. "In a place far, far away."

Dawson looked at him for a moment, his face serious, than broke out laughing. "Well, Mr. Frank you've earned them cattle. I'm good for my word. Saddle up and we'll start sorting. We can finish up come morning and you can be on your way. We ain't got enough room in the house, but the barn is mighty comfortable. You're welcome to stay there and have supper with us, assuming you've got your appetite back by then." He laughed, his eyes flickering to Philippe.

"The four of us always eat together," said Reuben quietly. Dawson nodded. "I mean all of you."

DAWSON'S OLDEST BOY, RICHARD, A YOUNGER REPLICA of his father, slid one large calloused hand over knots on the counting rope as the last of cows were herded through the chute from the corral into the open pasture beyond.

As young Michael and Philippe deftly organized the herd, Philippe occasionally shouted in a mixture of Spanish and English to Johannes, pointing and directing the tall Dane, who more often than not was failing in clumsy attempts to gather an animal. *Not quite like flanking a cavalry patrol, is it Viking?* Reuben smiled to himself.

A heavy hand slapped him on the shoulder, propelling him a step forward. Dawson was grinning. "That's three hundred cows and as soon as Richard is done recoiling that counting rope, he's gonna ride out, meet up with my middle son and bring in your bulls. I'm still thinking about you eatin' that glass." He moved his face closer to Reuben's, peering intently at him. "You feeling okay?"

"I feel fine," Reuben chuckled, "but the real test will probably come in a few hours."

One of Dawson's eyebrows lifted. "Good luck on that!" he said with a wide smile. "Well, I got two presents for you." He raised a bent forefinger and pointed. A longhorn cow, larger than most of the others stood proudly shaking giant twisted horns slightly from side-to-side. Beautifully colored in brown and white, with a white muzzle and graying cheeks, she craned her neck toward the cows being gathered by Michael, Philippe and Johannes. The twin, brass, square shaped bells hanging around her neck with a heavy canvas strap clanged with a tinny sound.

"That there is Queen. She's my best lead. She led over five hundred head up from Texas eight years ago. Same bells."

Reuben began to protest, but Dawson waved at him. "Son, you're smart. You got grit. I think you'll do just fine but..." He fell silent, his eyes fixed on some distant point in the rugged peaks to the west. He turned slowly back to Reuben, "...But this I know. The country you're headed into is harsh, unforgiving, unexplored, and unsettled. It's beaten and killed many men that called it home and knew its ways. You can't afford to get this herd spread out. Some you ain't never gonna find. Some will get picked off by Indians and rustlers. Queen and them bells will help keep 'em together, especially when the country gets rugged and steep." He looked at Reuben closely. "It'll be all of that, and more."

He stuck out a beefy hand and Reuben took it. "I wish you Godspeed. Me and Mama will pray for you." The leather of his jaw split into a wide smile, "I'll sell you cows anytime, but I ain't never givin' you a shot glass again. Them things have value."

Smiling, Reuben swung himself up into the saddle on Lahn. "Much obliged, Mr. Dawson. You never did tell me your first name."

Dawson looked up at him, the corners of his lips twitching slightly, the twinkle Reuben had noticed at the breakfast table back in his eyes. "Nope, never did. Most likely never will." Dawson surveyed the cattle now organized in a rough line twenty to thirty cows wide stretching several hundred yards. "Looks like you got yerself an outfit. That Mex and the boy knows cows." He chuckled, "But that tall blond? Seems like he knows a saber better than a lariat."

Reuben laughed, "You are a good judge."

Dawson half smiled. "By the time you get to where you're going he will know cattle sure enough. I'll open the gate. You can take old Queen out to the head of the bunch. She'll know what to do and so will they. Them bulls is less likely to wander. If I was you I'd keep them at the back of the line, it'll save you stragglers."

Reuben pulled down on the brim of his hat. "I'm sure we will meet again, Mr. Dawson."

Dawson looked at the cows and then up at the mountains. "Maybe so." He turned slowly and headed toward the gate.

EVENING CAME ON QUICKLY, THE SUN DISAPPEARING behind a jagged western rim, the last screeches of color reaching like painted fingers into a sky darkening from the east. Johannes reined in Bente, taking in the scene. He had been riding what Philippe called "drag" all afternoon. His clothes were covered with dust and interlaced with the smell of cattle and manure. Even Bente's long, thoroughbred-like legs had lost their luster. One cow split off from the rear flank, evading a lumbering bull trying to chase her back in.

Bente flipped her bay head back, her dark-tipped ears perked up and she whinnied. "By the love of God, you like this don't you, horse? Okay, let's go get her." They set off at an easy lope but four times the cow out-maneuvered them, refusing to turn back to the trail.

Johannes shook his head in disgust. The cow was thirty feet off, broadside. There was an unusual crescent moon shaped marking on her left cheek and neck. She seemed to be smiling, her big brown eyes taunting. Bente shook her head. "Well Bente, we can't out run her, it seems, so let's reason with her."

Johannes drew his gun and spun the cylinder, holding the pistol up to the cow. "All right you smelly beast. I'm not playing games with you. This is an Army Colt pistol. I imagine it kills cows just as well as it kills men. It's getting dark and I'm in no mood for any more of this, so what is it gonna be?"

The cow stared at them, bawled a long, low *moooo*, and then reluctantly wheeled, trotting back towards the herd as Johannes watched, astonished. "Well Bente, we have to have a talk with Reuben. He's all about ropes, whistles and hoots," Johannes laughed, "but it looks like there's something to be said for a bit of psychology." He slipped the pistol back in his holster, took a long look at the darkening mass of mountains to the west, and then dug his heels gently into Bente's flanks. "Come on girl; let's see what Philippe can whip up for dinner."

June 11, 1855

$\mathcal{A}$TTRACTION

REUBEN AND JOHANNES RODE SIDE-BY-SIDE, THE TREE
line of Trinchera Creek several hundred yards to the right,
its rough, uneven grouping of cottonwoods and aspens
stretching northwest into the distance like a great direc-
tional arrow. Around the broad valley rose treeless
foothills. Their rolling forms gave way grudgingly to distant
higher, sharper conifer-covered ridges of the San Isabel.
Further out, to the northwest, the sharp spines of the Sangre De Cristo Mountains glistened white with snow.

"I figure we are within a day of the Fort," Reuben said,
lifting himself in his saddle and craning backwards
toward the group of bawling cattle. "I'm glad we went
around this southern edge of the San Isabels, and
avoided La Veta Pass." One hundred feet behind them
was the clank, clank of Queen's brass bells. Behind her
by thirty feet was the vanguard of the cows spread out
an eighth of a mile on the wide valley floor. Johannes
watched his friend closely. He knew Reuben was pleased

with the deal he had made for the herd and the time they were making, but the young Prussian's expression had a worried, preoccupied edge.

"Johannes, do you think…"

"I don't know, Reuben. I honestly don't know whether she'll be there."

Reuben nodded and cleared his throat, "So, how is the King's Cavalry doing with the cows?"

Johannes shook his head and swore in Danish.

Reuben laughed. "If we don't spot the fort soon we'll make camp up there a few miles where the river bends north, get the cows watered and settle down early for the night. Zeb is not expecting us until tomorrow, and that Philippe is some cook."

Johannes smacked his lips, "Yes he is. That camp coffee of his is about the best I've had anywhere."

"Yep, but what do you think of him?"

Johannes began to speak, then abandoned his first instinctive answer, instead choosing his words carefully. "He is very capable, Reuben. I think he is honest and smart, but…" Reuben looked at him, waiting, "…similar to your first impression, he's the kind of man you want as a friend and never as an enemy. And, there is no in-between with him."

The young Prussian stared at him for several moments before nodding.

———

REINING IN LAHN A HALF HOUR LATER, REUBEN squinted into the distance. They were nearing the point requiring a decision to camp or keep moving. He pulled out Mac's telescope and extended the tube.

"What is it, *Señor* Reuben?" Reuben hadn't heard Philippe ride up over the grunts, muffled shuffle of cattle hooves, and the whistles and shouts of Johannes and Michael.

"I do believe that's Fort Massachusetts up there three or four miles."

"You are aware, *Señor*, that this fort is the only location on the Old Spanish Trail with reliable supply and repair facilities. It was only built in the last several years. At least it was not the staging point for Kearney's Army of the West." There was bitterness in his voice. "The gringo soldiers who stole my parent's land."

"Yes, Philippe. I know that Army staged at Bents' Fort. Randy gave me a bit of the history. I understand your anger. I can not imagine a greater injustice than losing one's land. You don't need to go into the fort. We will be here just long enough to obtain final supplies before the more difficult part of the journey."

Philippe sighed, then grinned, his facial muscles relaxing. "But you had nothing to do with that. So, we will soon meet the rest of your *estancia*. That pleases me. *Señor* Johannes has told me just a bit."

"Yep," was Reuben's tense reply.

"You're wondering if your *señorita* will be there?"

Reuben felt himself start in surprise. "Maybe."

Shrugging his shoulders, the vaquero observed, "One never knows the heart of a woman."

Reuben felt a pang of disappointment. *It's not like Johannes to have a big mouth.*

Sensing his thoughts, Philippe grinned. "No *Señor* Reuben, Philippe Reyes just knows the questions to ask. I think she shall be there."

Reuben threw him a sharp glance. "What makes you think so?"

"Because..." There was a sparkle in the Mexican's eyes. "Philippe Reyes is a romantic."

Despite himself, Reuben laughed.

AN HOUR LATER, THEY COULD CLEARLY SEE THE LOW-slung, meticulously constructed buildings of the army post, built to protect the sparse, but increasing settlement of the San Luis Valley.

The walls of the distant structure rose about ten feet, built of logs which blended with its backdrop of the uneven edge of forest where it had been constructed. The gentle roll of the valley floor and the gold, grey and green tones of sagebrush, grass and rock complemented the post's combination of peeled and unpeeled timbers. Just east of the fort was the tree line of Ute Creek, dwarfed by towering mass of Mt. Elbert. It appeared to be approximately one hundred fifty feet wide, built in a rectangular shape, and slightly shorter in the opposing dimension. Turreted bastions with firing apertures for cannons rose at several corners. A corral was off to one end. An American flag flew smartly over the scene from somewhere near the center of the compound which was completely enclosed by a stockade of pine logs, ten feet high. A number of wagons, buggies and horses moved to and fro. Others were tied off at various hitching posts. The blue of uniforms was visible at various points along the parapet which ringed the top of the walls of the fort.

Despite the warmth of the midday sun, Reuben's hands felt clammy and he noticed his heart beating more rapidly than normal. That, and the hollow feeling in his gut, fueled his annoyance with himself.

He turned at the pounding of hooves behind him. Johannes, wearing a mischievous smile, rode up. "Hey, Prussian, hand over that spyglass."

"What are you looking for?"

Johannes said nothing but rapidly extended the glass, stopping Bente's prancing with a gentle curse. After a moment, he lowered the glass with a big grin, handing it back to Reuben. "Look to the right of the Fort—north just a bit. I'd swear those are our wagons. One prairie schooner looks like the next but that makeshift freight wagon, the one that bastard Jacob had, is one of a kind."

Reuben was puzzled. "So what?" he snapped. "Zeb was leading them. Didn't you think they would be here?"

Johannes shook his head. "You are a stubborn fool. And what your words don't reveal, your eyes do, changing color faster than your mood. Put the damn telescope on the wagons and take a look behind the prairie schooner."

Reuben held up the glass.

"Reuben, see that red sorrel behind the wagon. That's Mac's horse, Red."

Reuben's heart jumped and he heard his own intake of breath. "It does, kind of, look like Red."

"Kinda, my ass. That's Red. Why you suppose Red would be tied up behind that wagon? Think Zeb brought that temperamental mare to ride?"

Reuben slowly lowered the spyglass, turning to Johannes, now grinning ear to ear.

"Don't just sit here like the dumb farm boy. Ride up there and kiss her."

"But..."

"But nothing. Show some enthusiasm. Remember that deal we made back on the train? I would teach you about women and you would teach me about cows. After the last week, you're well on your way to keeping your promise, unfortunately. Now I have to keep mine. Get your ass up there."

Reuben felt giddy. Shoving the telescope hurriedly back in his coat pocket, he spurred Lahn. Behind him he heard Johannes, still laughing, and then a shout, "And don't say anything stupid."

IT SEEMED LIKE IT TOOK FOREVER FOR LAHN TO COVER the mile between the cattle and wagons. Reuben's thoughts were jumbled. *Maybe Zeb just took Red as an extra horse. Maybe she just wants to see her father's land, maybe...*

Then he was there; dismounting before Lahn fully halted his run, the dust of their gallop catching up to them in a swirling cloud that billowed over the top of the canvas of the prairie schooner like an excited spirit. Taking a deep breath, Reuben half ran to the back of the wagon.

As he rounded the corner, Sarah leaned out the rear of the canvas, her blue eyes bright and smiling. "Reuben," she called out. *Much too loudly.* "We didn't expect you until tomorrow."

"We made good time, Sarah..." *My voice is way too anxious, calm down you idiot.* Reuben took a deep breath, "Sarah, I..."

His words died. Sarah had backed into the wagon. In her stead was a petite, trim figure with a shock of long dark hair, wide brown eyes looking into his and a radiant, but amused smile accented by the scar almost healed, but visible above her lip. "Mr. Frank, you are a sight for sore eyes. Did you roll in the dust to impress me?"

"I... I," Reuben looked down, realizing with a start the color of his clothes beneath the dust was barely discernable. He began to brush himself off.

"Reuben."

He stopped mid motion.

"I don't care about the dust. Help me down."

Taking a step forward, Reuben extended his left hand. Her fingers slipped over his perfectly. Holding her riding skirt, she descended the ladder, standing inches from him, looking up into his eyes.

She raised a delicate hand to the back of his neck and pulled his lips down to hers. Their arms wrapped tightly around one another and Rebecca rested her head on his shoulder. Reuben felt a huge weight of uncertainty lift. "I love you, Rebecca," he whispered.

"Reuben, there some things we must discuss." He could feel her lips moving against his throat. "I want you to know why I am here."

Reuben bent his head and kissed her neck. "We have plenty of time to discuss whatever you wish, Rebecca."

Rebecca pushed him away, but her hands remained entwined in his shirt. "Reuben, I want you to understand the situation."

"Rebecca, I..."

Sarah's exclamation interrupted him. "Who is that?" Sarah stood framed in the rear of the wagon, sun streaked red highlights shimmering in her hair, her blue eyes widened, her gaze fixed over their heads.

Reuben turned. Fifty yards away Philippe was riding toward them in an easy lope, back arched, shoulders stiffened, proud and handsome, his eyes fixed on Sarah. He reined in, his gaze momentarily shifting to Reuben, then to Rebecca.

Reuben realized with astonishment that from the time Philippe had left the herd to gallop to the wagons, he had managed to brush most of the dust off his finely fitted tunic and hat.

Sweeping off his hat, the aristocratic vaquero bowed low from the saddle. "*Señorita* Rebecca, I presume. I am Philippe Reyes."

Philippe's gaze again moved to Sarah. She stood in the rear of the wagon, each arm outstretched to the edges of the canvas, which formed the oval opening. Her lips were slightly parted, her chest rose and fell rapidly and, Reuben noticed, her eyes were wide, *very wide.*

Philippe bowed again. "I presume you, *Señorita*, are Sarah Bonney."

"Yes." Sarah's response was more a breath then a word. Rebecca darted quick glances from Philippe to Sarah, then back again.

A long silence grew more awkward by the second. Reuben cleared his throat. "Where is Zeb?"

"Sarah?" There was an edge to Rebecca's voice.

"Yes?" Sarah's eyes were still fixated on Philippe.

Rebecca shook her head, looking at Reuben. "He went to the fort to see what supplies they might have." Rebecca stared at Sarah. "Right, Sarah?"

"What? Oh, oh, yes, Zeb is at the fort."

Philippe smiled, again bowing from his horse to Rebecca, and then to Sarah. "I'm sure we will have ample opportunity to further converse."

His eyes still on Sarah, he wheeled Diablo and galloped back toward the cries of the cattle still a quarter of a mile away.

Reuben had a sudden vision of Sarah sobbing into Zeb's chest at Two Otters Creek, one long arm of the mountain man wrapped tightly around her shoulders, the other holding his coonskin cap—his exposed hair far more grey then Reuben had ever previously supposed.

June 11, 1855

$\mathscr{P}$RIMAL SURPRISE

"WHAT EXACTLY WAS THAT ALL ABOUT?" REUBEN'S BROW furrowed, his eyebrows low over a puzzled expression.

"What was what all about?" Rebecca tried to keep her voice nonchalant.

"Whatever happened here between Philippe and Sarah. You're a woman."

"So glad you've noticed, Reuben."

He chuckled. "I've noticed from the first day I saw you walking up the gangplank of the *Edinburgh* back there in Portsmouth, Rebecca."

Reaching up her left hand, she smoothed her delicate fingers down his cheek. *So handsome.* "I think Philippe is a rather dashing figure, obviously charming and well mannered. I imagine Sarah just found those qualities a bit surprising."

Reuben nodded, looking somewhat relieved, but a lingering doubt was evident in the purse of his lips. Rebecca laid her head on his chest, her thumb and forefinger playing with the heavy wool of his shirt. *I like the smell of cattle, dust and Reuben.* She closed her eyes, allowing the warmth of the sun to bathe her eyelids, trying to still the anxious, rapid beat of her heart.

Reuben had one arm around her. He cleared his throat, one boot scratching self-consciously in the dirt. "I can't tell you how pleased and relieved I was to see that you decided not to return to England."

Rebecca craned her neck upward. The deep green of Reuben's eyes unsettled her. She sighed, the butterflies in her belly mixing uneasily with the slight queasiness she had been feeling for most of the day. *I must tell him.*

"Reuben, before Philippe rode up, I mentioned that we needed to talk. It is very important to me—to us," she added hastily, "so that we have an understanding."

Reuben blinked. "An understanding?" he repeated slowly. "Pretty simple to me, Rebecca. I love you. You decided not to go back to England. We are together and I aim to—"

She raised her fingers to his lips. "Shhhh. Let me talk, Reuben. It's not so simple as that." Her stomach cramped, her neck suddenly clammy with sweat.

"You're turning pale, Rebecca. Are you all right? Are you sick?"

"No, Reuben, I'm not sick. Take me for a walk down to the river."

Reuben nodded at the scabbard on Lahn. "We should bring our Sharps."

"You bring yours, Reuben. The only thing I want to hold is your arm."

Reuben's eyes widened and he licked his lips, the same wondering expression on his face as a few minutes before when he tried to decipher the meaning of whatever currents had flowed between Sarah and the vaquero. Peering toward the fort, he asked, "When's Zeb coming back?"

"Not for a while, Reuben. We have time."

The spring sun warmed her shoulders. Her left arm was hooked to his right at the elbow. Beneath her right hand, she felt the hard muscle of his bicep. *We do fit well.* They walked slowly, enjoying the slight breeze that wafted down the valley from the west. The distant spines of the Sangre De Cristo Mountains rose abruptly to the southwest, sparkling, twinkling white. The voices and sounds of the fort were distant and detached. Reuben laughed as Rebecca pointed out circuitous paths between larger sagebrush to avoid tangling her riding skirt in the twisted limbs of the sweet smelling ground plants.

As they approached the tree line, two mule deer doe sprang up from their daybeds in the cottonwoods, watching them for one surprised, panicked moment. One whistled an alarm and they tucked their black-tipped tails and bounced off into the timber.

The river was chocolate, swollen by the melting snows miles upstream and rushing toward a far-off destination. He dropped back a step, leaning the Sharps against a downed tree trunk. Rebecca stopped and turned to Reuben, lifting her hands to his shoulders. "Reuben, I want you to know that when you touch me...," she felt the heat rise in her face and involuntarily looked down, momentarily breaking eye contact with him, "...when we are together it is...indescribable. I could never have imagined such intensity, such pleasure, such a feeling of impassioned completeness."

Reuben smiled. "And I—"

Rebecca shook her head and raised her fingers to his lips again. "Please, Reuben, I must finish this thought. You said that you love me. Perhaps we're too young to know what love really is. Maybe this is just some magical physical attraction." Reuben's eyes widened, wondering, looking down at her. Rebecca fixed her eyes on a button on his shirt.

"Please know, Reuben, that I trust you, more than any man other than my father. It is because of this trust and what we've shared between us, in our journey, losing Inga and Mac, that I always want you to know where I stand, even though at times...," she smiled, trying to still the tremble in her lip, "it takes me a while to utter the words." His cheek muscles twitched as she spoke. "I decided not to return to England at the current time— because I must see the land my father left. I must investigate his deathbed whispers about gold. With the death of my mother, the impetus to immediately return to the continent has been dulled."

Reuben's lips tightened. He was silent a moment and then spoke slowly. "One of the maps, drawn by that scout my father and Uncle Hermann hired, is missing. It was supposedly a map of potential gold or silver deposits around where we intend to establish the ranch. Perhaps there is some link."

Rebecca smiled. "Something else I've meant to tell you. Sarah has a map. I believe it is the missing chart drawn by your father's scout."

Reuben's eyebrows shot up. Rebecca thought she heard the echo of a blacksmith's hammer coming from the fort.

"Apparently, Jacob killed the messenger bringing the map to your uncle Hermann in New York. Happen chance. Bizarre coincidence. And it was his plan to file that map and try to exploit the resources whatever they may be, for his own account. Sarah was hoping that if the map bears fruit and it is through her that it is being returned, that you would take that into consideration."

Reuben nodded. "Of course." There was an edge to his voice. "Are you telling me, Rebecca that you are simply tagging along to the Uncompahgre as a matter of convenience, of transportation?" His eyes narrowed. There was a hint of grey in the green and his jaw tightened.

I'm so very poor at this. "No, no, Reuben. There is something strong and magnetic between us." She felt her face flush and fought back tears. "I felt it when I first laid eyes on you on the ship, before we ever conversed."

Reuben chuckled without mirth. "You didn't do a particularly good job of showing it."

"I was unsure, Reuben. I've never been in a situation like that, never felt attracted to a man as a woman." She felt a wave of frustration. *I am not saying this correctly.* "What I'm trying to tell you is I'm still unsure but on a different level. I am positive you and I have something unique and special. I just can't yet tell you that I love you, nor promise you that I will never return to England."

Reuben cleared his throat. Stepping away from her, he stooped down, picked up a rock and threw it forcefully into the muddy current. "What are you going to do with those creditors you told me of, your London house, the Aborigine servants?"

"I penned letters to each of the remaining creditors and enclosed them in an envelope with a letter of instruction to our solicitor. Randy promised it would be posted as soon as possible from Cherry Creek. I instructed the solicitor to sell the house giving the first twenty-five percent of the proceeds to Adam, Eve and Sally, which should set them up nicely. Their needs are rather minimal. The solicitor shall deposit ten percent into my account and then split the balance of the proceeds on a pro rata basis between the remaining five creditors of my father's trading business, simultaneously delivering my other letters to them. Those letters promise to pay the debts in full, explain the situation and make the case that their interests and eventual full payment are best served by my not returning to London at the current time."

"Well, you seem to have thought of everything." Reuben's voice was icy, but laced with a grudging respect.

Rebecca took the few steps toward him, setting her hand lightly on his upper arm.

When he did not respond, she gently yanked on his arm, turning him and wrapping both hands into the lapels of his jacket. She blinked back tears, feeling almost faint. She was sure he could hear the rapid pounding of her heart. "There is one other thing, Reuben. It is the most important."

"And that is?" he asked coldly.

She bit her lip at his tone, but despite herself, began to cry. "I am carrying your child."

Reuben's face went white. He blinked rapidly and his jaw slacked open. "What?"

"I believe I am pregnant, Reuben. With your baby."

"You mean *our* baby."

Oh my God. Rebecca Marx, you fool. "Of course. Yes, our child, Reuben."

"Are you sure?"

"I had not been feeling well for several mornings. Sarah suggested the possibility. I was incredulous but Zeb took me to the wife of the medicine man at the Arapaho village near town. She was very respectful. Zeb interpreted while Bird Song asked me several questions, put her hand on my belly and looked at my eyes and tongue. She assured me that I was indeed with child."

Taking a step back, Reuben sat down heavily on the fallen log next to where the Sharps leaned against the weathered wood.

Rebecca felt panic rising in her. "Talk to me, Reuben. Tell me what you're thinking. Please."

He was silent for a long moment then rose and walked to her, wrapping his arms around her waist, lifting her in the air and kissing her deeply. "I think," he whispered in her ear, "that Reuben Frank is a proud and happy man, and I'm honored to have you as the mother of my children."

The tense, anxious anticipation of this conversation that had infiltrated every minute of the days since Rebecca found out she was pregnant burst. *I promised myself I wouldn't do this.* She began to sob into Reuben's shoulder. "Song Bird said I would be more emotional than normal. I'm sorry, Reuben. I've been very worried."

Reaching down both hands, he placed them gently on her cheeks and lifted her face toward his. "There's nothing to be sorry about. I'm shocked, but thrilled. True, it will complicate things in setting up the homestead and necessitate certain changes to the house I planned to build, but I'm delighted, Rebecca." He grinned, his voice taking on a teasing tone, "And you being more emotional may not be a bad thing."

Rebecca chuckled through her tears, wiping her eyes with her knuckles. "She also said that I needed to be careful. My small hips might mean some difficulties at birth."

Reuben smiled absently. "Oh—you will be fine, Mistress Marx." Raising his gaze to the river behind her, he thought aloud, "So Zeb knows, Sarah knows. I know and you know. I guess Johannes is the only one who does not, other than Philippe and the young man we have helping us with the cattle."

"There's one last thing I must tell you Reuben but you must promise to never breathe a word of it to Johannes." Some of the light in Reuben's eyes faded to worry. "Promise me, Reuben." Rebecca began to sob again. "I hate it when I do this," she murmured into his shoulder, stamping her foot.

"It's okay, Rebecca. Tell me. I promise." Looking up into his face, she could feel streaks of tears on her cheeks, cool, blurring her vision. She blinked, trying to bring his features into focus. "When Inga died she was pregnant. She was carrying Johannes' baby." For the second time in a few minutes, Reuben looked shocked.

"Sarah and I have wrestled with this ever since Two Otters Creek. Inga was going to tell him that night, but, but...," she drew a deep ratcheting breath, "... that night never happened. On one hand, it is his right to know. On the other, we are convinced it will simply exacerbate the guilt and grief he feels."

Reuben shook his head slowly. "I understand why the two of you held off. He is just now beginning to show signs of his former self. I think one day he must be told but that is not anytime soon."

Rebecca wrapped her arms round Reuben's waist and squeezed, burying her head into the wall of his chest. Minutes passed before he tenderly pushed her away, holding her arms, his eyes boring into hers. "There is one more question, you know." He reached into his coat pocket and withdrew a bandanna.

Rebecca dabbed at her eyes with the cloth. "And what would that be, Mr. Frank?"

Smiling a thoughtful smile, he looked up at the sky, his teeth gnawing on his lower lip. "I'll think about it for a day or two, Mistress Marx, and then we shall have another talk." He leaned over, picking up the Sharps and nodded toward the wagons. "Let's get back."

Rebecca held his hand as they picked their way back toward the fort. *He is going to ask me to marry him. What will be my response?*

They walked past the day beds of the two deer they had spooked. The matted grasses of the nests were not parallel but at odd angles to one another. Rebecca felt an uneasy pang.

June 11, 1855

 BREMERHAVEN

"WHAT ARE YOU DOING WITH THAT DUFFEL IN YOUR room, Erik?"

Erik raised his eyes from the eggs and boiled potatoes. *I wanted to have this discussion at supper.* Isaac, almost three times his size, was glowering at him from across the breakfast table, but Erik was unflinching. "I'm packing for my trip to America."

Isaac and Helmon exchanged startled glances in dumbfounded silence. Then Isaac slammed his meaty fist into the kitchen table, almost cracking the wood. "You will do no such thing. I am the eldest. I run the farm. With father and Reuben gone, we need you here."

Erik dropped his gaze to his plate, scraping it with his fork and then lifted his eyes, staring back up into Helmon's angry glare. "No, brother, you don't need me. I'm just your *frau.* I save you the cooking and cleaning and the sewing," Erik looked from one to the other, "and endure the incessant arguing. There's no future for me here. I'm going to America to find Reuben and help him establish our family legacy over there."

Helmon opened his mouth as if to speak, then snapped it shut. Veins bulged in Isaac's neck. He looked apoplectic. "You think this is such a bad life we have here? Are you treated so poorly?" he shouted.

Erik pushed his plate away. "Poorly? It is your life that you have here, Isaac, not mine. And the fact that you do not realize how meanly you treat me, proves how little you care about my future."

There was a long silence. The flush in Isaac's face lost some of its intensity, and he looked deflated. "When do you leave?"

"Tomorrow, Isaac."

Without a word, Isaac rose suddenly from the table, the force of his legs pushing over the chair behind him with a crash. He strode to the door, crunched his felt hat over his head and stormed out. Helmon still sat at the table without a word, looking bewildered.

Erik rose and began washing the dishes.

Except for the brief, stiff, unemotional goodbye tinged with bitter anger that evening after supper, neither of his brothers spoke a word to him until just before an early bedtime.

Erik had turned down the covers, checking his duffel one last time, especially the secret false end he had carefully sewn into the heavy, canvas bag to hide his money. Glancing at his pocket watch, he shook his head. *Just three hours to sleep.* The door creaked open. It was Helmon, furtively looking over each shoulder for Isaac. He nervously held up the dagger their father had given him on his sixteenth birthday, then slid its thin, six-inch blade with curved tip into a well stitched and oiled burgundy sheath. Carefully placing the weapon into Erik's hands, he curled his younger brother's fingers around the leather housing the blade. "Be safe little brother," he whispered. "Godspeed. Father would be proud."

June 12, 1855

THE CLIP CLOP OF THE PAIR OF THICK-SHOULDERED Belgians pulling the wagon echoed up the wide dirt road into the early morning darkness. The damp air muted the sounds, giving their hoof steps a hollow distant tone. The sound was surreal as it reverberated between the tree trunks, stone walls and occasional dense hedgerow.

For the tenth time, Erik cast a quick glance over his shoulder at the dark bed of the wagon, making a mental list. *Have I forgotten anything? Violin case. Duffel.* His mind ran over the contents of the duffel.

He jumped at the sound of Rudolph's voice, though they had been sitting together on the wagon seat for almost three hours.

"I'm sorry, what did you say?"

Rudolph's pudgy, medium frame shook with quiet laughter. "We have gone to school together since we were three. I have never seen you as absent-minded as this morning, Erik, but no doubt very excited. I would be. I asked if the ship was departing Bremen or Bremerhaven?"

Erik blinked. "You mean there are two harbors? I had no idea."

He could feel Rudolph staring at him through the darkness and sensed rather than saw the movement of his hands as he shifted the lines to the traces. "Really? Weren't you in history class with me? Bremen is almost fifty kilometers up from the mouth of the Weser. In fact, there was no harbor at the mouth of the river until Bremen bought the territories there from the Kingdom of Hanover in 1827, less than thirty years ago. Now most of the shipping comes out of Bremerhaven."

"When I took Reuben to the SS *Edinburgh* last January—*it seems so long ago*—I'm sure we were at the harbor at the mouth of the river. The ship must be leaving from the same place."

"Let us hope so or you'll be late," Rudolph laughed. "Do you know where you're going Erik? I hear America is a giant country. Herr Burger told us in geography class there are places in the western part that don't have a single person, except for wild Indians, for hundreds of kilometers."

Erik tried to imagine all the lands from Villmar to Bremen without a human, but couldn't. "When I get to New York I'm going to my Uncle Hermann's. That's what Reuben did. I don't have Reuben's maps but I'm sure Uncle Hermann can tell me the directions. Though, I must admit that when I get to this place called Cherry Creek, I really have no idea of where to go from there. I'm hoping somebody will know Reuben or know where he went and can help me get there. I have plenty of money—the entirety of the one quarter father left to each of us. I have Reuben's too."

"Not much of a plan, Erik," said Rudolph dryly. "I hope that money is very well hidden. I would not flash it around if I were you."

"It is where *no one* will find it."

Rudolph sighed, "I must admit I am very jealous. I would love to see America. Everybody's talking about the grand, mysterious aura, the immenseness of the country."

The fading morning glow of the moon lit his friend's face as he turned toward Erik. "And the people, Erik— the people are supposed to be very tough, many of them rough and not given to manners at all." He chuckled, "Though I suppose if you live in a place where there's no one else for a hundred kilometers, manners are not all that important."

Erik swallowed and rubbed his fingers together. "I shall manage. I'm sure I will be able to find Reuben or perhaps he will hear that I'm in Cherry Creek and will seek me out. It can't be that far."

"I suggest that when you get to your uncle Hermann's that you have him draw or get you a map. I don't know, of course, but I think you're underestimating the sheer size of the country. All of Prussia is supposed to be just a fraction of the size of what they call the Territories, and the Americans recently added almost a quarter more to their land area with a place called Texas. I think they get in more fights than the British."

Erik laughed. "Yes, it seems to me that as proud of their military as the British are, they would rather not

battle the Americans again. Turn down here, Rudolph—
I'm almost sure this was the street that brought us to
the harbor. These buildings seem familiar and so are
these large, square street cobbles."

They fell silent for several minutes; then Erik saw the
dim forms of masts rising in the half-light above buildings.
"Yes, yes, I can see the masts! This is the correct street!"

The horses picked their way down the cobbled street
toward the edge of the harbor, their shod hooves click-
ing with a metallic ring on the hard surfaces. They
passed several docks, most still quiet at this early hour.
The black hull of a steamship materialized in the partial
light, the big white letters sifting and moving with the
billows of fog. SS *Edinburgh*.

As it had been that Sunday morning six months before
when Erik dropped off Reuben, the wharf was alive with
activity. Passengers crowded toward the gangplanks.
Shouts and curses flew through the sea air, mingling
with the creak of cargo nets lifting cargo high off the
dock and then lowering it into the hold. Officers and
seamen scurrying on the decks high above the wagon
barked orders. *The last time I was here there were tears
streaming down my face as I said goodbye to Reuben. Now
it is I embarking on the adventure.*

"Come on, Erik, I will help you with your things. I can't
believe you are bringing the violin. From what I've heard
about America, you would do far better with a weapon."

The memory of Helmon at his bedroom door the previous night tugged at him. For a moment, he was tempted

to show Rudolph the dagger. Instead, he forced a light laugh. "Even hard hearts soften to the sound of music."

"I hope so, Erik. I hope so," Rudolph muttered without conviction as he reached into the wagon for the duffle.

The two long-time friends embraced. "Please write me, Erik. I'm anxious to hear about America. You draw well—perhaps you could draw some pictures." Rudolph looked wistfully at the *Edinburgh*. "Perhaps someday I'll come visit you."

Erik hugged his friend, hefting the duffle onto his shoulder. "I hope so, Rudolph, I hope so."

"What about your brothers? Do you have their blessing?"

Erik shook his head slowly. "Anything but. They are self-centered and more interested in competing with one another than in my affairs or events of the world. They know nothing but the farm, nor do I sometimes think that they want to." He paused. "Though perhaps Helmon may at least understand."

"The sun is rising! Erik, it is time for you to board. Goodbye, my friend."

Erik shook Rudolph's hand and gave him another hug. "It is not goodbye, Rudolph. This is simply until we meet again. I shall write and, when you have a chance, send a letter with news of the village to me. Father told me a posting simply needs a name, then Cherry Creek, then Kansas Territories and then finally,"—he smiled—"United States of America."

Rudolph clambered back in the wagon, waved once and snapped the lines. The Belgians moving out smartly.

Erik looked after the wagon until it disappeared. Bent over from the weight of the duffel, he struggled toward the gangplank, suddenly wishing he'd eaten breakfast. At the bottom, he stopped, lowering the violin case and the duffel to the dock as the mate checked his name on the manifest and tore his ticket in half. Far up the gang-plank, he saw a mill of emigrants moving to and fro on the deck. His hollow gut surged with adrenaline. *Will I be predator or prey?* His hand closed on the dagger in his coat pocket. Clenching his teeth, he swallowed, stooped and picked up his luggage.

June 15, 1855

*T*HE NARROWS

THE CACHE LA POUDRE RIVER RUSHED, TUMBLED AND roared through the narrow chasm of rock. The lower temperatures at the higher elevation kept its boils tea colored, less muddy than down below. The angry flow threatened the narrow, rocky trail, already slick with shaded ice and partially thawed mud, its waters on the verge of eroding the soil clinging to the roots of the few tough cottonwoods that had weathered flash floods and spring thaws over the decades. *Soon, it will get warmer, and there will be no trail,* Black Feather thought with satisfaction.

The band rode single file, Dot right behind him and following her, Miguel. Turning in the saddle, Black Feather shouted through cupped hands over Dot's head, "Miguel, go on ahead to where it opens up above here. It ain't too far, maybe a couple hundred yards. Don't show yourself. Just check and be sure we are alone."

Miguel eased his grey mare carefully past Dot's mustang and Black Feather's big black stallion, who was tossing his head nervously at the powerful current. The

Mexican had to raise his left stirrup boot far behind him, almost on top of the mare's rump to avoid contact and even then, his saddle brushed Black Feather's leg as his mount moved warily past.

Black Feather craned back in his saddle again, staring at Dot's pallid face, bluish lips and half-closed eyes. Her shoulders swayed left and right as she tried to maintain balance even though the mustang stood still. A dull red bloodstain ran down the length of her pant leg along the calf. *Not doing all too well. She's gonna need some tending to.*

The renegade motioned with his hand and the band, still strung single file, began to pick their way up the almost submerged path. Raising his arm, he motioned them to stop a hundred yards further. *No sense talkin', no one can hear me over this racket.* Gesturing to the others to stay put, the renegade backed the stallion slightly. Leaning far to the back, he grabbed the reins of Dot's mustang and eased the two horses another twenty or thirty yards until he could just make out the form of Miguel through the newly leafed trees. The Mexican had stopped his horse at the edge of the widening of the floodplain, his thin frame silhouetted by the wider backdrop of patchy snow, golden spring grass and sagebrush. Glancing back over his shoulder, Miguel motioned him to come up. Black Feather passed on the signal to the men waiting behind.

Emerging from the Narrows, they hugged the toe of steep and rugged slopes rising above them to the north. Angular rocks, granite slabs, scattered pines and the occasional more magnificent, thick red-brown trunks of ponderosas proudly towering above all the other trees, dotted the rugged terrain. Though now several hundred yards from the river, the roar was still deafening. Using his hands, Black Feather motioned to everyone to gather around him.

Pointing backward with his thumb over his shoulder, he half-shouted, "Miguel, Chief, take up positions on the tops of those cliffs. You'll do better walking into position than trying to ride. Those hillsides is steep, slick, half-frozen like greased snot. No sense riskin' your horses." He looked south up at the sun already partially obscured by the high folds of the mountains across the river. "Figure we got four to five hours 'til dark. I'll send some of the boys up around then to spell you."

He looked from one man to the other. "Unless we get a spring storm, it should be a little bit warmer each day. When that river comes over the trail down there in the Narrows, we won't have to post behind us. Until then I want one man out front and two men behind us at all times. Everybody is gonna have to do their part." Several men shook their head and he thought he heard some grumbles but he couldn't tell with the rush of the river. "That or maybe have your scalp lashed to an Arapaho lance or a cavalry saber run through you while you're sleeping or worse if the bunch that sneaks up on us are like us." Several men half-smiled at the thought. "I will do my share too."

He looked sharply at Johnson. "When I'm on watch, Johnson, you will be responsible for the girl." Johnson blinked, then nodded.

Black Feather pointed to a small canyon another several hundred yards up around the toe of the hill they had been skirting. "Looks like it flattens out at the mouth of that little draw. Fairly level and steep enough for good defense behind us." He looked up to the sky again. "Probably get a bit more sun there, too. Tom, go up a quarter mile. There'll be some rocks that come down off that hill and another little draw like this. Must have been some slides up there. *Lots of them in this country.* Some of them rocks come about halfway across this floodplain to the river. It's a good spot. Get up in them boulders and keep your eyes peeled upstream. Ain't no trail to speak of on the other side but don't ignore it. You oughta be able to see anybody coming for quite a ways." Tom started to put his heels to his horse but Black Feather put out his arm. "And one thing to keep in yer mind, that sun finishes its day swinging across these hills, then sets almost up-valley. Wear the brim of that hat low or you won't be able to see nothing."

"Good idea, boss." Tom spurred his horse into a trot and moved upstream still hugging the toe of the hill.

"Well, what are you waiting for—summer?" Miguel and Chief glanced at each other and then wheeled their mounts, trotting back to some low pines where they tied them off. Slipping and falling every dozen or so steps, they began to pick their way up the slope, which would bring them to the top of the rock faces that plummeted into the Narrows.

"Johnson, let's get up there and get set up. Ain't gonna be warm nights this high, probably still frosting. I want to set up a bivouac for Dot. She's weak and bleeding. I might have to work on that calf and you might have to hold her like before." Johnson stared at the girl, now half slumped over, then looked apprehensively back at Black Feather.

"I think it will be okay for a fire if we keep it small and up that draw out of direct sight. Not many souls wandering around this high this early. Too late today, but tomorrow Chief and I will hunt up some meat. We both have bows. Way less ruckus. We'll all get our bellies full, some rest and get mended up."

Looking up river, Johnson lifted his chin toward the pass "How far you think to up there? I never been. Purty spot, though on the chill side."

Black Feather smiled. "Thirty miles, maybe a bit more. This here is midsummer compared to up there right now. Winter ain't quite over at ten thousand feet."

DOT WASN'T SURE WHERE SHE WAS. SHE FELT SUS-pended, dizzy, floating. Realizing instinctively she was half-unconscious, she concentrated on keeping her hands tight around the saddle horn, adjusting their pull and pressure when she felt herself slipping one way or the other. *Somebody put socks on my hands!* It was an effort, but she half-opened her eyes. *Mountains, and what is that loud roaring sound? My leg hurts.*

Then two strong arms were lifting her, sliding her gently sideways from the saddle. Her eyes flickered. A blurry, bronzed, swarthy face with a scar above thin lips belonged to the arms that wrapped themselves under her thighs and shoulders, carrying her with an uneven gait. She was lowered down on something soft and warm. Fluttering one eye partially open, she saw Black Feather's black and tan wool coat, the one he kept under his bedroll behind the saddle on his black horse.

His voice seemed far away. "You feeling okay? You with us?" *So tired.* She forced the one eye fully open. He was kneeling, staring hard at her as he carefully wrapped the folds of the greatly oversized jacket around her, tucking in the edges so it would not fall off. She realized she was shivering. "Cold," she heard a high, weak, female voice say as if from somewhere else, "cold."

"That's okay." The words came from the scarred lip. "We'll git a little fire going, get warmed up and some food in you. Going to have to work on that leg a little bit. It's opened up from ridin'. We gotta stop the bleeding."

"No, no, it will hurt." *That same far-off girl's voice.* She felt the coat collar getting snugged around her neck with tender roughness. "Yep, it'll hurt some, but if you keep bleeding it will be far worse than that. Don't worry none, you'll be fine."

Then everything went black.

THE NEXT MORNING THE SUN SHOWN PALE AND YEL-low from the east between the spires of rock that marked The Narrows, bathing their camp on the small alluvial plain at the mouth of the draw with relative warmth. Black Feather crawled into the bivouac he and Johnson had quickly but expertly constructed. The lean-to was simple but effective. They had lashed two poles, entry side higher, between two pairs of saplings, more or less evenly separated, then overlaid cut evergreen boughs on the top and sides. *Not square, but cuts the wind and stops the frost.*

Twenty feet into the little wash, four of the men huddled, stretching their hands out to a small fire crackling merrily and emitting the pleasant smell of pine pitch in its sparse smoke.

"Damn, *fuego*! First in *una semana*!" Miguel said in his thick, mixed English accent.

"Ain't much of a fire," Tom laughed.

"Well, may be small but it's doing the job on my frozen fingers," Johnson mediated.

Black Feather half-smiled to himself. *Sometimes it's the simple things.* He gently separated Dot's wool pant leg he had split the previous evening, carefully checking the areas he had cauterized with the glowing, red-hot blade of his knife. *Good thing she was passed out.* He brought his eyes close to her calf, shifting his position to allow more light along the area where the chunk of flesh was missing. *Bleeding seems to have stopped.*

She whimpered slightly. *Still out—probably better that way.* He backed out of the bivouac, rose and took several long steps to the fire. "Nice to see those flames, ain't it, boys?" They all nodded. Tom pointed to the blackened kettle sitting on a rock at the edge of the flames. "Hot coffee, boss. First in a week. We already had ours."

"Obliged, Tom. Throw me that cup." He took a long swig of the black, very hot java. "I'm goin' up river and spell Chief. Keep your eye on the girl, Johnson." The men round the fire all looked at one another. "Just your eye." Impelled by the deadly tone in his voice, they immediately turned their faces back to the flames.

"I'll watch after her. She'll be fine." Johnson's tone was reassuring but permeated with a subtle, odd distraction, which caught Black Feather's attention, suddenly triggering a long forgotten memory. *I wonder if he's been thinkin' about that gold he and I took from them pilgrims and buried in secret over on the Yampa years ago.*

Black Feather held Johnson's eyes for a moment, then nodded. "Come get me if she starts bleeding again." He looked around the small circle. "When it warms up toward midday Chief and I will go get us that meat. I wanna use the bows. No sense making gun noise. Might be an elk back up from winter grounds and I'm sure there's mule deer. They will be bedded down, easy to spot and we can put on a sneak. Tonight we'll have ourselves fresh steaks."

Tom grinned. "Meat, fire and coffee, I might just live here." There were guffaws from all around the fire.

Smiling, Black Feather walked a few uphill paces and unhitched the stallion tied with the rest of the horses to the tether line slightly further up the draw.

CHAPTER
25

June 15, 1855

JOCKEYING FOR POSITION

A STEW OF FRESH RABBIT, SMALL WILD SCALLIONS AND potatoes bubbled merrily inside a large, black iron kettle suspended from a tripod of lashed green limbs over the fire ring. Sarah reached for another broken branch of aspen, placing the small log on the fire, positioning it so the flames were centered under the rounded cauldron.

"*Señorita* Sarah, your fire is perfect. Have I told you how much I like your cooking, too?" Philippe flashed a wide grin at her from across the fire. His thin, wiry frame was fully stretched out on the ground, his ankles crossed far enough so his spurs didn't dig into his shins, his head resting on a hand supported by one elbow planted on his bedroll. The orange glow of the fire deepened the tanned, olive tones of his skin and reflected off the bright white of his teeth. Sarah raised her head acknowledging the compliments with a smile. Realizing her eyes had been fixated on his lips, she busied herself stirring the stew again.

She could feel his gaze, sense his eyes examining one part of her body, then another. *Why is my heart beating so rapidly? How does he do this to me?* Keeping herself fixed on her stirring, she asked, "How are the cattle, Philippe? Are they behaving?"

"Behaving?" Philippe threw back his head and laughed. *I like his laugh.* "Behaving, *Señorita* Sarah? Cattle never behave. There are always problems. Sometimes *grande*, sometimes *pequeno*. These are good cattle that *Señor* Reuben purchased. Strong, they have stamina and they have not been losing weight despite the rugged nature of the country but they are not used to mountains and trees and fast-moving creeks. After being raised on that parched grass down on the flats, they want to linger around the sweet, green grasses that grow this high, especially these early summer, tender young shoots of grasses. For cattle, they are always the most tasty."

There's something in his tone. Sarah glanced up from the stew. Philippe's eyes were glowing. Sarah was sure it was more than a simple reflection from the flames. She looked hurriedly down at the stew again.

"I've been very busy, *Señorita* but soon the cattle will become accustomed to this type of trail and settle down. Then I might have a few spare hours...." He paused. Sarah realized she was moving the long ladle around the pot far more vigorously than necessary. "I've asked you before, *Señorita* Sarah, will you take a walk with me when the time arises? I would be honored."

I'd love to. She caught the thought before it became words rising from her throat. "I would be flattered, Philippe but..."

"But?"

Sarah tried to formulate a response.

"But?" The look Philippe cast at her was a bit too knowing. "*Señor* Zeb?" he asked.

She wiped her hands down the front of the thick knapped waist apron draped over her grey, wool pleated traveling dress and tied at the back. *How did Rebecca manage to find an apron at Gart's Mercantile?* Looking across the fire at the vaquero, her eyes involuntarily followed the taper of his shoulders to his hips. "Yes, Philippe, Zeb. He is a very good man, you know. He's been very kind to me and..."

"And?"

"And, we talked."

"Talked?"

"Yes," She stammered, "Yes, we talked about perhaps being together after we get settled in the Uncompahgre."

"I see." A smirk played with the corners of Philippe's lips. *Those lips.* "*Señor* Zeb has not asked you to marry him, has he? You are not betrothed?"

With a conscious effort, Sarah slowed the circular rate of her stirring. "No, no I don't believe we're engaged," she replied slowly, "and he has never really said anything about marriage."

"Forgive me, *Señorita*. Perhaps I am being too forward, but I presume it is *Señor* Zeb's child that you are carrying?" Sarah's knees suddenly felt weak. Taking a step back, she sat down heavily on the log Johannes and Zeb had dragged close to the fire for a seat, leaving the ladle in the kettle. She pressed her lips together tightly trying to still the quiver she felt creeping into them.

Blood rushed to her cheeks. *He has no right.*

"I am surprised at you, Philippe. You have always been a gentleman. That is not a thing to say to a lady."

Philippe's eyebrows shot up, his eyes widening in the firelight. He sat up quickly, leaning slightly toward her. "I'm sorry, *Señorita*. I did not intend to be rude nor prying, but..."

"But what?" Sarah snapped, surprised at the defensive intensity in her tone.

"But you are an extremely beautiful woman...." He waved his hand, searching for the right words, "...It's—obvious, I think. That you are with child adds to your beauty. I was not trying to intrude; I was just trying to understand. Forgive me."

This is how it's going to be with everyone. Sarah blinked rapidly but to no avail—the fire blurred. "Well, Philippe, since you are so curious, let me tell you...."

Out of the darkness, a cheerful but tired voice boomed, "What's that I smell?"

Both their heads snapped toward the sound and a moment later Reuben and Zeb leading Lahn and Buck materialized into the outer bands of firelight. They tied off the horses on two aspen trees near where Philippe had tethered Diablo.

Reuben walked purposefully toward the fire, oblivious to all except the stew but Zeb stopped suddenly, looking sharply at Sarah, then Philippe and then Sarah again, his eyes narrowing. Philippe scrambled hurriedly to his feet, buttoning his tunic and setting a thick woven black and white serape over his shoulders. Replacing his hat on his head, he gave it a tug forward to settle the black, broad brim over his forehead. Zeb had not moved.

"Hello, Zeb." Sarah tried to smile brightly. *Why am I feeling guilty?*

Zeb nodded curtly at Philippe. "Philippe."

"Hola, *Señor* Zeb and *Señor* Reuben."

Reuben's attention was diverted from supper by the tone of the voices of his two friends. His facial muscles tightening, he looked from one to the other, finally shifting his eyes to Sarah. "Sarah, you plan on cooking that ladle along with the rabbit?"

"Ooohhh, I forgot." Sarah stood, reaching out hastily and pulling the long handled, deeply dished spoon from the kettle.

Reuben's voice softened. "How is Rebecca?"

Without meeting Reuben's eyes, Sarah forced a tone of optimism into her voice. "I think she's better, Reuben. She is sleeping." She glanced at Zeb, then quickly at Philippe.

Philippe was silent, shifting his shoulders to adjust his serape. Sarah looked away as he looked up at the sky. "It will be chilly this night as high as we are. I will go out and see how the boy and Johannes are doing." He chuckled. "*Señor* Johannes especially." He bowed slightly. "*Señor* Reuben, *Señor* Zeb." Turning toward Sarah, he swept off his hat, "*Buenas noches, Señorita*

Sarah." He wheeled, walking off into the darkness toward Diablo.

"THAT WAS DELICIOUS, SARAH." REUBEN SIGHED AS HIS fork scraped the last of the stew from his tin dish.

Sarah cast an anxious glance at Zeb, who squatted by the fire eating slowly, a frown playing on the chiseled features around his eyes.

"Is Rebecca really feeling better?" asked Reuben, his gaze turning toward the dark wagon.

Thankful for the distraction from Zeb's awkward silence, Sarah spoke in a low tone, "I don't know, Reuben. She rarely complains but I know she is nauseous for several hours every morning and she is very tired early. The last two nights I had to bring her supper in the wagon and wake her up or I fear she would not have eaten at all."

Reuben pursed his lips, a look of concern evident on his face. "Bouncing on these two-wheeled rocky ruts can't be comfortable for her." His eyes flickered toward Sarah. "Or you. How are you feeling?"

Unconsciously, Sarah's hands fell to her belly, which over the last week or two had begun to push against the fabric of her wool dress. She could no longer fit into any of her corsets. "I'm feeling fine, Reuben. Once in a while I am a little queasy." She tried to make her voice light and airy. Zeb stopped eating, and sat staring at his plate, listening.

Reuben dampened a burp with his hand. "Excuse me, Sarah. Please consider that a testament to your good cooking. I might add, you're doing a fine job of driving that freight wagon. I am sure that rig is difficult to handle on a trail like this."

"Thank you, Reuben. I do notice the horses are struggling a bit on the steeper uphill grades. How much farther is it?"

Zeb's eyes remained fixed on the fire and his voice echoed off his plate. "Eight, mebbe ten days, I reckon. Assuming that shortcut's passable, and we don't get caught by a late spring snow. That would hole us up for a few days. Don't wanna be driving wagons up and down these hills, especially down, in a muddy, snowy slick."

He reached down, picking up a stick and tossed it into the fire. "Right now we are on the east side of the pass. Toward the top we'll branch north down through Little Medicine. Narrows real tight, then opens up a bit. There's some hot springs the Utes use, too. Got more passes to work our way across, and they're steeper, particularly that Red Mountain Pass. That trail is nothing but switchbacks going up. Some slopes you probably couldn't ride a horse straight up. Some parts is so narrow that if you meet another wagon comin' the other way—which ain't likely—it might take an hour to get them both in position so the one that passes by doesn't drop off the edge."

He chortled, but Sarah detected little humor in his tone. "One good thing is those damn cows won't have any place to go. Have to follow the trail just like us, although probably be strung out for a half mile or more behind the wagons." He stood up, stretching his legs. "We ought to check them loads before the Lost Trail shortcut. You don't want anything shifting or sliding on those grades, or falling out the rear on one of them mules."

He raised his eyes to Sarah with a look that was kind, but edged with worry. "That stew was good, Sarah. I think I'll break off tomorrow for a few hours when we get a little lower and see if I can shoot us a deer. Won't take more than a couple hours to butcher and salt. As little as you women eat, it ought to keep us going for the better part of a week. It ain't often I luck out and get three rabbits in one day. Anything less wouldn't be much of a stew."

A gentle snore from the log caught their attention. Reuben's chin was on his chest, his boots stretched toward the fire, his hands clasped over his stomach, fast asleep.

Leaning over, Sarah reached out to shake him but stopped mid-motion at Zeb's voice. "Let him be for an hour or so, Sarah. He's been putting in longer hours than all of us but Lord knows, no one's had much shuteye. I'll ride back out. Each of the boys can come in one by one and get themselves fed. I think me and Johannes have the first half of the night anyways. The boy and that Mexican go from then 'til sunup. Come on over here for a minute."

Zeb walked twenty feet from the fire and away from the wagon and Reuben. Sarah followed. He turned sharply, his eyes holding hers. "That Mexican bothering you?"

"No, no, Zeb; he is not," She said, surprised at the brusque directness of his inquiry.

"You'll let me know?"

"Why, of course but Philippe has been a complete gentleman."

Zeb searched her face for a long moment then nodded, dropping his voice, "Tell me the whole truth on Rebecca."

Sarah glanced over her shoulder toward Reuben, still snoring by the log. "Actually, Zeb, I'm worried about her. I think she's having some type of difficulties. I just can't tell, and every time I ask her, she insists that she's fine."

Zeb's lips twitched underneath his mustache, "She's awful narrow hipped. There's some type of concoction the Sioux brew up for slightly built women when they're with child to ease things." He shook his head. "Damned if I can remember what it is. The Utes use it too."

"Perhaps we will run across some Indians and we can ask," Sarah suggested hopefully.

Zeb's eyes clicked down to hers. "I think it's best if we don't run into any Indians between here and the Uncompahgre. These southern Utes ain't all too friendly. They've tangled with the troops out of Fort Massachusetts several times. Once we get over there, it's Chief Guera Murah and his son, Ouray and their band. You can get along with them mostly. Mebbe Ouray's wife, Black Mare, or one of the other women in the tribe would help." Raising his eyes to the wagon where Rebecca slept, he shook his head. "We're just gonna have to do the best we can." He shifted his gaze back to Sarah. "If she gets any worse, come talk to me. Don't tell Reuben. He's worried enough about her as it is and he has a lot on his mind. The going's tougher than he thought. He sure knows cattle but he ain't never moved them in country like this," Zeb looked up at the sky, "especially racing against time."

Sarah felt a pang of alarm. "Race against time?"

"Yep. The longer this takes the more likely we are to lose cows one way or the other. A shorter time would be better for Rebecca and you and...," he paused, "...this here's gittin' to be the end of June. First snow's likely to fly mid-September where we're headed. That don't leave a lot of time to set up a homestead that'll keep the wind and snow out and the heat in." He looked down at his calf-high, thick elk skin moccasins and rubbed one toe in the dirt. "I figure you're due sometime around December and Rebecca, as near as I can figure from what you've told me, sometime around February or March. You women ain't Indians. You can't be havin' babies out in the open or in some drafty wagon or lean-to."

"Oh!" Sarah raised one hand over her mouth. "I just hadn't given it much thought, Zeb. We're greatly complicating what you men need to do."

Zeb smiled tenderly at her. Raising one rough thumb to her cheek, he stroked it softly from her cheekbone to her throat. "We know you ain't. I think we're all delighted to have you along." He smiled. "I know I am. It just makes for other considerations, that's all. Nothin' that can't be handled; just gotta be kept in mind."

June 16, 1855

$\mathcal{T}$HE PROPOSAL

REUBEN AWOKE WITH A START. SARAH CROUCHED BESIDE him, pushing gently on his shoulder. "You needed the sleep Reuben; and Rebecca's awake." Sarah nodded with her head toward the wagon, its canvas top illuminated by the dull glow of the oil lamps. "I just took supper to her."

Raising his fists, Reuben rubbed his eyes, blinking. Overhead, the sky was a dark canopy punctuated by countless stars. The leaves of the aspen grove that cradled Blue Creek and the east side of Wolf Creek Pass fluttered, lending a textured rustle to the breeze sighing through the scattered conifers on the slope above them.

His fingers had stiffened from the cold. "Chilly," he said, flexing his hands.

Sarah smiled, snugging the blanket she had wrapped around her shoulders up close to her neck. "But clean and fresh," she too raised her eyes to the sky, "and beautiful. It would take a lifetime to count all those stars."

Reuben chuckled. "Several lifetimes." He rose to his feet, glancing at the wagon and then at Sarah.

"Go on, Reuben. She would love to see you. Between her feeling a tad sickly and retiring early these past few nights, and the non-stop schedule that you and the others are keeping...." Sarah's voice trailed off and she returned her stare from the night sky to his, "a little time together would be good. I'll straighten up around the fire."

Reuben turned, walking toward the wagon. He patted the pocket of his britches, feeling the round outline of the ring he had purchased when he slipped into Fort Massachusetts. *Such a cheap little ring, but there was no choice. I will get her another at the first opportunity.*

His knock on the tailgate of the wagon was answered with a cheerful, "Reuben? Please come in."

Reuben untied the rear canvas and lowered the tailgate. Not bothering with the ladder, he sprang onto the back of the wagon, closing the tailgate and re-lashing the canvas behind him. It was noticeably warmer inside, the gentle wind stirring the canvas top, the oil lamps emitting heat as well as light. Rebecca sat on her bedroll, the extra blanket pulled up to her hips. She had donned one of her lighter jackets over her chemise, but the silky cream of her undergarment was visible in the jacket's open lapel, as was the smooth, creamy flesh below the sheer material. Suspended over a hint of dark circles, her slightly puffy eyes seemed welcoming. She had obviously brushed her hair, but her dark locks had a wild, unkempt look. *So is this the time to ask? What are these butterflies? It's ridiculous to be nervous; she's carrying our child.*

She placed the tin plate Sarah had brought her on top of the flour barrel. Shifting her hips toward the inside of the bedroll, she patted the makeshift bed next to her. "Perfect timing, Reuben. I just finished supper. Come over and sit. It seems we haven't really talked in days." Tipping her face slightly, she batted her eyes. "And if I'm not too disheveled looking you might even kiss me." Her smile both challenged and teased.

Reuben's eyes shifted momentarily to her tin plate. *Only half eaten.* He walked the several steps to her bedroll, seating himself beside her and nodded at the plate. "People that don't eat normally don't feel well. If you wish, I would be happy to feed you." He laughed. "See, I can be romantic."

Rebecca's eyes were fixed on his lips. Reaching out both arms, she clasped her hands behind his neck, pulling his face toward hers. "I would rather you kiss me."

Their lips met, slowly, just a tingling brush at first, then melded into a warm, passionate kiss. Reuben's arm wrapped around her back pulling her body to his. Cradling her cheek to the muscular trough of his shoulder and neck, she sighed deeply. "I have missed you, Mr. Frank. It's ridiculous. We're on the same little wagon train."

Reuben laughed. "Yep. Two wagons and three hundred cows."

She nodded her head into his shoulder, giggling. "Yes, not quite like the long line of wagons in our journey from St. Louis to Cherry Creek...or the endless parade of buggies and coaches in front of the theatres in London." Reuben felt himself tense. *Why in this place, at this moment, would she mention England?*

Drawing back her head, her eyes were wide and animated. "These mountains, Reuben, they are beautiful —stunning. Every twist and turn of the trail is an entirely different vista. The south slopes are completely different from the north slopes and every few hundred feet going up or down, the vegetation and leaves seem to change. I never knew."

Reuben half chuckled in agreement. "I had an inkling from the scout's letters to my father but I had no real idea either." He raised his hands to her shoulders, pushing her back gently. "Rebecca, we have to talk." He looked at her sharply. "First, how are you feeling? *Really.*"

Her eyes flickered from his for an instant and then returned his searching gaze. "I feel more tired than normal and once in a while for a brief spell in the mornings I feel nauseous."

Reuben looked closely at her. "It does not appear that you are eating much either."

She giggled. "I may not eat all of my supper Reuben but each morning I prepare quite a bundle of snacks. For some reason I'm craving pemmican. Every time the wagon is in a relatively controllable stretch of trail I find myself eating." She rolled her eyes. "So, when I'm completely fat, round and waddling around like one of those cows of yours, will you still kiss me like that?"

Half a question, half worried. "I don't believe, Mistress Marx, that you ever have to worry about Reuben Frank not kissing you—often." Her facial muscles relaxed slightly and her eyes sparkled.

"Rebecca," Reuben looked down at his boots and then back up at her. "I've been giving this a lot of thought. Our child can't be a bastard. He needs to have the name of his father. I know how little villages work. Folks' favorite pastime is talking about tidbits concerning others—whether accurate or not. They will love discussing our child, and the wanton Englishwoman who is the mother but not married. Grist for the gossip mill."

Rebecca's chin lifted. "Then we shall not go to town."

Reuben shook his head. "There will be no getting around having to trade with someone. Based on the maps, there are only two tiny human camps within a day or two's ride of the Red Mountains and they are primarily Ute villages...depending upon exactly where we decide to locate the ranch." He tried to smile, "As I understand it from the scout's notes, sometimes there is trading at the remnants of Fort Uncompahgre, but the Mexican trader that built it, Antoine Robidoux, abandoned it in the forties. And its eighty miles away at the confluence of the Uncompahgre and Gunnison Rivers."

"I see," she said slowly. "And don't forget my land *and* gold, Reuben."

Reuben stared at her. *I need to choose the right words.* "Rebecca, about your land. It will be interesting to see where it is situated relative to the general location of the ranch. The scout recommended the area at the lower end of a certain creek before it empties into the Uncompahgre River for the homestead. But I didn't see that creek on your map." He looked at her intently. "Don't get your hopes up on gold. I know similar rumors have bubbled up from my father's scout and in his maps, and from your father's travels and your map, but don't set yourself up for disappointment."

Her eyebrows lowered into a slight frown and the line of her lips thinned.

I know that look, he thought. "What I mean to say is, at the least, I'm sure your land is breathtaking. It may have timber resources on it. I'm sure it is suitable for cattle and perhaps has good water for hay. Neither one of us will know until the time comes."

"I believe, Reuben," her eyes did not waiver from his, "that my dear father's bequeath will be all of that, but I have this feeling that there may well be more."

Reuben took one of her hands between both of his, taking in a deep breath and holding it for a moment before exhaling. "It will be what it will be, but, what is, is. You and me." He reached out his other hand placing it lightly on her belly, partially concealed by the bedroll. "Us. I'd really planned to bring you flowers, drop down on one knee with the sun beating down and a huge expanse of one of these views around us." Chortling, he shook his head. "But at this rate..." his voice trailed off.

Her eyes were wide, her lips slightly parted. "Are you proposing to me, Mr. Frank?"

"Yes," stammered Reuben, "Yes, I suppose I am."

She leaned back into the blankets keeping her hand sandwiched between his. "Reuben, our child can most certainly have your last name."

Reuben felt a wide smile rapidly broadening on his face. Freeing one hand from hers, he began to reach into his pocket. "You mean..."

She held up her hand, "No, I mean your child, our child, can certainly have the last name of Frank but I will have to think more about marriage. That could be very confining, you know."

"Confining?" Reuben felt a flash of anxious, confused anger. Even the ring pressing against his thigh felt hot. He withdrew his fingers from his pocket as unobtrusively as possible and stood, pacing two steps, then turning and pacing again, suddenly wishing he could stride right out the damn wagon. *Confinement? She's not the only one who feels confined. I'll be damned if I will have to convince the woman carrying my child to marry me.*

"I've been honest with you, Reuben," she said, looking up at him earnestly. "I don't know what I may find on or about father's land. I have responsibilities in England. They may not be able to be handled satisfactorily unless I am there. What if I did have to go back?"

Reuben stood still, staring at her. "You mean if you choose to go back."

Rebecca was silent, her eyes blinking several times. "Yes, Reuben. If I choose to go back. What if for whatever reason, I did not return or something happened to me, or to you? We would be married, not even knowing, unable to move on with our lives, constrained by some distant tether."

"Distant tether?" *Get that edge out of your voice, Reuben.* He turned and stepped away, his back to her. Taking a deep breath, he turned back, walked over and sat down on the bedroll next to her, dropping his hand gently to her belly again. "This is not a tether. This is a bond. Unbreakable. Forever. We have a child to consider, not just ourselves. What would you propose to do with our son or daughter if you decided to traipse back to Europe?"

A startled expression flashed across her features, and Reuben thought she grew a shade paler. "I...I hadn't thought of that, Reuben."

Struggling to mask his hurt frustration, he leaned over, kissing her softly but quickly on the lips. "I didn't think so." He stood, looking down at her, one hand still holding hers. *Thank God I didn't pull the damn ring out.* "Think about these things, Rebecca, as will I. It would never be my intention to bind a heart to mine that did not wish to be bound but there are realities."

Her eyes widened and she tightened her grip on his. "I'm sure that together..."

Putting one finger to his lips, Reuben focused on keeping his tone level. "We can talk about it in a few days. Get some rest. Tomorrow will be a hard day. We're pushing down through the gap and if that short cut of Zeb's is open, I'd like to make Farmers Creek before dark and camp there. We still have a long ways to go, Rebecca. From what Zeb says, the trail will become more difficult, the mountains higher, more rugged, and," he forced a grin, "even more spectacular."

They held each other's gaze for an extended moment, then Reuben turned, letting go of her hand. "I will tell Sarah to come on in. She's probably freezing out there."

June 16, 1855

SENSELESS

EAGLE TALON RODE GLUMLY, GLANCING OCCASIONALLY over at Walks with Moon, the tails of the long poles of the travois dragged by her mustang scratching across the rough ground.

The People had been moving steadily eastward in their continuing quest for tatanka. As he had each day just after sunrise for the past three suns, Eagle Talon sought to ride into a scouting position toward the front of the line, fanning out to the flanks with the other esteemed scouts, a customary position befitting a maturing brave with eight eagle feathers. *And five more if the Council ever decides to count my coup against the Pawnee.*

On each occasion, Flying Arrow had halted Eagle Talon, riding back toward him as he sought his traditional position. Flying Arrow said not a word, but his stern look and slight nod of his chin toward the rear made words unnecessary. Each day, Eagle Talon moved toward the back of the moving camp, pretending to ride with the *akacitas*, the men whose job it was to guard and police the line. He avoided riding next to his friends, Three Knives and the others, also shunned by the Council.

The travois that Walks with Moon's mustang pulled, two shorter poles across and latched with rawhide at the horse's withers, was loaded with the family's possessions—rolled tipi and parfleches filled with ceremonial items, food, utensils and clothing. Behind her stretched Eagle Talon's other fourteen horses, mostly mustangs, in a trailing tether behind two ponies, their lead rope clutched tightly by Walks with Moon. Both of those horses were laden with lodge poles, strapped to their sides and balanced equally. The horses whinnied and shuffled, as disgruntled as Eagle Talon, as the irregular long line of women and children, horses dragging travois and younger, less experienced braves and teenagers passed him, the dust from the movement softly sifting toward him.

Eagle Talon's shoulders and neck felt stiff. *I cannot wait until the shame is over but what if the Council decides to extend it?* He shifted his gaze beyond the moving throng to the vast emptiness that seemed to swallow the tribe. The occasional, distant figure of a rider could be seen dipping and emerging on the gently contoured landscape, only to disappear in the next small draw. *I should at least be one of the akacitas. It is bad enough I am not part of the advance scouts.*

He nudged his horse forward and rode up to Walks with Moon.

"Husband." Walks with Moon looked at him, her eyes quizzical, wider than normal and concerned.

Eagle Talon dropped his eyes from hers.

"The shame is not over," he said, knowing her thoughts, "until the Council pronounces it so."

Leaning sideways toward him from her mustang, Walks with Moon placed a deliberate hand lightly on his thigh. "Eagle Talon, was not Flying Arrow pleased that you discovered the dark-skinned ones? You told me that he seemed impressed by your contact with them and your gesture of friendship."

Eagle Talon wagged his head slightly, again fixing his gaze to the north hoping to catch another glimpse of one of the scouts, perhaps riding a high ridge, scanning the horizon, protecting the tribe. *As I should be.* He jerked as Walks with Moon dug her fingernails into his flesh. Spurring his mustang slightly so that her hand fell from his leg, he snapped, "Why do you scratch me woman?" Immediately knowing the answer and feeling sorry for the irritation in his voice.

Walks with Moon's lips compressed, the almond shape of her eyes narrowing. "Feeling sorry for yourself will do us no good. You made a decision with the Pawnee. You thought it was right. You saved lives, even if they were hairy-faced-ones. And you believe you've met your spirit brother. Then eighteen suns ago you ran into the dark-skinned ones. You're the only warrior in this tribe who has had this kind of contact with hairy-faced-ones, and the only person to meet dark-skinned ones, though we have heard of them. Spirit has purpose in all this, Eagle Talon. Sunshine always follows rain."

She edged her mustang next to his again, reaching out and taking his hand, placing it on the taut leather covering the now very pronounced rounding of her belly. "And our son is on the way, my husband." She held up her other hand toward the sky, which sparkled with an early summer morning's promise. "The sky is blue." She smiled slightly. "If we are riding at the rear, at least you will be by your friends. You are all in shame. You're not alone, but..." Her face grew serious. "...I know there is some greater purpose in all of this for you."

Eagle Talon felt his shoulders slightly relax. Again, he had that feeling. *There is still something, some undisclosed matter that she is not sharing.* He gently rubbed her belly and tried to force a smile.

"I think, my husband, that Flying Arrow does not look pleased." She squeezed his thigh. "Patience Eagle Talon. The shame will be over, if not at the end of this moon, then in the next. The designs of Spirit will become apparent over time. I am your wife. I believe in you. I have faith in the course Spirit has set for us." She laid her hand lightly over his. "Nothing happens without reason. There is a destiny to be fulfilled. I know this." She looked away. "I have heard it spoken."

Eagle Talon felt himself jerk again. "You have heard it spoken? By who?"

Walks with Moon swallowed, her lower lip shaking slightly. "It was the night you returned, after your battle with the Pawnee. I've not talked about it with you because...," looking briefly away, she searched for the right words, "you have much burdening you right now." She raised her eyes to his. "It was Talks with Shadows."

"Talks with Shadows?" Eagle Talon snorted. "You believe in the ramblings of Talks with Shadows? I thought you and your friends often tease her about her premonitions being wrong and you, yourself told me that most of them were pretend—just an attempt by her to get attention."

Walks with Moon returned his derisive stare with unflinching, steady eyes. "This was different."

"Then tell me...."

She shook her head firmly, jutting out her chin, her cheek muscles tightening, "Not now, husband. Sometime soon. Just know there is a purpose in all this."

Eagle Talon's mind raced, imagining but his train of thought was broken by a shout from Pointed Lance. "At least back here in the rear of the column we can talk as long as we pretend not to."

Eagle Talon looked quickly at his friend, and then the faces of Brave Pony, Three Knives and Turtle Shield, who rode together as a pack, their families' travois and horses separated by three or four lance lengths in which camp dogs trotted. All of his friends were smiling, but all stared rigidly ahead, none of them looking at one another. Even Pointed Lance had not turned his head while speaking.

Eagle Talon's gaze shifted to Talks with Shadows and was surprised to see her staring at him, then Walks with Moon.

She slowed her pony, allowing Turtle Shield, her husband, to move ahead of her and then angled her horse dragging their travois toward their mounts, which were plodding forward, moving with the flow of the tail end of the village.

Talks with Shadows drew abreast of them, turning her horse parallel, a lance length away. "You have not told him fully, yet." Walks with Moon's mouth dropped open and she cast a startled glance at Eagle Talon, himself surprised at the other woman's comment. *Not a question, but a statement. She couldn't have heard us.* Talks with Shadows nodded her head once sharply. "That is good my friend Walks with Moon. It is not yet time." Without another word and without looking back, she gently spurred her pony, whose pace quickened as she moved to catch up with Turtle Shield.

Eagle Talon extended a muscled bronze arm, gently but firmly wrapping his hand around Walks with Moon's bicep. "Wife, what is this? You cannot keep such a thing from your husband."

Walks with Moon looked at him, blinked and shook her head slowly, "As we've told you, it is not yet time."

Eagle Talon felt his already simmering boil of anger and frustration rise inside of him. "Wife, by—"

Walks with Moon shook her head emphatically and then stared at him, her brown eyes earnest, "Trust me, Eagle Talon. Trust your wife. I will tell you only this." She placed her hand, fingers spread wide, on her belly and again bit her lower lip, staring straight ahead. "We are misjudging the hairy-faced-ones."

"You mean Ray-bec-ka and Roo-bin?" asked Eagle Talon incredulously.

"No, no." She shook her head. "Not them. Not them at all. The many, many hairy-faced-ones that will be coming. It will not be the same for The People in ways we do not yet understand."

Eagle Talon clenched his jaw, the wrath inside him shifting targets. "Then, we will fight them and drive them away," he said fiercely.

Walks with Moon's eyebrows hunched in a worried frown. "No husband, we shall not drive them away." Then she fell silent.

EAGLE TALON SHIELDED HIS EYES FROM THE SUN, SCANning the head of the column. The sun was high now, nearly past its midday zenith. He stared morosely up the column led by Flying Arrow's lance pointed to the sky. Behind the Chief was Tracks on Rock, the bright colors of the beaded vest covering his broad shoulders occasionally visible as the throng of The People behind parted in their movements. Far beyond them, there seemed to be faint, but growing and evermore distinct, light brown twirls. *Riders? The advance scouts! They must've found tatanka!*

The billows of dust grew closer. It was indeed two of the braves posted far in front of the moving band, returning at full gallop. Flying Arrow raised a long arm in the air and the progression shuffled to a halt, various members of the tribe looking at one another with questioning stares—except he and his friends who kept their eyes fixed ahead of them.

There was a distant shout and one of the braves began to ride back alongside the line at full gallop. To Eagle Talon's astonishment, the scout reined his horse in abruptly as he approached them, skidding to a stop in the loose sandy soil, talking excitedly, and gesturing at Eagle Talon and his friends. "Flying Arrow wants you at the head of the line immediately. You need to see something." The brave's face was both animated and agitated. Greatly puzzled, Eagle Talon and his friends exchanged looks with their wives and then furtively at one another.

"Let's go," Eagle Talon called out quietly. The five warriors spurred their ponies into a gallop along the flanks of the long trail of The People.

As they drew their horses up near Flying Arrow and Tracks on Rock, a number of other braves were gathering. Flying Arrow and Tracks on Rock's angular features were etched in expressions of somber anger.

Turning stiffly to one of the warriors who had ridden in from an advance position, Flying Arrow commented, "Show us." His voice was cold and emotionless.

The brave wheeled his pony and followed by the two chiefs and twenty-one warriors; the group advanced at a quick lope toward the southeast. They rode silently for several hours, the muffled sound of so many pony hooves creating a rhythm that flowed up and down the rolling hills, now covered with the gold-hued green of early summer growth. Nearing the crest of one rise, the advance scout pointed. Flying Arrow raised his hand then lowered his arm halfway. The party slowed their advance, the instinct and training of generations causing them to separate and fan out, their horses shaking their heads with impatience, moving slowly, step-by-step, toward the crest of the hill, the view beyond expanding as they ascended the rise until finally gentle swells of a valley bisected by a small creek with occasional alders, willows and two lone cottonwoods was fully visible. There was a collective gasp and several braves murmured under their breath. Eagle Talon was unsure whether he joined into the single voice of dismay. Strewn across the valley floor and rising up the cusp of higher land around the creek, were the red glistening mounds of over sixty buffalo, strewn haphazardly and grotesquely in rotting death. Their carcasses were completely intact except their hides had been removed. Eagle Talon was sure, even at a distance, that he could hear the drone of flies swarming around the spoiling meat, the animals' insides distended with bloat from the heat. *This many of our brothers would have kept the entire village for almost a winter. Who would do such a thing?*

Flying Arrow squared his bony, aging shoulders. Slowly, deliberately, he turned his mustang until he was facing the line of warriors. "The scouts reported to me that, late before the last sun set, they heard the sound of many guns. They had been trailing this herd of our brothers, determining their course of travel before reporting back to us so that we could intercept them. They watched from that ridge..." his arm rose, a thin, crooked forefinger pointing with a slight tremble at a ridgeline twenty arrow flights distant..."as seven hairy-faced-ones skinned these slaughtered tatanka." There was a catch in his voice. He paused, then swept his arm out over the expanse of bloody carcasses. "They skinned them, piled the hides in a wagon over other older hides and then moved south." There was the slightest tremble in his voice as he added, "They took no meat. They did not clean a single animal. All the meat is now ruined. These brothers will feed no one." He shook his head, pressing his lips together grimly.

Eagle Talon could not tear his eyes from the carnage, his stare shifting rapidly from one wasted, decaying carcass to another. *Senseless.* Walks with Moon's face clouded his sight as he recalled her words. *"It will not be the same for The People in ways we do not yet understand."*

June 17, 1855

*L*UCKY ENCOUNTER

"SERGEANT, GET THOSE TROOPERS IN LINE."

"Straighten up, lads. Line up those columns."

Lucy's eyebrows shot up over eyes suddenly twice as large as normal. Looking down from astride the mule, she opened her mouth to speak but Israel raised his forefinger to his lips. "Shhhhh. Might be soldiers down in them thick trees close to the river," he whispered.

He looked quickly around. A thick stand of heavy trunked cottonwoods was directly in front of them, like the icing on the cake of the horseshoe bend in the river that curved in their direction several hundred yards away. Downstream, the South Platte tapered, glistening through less dense trees in a west sinking sun, its rolling current framed by white, jagged peaks rising in the distance.

The mule stood at nervous attention; its grey-white muzzle pointed directly toward the source of the voices, one ear forward, one ear back. Lucy's cheeks were twitching under her eyes. Reaching up, Israel set one gnarled hand on hers and squeezed.

"Israel, which side of that line you was talking about, between freeman and slaves, do you think we're on?" Her voice was an anxious hiss.

"Don't rightly know," Israel answered quietly. "It's called the Mason-Dixon line. Not sure if it even goes this far west. Weren't nothing in the papers describing what happens to it near the mountains." He looked furtively around. "But one thing's for certain sure; we ain't come this far to get turned in 'cuz we be on the wrong side of a line some white men drew up. Let's get over in them trees and hope those soldiers, or whoever they are, pick another route out of the stand."

Lucy sucked in her lower lip and bit on it, nodding assent.

"We'll get maybe twenty feet inside them trunks," Israel breathed. "Have a little room to move and still be hidden. Hopefully, we'll just blend into that grey bark. Let's go! We can't stand here in the open."

As quietly as he could, he led Sally and his wife toward the tree line. *Our clothes is mostly dull colors.* He looked down at the grey, threadbare jacket that hung halfway to his knees, *'cept Lucy's bandanna.* "Take that bandanna off, woman."

Lucy blinked, an understanding flitting across her expression. She hastily pulled the bandanna off her wiry, salt-and-pepper hair, scrunching up the colorful cloth and holding it in her hands so it couldn't be seen.

"By the twos, sergeant."

"Yes, sir. By the twos, troopers. Smart about it now. Might be a general outside this tree line waitin' to review you." There was muffled laughter from a group of men.

Israel felt a slight lessening of anxiety when they reached the cottonwoods. Melting into the timber he looked behind him several times to make sure they would be hidden, or at least obscured by the outer band of trees to any eyes riding out into the open country where they had been just seconds before.

"Move them out, Sergeant O'Malley."

"Yes sir. Forwaaaard ho-oooh!"

"Don't wait for me sergeant. I will take over lead of the column once we are out away from the river."

"Yes, sir."

The voices were clearer now, nearer. The mule's nostrils were flaring. *Don't be thinking about making no sounds, Sally.*

Israel could hear the muted thuds of a number of horses hooves punctuated by the occasional snort and crack of branches downed by winter winds.

Now there were glimpses and flashes of blue sifting momentarily into sight, then disappearing as the riders moved through narrow alleys in the timber at what appeared to be a perpendicular angle to them. He exchanged a quick glance with Lucy.

Israel had positioned the mule's nose into a particularly thick cottonwood trunk between them and the riders. *Keep the big animal's shape head-on rather than sideways.*

A hundred yards from them, the first of the column of riders quick stepped from the tree line, their forms and uniforms clearer outside the trees. *Army, sure enough, but how many and which way they goin' to turn?*

The cavalry troops did not turn. They continued to ride straight northeast.

Some of the tightness left Israel's shoulders. He turned to Lucy, a slight smile beginning to form, then freezing at the distinctive click of a pistol hammer being cocked.

Lucy pressed her lips together hard to stop their trembling and the mule shifted his weight from one shoulder to the other without moving.

Israel slowly leaned over, inches at a time from behind the cottonwood.

A medium height man in a blue uniform with gold buttons stood twenty feet from them. Partially concealed by a tree, he had drawn his pistol, which pointed at them from the waist. He led a dark sorrel horse draped with a blue and gold blanket underneath a saddle, to which was strapped a saber and rifle scabbard. His wide-brimmed hat had an insignia of crossed swords centered on the crown; a braided, gold headband with twin tassels wrapped the base of the crown where it met the brim.

"Who else is behind that tree with you?" The man's voice was wary, but not hard. He wagged the muzzle of the pistol slightly. "Come out where I can see all of you." Israel took two steps to the side leading Sally and Lucy into view. He noticed two straight golden bars on both of the soldier's lapels. *An officer.*

The officer's eyes carefully searched Lucy, scanned Israel and then roved the length of the mule. "You are not armed?"

Israel removed his hat. "No, suh; all we got is a knife for camping and filleting fish and such."

The officer lowered his pistol but didn't holster it. He took a few steps toward Israel. "What's your name, where are you from and where are you going?" Israel shifted his eyes to Lucy. *Let me do the talking.*

"We is Israel and Lucy Thomas. We come from the east and we're hoping to settle out there to the west, somewheres over them mountains."

"That your wife?"

"Going on twenty-five years," said Israel, casting another quick glance at Lucy. There were tears streaming down her face and the trembling of her lips overpowered the clench of her jaw.

"Where exactly are you planning on going? Those mountains go on mostly forever. Give me a specific place that you're headed to? Kinfolk?"

Israel swallowed and realized he was nervously playing with his hat. We're headed to a place we never seen but we heard about. It's called Uncompahgre."

The officer's eyes widened. "That's clear down southwest. Some of the most remote country there is." His eyes narrowed. Israel was sure he detected a click of realization in the officer's expression. "I'm Captain Henderson, C Squad, F Troop, United States Army, Second Cavalry. We are based out of Fort Laramie, which is a good ways to the north." He smiled. "Actually, we are based out of these saddles. Haven't been back to the fort for weeks." His stare was stern but softened as his eyes rested on Lucy. "Let me see your papers. The Army is the law out here, you know. There's treaties and such that we are bound to uphold."

Israel felt his heart sink. "Papers?" he repeated slowly, trying to buy time to think.

There was a hint of stern concern in the captain's face. "Do you have your papers?"

Israel sighed, then drew his shoulders back. "We got our papers. They's wrapped up. They is on newspaper so dry it could break apart."

The captain's eyebrows raised. "That's it?"

Israel felt sick to his stomach. He nodded slowly.

"Let me see those papers."

Israel hesitated. Captain Henderson smiled, "I'll be careful."

Israel went back to the saddlebag draped over Sally's rump and withdrew the several pages of old, yellowing *New York Times* carefully wrapped in a handkerchief and pressed between two thin pieces of wood as protection. He delicately handed the bundle to Captain Henderson. *Gotta get the tremble out of my hands.*

The officer looked surprised. "You can read?"

"Mistress of the plantation taught me, though she weren't supposed to."

The captain's eyebrows arched as he quickly scanned the still folded newsprint. "These are not official papers, Mr. Thomas. What is this?"

Israel straightened his shoulders again, shoving his hands in his pockets to hide the shake in his gnarled fingers and looked with a steady gaze square into Captain

Henderson's eyes. "That there is a cutout I made from part of an article in that *New York Times* paper."

The captain began to unfold the brittle, yellow sheet. A small corner of it cracked and fell fluttering to the ground.

"I'd be obliged if you handle that carefully, suh; it cracks easy. One of the first things I ever read after the Mistress taught me. I aim to keep it; mebbe pass it on my kinfolk if I ever find them."

The captain glanced sharply at Israel but slowed his unfolding, gently unbinding each layer of newsprint from the next. He paused momentarily, looking up from the task. "Mr. Thomas, these are not official papers. I ask again, what is this?"

Israel lifted his chin, "It is the Constitution of these United States. And there's one part of that I want to especially point out to you, captain, suh."

A puzzled expression flashed across the captain's face; his shoulders lifted in a partial shrug and he continued the process of unfolding the paper, finally holding both edges, one in each hand. His eyes moved rapidly back and forth over the print, every so often lifting to Israel's face and then back to reading.

Israel took two steps so that he was next to the officer and extended one long, skinny dark finger pointing toward the top left of the long columns of print. "Captain suh, read these words if you would please, where it begins with *All men are created equal....*"

The captain turned his head sideways to Israel, a look of understanding suddenly replacing the authoritative expression he had worn to that point. He cleared his throat. "I'll do that Mr. Thomas. Matter of fact, I will read them aloud. *We hold these truths to be self-evident, that all men are created equal, that they are endowed by their Creator with certain unalienable Rights, that among these are Life, Liberty, and the pursuit of Happiness.*"

After reading the first line, he raised his eyes to Israel's and completed the entire preamble, his eyes never returning to the page. "*That to secure these rights, Governments are instituted among Men, deriving their just powers from the consent of the governed—That whenever any form of Government becomes destructive of these ends, it is the Right of the People to alter or to abolish it, and to institute new Government, laying its foundation on such principles and organizing its powers in such form, as to them shall seem most likely to affect their Safety and Happiness.*"

Israel let several seconds of silence lapse. "You see, captain, these *are* my papers and they're her papers," Israel pointed at Lucy who was watching the exchange wide-eyed, "and they're your papers. Matter fact, suh, seems to me you wear that uniform because of this paper and it seems to me there's no papers more important than the one you got in your hands."

Captain Henderson began to speak, but instead turned his head toward the sound of a horse coming at a gallop.

The rider reined in ten feet from them. The newcomer was stoutly built with wide shoulders and a shock of brown hair with a reddish tint underneath a blue Army cap with a black bill. There were stripes on his sleeves. "Sir?" He had drawn his pistol.

Captain Henderson glanced at the newcomer's weapon and then at Israel and Lucy. "That's all right Sergeant O'Malley. At ease. You can put that away." The sergeant's bushy red eyebrows surged upward. Shaking his head slightly, he reached over with his left hand opening the flap of the holster on his hip and shoving the pistol back into it with his right, taking care to fasten the holster flap after the gun was sheathed.

"Came back to check on you, captain."

"Yes, sergeant, by happenchance I saw Mr. and Mrs. Thomas here through the trees, and came over to investigate their papers."

The sergeant's eyes moved from Israel's face to Lucy's, back to the captain's and came to rest on the large yellowed paper in the officer's hands. "Don't look like no papers I've ever seen before, captain. We gonna take them back to the fort?" The tone of the sergeant's voice made it clear he believed he already knew the answer and he raised himself in the saddle partially lifting one leg, beginning to dismount.

"At ease, sergeant. No need to dismount." Captain Henderson's eyes were fixed on Israel's even as he was talking to his noncom. "In point of fact, these here papers are in perfect order. Might be the most complete set ever presented to me." The corners of the captain's mouth turned up in a suppressed smile and his eyes were kind. *Maybe even respectful.* Without taking his gaze off Israel, he carefully refolded the page, reaching out a hand and taking from Israel's the handkerchief and two thin protective wafers of wood. He wrapped the old paper in the cloth, positioning the wood pieces firmly and gently on either side of the refolded article and then presented the rebound document to Israel.

"Sir?" The sergeant's voice was filled with puzzlement.

"You're free to go Mr. and Mrs. Thomas." He shifted his gaze to Lucy, drew himself up and saluted smartly. "My apologies, ma'am for delaying your trip." Captain Henderson turned back to Israel. "If you're headed to that destination you told me of when we first met, I think, if I were you, I would take a less settled route, though it might be a tad more arduous and the journey several weeks or two longer than following the Platte down to Cherry Creek and taking the usual route over Kenosha Pass."

"Sergeant, hand me that pad and pencil of yours. I'm going to draw a map for the Thomas'." The captain smiled at Israel. "Going to take more than one page with these little sheets, but I'll number 'em. Stand behind me while I sketch them out. It will help you remember."

Israel could feel Lucy's questioning stare on the back of his head. *What's he drivin' at?*

Captain Henderson's pencil scratched industriously. "I would recommend you cross the South Platte several miles upstream from here where it widens out. If you keep a west northwest course, you will hit a large creek about a hard stones throw wide. That's Lodge Pole Creek. Follow it 'til it joins another slightly larger river. That's the Laramie River. Work your way upstream. The going is mostly flat 'til you hit the abrupt toe of the Medicine Bow Mountains south of the Snowy Range."

He chuckled. "You'll be able to see them peaks, and you'll know why they got that name. A short ways into the mountains the Laramie bends hard south, and a smaller creek comes in from the west. It will seem like the better trail goes up the Laramie, but not at your age or as old as that mule is." He nodded at Lucy. "Gets too steep."

Good Lord Jesus, he's tellin' us how to stay free!

Follow the smaller creek west 'til it peters out. The trail is not much, but it will do. Some of the prettiest stands of straight-trunked lodgepole you will ever see. The climb is gradual enough, and the Arapaho call the top Fox Park. On the west side, the trail follows several small drainages down and though faint, is easy to travel. Stay out of anything that looks boggy or around beaver dams. That mule will sink into her belly. The valleys will get wider until you come out above a tremendous big area called North Park. You'll see the signs and tree line of a river out some miles. That would be the North Platte and there's a canyon to the east there, Northgate. Might be a good place to hole up a few days and rest. It's good fishin'. Follow the Platte until it bends north, then keep heading west across and next to a number of smaller creeks and rivers—the Canadian, Michigan, Grizzly and Willow Creek."

The captain's pencil paused as he stared into the trees and thought. "At the west side of North Park are the Buffalo Mountains. You'll take Muddy Pass below, and then Rabbit Ears Pass higher up which is marked by two tall columns of rock at the top. Can't miss them. This is a big high stretch, and if your bones are aching when you get over, there will be hot springs on the west side. You'll see the steam rising in the morning just up from the valley floor if you keep your eyes sharp.

"Once you're over Rabbit Ears Pass it flattens out quite a bit. The river over there is the Yampa. It runs mostly east-west until you get about fifty miles from the west side of Rabbit Ears, where it bends south. Follow that bend. The Yampa will turn back north, but you keep heading south, sticking to the lowest areas and those trails will bring you all the way down to the Colorado River. You'll know you're halfway to the Colorado when you cross a good sized river flowing mostly east and west. That's the White." The captain drew another line on the page.

He looked up at Israel, pointing the pencil at him. "That Colorado is a big, powerful river. First really good crossing is about seventy miles down from where you will come down on it, just above where the Gunnison River comes in. Some call it Grand Junction. Cross there. There is a short cut, and a crossing by Brush Creek, but it entails another pass. I think the less up and down for your mule and your wife, the better. And," he looked hard at Israel, "If the river has not yet dropped from the melt, you hole up until it does or you will all be swept away."

Israel knew his eyes were wide from the building surprise at the wealth of detailed information the captain was sharing. He nodded vigorously, glancing quickly at Sergeant O'Malley. *Them eyebrows of his get any higher, his cap's gonna eat 'em. I ain't the only one flabbergasted.*

Captain Henderson began to draw again. "Follow the Gunnison River upstream to what's left of an old fort, Fort Uncompahgre, on the south bank. He craned his head back and up at Israel. "From here on, I'm less familiar. Only been down this far south two or three times. Once in a while I hear about various folks setting up a temporary trading post in what's left of the fort, until they get run out by the Ute. This spot is a very large delta formed by the confluence of the Gunnison and the Uncompahgre. From there, follow the Uncompahgre up river to wherever you want to wind up. You'll certainly be seen by Injuns, though you may never know." He pursed his lips. "But I don't think they'll bother you on account of your age, you being Negro, and..." his eyes flicked to Sally, "...how old that mule is." His one eye hidden from Sergeant O'Malley by the bridge of his nosed closed in a quick wink. "It's a long way, for sure, but less people and less chance of running into..." The captain paused, "folks who would take from you what is yours."

"Thank you, captain. Those there might be the best directions we ever received. How long do you reckon it will take us to get to where we are headed going that way?"

The officer's eyes flickered over Israel's legs, appraised the mule and lingered on Lucy's swollen ankles. "I would say, Mr. Thomas, that traveling at the rate that would best suit you would put you up in that country at the first to mid part of September." He paused. "Just so you know, winter can start up there any time around then. It all depends on the year." He looked from one to the other of them, then abruptly turned, taking two steps to his horse and lifting himself stiffly into the saddle. "May the good Lord look after you." His head swiveled toward his sergeant. "Sergeant, let's rejoin the troop."

Sergeant O'Malley's eyes were still wide and his jaw slack. He looked at Captain Henderson, blinked, shoved his wide shoulders back and stuck out his chest. With a nod to Israel and Lucy, he wheeled his horse, as did Captain Henderson and the two of them burst from the trees at a fast canter headed northeast toward the distant cloud of dust that was their patrol.

June 19, 1855

 $\mathscr{P}$REMONITION

Chief smacked his lips, sucking and licking each of his fingers slowly their entire length, then wiped his hands on his already filthy leather leggings. "Mighty damn good—three days taking it easy, fresh deer meat, a fire, not looking over our shoulders. Yep, damn good."

The men around the fire, most holding chunks of meat and chewing, nodded. Tom wiped his mouth with the forearm of his sleeve. "Yep, I watched that whole thing. Had a perfect vantage point from them rocks you put me in up valley, boss. Chief kept them does' attention and you did that sneak. Bit too far for me to see, but looked like a hell of a shot. Couldn't a been much more than her head stickin' up above that rock they was bedded behind."

Black Feather squatted, slightly to the side of the group, devouring steaming, dripping flesh hanging off a thigh bone. "Worked out good. They was fixed on Chief. Never saw me coming. Might've knocked down another one if they had stuck around a second longer."

Still chewing, he swiveled his head toward Dot. "You get enough to eat, girl?" She was sitting on a log positioned by Johnson as a seat for her near the fire. Her pale face, framed by scraggly blonde hair, lifted, her gaze looking up over the slab of venison in her hands. Still chewing, her lips greasy from the meat, she smiled and nodded.

Johnson looked up at the stars, bright and white in the still deep black of the mountain night. "Been a while since we knocked over some loot, boss. I'm sure there's a couple of settlers down there in North Park and might be some wagon or buggy traffic along that Platte trail between the Rawah and the Buffaloes. The river ain't far from the toes of the Zirkel on the north side of the valley. That's rugged country; easy to escape into if we need if I remember. And last time we was up that way from the west, weren't much cavalry patrols."

Wiping his mouth with the back of his hand, Black Feather belched. *He remembers that gold we hid too. We came in from the southwest back then. He ain't never been to North Park from the east before.*

Taking another bite of venison, Black Feather chewed slowly, thinking. "That snowpack oughta be getting down on Cameron but there can still be some tricky spots and don't figure there's been any traffic. Folks don't much start coming over the divide there 'til sometime in July." He looked around the fire and then back to Johnson. Several of the men glanced between he and his second-in-command, waiting expectantly. *They are getting a mite antsy.*

"I'm thinkin' travel might be easier in four or five days, and she..." he nodded toward Dot, "...should not travel 'til her leg's past opening and bleeding again." *She has seen enough killin'. Gonna try and shelter her from that here on in.*

"Well, maybe boss, some of us could go up ahead. Scout out the pickins' and see what's doin' on the other side of the hill."

Black Feather rose. Turning, he hurled the thighbone out into the darkness. *Crazy fools go down there and get caught, and then cavalry or some bunch of vigilantes will be comin' after us.* He raised his eyes into the darkness toward the ten thousand-foot peaks of Cameron Pass. *Spring snow ain't gonna be too stable up there either.*

Taking a step to the fire, he sat cross-legged, his hands out to the heat. All of the faces in the circle of the flames were fixed on his, the flickers of firelight dancing ghostly, red shadows across their eyes and cheekbones. "Tell ya what, Johnson. Take whatever of the boys want to go and head on over that way, but just watch. Don't be knocking over anything 'til I catch up. Will be less than a week, maybe just a few days. We can't afford to make a mistake as few as we are now and we don't want to get chased from here to hell by who knows who. If there's something worth taking, it'll be there the next day too."

The men glanced at one another and nodded.

"Okay, boss. That's a good plan. Who wants to come?" Johnson asked, shifting his glance to Tom, then Chief, then Miguel and the rest of the men. All of them nodded. "Okay, we'll be lighting out of here after sunup tomorrow. We'll camp this side of the pass so we don't get caught up on top in the dark. Then we'll head over and drop down into North Park the day after." Johnson fixed his eyes on Black Feather. "You gonna be okay, boss? Sure you don't need one of us to stay behind?"

"I think me and the girl will be just fine, Johnson. Hank, didn't you say that the river is up over the trail in the Narrows?"

Hank, a burly man with pudgy cheeks, narrow slits for eyes and a dark complexion, looked up from his meat, nodded and took another mouthful of the steak he was holding in his hands.

June 20, 1855

"Colder," said the tiny voice. Black Feather looked up from the small honing stone on which he was sharpening his blade. Alone with Dot this day past, his mind had been riding the past, his guard letting up some.

"Yep it's definitely colder...." His eyes strayed up toward Cameron Pass and Nokhu Crags rock. The high peaks were gone, obscured by a dense, boiling grey-white cloud. The cloud cover settled almost down to their camp above the Narrows, the edge of the high elevation storm dissipating with uneven, serrated edges into a blue sky. His mother, Sunray, had told him of such cloud for-mations, *shaped by the strong breath of Spirit high above the earth.*

With that thought, the numbing, gut wrenching mem-ory of the day she had been taken from him again welled up. His eyes searched the hillsides around them for any hostile movement as they did every few minutes, then shifted to Dot. She was bundled up in his black and tan wool Army coat, hunched over and shivering. *And they killed that defenseless old horse. Never even kicked anybody in her life. My mother, my pa, and old Dot. In a matter of hours. No warning. And I did nothing.*

His eyes fell to the knife in his hands, its cutting-edge poised against the whetstone. *Until later.* He recalled the heavyset man moaning in pain after six weeks of torture, begging for his life, the young teenager Black Feather had been looking into the doomed man's panic-stricken eyes. He had found grim satisfaction in the bloody gurgle rising through the killer's lips and his windpipe as the compulsion of revenge slowly, deliberately, propelled the knife's edge across the front of the killer's throat. *This very blade.* Shaking his head, he shoved the whetstone into one pocket of the wool coat. Standing abruptly, he sheathed the knife, focusing once more up valley. *Sure hope they had sense enough to get up and over before that storm or the patience to wait it out.*

"Dot. I'm gonna build this fire up a little bit. You get closer to it and you'll be warmer. I'll tip this big rock up next to it. After it warms, it'll be like a reflector, get more heat coming at you. We'll cook ourselves some venison and boil up that wild asparagus we found yesterday. Early growth, but I figure we got enough to make a dent."

The girl tipped her face up slightly from where it was buried under the fully extended collar of his coat. Just her nose and big blue eyes were showing. She blinked.

"Are the horses cold?"

Black Feather had begun to slice chunks of venison from the single front shoulder remaining of the doe's carcass hanging from low branches of an aspen tree thirty feet from the fire. He stopped cutting and craned his face toward her, "You know, that's the first full sentence you've said in a spell. You do well when you're talking about horses." He pointed with the knife at the mustang and stallion. "See that fuzzy hair they've grown over the winter?" Dot tipped her head just enough to see over the collar. "This ain't bad for spring grass, they still got most of their winter coat, and there's not a rib showin' on either one of 'em."

The meat cut, Black Feather strained to roll the large triangular boulder so that one diagonal flat granite side was tucked in close to the flames. "Move in here a few feet across the fire from the face of that rock." He again looked toward the pass and the seething weather above them and pursed his lips.

"I think your leg is about the point it won't open up again. How's it feel?"

Dot's eyes peered at him from under heavy lids. She raised her mouth just above the coat collar. "Better."

"Good. I was worried about you there for a while. Figure we'll start to catch up with the boys tomorrow morning. By then this wind will die down and whatever weather's going on up there will have skedaddled. Best eat up tonight. No time for breakfast in the mornin'. I want to get started before daylight."

June 20, 1855

Storms on the Pass

Sarah and Rebecca huddled under a shared blanket. The hiss of snow against the canvas wagon top ebbed and flowed in intensity with the howl of the wind, the heavy fabric bowing between the arched wood ribs, then billowing out from the sides of the wagon as the swirling gusts changed direction. The suspended oil lamps swung slightly from the buffets of the storm, ever changing the pattern of shadows their light cast across the goods and bedrolls in the wagon.

Rebecca felt the redhead shift as the back gate of the wagon opened with a hurried thud and two long arms reached in with a wind-driven boil of snow, pulling out the ladder. Johannes, then Philippe, followed by Michael, clambered into the wagon scooting underneath the tied canvas back, not wanting to open it to the tempest outside. One by one, they straightened up, their shoulders and hats covered with snow.

"Michael, shut the tailgate," directed Johannes. The tall Dane peeled off his leather gloves, letting them drop with a sodden splat near the tailgate. He rubbed his hands together vigorously, flashing a broad smile. "Good evening, ladies. We expected to see you outside by a fire, busy stirring a big, hot pot of Sarah's stew, ready to feed the hungry cattle crew."

Good to see glimpses of the old Johannes from time to time. Reuben and Sarah were right. It was best not to say anything. Smiling back at him, Rebecca retorted in an overly serious tone, "You should've come to the wagon earlier, Johannes. You would have seen us huddled out there in the cold and the dark sacrificing our comfort for you men," she began to laugh, "but the snow kept putting out the fire."

Johannes began to step toward them, but Sarah raised an arm from beneath the blanket. "Oh no, no you don't. Don't take one step in here, Mr. Svenson, until you take off that sopping gutta-percha and that hat. You're already dripping over everything. Rebecca and I just got warm."

Johannes and Philippe exchanged amused glances. Michael was already dutifully following Sarah's instruction, his eyes periodically looking up at the two women, then settling on the floor again as he shed his poncho, hat and gloves.

Johannes snorted. "You ladies were not out trying to start any fire, but," he added with a mischievous grin, "just imagining that scene makes us feel looked after."

"How dare you question us, Johannes?" Rebecca faked indignation, trying to maintain a straight face, but to no avail. Both she and Sarah began to laugh. "You know us too well. We have, however, laid out the pan bread we made yesterday, honey and the last bit of butter. We should've brought more of that."

"And some pemmican you can roll in those thin round bread things Philippe showed us how to make the other day," added Sarah looking brightly at the vaquero.

Philippe chuckled. "They are called tortillas, *Señorita* Sarah, and when you roll them over some type of content, even pemmican, they are called burritos."

Rebecca turned her head to Sarah. The redhead was staring back at Philippe who was untying the colorful bandanna wrapped around his neck, its two tails tucked deep into the lapel of his tunic. She cleared her throat. "How are Zeb and Reuben doing out there? Such a horrible night to be out."

"They are fine," responded Johannes. "We have the cows pretty well bunched together. They are concentrated in small groups, staying close to one another for warmth I suppose and they're not about to move out from the downwind side of the various clumps of trees they have gathered behind. Given this hellish weather, we are rotating three hours on, three hours off, tonight." Johannes shook his head disgustedly. "This is June. It's supposed to be summertime."

Philippe chuckled. "*Sí, Señor* Johannes, but apparently the weather gods on top of these passes don't keep calendars. One can only imagine what December or January would be like." He turned his attention to Michael. "*¿Como esta, muchacho?* Warming up?" Michael threw another quick glance at Rebecca and Sarah, then diverted his eyes down to the floor nodding his head, "Yes...yes...yes, sir," he stammered.

"Good!" Philippe clapped his hands. "Good! So the *señoritas'* reward for our promptly obeying their commands is that we may now make the looong walk to the food." He gestured to the trays and plates Sarah and Rebecca had set out for them more than an hour before, a mere few feet away from where the men stood.

Sarah giggled. "Well, of course, Philippe. We would be honored to have you dine with us."

Rebecca watched Johannes' eyes shift rapidly from Philippe to Sarah. *Sarah —you are being far too transparent.* "We shall even let you sit, as long as your pants are halfway dry. If things get wet or damp in here, they take forever to dry out."

"Yes, ma'am." Johannes threw her a mock salute.

In a repeat of the scene three hours earlier, the tailgate opened with a thud, and snow curled under the closed canvas rigging, rising in a blown column in the relatively heated air of the wagon, the flakes melting as they rose, then disappearing, falling in droplets to the floor. Reuben rolled under the canvas, followed by Zeb on his hands and knees. Zeb rose to a crouch, reaching back out into the snowy darkness, pulling the tailgate up behind them. Sarah, her head resting on Rebecca's shoulder, jolted awake.

"We would appreciate—" Rebecca began to speak, but Reuben held up his hand with a smile.

"Johannes gave us the word. You might say we have been pre-instructed. Take off all our wet gear here before we take one step." He laughed. "Do I have it right?"

Reuben smiled and Zeb, now standing, chuckled, his fingers busily working the ice and snow out of his mustache. "I'll just hunker down right here on this barrel by the tailgate. These leather leggings are wet through, though this fringe will dry 'em soon enough. Reuben, would you mind fetching my food for me?"

Reuben turned from hanging his gutta-percha over the cross brace suspended side-to-side from one side of the top of the rearward arched canvas support to the other, an idea of Zeb's, lashed into place for just such a purpose. He took the several steps to the food the two women had laid out, preparing two plates, cutting large slices of the pan bread for each, and smearing gobs of butter and honey over the top of thick cake-like squares. He hesitated, surveying the tortillas and the adjoining dish of pemmican, looking at Rebecca and Sarah with a puzzled expression. "Those round pieces of bread are called tortillas. You roll the pemmican up in them and then you have a burrito." Sarah beamed helpfully.

"Really?" said Reuben, his eyes sliding to Rebecca's.

Reserved. He's been like this since he tried to propose. Waving her hand in the air, Rebecca forced a light and airy tone, "Yes, really. Actually quite delicious."

"Just bring me pemmican, Reuben. I don't need any of them tortillas." Zeb's voice was flat except for the word 'tortillas' to which he had added a sarcastic inflection. Sarah's face blanched.

Reuben paused, looking back over his shoulder at Zeb from his stooped position, his hands frozen, one holding a tortilla, the other about to sprinkle pemmican on it. "Sure, Zeb."

Rebecca fixed her eyes on Zeb. *Best to cut this conversation off.* "Zeb, are these types of storms common in June?"

"Much obliged, Reuben," said Zeb, reaching up for the plate the young Prussian extended to him. With his thumb, forefinger and middle finger the mountain man picked up a clump of pemmican, dropping it in his mouth and chewing. "Sure are, Rebecca. I've seen snow like this in July, this high, sometimes August. I reckon we're over eight thousand feet. The Gap is around six thousand and Wolf Creek, behind us, tops out at more than ten thousand feet, if I remember correctly. We holed up here on the east slope of this next ridge, 'cause the west sides of these hills get way more snow." He tipped his head back, dropping another mound of pemmican into his mouth and chewing. "Good thing is, it won't last long--usually. I bet tomorrow there ain't a cloud in the sky and it'll warm up right quick. By noon, this snow'll turn to muddy slush. We'll be stuck here at least a day."

Reuben's head snapped up. "We're going to lose a day?"

"Better than losing a wagon on slick slopes." Zeb's tone was matter of fact.

Rebecca was struck by a sudden memory. Trying to keep the alarm out of her voice, she peered at Zeb. "I saw an article in the newspapers back in England—

I believe on the Alps. They talked about snow sliding off mountains under the right conditions."

Zeb looked at her with respect for a moment, then nodded, still chewing. Swallowing, he wiped his lips with the back of his hand. "Yep, them is called avalanches. They can sweep down off a ridge and take out everything in their path, even the biggest of trees. Quite something to see." He paused, obviously lost in a memory, then catching the look of alarm on Rebecca's face, added quickly, "But we're fine here. Checked it out before we chose this spot. Ain't much of a north slope above us, which is where the snowpack is mostly this time of year. That south slope is steeper and higher but there's only patches of snow left. We'll be fine."

Rebecca breathed out, relieved. "I thought there were just going to be two riders out at any time tonight."

Reuben, sitting on a keg next to the bedroll near Rebecca, took a bite from the burrito, a large portion of the pemmican falling out of one end. "Remind me to wrap these things tighter next time." He picked the pemmican off his leggings and threw it back on his plate. "Philippe should be in shortly." At the mention of Philippe's name, Rebecca noticed Zeb's gaze dropped to his plate before Reuben continued on. "He just wanted to make sure Michael and Johannes was all set up. Shift after this, he and I will go back out and Johannes and Michael will come back in. Zeb gets to have two shifts off. Figured that would be fair since I broke my promise that he wouldn't have to spend any time with cows."

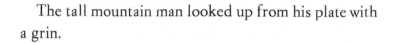

The tall mountain man looked up from his plate with a grin.

OPENING HER EYES SLOWLY, REBECCA'S GAZE ROVED THE interior of the wagon. Sarah lay on the bedroll next to her, breathing rhythmically, both of them still under the same blanket. *The winds have died down.* Reuben sprawled on the wagon floor below her, his chin on his chest, arms crossed and legs extended in an uncomfortable position in the narrow space that formed the small walking corridor between Sarah's empty bedroll and hers, and the stores and supplies carefully piled on either side of the wagon bed. Snoring more deeply, Zeb had tipped back the barrel he sat on, leaning his shoulders against the rear corners of the canvas.

A horse whinnied at the rear of the wagon. The tailgate slammed open and Philippe crawled in on all fours. Rebecca felt, rather than saw, Reuben's head snap up. Sarah sat up suddenly next to her.

"*Hola!*" said Philippe cheerfully, sliding his gutta-percha over his serape, then reaching up and taking off his hat, shaking it. *Not snowing nearly as hard,* Rebecca noticed. Philippe's smile froze as his eyes met Zeb's. He shifted his eyes to Sarah, breaking the icy stare between the two men first, then looked at Rebecca, his grin forced. "*Este vaquero* is hungry, Señoritas." He began to peel off his serape.

Throwing off her part of the blanket, Sarah rose quickly. "You are wet, Philippe. I will fix you a plate." She smiled.

An impossible situation from which to distract attention, Rebecca looked quickly at Zeb. He still leaned back on his barrel, his posture relaxed, but the eyes he fixed on Sarah were as stormy as the swirling snow outside.

Rebecca felt her jaw tighten as she watched Sarah prepare Philippe's food. *Two men after you, and you are hurting the one who has stood by you and the kindest of the two.* Rebecca looked away, focusing her gaze on one of the gently swinging lanterns. *And you do have choices, my friend.*

June 20, 1855

BURIED PAST

THE STUNNING BLUE OF SKY JUST BELOW THE PASS CON-trasted sharply with the dark green of conifers and intermittent steep meadows on the north side of the narrowing valley. Heavy snow still packed the north face of the steep mountainsides and many of the tree branches on the lee side of the lodgepole, spruce and fir supported five or six freshly fallen inches disgorged by the thick clouds they had seen the afternoon before. North, on their right, was the river, swollen with melt and chunks of ice, but almost clear and a fraction of its size at the Narrows. They had ridden hard and the horses were sweating in the warm spring sun of mid-afternoon, which had softened the newer snow of the day before to a heavy wet layer over the pack of previous storms. Their horses moved slowly, stepping tentatively, their hooves breaking through the spring crust and sinking into the corn below. Black Feather's careful scrutiny found no tracks. *Must have filled with the wind before the sun set it up.*

The twists and turns of the evermore narrow canyon above them were more defined. Rising several miles to the northeast were the abrupt faces of Nokhu Crags rocks, grey-brown and proud against the spring sky. Black Feather let the stallion pick its way, concentrating instead on a continual close survey of the intermittent avalanche chutes and areas of little timber on the north face.

He shifted his gaze to a movement deep in the trees by the river, his hand instinctively beginning to draw his Smoothbore. A riderless horse limped into view, dragging his left rear leg, struggling. Black Feather felt his jaw muscles tighten. *Don't look good.*

Several hundred yards further, as the invisible trail began to steepen, he thought he saw a dark mass in the snow on the north side of the canyon above them. "Dot, follow me. Keep your eyes on me and do what I tell ya. Stay close."

As they neared the dark aberration in the field of white, his initial fear was confirmed. A body, half-buried, only the shoulder and head visible, jutted up from the edge of a jumbled mass of giant snow wedges and balls of frozen ice extending far up the hillside. He reined in the stallion, his eyes traveling high above them, just below the northern ridgeline where avalanche chutes emptied into a meadow above scattered trees, some newly snapped in two. He spurred the stallion. The horse whinnied in protest, hunching his back, bucking and floundering through the deepening snow one jump at a time, moving its front legs forward, then catching up with a push from its rear haunches. Behind him Dot's mustang also lurched through the heavy snow cover but she gave him his head, her small frame moving easily with him.

Reining in several hundred feet from the buried body, he turned to Dot. "Dismount here. You stay with the horses. If I yell, you don't think; you don't look. Leave the horses and just run as fast as you can for those trees." He pointed to a particularly thick stand of trees slightly off the trail, south and behind them fifty yards away. "Get on the river side of them and hunker down."

Dot nodded, her eyes very wide. "What's that?" She held up one small finger poking partially through the sock he had fashioned into a glove for her, pointing at the dark object up ahead of them.

Black Feather compressed his lips. "Not sure," he lied, "but stay here."

He drew the Smoothbore from the scabbard and began to move carefully through the snow a few steps at a time, stopping, scanning the hillside above them. From this angle, he could now see the great jagged crack in the snow surface high in the chute where the new snow, and part of the old melted and refrozen snows, had separated in a slab.

By the angle of the twisted back, it was clear the rest of the man's torso and legs were buried at a deep angle. *Johnson!* Black Feather knelt and reached out a hand to the man's coat. There was a low groan from the form.

Damn, the sonofabitch is alive. Turning his head back toward Dot, he opened his mouth to yell but then stopped, looking at the slope above them. Instead, he extended his arm, waving his hand rapidly, motioning her to come. She started leading the horses and Black Feather gestured firmly to her to leave them. *No horses.*

She made better time than he did, her much lighter frame not sinking into the tightly compressed tailings of the slide. Black Feather concentrated on carefully digging out the buried shoulder. He put his hand on Johnson's cheek. *Very cold.*

Johnson's eyes fluttered open and he turned his head slightly, grimacing in pain through blued lips. At first, there was no recognition in his eyes and then they widened slightly, dully. "Boss, boss," he said weakly, "avalanche."

Black Feather nodded, focusing on moving snow away from Johnson's back with both hands, which he had wrapped in bandannas. "Damn miracle you're alive, Johnson. Where are the rest?"

Johnson's words were slow and thick, punctuated by long pauses. "Yesterday afternoon. Told them to wait for that new snow to end and set up. Got talked into it," he coughed. For the first time, Black Feather noticed the caked, frothy, pink spittle coating the blue of his lips. *Ribs got crushed, must be one through a lung.*

"Take it easy, Johnson. I'll dig you out of here, get a fire going and get you warmed up. Give me a little help. I'm gonna lift on your shoulders so I can dig below you." Black Feather began to lift on Johnson's shoulders but his lieutenant screamed in pain. "Don't move me. My back's broke. Can't feel nothin' below my waist. Hurts something terrible above that."

Dot was now standing beside them, her hand over her mouth, eyes twice their normal size, blinking rapidly, teary trails zig-zagging on her cheeks. *Johnson had always been kind to her.*

Black Feather turned back to the critically injured man. "The rest of the men?"

Johnson barely wagged his head, scrunching his eyes in pain. "All gone. Single file. I was drag. Was a roar like one of them tornadoes on the flats. Happened in an eye-blink. They're all gone." He coughed again, little flecks of blood turning the snow pink around his face. "This was the downside edge. My horse saved me. Tried to swim out of it." He opened his eyes wide, suddenly remembering something. "Boss, seen my horse? Saved my life."

"It's okay Johnson. I know where your horse is. We'll take care of him. Just relax."

Breathing in shallow, rapid breaths, Johnson slowly lowered his head to the snow again, "Got any of that whiskey I lent you for the girl?"

Black Feather swallowed. "There's some left."

"Sure would..." he coughed and groaned, "...like to have me a sip."

Motioning with his head to Dot, Black Feather spoke softly, "Go back to the horses. Careful, like I told you. Remember where you go if I yell." She nodded vigorously, her eyes wide and filmed. "Look in that smaller saddlebag of mine, left rump of the stallion, right behind the big one. There's a bandanna wrapped around that whiskey bottle. Pull the whole thing out, then walk slowly back here keeping your steps in the tracks that you made. Leave the horses there."

Her head bobbed up and down, she took another long look at Johnson, then turned, hurrying back toward the horses.

"Johnson, gotta get you outta here or you're gonna die. Just plum unbelievable luck you're still alive."

Johnson tried to chuckle but his face cracked in pain, more blood oozing from his mouth. "Boss, bottom half of me is broke. Top half of me so froze I can't feel nothin' but the hurt in my back." Without moving his head, he rolled his eyeballs toward Black Feather. "You and I both know I'm done. I'd just like to have me a sip of whiskey and then ask you in return for all these years we rode together, to do what you got to do."

Black Feather relaxed his legs, sitting back from his knees to his heels. "I'll do that for you, Terry."

Johnson's eyes flickered open, "You ain't called me by my first name in years, boss. You gettin' sentimental?"

Black Feather half-smiled, watching Dot struggle back toward them through the snow. "Maybe I am and maybe I ain't, but I'll do what needs be done."

"Thanks, boss." Johnson's shoulder seemed to relax under the wool fabric of his coat. Opening his eyes again, he slowly licked his lips, "Remember when you and I knocked off that wagon down there in the Yampa River country the other side of the Buffaloes some years back?"

Black Feather nodded. "I ain't thought about that for years 'til the other day down by the Narrows. Almost forgot."

"All last night, I was freezing. I was certain I was never gonna make it to morning." He coughed and lowered his face to the snow, closing his eyes tightly. "Figure we done the right thing burying all that gold jewelry, dishes and the like we took from them pilgrims and never tellin' the rest of the boys 'bout it?"

"Yes, Johnson. That job was just you and me. The boys were fifty miles away. We was going the opposite direction. If you remember, there were some people after us."

"What'd you figure that stuff was worth back then?"

"Mebbe five hundred to one thousand dollars. Might be more now."

Johnson hacked up blood, then wheezed with pain. "The girl back?"

Black Feather raised his head. "Not yet, a minute or two."

"Let me talk quick then. You give my half to that girl. You make damn sure she goes to school. I know you got a soft spot for her." His eyeballs swiveled up to catch Black Feather's stare. "I'm going to do the right thing going out and your past is buried up here. Use it to get her going."

Black Feather realized he had unconsciously raised one sleeve of his tunic and wiped an eye.

"I sure as hell will do what you asked, Terry. Mebbe I'll throw in my half too."

"Good, boss. Good."

Dot reached them. "Give me the bottle," Black Feather said quietly, reaching out and taking the whiskey from her small, violently shaking hand.

"I'll hold the bottle for you, Terry. You gonna have to turn your head just a bit or this rotgut will be in the snow."

His eyes squinting tightly, Johnson slowly turned his head toward the sky, his bloody lips open. Black Feather held the glass bottle close, tipping it carefully until a small trickle of amber liquid driveled into Johnson's mouth. The doomed man's lips closed, some of the whiskey spattering off his nose.

He swished the whiskey around in his mouth, then swallowed. "Damn, that's good. Give me another, boss." Johnson had three more sips, then coughed blood. *Thicker this time.*

"Send the girl back to the horses, boss," he said weakly. "She don't need to see this."

Black Feather stood slowly, lifting the bottle to his lips. Tipping his head back, he drank the remainder of the whiskey in one gulp, then hurled the bottle into the snow above them. "Damn."

Extending one hand, he gently touched Dot's cheek, looking down at her, trying to smile. "Good job. Go on back and stay with the horses. Johnson needs some privacy." His eyes shifted back to Johnson and then returned to hers. Nodding, she wiped her eyes and began the walk back to the waiting stallion and mustang.

Pivoting to make sure his body blocked her line of sight if she turned, Black Feather knelt and began to draw his pistol, then hesitated, looking up at the snow field above them.

Johnson's eyes fluttered open. "Boss, you fool. Put that pistol way. She'll know what's going on sure as hell. Use your knife."

Plus mebbe trigger another slide. Black Feather straightened up slightly from his hunched over position, shoving the half-drawn pistol back into his belt, then drew his knife, casting furtive glances behind him.

Johnson rolled his eyes sideways toward him and blinked. "Take my Colt. I don't think it's buried too deep. No sense leavin' a good gun up on this mountain." He coughed, groaned and then relaxed his head on the red-hued snow. "Just make sure it's once to the heart," he rasped, "Been good riding with you, Samuel."

Black Feather almost dropped the knife in startled surprise. Johnson's bloody lips cracked in a pained half-smile. "Never did tell you, sometimes you mutter in your sleep." He closed his eyes. "I'm ready."

Black Feather positioned the point of the blade over Johnson's heart, its tip gently steadied in the wool over his chest. He raised one hand slowly, then slammed it down on the hilt of the knife driving the blade in fully. An involuntary spasm wracked Johnson's body, he gasped, his lips quivering a glistening pink in the sunlight and then he was still.

Black Feather withdrew the knife, wiping it carefully on Johnson's jacket until the steel was clean, then plunged his arm bicep deep into the snow covering Johnson's torso where he supposed his belt might be, groping for the dead man's pistol.

When he returned to the horses, Dot was standing quietly, one hand on the mustang's shoulder, her eyes wide and teary. "Johnson?"

Black Feather looked at her for a long moment, and shook his head. "He was too bad hurt, Dot. He's dead. He ain't on this earth no more, but he was thankful you brought them sips of whiskey."

Dot's lips trembled. Black Feather stepped to her, putting his hands on either side of her shoulders. "Look up at me. All things die one day. It'll be my turn someday, and sometime long, long from now, yours. It is the way of things. I need to take care of his horse. No need letting it suffer or starve. Then, let's saddle up and work our way up real careful like. We'll stick close to these trees. Anything happens, a loud sound, or if I yell, you don't think twice. You just head down to the thickest trees and behind them as far as you can get and you'll be fine."

Dot looked fearfully above him toward where the avalanche had begun. Black Feather squeezed her shoulders. "I think we will be okay and this snow is set up enough, but no way of knowin' this time of year. You got ground that's warming, snow's frozen and refroze into little ice balls and then new snow on top of that..." His voice trailed off.

She looked up at him, her expression stricken. "Where?"

For a moment, he didn't understand and then he smiled. "Can't believe I'm saying this. We're gonna head down into that North Park country they was headed toward and then over another range, which is called the Buffaloes. Has two twin rocks towards the top—looks like the ears on a rabbit. On the other side, there's some hot springs that make funny sounds. The Indians say it's Spirit talking from the earth. White men swear they are like the chug of a steamboat. Maybe we'll stop there for a day, then head down to a place we call the Yampa." Black Feather looked to the west. "I got a promise to keep."

June 21, 1855

RIFT

"Simply amazing how men can make such a mess," Sarah chirped, sweeping dirt and mud from the rear of the wagon out over the open tailgate with the small hand broom Rebecca had insisted be kept in the wagon. Rebecca, busy cleaning toward the front of the wagon, did not respond. *She has barely said a word all morning.*

Sarah lifted her face to the intense sunlight streaming in the partially unlashed rear canvas. The wagon was a speck adrift in an unending sea of dazzling white, the small meadow that had been the overnight home to the wagons ringed with a mix of spruce, fir and aspen. Towering peaks surrounded the scene. To the west and north several exceptionally sharp-peaked mountains rose above the top of the pass, their highest points tapering upward in long jagged edges. Light green streaks of aspen flowed unevenly up the mountains' lower elevations into the darker green of the higher coniferous cover.

A steady drip of melt sparkled from branches, leaves and spruce needles in the sunlight. Intermittent cascades of snow clumps rained down as the limbs supporting them bent just enough to release their leafy bond. Tumbling to the branches below, gathering in size and falling ever more rapidly, uneven mounds of fallen snow soon covered the base of the trees. Cocking her head, Sarah listened carefully, deciding after several minutes that the only sound attributable to the aftermath of the storm were the subtle sighs and pleasant soft hiss of yielding snow.

Turning her head back over her shoulder, she tried to focus on Rebecca but her vision, adjusted to the blaze of light outside the wagon, saw only dark forms. She squeezed her eyes together, colored shapes flaring and exploding on the back of her lids. *Remarkable. The brightness is blinding. I shall have to ask Zeb what one does to protect the eyes.* Slowly, the image of the interior of the wagon began to lighten.

Rebecca, busy straightening the bedroll they had shared the previous night, had already stacked the plates to be carried out and washed. The tin baking tray holding the remnants of the pan bread and tortillas was covered with wax paper, ready to be put away. The remaining pemmican had already been stowed.

Sweeping the last of the snow from the tailgate, Sarah then backed into the wagon and stood. "Zeb was certainly right about this weather. The sun is incredibly warm. If there wasn't snow on the ground as evidence, one would never even know there'd been a storm." Sarah waited, but Rebecca neither turned nor responded. *Odd.*

Straightening suddenly, Rebecca put one hand just below the waist of her black wool traveling skirt, swayed and then sat down heavily on the bedroll staring straight ahead, her jaw tight. Taking two quick steps to her, Sarah sat, putting her arm around the brunette's shoulders. "Are you all right, Rebecca? Feeling sick again?" Rebecca's face was pale and drawn, her lower lip trembling. She took several very deep, rhythmic breaths slightly restoring color to her cheeks.

She turned her head to Sarah, "I'm all right, Sarah, but are you?"

Sarah drew back in surprise at the intensity in her friend's narrowed eyes and frigid tone.

What is she talking about? "I'm fine, Rebecca."

"Are you?" snapped the brunette.

Sarah blinked. "Whatever are you talking about? Are you angry about something? You and Reuben seemed to get along fine last night. Perhaps a little distant but—"

"No, Sarah; it is you I am talking about. Your behavior has been surprising..." Rebecca paused, her eyes still boring into Sarah's. "In fact, reprehensible and shocking."

Dropping her arm from Rebecca's shoulder, Sarah slid herself down the bedroll, creating a separation between them. "What? What are you possibly talking about?"

"Your overt flirtations with Philippe." The muscles in Rebecca's cheeks twitched and her jaw set in a grim line. "You're hurting Zeb, terribly—a kind soul who has protected you for months, fought for you, lent you weapons, saved us from disgrace and who-knows-what when you killed Jacob after that beast almost raped me." The corners of Rebecca's mouth quivered and a tear rolled out of one eye and down her cheek.

"Rebecca, I don't know what you're talking about. I would never hurt Zeb." Sarah reached out a tentative hand toward Rebecca but the brunette yanked her arm away. Sarah sighed, "We are both just emotional now, being pregnant and all."

Rebecca lunged to her feet, turning and glaring directly down at Sarah. Eyes blazing, she stamped her foot. "Are you that blind to your own actions? I'm surprised at you Mistress Bonney." Her voice rose. "Ever since Fort Massachusetts, you have ogled and flirted with Philippe, even in front of Zeb." One corner of her mouth drooped indignantly. "Paying attention to him while ignoring the man who offered to take care of you and your child, despite knowing your history and your condition."

Sarah was shocked. She opened her mouth several times to retort, but no words came out.

The lack of response infuriated Rebecca further. "Answer me!"

"I...I don't think you're correct, Rebecca. If anything like that happened it certainly hasn't been conscious on my part." Sarah could feel the hot scald of tears below her eyes, their trails cooling as they descended her cheeks.

"Really," snorted Rebecca, her voice rising to a fierce shout. Her shoulders were shaking, and the twitch in her cheek grew more pronounced. She stamped her foot again. "Really? You served Philippe supper last night, but ignored Zeb. Really? Utterly outrageous!"

Sarah put her hands out. "Rebecca, sit down. It's not good for you to get so worked up."

"This is not about me, you trollop. You have become confused about what is important." A strange expression passed across her features and her jaw relaxed suddenly, her eyes widening in some focus of sudden realization.

Sarah felt a cold shudder run through her body and the heat rising in her cheeks at the slur. Standing abruptly, she leaned forward with her chin, on tiptoes, waving her arms. "How dare you call me that? My condition is not my fault. I was raped. What about you? You were willingly with a man before you were married..." she waved her hand at Rebecca's belly, "and now see what position you are in."

Rebecca's attention returned to Sarah, the brunette's face turning scarlet and then immediately pale. She sank down to the bedroll holding her stomach.

June 21, 1855

UNDER A HIGH COUNTRY SUN

"THIS GLARE IS BLINDING," GRUMBLED REUBEN, PULLING the brim of his hat even lower over his eyes.

Zeb chuckled, one long leg folded up over Buck's neck just in front of the saddle horn, his rough fingers rolling a smoke. "If I remember correct, you boys thought it was funny when I smeared charcoal across my cheek bones this morning."

Reuben laughed. "So we did, Zeb."

Focusing on the cigarette paper, the mountain man did not look up. "Cuts that glare off your cheeks a mite. You wouldn't think so, but it does." He raised his eyes briefly to Reuben's cowboy hat. "Days like these I wish I had one of them broad brimmed hats rather than this fur cap." He tipped his head slightly to the left. "See where that snow is about melted off on the southwest rises, yonder? Just look up there in the brown and green. Get them eyes off the white for a spell and rest 'em."

"In Villmar, we have bitter cold, and snow, but nothing like this glare and the snow never melts as quickly." Eager to resume their journey, Reuben added, "Maybe we can start moving this afternoon."

Zeb's thumbs and forefingers stopped their rolling motion as he searched Reuben's face for a brief moment before returning his eyes to the smoke. "Moving this afternoon? You know the answer to that, son. One of these horses goes down, someone gets hurt, or a wagon slides off into a draw? We'll lose way more than an afternoon."

Reuben swallowed his impatience. *Can't argue with that logic.* "Well, the cows look settled down. I am going back to the wagons and grab some lunch. Be back in an hour or so. Then you can head in."

Zeb licked the cigarette and ran it under his nose, inhaling deeply. "And check on Rebecca."

"Yes, and check on Rebecca."

Holding the cigarette up to the sky, Zeb examined it critically. "No shame in it, Reuben. When a woman reaches out and grabs your heart, she's under your skin. Just the way it is."

Reuben nodded, unlooping his reins, which he had wrapped once around the saddle horn.

"And tell Sarah," Zeb added, "she ought to wear a bandanna over the bridge of her nose and around her face. That fair skin of hers will burn quick this high up with the snow."

Reuben started to reassure his friend he'd pass on the message, but Zeb was busy holding one lapel of his

fringed buckskin jacket out from his chest, reaching in
for his flint pouch with his other hand.

LAHN'S HOOVES WHISPERED THROUGH THE SUN-SOFT-
ened remnants of the storm. At the short, steeper incline
that separated the small plateau with the milling cows
from the clearing nestling the wagons, Reuben was startled when the big palomino slipped. The horse raised his
head and snorted, setting his front hooves and instinctively lowering his rear haunches, sliding thirty feet to
the bottom of the little rise without taking a step. At the
bottom, Lahn straightened up and shook. Reuben turned,
looking back over his shoulder at the long, heavy skid
mark. *Yep, Zeb was right.* With more caution, they worked
their way through scattered aspens toward the wagons.

He was surprised to see Sarah sitting in front of a
small but blazing fire, hunched over, her elbows on her
knees, her hands extended palm down toward the flames.

She didn't look up as he dismounted. "You're getting
mighty good at starting those fires, Sarah."

Her eyes rose to him briefly, then sank back down.
Are those tears? "Zeb told me to tell you to make sure
you wear a bandanna over your nose and cheeks." She
nodded without looking up. *Strange. Maybe she's not feeling well, but then she'd be in the wagon.* Reuben decided
to say nothing further, instead leading Lahn to the
wagon and tying him off on the customary rear wheel.
The tailgate was open and the rear flaps partially tied
back. A long ribbon of sunlight beamed its way deep into

the wagon interior. Rebecca lay on her back on the bedroll, her legs drawn, bent knees in the air.

"Rebecca, you okay?"

At the sound of his voice, her face shifted toward his. She sat up slowly, swinging her legs to the wagon floor. Reuben put his hands on the tailgate readying a vault into the wagon.

"No, Reuben. If you don't mind, we just got through cleaning up. I'd be happy to make some lunch and bring it to you." She raised a delicate hand to her eyebrows looking out beyond the rear of the wagon. "Such a beautiful day. I would love to get some sun. Would you take me for a walk?" Her voice was hopeful. *And something else.*

Reuben tried to mask his surprise. "Sure I would. Snow's mostly down to a couple of inches. If you don't mind sliding through some, we can get a little ways up on that southwest face. The snow is gone on those exposures, though it is sure to be wet. You can fix me up that meal when we get back."

Rebecca smiled and, using her arms, pushed herself off the bunk and cautiously rose. She swayed once from side-to-side, then straightened her shoulders, walking to the rear of the wagon. "Help me down, Reuben." She crouched on the edge of the tailgate, reaching out her arms. Reuben placed his hands on the perfect curves of her body above her hips, lifting her easily and gently down to the ground. She looked up at him and smiled weakly. "Thank you, Mr. Frank." Her eyes shifted toward Sarah briefly, a cloud passing across her features. "Let's walk in that direction," she said, pointing away from Sarah and the fire.

Reuben's eyes darted to Sarah, then back to Rebecca. Though only thirty feet away, Sarah had not acknowledged them. The redhead remained fixed on the flames, seemingly frozen in the same position he had seen her a few minutes before.

"Okay, Rebecca. One direction is as good as the next I suppose." He walked over to Lahn, slipped the Sharps from its scabbard and with Rebecca's right hand firmly clasped around his upper arm for balance, they began to walk slowly uphill, stopping occasionally for Rebecca to catch her breath.

"Johannes says there is way less air at this altitude. We're all feeling it a little bit. He told me of some campaign in the foothills of the Alps—some conflict or other. The Danish Army even gave out papers telling the troops the air was twice as thin in the mountains as at sea level. I think it's one of the reason the horses pulling the freight wagon are having some problems."

They had reached a small clearing mostly devoid of snow on the side hill. A twisted, grey and black aspen trunk canted at an angle low to the ground, its fall arrested by the fork of another tree. Rough pieces of its ancient bark hung by stubborn threads waving in the light breeze. A single strip of snow clung to the shadowed ground beneath the leaning trunk. Splotches of the canvas tops of the wagons were visible through fir branches and white trunks of still standing, younger aspens. They could hear the muted bawls of cattle and the occasional faint drone of voices, though their owners were indistinguishable.

"Let's sit here, Reuben. Such a lovely spot. What are those mountains straight out there, the jagged ones, and the ones there to the right?"

"To the north," corrected Reuben.

Rebecca smiled at him. "North. What are they?"

"They are all part of the great San Juan Range," he chuckled. "Those to the right—"

Rebecca laughed. "Point made, Mr. Frank. To the north."

Reuben grinned into her eyes. *So pretty.* "I checked the map yesterday before the snow moved in. To the north that would be Red Cloud Peak, Slumgullion Peak, and the highest one out there, the one that kind of hooks at the top," he grinned widely, "is Uncompahgre Peak. Sculptures of God. The scout notated many of these were almost three miles high. Now those there tallest to the west?" He raised his arm, pointing. "Farther out is Lizard Head, and that one closer in and slightly north— I can't pronounce the Ute name. The closest is Pole Creek Mountain. And from what Zeb tells me," he closed one calloused hand around hers and squeezed, "those mountains in-between Lizard Head and Pole Creek that have a sort of triple top, with red showing through where the snow has been blown off or melted? Those, Mistress Marx, are the Las Montanas de Rojas, the Red Mountains. They are where the maps end."

Rebecca's eyes widened, her mouth opening in a gasp. "Really?" She squeezed his hand back, hard. "That's the place mapped out by your father's scout and my dear father?" There was wonder in her voice and she bounced their hands up and down excitedly in her lap. "How much farther? How many days until we are there?"

"I asked Zeb the same thing this morning. That's when he pointed out the Red Mountains." He smiled at her. "I was just as excited as you are. In fact, I still am but, there's a lot of country between here and there, most of it twisty and up and down. We have the Gap tomorrow, then Lost Trail, if it's open, the west short cut to Red Mountain Pass. Zeb thinks that's the shortest way, but he supposed it would be at least four or five days assuming it is dry and we have no mishaps. And, if we have to go all the way around to the Gunnison, we have several weeks ahead of us."

"Oh, my," she breathed, leaning her head against his shoulder. "We've come so far, Reuben."

"We have indeed, Rebecca." He closed his eyes allowing the sun to warm his eyelids and his soul to absorb the energy of the moment and the vista. "It is more than just raw, unending, rugged beauty, though." He wrapped his arm around her as she raised wide, misted eyes to him. "It is freedom. A place to build whatever life one chooses." Tucking her face to his shoulder, Rebecca moved her head in agreement.

Reuben lowered his cheek to her hair. *I do love the way she smells.* She raised her fingertips to her face with a swiping motion. *She's thinking about Inga.* Reuben took the rifle from his lap, setting its butt plate to the ground and snugging the barrel into a large raised knot next to him. Hugging her, he whispered, "Yes, Rebecca. Inga would have been excited, too. Perhaps we will build some kind of stone markers for her and Mac down on the ranch. Kind of a tribute."

One of Rebecca's hands knotted up in the open front of his jacket. She sniffled, then raised a teary face to his. He leaned his head down and kissed her, her other hand curling in the open collar of his jacket as her tongue traced his mouth. "I like the name Frank," she said in a whisper, nestling her head in his chest.

Reuben's gaze flicked down toward her hair, thankful she couldn't see the surprise in his face.

"Rebecca Frank. Rebecca Elizabeth Frank." she said in a soft voice. "I think that's a fine name."

A surge of adrenaline carried on the wings of butterflies coursed through his body. He pulled away slightly, lifting her face with fingers gently placed under her chin. "You mean..."

She moistened her lips and swallowed. There was a blush to her cheeks and a sassy twinkle shone through the moisture in her eyes. "I believe, Mr. Frank, that you mentioned something in your first clumsy attempt to propose about being down on one knee under a warm high country sun and expansive views surrounding us."

Reuben's mind was a racing jumble, her meaning finally registering with him. He stood so quickly she almost lost her balance before he hurriedly reached out and saved her from toppling over backward, both of them laughing.

He fumbled with the leather glove on his right hand, then raising the side of his coat, dug in his pocket for the ring, Rebecca's smile tender with amusement. He no sooner extracted the simple band of metal than it slipped from his fingers, falling into the thin strip of snow hiding under the log. Flustered, he looked frantically down around his boots and Rebecca started to laugh.

She pointed, "Right there, Reuben, a few inches in front of your right toe. You see where it made a mark in the snow?" He knelt, one hand feeling blindly for the ring as he lifted his eyes to hers, embarrassed. *What a clumsy oaf.*

As if reading his mind, her eyes twinkled. "Yes, you are, dear Reuben. Isn't it a good thing you only have to do this once in your life?"

Reuben lost himself in the loving intensity of her stare and their eyes locked, unblinking for what seemed like forever. He smiled. "And, milady Marx, isn't it a good thing you shall only have to endure this spectacle once in your lifetime?" Rebecca giggled as his fingers found the ring. Wiping it on his jacket sleeve, he took her hand. "I love you, Rebecca Marx. I'd be honored if you'd be my wife."

Rebecca's cheeks reddened further and she looked deeply into his eyes with an unflinching gaze, as she added softly, "And the mother of your children."

Reuben suddenly felt hot, the sun intense on his shoulders. Sweat trickled from his armpits down the sides of his chest.

Rebecca's eyes had not left his. "I ask only one other promise in addition to all those this moment means for us..."

I'm not sure she has ever really looked at me this way, Reuben thought, lost in the magnetic emotion radiating from the brown of her eyes. "And that would be?"

"And that would be, Reuben, that though our hearts and bodies will be eternally promised and bound, that each of us swears to never attempt to subdue the spirit of the other."

What exactly does she mean? His leg muscles tensed, as if readying to stand. *Don't overthink this Reuben, you idiot.* He forced himself to relax. "I agree, Rebecca."

"Then, Reuben, my answer is a very happy yes!"

He splayed her fingers out in his hand, trying to control the tremble in his own and slipped on the ring. "And, I have one question for you."

Her eyes, filmy, happy and glittering in the sun, rose from the ring. "Yes?"

"Our children. I'd like to raise them, as best we can, out here in the middle of nowhere, in the Jewish tradition."

Rebecca smiled radiantly. "Funny you should mention that, Mr. Frank. I was going to suggest the same." Her lips curled into a teasing grin. "I believe this is the time that all the books say that you are supposed to kiss your betrothed."

Grinning, Reuben stood, lifting her from the log. "It seems we've been reading the same books," he murmured in her ear, and then he kissed her deeply, fully, the melt of their lips endless, the heat of their touch warmer than the sun. They clung tightly to one another as their lips parted, slowly, reluctantly. She looked up at him with a slight tremble in her chin and a smolder in her eyes. "Tell me, Reuben. Tell me about the house we shall be building."

We shall be building. Reuben savored her words, letting them echo in his mind. *First time I've ever heard it put that way.*

June 21, 1855

TAKING NO CHANCES

RISING UP IN HIS SADDLE, PHILIPPE SHIELDED HIS EYES against the glare with his hand under his hat brim. "It appears, *Señor* Johannes, that *Señor* Reuben is going back to the wagons." The vaquero glanced up at the sun. Smiling, he turned to Johannes. "I believe it is time for midday kafee, *sí*?"

Johannes nodded, but could not force a smile. *Maybe if he knows more of the history of Sarah and Zeb it might calm things down a bit.*

Philippe swung out of his saddle with one smooth motion, his eyes darting around the ground. "The trick will be to find enough dried wood for a fire." He straightened and turned toward the muffled sound of hooves approaching, as did Johannes. It was Michael, riding down from above.

"Them's...them's...them's..."

"Take a deep breath, Michael. Say what you want." Johannes kept his voice as kind as possible.

The young man drew a deep breath, held it, then exhaled. "Them's... Them's two cows missing. Seems like... they... they went back up from... from where we come the... the... the day before." He sighed, a look of relief flashing across his face at getting his thought out.

Philippe looked at him hard for moment, then raised his eyes to Johannes. "It is unusual for cattle to go uphill into heavier snow, especially away from the rest of the herd." His eyes narrowed. "Let's see if we can find them." Michael nodded energetically and began to turn his horse.

"No, *muchacho*. You stay here. Make sure none of these other cows wander off. *Señor* Johannes and I will go up and find them."

Johannes watched Philippe step close to Diablo, getting ready to mount. *He thinks it's more than just two cows wandering off.*

The vaquero sprang into the saddle and he and Johannes trotted back toward the summit of the pass, Philippe slightly ahead. When they were out of Michael's sight, the Mexican raised his arm out to the side, palm down. Johannes slowed Bente's gait, reining in abreast of the black horse. Philippe leaned down and back, sliding the Smoothbore from its belly scabbard with a practiced motion. He checked the load, then pointed to a partial track twenty feet away, half visible on the edge of a patch of retreating snow. Looking quickly around, Johannes drew his Sharps carbine. Dismounting, the two men led their horses over to the partial imprint, which in the blaze of sun became fainter even as they watched.

Philippe knelt, examining it closely. "*Indio.*" Johannes eyed the faint trail rising to the east, no more than a swath through the trees punctuated by the occasional ripple of a wagon wheel rut marring an otherwise smooth snow surface. The trail curved up an incline back toward the top of the pass still two miles distant. Johannes searched the terrain, thinking. Keeping his voice to a whisper, he pointed, "Let's work our way up to that rocky point. We ought to be able to see a ways up toward the trail and maybe down the backside of the rise. Might be enough snow left to see movement."

Philippe's eyes followed his outstretched arm. He nodded once, and without a word began a fast-paced climb toward the rock outcroppings two hundred feet away and fifty feet in elevation above them.

Johannes followed, casting his eyes left and right, every few steps turning around, peering intently behind them. Breathing heavily they reached the rocks, stopping for a minute to catch their breath. They clambered up between the reddish-brown boulders that poked from the snow, one or the other of them slipping with every second or third step, catching themselves with their free hand on the steep slope, the other hand clutching their rifles. At the top of the boulder-strewn rise was a huge, angular rock more red than brown. A vein of milky white rock ran diagonally from top to bottom across its entire length, glistening dully in the sunlight. *What is the name of that rock? Quartz?* A memory of something he read somewhere stirred in Johannes' mind but he couldn't place it. His attention was diverted by Philippe, five feet above him, hatless, peering carefully over the top of the large uppermost rock.

The Mexican held up two fingers behind him. In a barely audible whisper, he hissed, "*Dos Indios* and the cows." Philippe edged down on his belly from the lip of the ridge. Rolling partially to his back, he grinned at Johannes, still below him. "I think, *Señor* Johannes, they want *Señor* Reuben's cattle." He pulled one, then the other of the twin onyx-handled Navy Colts from his belt and spun the cylinders, checking the loads.

Climbing the last few steps to Philippe, Johannes' boots slipped out from underneath him several times, forcing him to catch himself on the rough edges of rocks. Together, they slowly raised their bare heads over the rock. The approximate line of the trail curved above and behind them to the east. On the opposite sides of the rocky point, to the north, was a small alpine valley, a narrow drainage through its center, water showing dark against snow where it had melted, collecting in what would be a small stream when the mountain thawed in the coming weeks. Fifty yards below them two Indians fully clothed in heavy, fringed leather shirts and leggings moved at a fast walk, each of them holding a stick that they snapped occasionally across the rumps of the two missing longhorns.

Johannes estimated the downhill end of the meadow to be no more than two hundred fifty yards away. Two light colored horses, dark spotted like leopards, stood in the shadows of the wall of dense green conifers that marked the end of the open space.

"Well, let's go get those cows back." Johannes rose to a half crouch and began to scoot around the edges of rocks. "Stay low so we don't skyline ourselves," he said, realizing immediately that the vaquero needed no such warning.

Philippe grabbed his arm, a strange light in his dark eyes. "*Señor* Johannes, allow Philippe the honor of retrieving *Señor* Reuben's cattle. Stay here, *mi amigo*. Cover me with the rifles." He leaned his Smoothbore against the rock.

Johannes opened his mouth to protest but Philippe was already on the move, creeping with stealth around the edge of the huge boulder and disappearing out of sight. "Shit," muttered Johannes to himself. He wiggled his lanky body slightly higher up on the rock and slowly, avoiding any rapid movement that might attract the Indians' attention, got the Sharps in position, drawing a bead on the taller of the two braves still moving steadily downhill. He couldn't see where Philippe was or what the vaquero was doing on the other side of the rock.

The smaller warrior in the rear glanced behind him, then again, stopped, and shouted, dropping his stick. His larger companion turned, looking back toward Johannes' position. The tall Dane spread his legs to stabilize his upper torso, snugging the smooth-grained stock of the Sharps against his cheek, raising his eyes once to make sure the path of the bullet would not hit the far edge of the rock slab. Looking quickly downward at Philippe's Smoothbore resting a few feet below him, he practiced mentally how he would lay down the Sharps, reach for and pick up the Smoothbore, aim and fire the second rifle. *Now where the hell is Philippe? Have they seen me or him?* His body jerked in surprise and his eyes widened as Philippe came into view, his back to him, walking slowly, but steadily directly at the two warriors. The braves glanced at one another nervously, obviously perplexed. The larger of the two appeared armed only with a lance. The smaller man had a bow, which he shifted off his shoulders, drawing an arrow from his quiver and notching it. Philippe kept advancing toward them until no more than sixty feet separated the three men. The smaller Indian screamed, simultaneously raising and bringing his bow to draw. Philippe's right hand flashed and a report echoed through the little valley, rumbling in echoes as it receded down the canyon behind the spotted horses prancing nervously at the sound of the shot. The Indian with the bow sank to his knees, releasing the arrow into the snow twenty feet ahead of him and toppling over face first.

Philippe stopped walking. The vaquero shoved the pistol back in his belt and stood, silent. With a wild scream, the larger brave ran at him, his arm high and locked, gripping the lance. Johannes drew back the hammer of the Sharps. *Jesus, Philippe. Move or shoot. You're going to be in my line of fire.* Twenty feet from Philippe the muscular brave slowed, planting his left foot, cocking his lance arm further preparing to hurl the spear. Again, Philippe's right hand moved in a blur, and there was another report. The lance flew from the warrior's hand, his head jerking, his body flying backward in an arch that lifted his feet from the snow. His body landed on his back and neck, his shoulders driving into the snow, skidding several feet before coming to a halt.

"I'll be damned," Johannes muttered, watching the vaquero walk from one Indian to the other, kicking each of them.

Johannes stood quickly, skirted the edge of the rock, then, one rifle in each hand, half slid, half slipped down the bank. Philippe walked briskly toward the two spotted horses, slowing his pace as he neared them. He raised his hand, then the other, one to each horse, gathering their lead ropes with a quick darting action. After some initial resistance, the ponies calmed, allowing the Mexican to lead them back toward Johannes and the two corpses. The confused longhorns trotted twenty feet this way and that, stopping, shaking their heads and bawling. Johannes looked closely at the dead Indians. *Young, perhaps mid-teens.* The brave with the bow had been shot directly through the heart, the other in the forehead just above his eyes.

The vaquero drew closer, a wide smile on his face. "*Señor* Johannes, I've always wanted one of these leopard ponies. One for you and one for me. I'll lead them out. Can you push those cows along? They will probably follow the horses." Johannes's eyes flickered quickly from the bodies, to Philippe's toothy grin, to the cows. *Cool customer.*

"You didn't have to kill them," a low voice came from the edge of the trees.

The spotted horses pulled on their lead ropes, prancing sideways. Johannes and Philippe both jumped, Philippe's free hand reaching for his pistol. It was Zeb, virtually invisible in a clump of three aspens at the edge of the tree line not more than fifty feet from them. Philippe exhaled visibly, relaxing his hand and lowering his pistol. Johannes stopped his one-handed swing of the Sharps.

"*Señor* Zeb, that's a good way to get shot, sneaking up on people."

Zeb stepped from the trees, his Enfield cradled comfortably in one arm. "I just moved natural like. If these two youngsters had been grown up braves, or with other warriors, you'd both be dead and scalped." Philippe's lips pressed together. The mountain man walked slowly to the two bodies studying their colorfully beaded leather clothing closely. "San Luis Valley Utes. The Mouache tribe teamed up with the Jicarilla Apaches and massacred fifteen men and women at El Pueblo over Christmas. Took two or three others captive. Them two bands of Indians been raiding and killing since the forties, maybe earlier. They've fought with the troops out of Fort Massachusetts several times—and the army is on their trail right now, from what I learned at the fort." His eyes rose east toward the pass, "their winter camp is usually down low on the South Fork, east side of Wolf Creek Pass, sometimes north, nearer to Conchopata. Probably seen us come up and been shadowing us for a couple of days. At least they weren't the Uncompahgre band."

"Band?" questioned Johannes.

Zeb nodded, one set of fingers stroking his mustache. Leaning over, he spat a wad of chew to the side. "Chief

Guera Murah's tribe, the Tabequache of the Uncompah-gre band of Utes. Their winter camp is on the other side of these mountains down on the Uncompahgre. They are the least warlike of all the Utes. He and his son, Ouray, who is sub-chief, can be good friends, but if these were theirs, there won't be much chance of that, and they can make life hell over there." His busy eyebrows fell over his eyes in a frown as he looked at Philippe. "You didn't have to kill them. They was just kids trying to count coup. We could've spooked them out of here."

Philippe half-raised his head, returning Zeb's stare from under the brim of his sombrero. He spun the cylinder of his Colt, replacing the spent cartridges and flashed a cold smile. "Or, *Señor* Zeb, they could have followed us, decided the women were better than the cows, and been even more trouble. Philippe Reyes takes no chances."

CHAPTER
35

One the Eve of June 22

*D*ISPUTED TRAIL

ZEB CHEWED CONTENTEDLY, SQUATTING BY THE FIRE, HIS
Sharps within easy reach. Across from him, Reuben and
Johannes sat on a log, hunched over eating, shoveling in
spoonfuls of pan bread smothered in gravy. Zeb swallowed, his eyes roving the ridge tops and the layers of
peaks beyond, their craggy, endless summits disappearing into a rose-hued twilight. Soft silver shimmers of a
half moon rose to the east, playing tug-of-war with the
dying light of the sun. Rebecca stood slightly to the side
of the fire, a pleased expression on her face as she
watched the men eat.

"You outdid yourself on this gravy, Rebecca," Zeb said.

"Thank you Zeb. The ingredients, of course, are an
old family secret." She laughed.

Looking up from his plate, just a semblance of his
usual smile evident on his lips, Johannes concurred with
Zeb, teasing, "Rebecca, I can just imagine you in that

stately townhouse in London busy preparing pan bread and gravy breakfast every morning."

Reuben, in the middle of swallowing, choked and coughed, spitting some of the pan bread into the fire.

"You are clumsy today aren't you, Mr. Frank?" Rebecca's smile teased back, but her eyes were unmistakably tender in the glow of the firelight.

Zeb studied Rebecca's face. Her eyes had not left Reuben. *She's mighty happy for some reason tonight.* His gaze shifted to Johannes. *Johannes is still thinking about them two young warriors.* Zeb took another bite, turning his attention back to Rebecca, curious.

Sensing his stare, Rebecca cocked her head at the coffee pot, and smiled, "More coffee, Zeb?"

"Thank you, ma'am; I would."

She stooped over, reaching her left hand for the kettle, which rocked and simmered on the side of the fire. In the firelight, Zeb caught the glint of gold on her finger. He stopped chewing, glancing quickly at Reuben who was still half-coughing, then smiled into his plate. *He finally asked and she finally said yes. About damn time.* He cast a quick glance over his shoulders at the wagon and its dimly glowing canvas top. *Strange, Sarah has not come out.*

Keeping his tone matter-of-fact, he pretended to focus on cutting another wedge-sized piece of pan bread, spinning the chunk around the gravy with his fork. "I don't know, Reuben. Seems a pretty gal out here where there ain't none, who can shoot as well as a man, and makes the best pan bread and gravy in the San Juans, just might be a catch." Rebecca, in the midst of carefully pouring coffee into the tin cup by his foot jerked, spilling some of the steaming brew on the ground.

Reuben's eyes clicked up from his plate. "Well, just so happens I agree with you, Zeb." The young Prussian smiled widely at Rebecca. "We were going to wait 'til tomorrow night after we get through Little Medicine, but this is as good a time as any." Johannes stopped chewing and straightened up, his mouth still full, his eyes darting between Rebecca and Reuben. Smiling warmly at Rebecca, Reuben stood up and held out his hand. Taking several steps, the brunette reached out to him and twined her fingers in his. "This Prussian farm boy got lucky yesterday," Reuben said with tender pride, "The finest woman this side of England said she'd marry me."

The couple looked at each other, broad smiles on their faces. An ache flashed through Zeb's heart. *Wish Sarah was here to see.* Johannes jumped up to his feet, spilling his supper. "Well, I'll be go to hell." He grabbed Reuben's hand, shaking it energetically. "Congratulations, farm boy. It looks like good sense can seep into any brain."

Johannes turned to Rebecca, stretching out his arms, "And to you, milady Marx, I offer my condolences." Everyone laughed. "Give me a hug while you're still single." She and Johannes embraced warmly.

Zeb stood, reaching a long arm across the fire to shake Reuben's hand. "Congratulations, Reuben." He slipped off his coonskin cap, smoothing back his hair with one hard hand and faced Rebecca. "I'm happy for you, Miss Rebecca. I was beginning to think the two of you might be old and grey like me before you got this thing settled." Laughter again echoed around the little clearing. Zeb hitched his head toward the wagon, "What did Sarah say?"

He was surprised at the sudden change in Rebecca's face. "I haven't told her yet, Zeb."

More here than meets the eye. "She gonna join us for supper?"

Rebecca returned his gaze with a steady eye. "I doubt it. I don't think she's feeling one hundred percent."

So, when's the party?" asked Johannes enthusiastically.

Reuben's brow wrinkled, "Party?"

The tall Dane shook his head in mock incredulity. "The wedding, Reuben, the wedding. Even Prussians have weddings, don't they?"

"Oooohh." Reuben and Rebecca exchanged quick glances. "We never talked about it." Johannes caught Zeb's eye. They both tried to stifle their laughter, but it was to no avail. Holding his stomach, Zeb collapsed back on the ground and Johannes sank to one knee.

"What's, what's, so funny?" stammered Reuben.

"Reuben," Johannes gasped, trying to catch his breath, "the wedding is the most important part."

Rebecca began laughing, too. "I think, Johannes, we were both so shocked that he asked and that I said yes, that we never even gave a thought to the next step."

"Zeb, I know there are no rabbis, but are there any preachers within one hundred miles of where we're headed?"

Shaking his head, his laughter finally under control, Zeb chortled. "None I know of, Reuben." Reuben and Rebecca exchanged questioning looks.

"But," said Zeb grinning and raising one hand and forefinger in the air, "Chief Guera Murah's medicine man is an old hand at weddings. Course, they are Indian style...." He began laughing again. "...I'd venture you'll be the very first white eyes he's ever married off."

"An Indian medicine man?" asked Rebecca slowly.

Zeb looked at her. *She ain't protesting. Just can't quite believe what she just heard.* "Yep, they know how to throw a shindig, too. The chief's wife died some time ago, Rebecca, but if you get along well with Ouray's wife, I bet she could find a fine doeskin wedding dress for you somewhere in the village."

Rebecca raised a hand to her mouth. "Oh, right, a wedding dress. I had not thought of that, either." Zeb looked at Johannes and they again broke into laughter.

Johannes' eyes focused toward the wagon. Zeb turned. Sarah stood ten feet away, watching them, forcing a small smile to curl her lips.

"I heard everyone laughing and came out to see what was happening." She looked at each of them in turn. Reuben turned his head expectantly toward Rebecca but she was silent. The Prussian cleared his throat. "Sarah, me and Rebecca got engaged yesterday and that seems to be a source of much amusement for these wild men."

Sarah's head jerked slightly, her eyebrows rising. "Well, I see. Congratulations Reuben." Her tone changed subtlety. "I am happy for you, Rebecca." Rebecca nodded curtly.

The redhead pressed her lips together. "I'm not feeling completely well this evening." Zeb opened his mouth to speak, but she caught his eye. "No Zeb, I'm fine. Just tired. I would love to talk with you though, when you have a moment in the next day or two." The look she threw him was hopeful, almost pleading.

Zeb twirled the coonskin cap in his hands. "Sure, Sarah. Anytime."

Sarah turned to Rebecca and Reuben. "Congratulations again. I'm really very glad for you."

Lifting the woven riding dress, one hand on either side of the hem, she began walking back to the wagon. Zeb watched her for a moment before turning back to the group around the fire. Rebecca was staring after the redhead, her lips pursed. Reuben turned to Johannes, their conversation happy and animated.

Eventful day, Zeb pondered, slipping on his coonskin cap. "Johannes," he said, "what say you and I ride out and spell the boy and that Mexican?" Reuben began to reach for his rifle but Zeb held out his hand. "No, Reuben, I ain't got much experience about all this but I know you just got betrothed. Why don't you spend some alone time here at the fire with your bride-to-be? You can join us later. Besides, I'm sure you want to tell Michael and Philippe yourselves. We won't say nothing. It'll be a surprise."

"Thanks Zeb," said Reuben, smiling down at Rebecca. He looked back up, "When are we going in the morning? Early I suppose."

Zeb pulled the cap snug around his greying hair and over the tops of his ears. "Nope. I figure maybe midmorning. This snowmelt is gonna set up overnight—be like ice early in the morning 'til the sun works on it a bit. Midmorning will give me time to make sure that freight load is cinched up tight, too. The steepest part of this trip is still ahead of us. Down through the Gap to Little Medicine tomorrow, then up that Lost Trail cutoff, a shortcut I've used and then up to the last part over Red Mountain Pass and the Divide. And if that shorter route is snowed in or blocked..." he paused, thinking, one hand stroking his mustache, "...then we'll have some tough choices to make. Probably have to head north up the Old Spanish Trail, then follow the Gunnison River to the Uncompahgre River and come in towards Red Mountain from downstream. We ain't there yet."

June 22, 1855

JOHANNES RODE WITH THE SHARPS ACROSS HIS LAP, lost in the brilliant grandeur surrounding him, enjoying the warmth of early summer sun. He could see the trail and canyon leading to Little Medicine stretched below them a number of miles away, the layers of mountains stretching endlessly in all directions, each range painted with its own brush, dipped in a different color from nature's palate.

Ahead of him straggled the last cows in the long, narrow line of cattle. Bente's ears flicked at the faint ding, ding, ding of the lead cow's bell, far to the front. Hips and shoulders swinging ponderously, the cattle picked their way downhill, occasionally sliding on the remnants of snow or plentiful mud. The column of cattle, five or six animals wide, was hemmed in on one side of the narrow trail by heavy timber on the uphill slope and a steep drop off on the other. Michael and Philippe were spaced out one hundred fifty yards between them on the more thinly treed downhill slope, sliding and occasionally falling as they led, rather than rode, their horses on the slick side hill. The sky capping the never-ending spires of mountains shown bluer than Johannes had ever seen. *Grander than the Alps.*

Leaning forward, he patted Bente's neck as the sleek mare picked her way down the trail, gingerly avoiding mud and noticeably shying from anything that had the appearance of ice, setting her hooves down slowly, testing their footing. *Smart horse,* Johannes thought appreciatively. *She's been in the mountains before.*

The trail temporarily lost some of its incline as it wound around the outside edge of a small bench, which flattened and fanned out several hundred yards from the toe of large, almost vertical brown-red rock faces interspersed with narrow chasms of steep, very densely forested bands of conifers. The bench fell off steeply again from the southwest edge of the trail. The timber between the herd and the rock slabs was dense but not completely impenetrable, a mixture of competing aspen, lodgepole and spruce. Snow had lingered in the shade of this large stand of trees, aided by a slightly northern exposure. One of the last cows in line stopped walking, twisting her horned head back at Johannes, challenge in her big brown eyes. A crescent-shaped grey area extended from her chin to her shoulder.

You again, Johannes shook his head. "You remember that pistol I showed you the other night?" he called aloud to the cow, "Don't you forget." The bovine lowered her head, craning her neck in a long *mooooo*, and then suddenly bolted from the tail end of the herd into the timber.

"Damn, I really am going to shoot you." He raised up in the saddle, one hand to his mouth and whistled. The nearest rider was Philippe. "Stray!" Johannes shouted, "Off into the uphill trees. I'll get her." Philippe took off his hat and waved it, indicating he had heard, and Johannes redirected Bente's attention to the timber. The vaquero had already broken from his place below the line of cows and was leading his horse back toward the rear to replace Johannes at drag.

Bente picked her way down to the spot where the troublemaker had disappeared. Even at a quick trot, the cow's tracks were clearly visible—a slight, narrow trail that wound through the trees. "Okay, Bente," Johannes said, annoyed. "Go get her." Bente shook her head, hesitating. "Come on, girl; we can fit through there."

With tentative steps, the grey, tall bay mare squeezed through the trees, the trail so narrow that her rump brushed trunks and several times the barrel of Johannes' Sharps did likewise, making a dull thud as the metal glanced off a tree. Johannes looked upward at the overhanging branches, too low to rest the rifle on his leg, muzzle in the air. He reined in the mare, slipping the long gun back into its scabbard. *No need of it in here anyway.*

Fifty yards into the woods, Bente slowed, occasionally shaking her head up and down, jingling the hackamore. "Come on, girl." Johannes clicked at her, "These are just trees." *That cow can't be far. She sure as hell is not going to go up those cliffs.* "Bente, what's the problem?" Johannes dug his heels lightly into the mare's flanks but the horse refused to move faster. He dug them again, harder. "Bente, we don't have all day." Bente's ears were stiff and alert, her nostrils flaring, her eyes fixed on what appeared to be an open area barely visible ahead through the trees. *Must be a little meadow.*

The bare whisper of the breeze suddenly reverberated with a terrified bawling, which ebbed, then rose in intensity until it ended abruptly. Bente quivered, trying to turn in the thick trees. "Dammit, Bente." Johannes kicked his heels into her sides forcefully, then again. She took two unsteady jumps forward breaking into a small clearing that backed to a steep rock face just forty feet away.

It all happened at once, without warning. The frantic cow lay on her side, futilely kicking her legs, her body writhing, red spreading through the snow where her neck and head were pinned by a massive, cinnamon-brown shape. Johannes' hand instinctively closed on the pistol in his belt. Bente tossed her head, her eyes rolling back, wide and white. She rose almost vertical on her rear legs, front hooves slicing the air above her head. *Bear! Grizzly bear!* The horse's wild rearing took him by surprise, one hand already committed to drawing the pistol. Johannes grabbed desperately for the saddle horn, dropping the reins but too late. He was already far back over the mare's haunches, his outstretched fingers a foot short of the saddle horn and losing ground. He slid off the back of the horse, hitting his shoulder and head on a tree, then another, landing partially on his side in the snow, his chest wedged between three aspen trunks, the force of the blow knocking the pistol out of his hand and into the snow.

The bear looked up from the still weakly kicking cow, small beady eyes fixed on him. Bente reared again, her hooves flashing close to Johannes. He twisted his hips and legs to the side. Wild eyed, she bucked twice, turning in midair and landing in a panicked gallop, kicking snow and earth high into the air. With stirrups flapping and reins trailing in the snow, she sped back down the disputed trail. Johannes, still on his side, his shoulders and torso hemmed in by the trees, desperately groped for the pistol under the snow.

Rising to full height, the bear snarled, shaking its head, droplets of red-tinted saliva flying from its jowls. The sun shown off its hair, the massive form glowing reddish-brown. The animal twisted its head, opening its mouth in a furious, rending roar, its steely eyes fixed on Johannes. Flattening back its ears, it gnashed and clicked its great bared teeth, drooling, then lunged forward on all fours, its muscled mass bounding toward him.

Desperate, Johannes found the Colt, his fingers wrapping around the grip. The bear was almost on him just feet now separating them. He heard the bear breathing, and smelled the foul stench of its breath. Wrenching himself partly onto his back, he swung the pistol upward over his head, then down between the trees, leveling his out-stretched arm. He fired as the raging grizzly lunged at him, its mammoth front quarters frustrated by the rigid tree trunks in which he was pinned. Another fearsome roar erupted. Bloodstained teeth gnashed the air mere feet from his face. Then a flash of claws, curved silver with white tips longer than a man's fingers, shredded the sleeve of his coat, knocking the pistol from his hand.

The grizzly eased back a step, bending its massive neck, teeth bared, gnashing at the inside of its front shoulder. *Must be where the bullet hit.* Working his hand underneath the snow and trying not to distract the bear, Johannes felt for the hilt of his knife on his belt. Before he could draw the blade from its sheath, the bear was on him again. Rolling partially to his stomach, trees bruising either side of his chest, he wrapped his hands over his head. Powerful jaws clamped on his calf halfway between his knee and his foot. Groaning in shock and pain, he willed himself not to move, a primitive instinct warning him that his limb would be torn to shreds if he attempted to yank it from the bear's teeth. Suddenly, from close by, the roar of a rifle cracked the air, and then the rapid succession of shots from a six-gun.

Johannes raised his head, trying to watch from the cor-ner of his eye. The bear screamed in rage, releasing his grip on Johannes' calf, rolled over on its back, then righted itself and stood erect, raking the air with outstretched claws at Zeb, twenty feet away. *Three feet taller than me!* Reuben stood several feet to Zeb's side. The mountain man was loading another cartridge into his Enfield. Reuben's eyes darted from the towering grizzly to the open cylinder of his Colt as he jammed in more shells.

The enraged bear thrashed its head side-to-side, screaming. Through the din came Zeb's voice, calm and sure, "Don't move, Johannes. Don't move a muscle."

The bear dropped to all fours as Reuben finished reloading, bunching its rear haunches to spring. Fire leapt from the muzzle of the Colt as Reuben crouched, palming the hammer. The Colt belched flame again, again and again, and one of the bear's eyes seemed to explode in a mist of blood and flesh.

Zeb steadied his musket for another shot. The roar of a long gun exploded almost over Johannes' head, the sound deafening. Twisting his eyes away from the bear, he saw the beaded, heavy-stitched moccasins of Philippe. The vaquero stood over him, his Smoothbore smoking.

The grizzly rose in the air, its unearthly screams rising from the depths of hell, one great paw clawing at its missing eye, blood foaming from its gaping jaws as it advanced toward Zeb on its hind legs.

Reuben was frantically reloading again. Zeb knelt in the shadow of the snarling beast, resting one elbow on his knee, the Enfield inclined at a steep angle upward just ten feet from the attacking bear. Smoke erupted as the muzzle disgorged its one-ounce lead bullet. A pulsing, fountain stream of red squirted from the bear's throat, the back of its neck exploding toward the sky in chunks of bone, flesh, and fur. His roar gurgled, one paw slicing the air as its cinnamon-brown body fell sideways and lay still except for the slight twitching of its rear paws.

June 22, 1855

$\mathscr{S}$TITCHES OF RAWHIDE

REBECCA HALF STOOPED, HALF CROUCHED NEXT TO ZEB who was seated on a keg, bent over Johannes' bloody leg. Johannes' lanky form lay stretched out on Sarah's bedroll, belly down, both of his hands outstretched, white knuckled, clutching the handle of one of Rebecca's trunks. His forehead was buried in a rolled up blanket, the ends of a stick wrapped in a handkerchief protruding from his mouth.

Lifting her eyes, Rebecca surveyed the somber faces crowded into the wagon. Sarah stood to one side, her face white. She cast an anxious look at Reuben but avoided returning Rebecca's stare. Reuben's worried gaze roved the full length of his friend's body, his eyes lingering on the mangled calf. "How are you doing, Viking?"

Johannes nodded his head slightly.

Zeb turned his head to Sarah, "Put those last two strips of that rawhide I cut thin into that boiling water out there on the fire, like the first ones. When they boil for about five minutes, bring the pot, water and rawhide in to me."

Rebecca turned her eyes from Sarah to watch Zeb. Beads of sweat rolled down his forehead from underneath his unkempt, grey-streaked hairline. She stared, fascinated with Zeb's careful treatment of Johannes' wound. Zeb had spent the last hour stitching Johannes' skin together with a sharp awl, fashioned from an elk bone, looping thin rawhide stitches back and forth, closing the damaged skin around the gaping puncture marks that circled Johannes' leg.

The mountain man straightened up, shifting his shoulders and wiped his brow with his forearm. "You can relax now, Johannes. Two more sets of stitches and we'll be done."

The tension in Johannes' body eased. Letting go of the handle with one hand, he took the stick out of his mouth and turned his head sideways with a weak grin. "My teeth hurt so much from biting down on that damn stick, I had forgotten about my leg." A feeble smile played across Sarah's lips. Reuben and Zeb chuckled guardedly.

"Rebecca, bring me that bandage pouch again, and pull out that medicine whiskey." Rebecca rose from her crouch next to Zeb, reaching across the back of Johannes' legs and handed Zeb the leather bag. Zeb shook his head, "I shoulda told you fellas more about them bears."

Johannes lifted his face from the blanket, rolling his eyes back at Zeb, "Yes, you should've. Though those scars on your face should have been warning enough. Damn, they are huge."

"And tough to kill," added Reuben grimly.

From the tailgate where he squatted, came Philippe's voice, "*Sí, Señors*, dangerous and angry, always. One bear I saw in the Sangre De Cristos—a mother bear with two cubs— killed five *indios* even with eleven, well-placed arrows sticking out of her. The last Indio she chewed buried his knife in the bear's neck, as many as three times, before that Smoothbore of mine broke her back. It still took four more shots. Angry she-bears, they are the worst."

"Let me see that arm while we're waitin' on Sarah." Johannes extended one arm behind him, stiffly holding up his wrist. Rebecca leaned closer as Zeb peered at the deeply scratched forearm closely, rolling it one way, then the other. "This swipe with his paw is what knocked the pistol out of yer hand?"

Johannes nodded into the blanket, "Yes. That was a bad moment."

Zeb's eyes flickered to the back of Johannes' head, his lips pursed tightly. "I just bet it was."

Johannes turned his head again, "I want to thank all of you for coming to help me."

"We was just lucky to see Bente bolt out of them woods. Knew something was up right off. That one shot you got off from the pistol give us a bead on where you were. Otherwise," Zeb paused, "it might've been a different ending."

Johannes' rejoinder was muffled by the blanket. "Might have been? You mean would have been. That damn grizzly must have been French." Everyone exchanged puzzled glances.

Rebecca's eyes roved from one man to the other. *If they won't question, I will.* "Why do you think the bear was French, Johannes?"

Johannes laughed into the bedroll. "I was waiting for somebody to ask. The two times in my life I've been wounded before were both in that calf. One time, a mini-ball from a French musket grazed it. Didn't do much damage but stung like hell for a week. The other, was a lucky cut from the saber of a French Cavalry officer. Fortunately, not too deep. The French like that calf. So, the bear had to be French." The tension eased and everyone laughed.

"Here's the water, Zeb." Rebecca turned to see Sarah standing outside at the tailgate below Philippe, steam curling from the pot. Philippe extended his hand. "Allow me to assist you up the ladder, *Señorita* Sarah."

The gesture irritated Rebecca, especially when she saw Zeb tighten his lips as Sarah stepped up into the wagon and held out the pot to him. "Careful Zeb," she warned. "It's very hot. Take it by the cloth I wrapped around the handle." Further annoyed by the comment, Rebecca almost snapped, *Don't you think Zeb knows that?*

Placing the pot on the wagon floor next to him, Zeb dipped the awl into the scalding water, swishing it around, then deftly scooped out one of the very thin strands of rawhide he had cut prior to beginning the procedure.

Holding his left hand out over Johannes' calf, he looked quickly at Rebecca. "Pour some of that whiskey over my fingers. It's okay if it drips on the calf." Holding the point of the awl in his whiskey-soaked fingers, he deftly threaded the eyelet with the rawhide. "Better put that stick back in your mouth, Johannes. One good thing is, them other Frenchie scars of yours is all gone. That bear's jaws took 'em out. The only ones you gonna have from here on is these bite marks. You're mighty lucky he didn't crush your leg."

Johannes paused, the stick halfway to his mouth, "Instinct told me that if I moved while my leg was in his mouth, he really would've torn it apart, but it wasn't easy to keep still."

"You was right," Zeb squinted as he placed the sharp point of the awl on the side of one puncture mark, an inch and a half across and more than that deep. "I saved these big ones from his front fangs for last."

Philippe stood, leaning under the canvas to get a closer look. Dropping to her knees from her crouch next to Zeb, ignoring Sarah, Rebecca leaned over Johannes' foot, fascinated as she watched Zeb's careful work. "So what happens when the wound heals, Zeb?"

The mountain man didn't respond, instead concentrating on pushing the awl through the skin on the opposite side of the wound. Johannes' winced and grunted. Zeb drew the pointed, polished sliver of bone through the flesh, raising his hand, slowly drawing the leather tight across the wound, almost closing a part of it, and then prepared to repeat the procedure with the next stitch. "Well, if it don't get infected, good thing about this rawhide is, it will just fall off or grow into the skin." He shook his head. "If it gets infected, that's a whole nuther story. Then you have to take the stitches out, open it up, clean it and start over."

Rebecca reached into her skirt pocket, pulling out a handkerchief and gently patted Zeb's forehead. "Let me get that sweat out of your eyes, Zeb."

"Much obliged."

"So, if there's no infection, Johannes will be fine?" Zeb stopped in mid-stitch, looking at her with concerned eyes and then up at Reuben. "Depends on hydrophobia." Rebecca threw an alarmed look at Reuben, whose eyes had widened at Zeb's words.

"Hydrophobia?" Rebecca gasped. "Here, in America?"

"The disease is everywhere Rebecca," said Zeb quietly, drawing the next stitch closed across the wound. "Some say it comes from the mouth juices of an animal that's sick."

"In England, the common people believed it was a monster that spread it, a very grim monster."

Shaking his head, Zeb kept his hands still for a moment. "Well, it's monstrous, that's for sure. People that gets it, die."

"That's cheerful," Johannes muttered, his words barely decipherable as he mouthed them through the stick clenched in his jaw.

A surge of anxiety shot through Rebecca as she thought of the amputee she had seen in England, his limb cut off because of the disease. He had died despite the extreme attempts by doctors to save his life. "How... how do you know somebody's contracted it?" she asked.

"Takes about two weeks," Zeb said, his voice flat, "and then you know. It ain't pretty. When I first came out here, trapped with a young fella about as dumb as I was. We was together about six months. Damn fool set a beaver trap in a bank hole 'stead of the water. Reached in to check it a few days later, and got bit by a raccoon. Two weeks later, he came down with the hydrophobia sickness."

"What happened to him?" Rebecca felt queasy. "Did he die?"

"Yep, he did. In the end, he asked me to shoot him, but by the time I made my decision, I didn't have to."

"Heartening," came Johannes' muffled voice again.

Zeb straightened. "That'll do it, Johannes. You're all stitched up as best I can. Rebecca, sprinkle some whiskey on there. Johannes, it's gonna sting like all get out."

Johannes' body tensed, then shook as Rebecca applied the whiskey to the series of stitches encircling the calf in two ragged lines. "I'm pretty sure the only thing he got was skin and muscle and nothings broke. It'll grow back. You oughta ride in the wagon for a few days so the bleeding stops and them stitches firm up. As they dry, they'll draw that skin together even more."

Johannes freed his hands from the trunk handle, reaching down and taking the stick out of his mouth. "We ought to give you the title, Doctor Taylor."

Zeb chuckled. "I've been called worse."

Reuben reached down, patting Johannes' shoulder. "Looks like you have a few days off, Viking." He turned to Philippe. "Why don't you go on up and tell Michael everything's fine down here. Poor kid's eyes were so wide when we carried Johannes out of the trees, they ran from his hat to his chin."

Philippe chuckled. "*Sí, Señor* Reuben. When I left, he had his pistol out and was moving his head around watching for another bear so fast I thought he might break his neck." The three men laughed.

Men. Rebecca shook her head disgustedly. *Not funny.*

Johannes started to roll over but Zeb put a hand on his back. "Nope, stay on your belly. Let them stitches set for an hour, then you can turn over. Rebecca, real careful like, wrap his whole calf in that gauze from the pouch. Try not to touch the wounds with your hands." Zeb held up the nearly empty glass whiskey flask. "After his leg is wrapped, sprinkle just a dab of this whiskey on the gauze. Hopefully, there'll be a little left if we need it. I'm gonna head up and skin that bear, and maybe cut some slabs of meat out of the rear haunches of that cow if it ain't spoiled."

"Do you eat bear, Zeb?" Rebecca asked.

"Yep. I don't recommend it in the spring when they've come out of their winter sleep but it can be tasty in the fall, particularly if they been feeding on berries."

The sounds of Philippe and Reuben riding away at a lope receded from the wagon. Zeb stood, turning to Sarah, "You said you wanted to talk?"

Rebecca turned her head and looked at Sarah, their eyes briefly locking. Sarah quickly shifted her gaze to Zeb. "Yes. Please Zeb, let's do."

Pointing out the rear of the wagon, Zeb suggested, "There's a flat rock over yonder about fifty yards in the sun. Let's stroll out there and set for a while; then I'll head back up and do what needs to be done."

Rebecca watched the two of them walk toward the rock, several feet separating them as they moved.

"I'm done now, Johannes." Rebecca shoved the cork back into the whiskey bottle.

Johannes breathed in deeply and exhaled. "Whew, glad that's over."

"I think Zeb did a fine job. He was very careful."

Johannes chuckled. "But none too delicate." The Dane partially lifted his head, rolling his eyes back toward her. "You have a really good man there in Reuben, Rebecca. I'm happy things have worked out for the two of you better than it did for me and Inga. And, you'll have a child to share soon, too. Can't get much better than that."

Thinking of Inga's unborn child, a child Johannes had never known, a welling of guilt gripped her chest. "You need to rest. Reuben has decided to camp here for the night. The trail gets narrower toward Little Medicine and there are only a few hours of daylight remaining. If Zeb's shortcut works, sometime in the coming days we are going across what he calls the Divide. He says on the other side every drop of water runs to the Pacific, and on this side all water runs to the Atlantic or the Gulf of Mexico."

"The Continental Divide? Well, I'll be in the saddle for that!"

"But Johannes—"

Johannes cut her off, "I'll be fine, Rebecca. Had far worse and besides..." he turned his face to the blanket with a wide smile, "I'm not missing it. Not many times in a man's life does one get to cross the divide of a continent."

CHAPTER

37

June 23, 1855

DREAM DANCER

KNEELING, WALKS WITH MOON EXTENDED HER ARMS, pressing the sharp-edged granite stone hard against the buffalo hide stretched between cottonwood stakes imbedded in the ground and drew the stone back toward her knees. Soon, the hide, laying hair side down on the early summer grass and already stripped of its blood, fat and tissues, would be ready for a vigorous rubbing of mashed and boiled tatanka brains.

Pausing to let her arms rest, she shifted slightly, spreading her knees to give the pronounced rounding of her belly more room as she bent over the hide. Waving one hand to brush away the flies that buzzed around her and hummed above the boiled brain emulsion, she smiled at Eagle Talon sitting cross-legged in front of their tipi. "I am pleased you managed to kill one of our brothers even though hunting alone. We now have two tatanka for winter, the one Soaring Eagle gave to us when you were away and this one that Spirit provided today."

Shifting his stare from off into the distance, Eagle Talon scanned the hide and then his wife's figure, lingering on the tight leather around her middle. "I would like to help you, Walks with Moon. This is much work for you when carrying our child."

"Thank you, husband, but this is not the work of a brave." She smiled. "Besides, Pony Hoof finished tanning their last robe just two days before she gave birth to their daughter. I will not have my friends thinking I am weak or spoiled." She thrust her chin out to where their ponies grazed. One, a handsome, muscular tobiano mustang, limped, dragging its right rear hoof as it moved slowly through the grasses. "How is your horse today?"

Eagle Talon shook his head slowly. "The horn did not bury itself too deeply. I do not think any damage was done, other than the ripping of some muscle and hide. I cleaned it and packed it with plantain poultice." He studied the pony. "The next sun or two will tell the story. If the bleeding stops and there is no infection, all will be fine. If not..." his eyes squinted, "I will have to open and re-clean the wound. He will not be able to be ridden until we get back to winter camp, perhaps later." He shook his head sadly. "My best horse."

Walks with Moon wiped the sweat from over her eyes with her forearm, hunching down again over the staked hide, remembering part of the story Eagle Talon told her the night before. *One of our brothers detached himself from the rest of the herd. I rode quickly to within three lance lengths. The first arrow was behind the shoulder, perhaps a bit high. He stumbled. The second arrow, in his neck above the shoulder, found its mark. He went down and then rolled to his side, spilling much blood.*

"Tell me the story again, beginning where your mustang protected you," she requested, knowing it pleased him to recount his pony's bravery.

Eagle Talon smiled at her. "I dismounted," he said, "and had already drawn my knife when the bull lunged to his feet."

With his finger, he traced the story in the sand between his crossed knees.

"Hunting alone, there were no other riders to distract him. The bull turned quickly, charging at my pony. Bravely, he stood between us, jumping away at the last moment, but a horn tore through the back part of his haunch."

Eagle Talon shook his head, remembering. "Fortunately, I had my lance." He added disgustedly, "At least I had that much presence of mind. The tatanka collapsed to its forelegs. I thrust the lance into the back of his neck."

Absorbed in the story, Walks with Moon stopped scraping the last bits of residue.

"You know the rest..." he said, raising his eyes to hers.

They both fell silent. The only sounds were the soft sigh of a gentle breeze, just strong enough to bend the very tips of the grasses, the distant, almost inaudible murmur of the creek and the wet scrape of the rock against the hide.

"It is now two suns past the end of the first moon since the Council's decree. It is obvious they are not going to lift it." His voice was flat, but Walks with Moon detected the concealed disappointment in his tone.

Fighting the impulse to look at him, she concentrated instead on the hide. "Have you given any thought to what we might name our son?"

"You keep insisting that we will have a son, Walks with Moon. This seems based entirely on the ramblings of Talks with Shadows from the little you've told me."

Walks with Moon paused, then resumed her draw of the stone. *His frustration and the injury to the horse have made him ill-tempered.* "Well, husband, if it is a daughter we shall choose a different name, but what name would you prefer for a son?"

Eagle Talon's silence prompted her to look back over her shoulder at him. His stare at her was hard until their eyes met, then his bronzed features softened and his lips lost their tight press. *He knows I'm trying to distract him and he is pleased.*

Eagle Talon reached over to the small leather pouch filled with pemmican she had set beside him, gathering some of the dried meat in his fingers, tipping his head back and dropping it into his mouth. He chewed thoughtfully. "If Spirit blesses us with a son, and Talks with Shadows' visions are for once proven correct," he chuckled "then I think we should name him Dream Dancer."

Walks with Moon let go of the rock, straightening up and looking at him for a long moment. "Dream Dancer," she repeated slowly, and smiled. "A fine name, Eagle Talon."

Eagle Talon grinned back at her. "And when, wife, may we expect..." he paused, "...our son to join us?"

"I don't know exactly, husband," feeling the heat rise in her face. "There could have been many times when we began his life. Eagle Talon's smile broadened and he nodded his head, "I have talked with Turtle Dove. We believe it will be in *canwapegi wi*, when the leaves begin to golden, perhaps during our journey back to winter camp."

Eagle Talon nodded, the smile leaving his face. "Let us hope that by that time the father of Dream Dancer will once again ride in front, as the eyes of the People, so that his son will be proud."

THE SUN WAS LOW TO THE HORIZON, CASTING LONG shadows on the grasses surrounding the camp, patches of shade in ever-growing crescent shapes on the east faces of the gentle swells of plains. Walks with Moon had begun rubbing the brain mash into the hide to soften the leather. Restless after having visited the mustang, Eagle Talon rose from where he was seated cross-legged in front of the tipi, his mind on the injured tobiano. *The bleeding has stopped, but the outer edges of the gore is forming puss and the pony's muzzle is warm. If it is no better when the sun rises, I shall have to open and re-clean the wound and repack it with a new poultice.*

The sound of a horse approaching at a lope arrested his attention. *Three Cougars!* The brave slowed his horse at a nearby lodge, leaning far over its side to speak with Talks with Shadows, Turtle Shield's wife. Three Cougars straightened, digging his heels and directing the pony toward their tipi at a fast trot.

Eagle Talon halted his stride out toward the injured pony. Three Cougars looked at him, then quickly away, instead reining in the mustang next to Walks with Moon. "Fine hide, Walks with Moon. It will make a good robe."

Holding one hand out to block the setting sun, Walks with Moon looked up at the brave. "Thank you, Three Cougars."

Studiously avoiding Eagle Talon, who was now just a lance length away, Three Cougars spoke to Walks with Moon, pointing behind him, "Tell Eagle Talon that the Council is assembling. He is summoned by Flying Arrow and Tracks on Rock."

Walks with Moon's eyes widened as she and Eagle Talon exchanged quick glances. "What is it about Three Cougars?" she asked, an equal mixture of concern and hope in her voice.

"The Council has not confided in me, Walks with Moon. But they expect Eagle Talon, Pointed Lance, Brave Pony, Three Knives, and Turtle Shield when the sun can no longer be seen." His eyes rose involuntarily to Eagle Talon, again quickly averting his gaze. "Please tell Eagle Talon." He wheeled his pony, urging it into a lope in the direction of Brave Pony's lodge.

Walks with Moon looked up at Eagle Talon from where she knelt, a slight quiver in her lips. "Husband, do you suppose..."

"It can only be one of two things, Walks with Moon," Eagle Talon interrupted her. "They will lift the shame, or they will not," he said.

EAGLE TALON SPRANG FROM HIS MUSTANG BY THE Council Lodge. He had hurriedly braided eight feathers into his hair, cleaned his hands from the stains of his horses' wound, and had rubbed himself with sage. His four friends had already arrived, their horses milling around the lodge. All the warriors stood stiffly, not looking or talking to one another, their faces anxious. The highest lines of the gentle ridges around the camp glowed with a fading golden sheen. *Like the fringe of deer leather in sun.* Daylight was remembered only by the slightest of shallow halos of fading rose to the west.

The lodge flap opened roughly and the wizened face of Horse's Leg, one of the Council members, poked out, looking at each of them in turn. "Come," he commanded.

When none of the other braves moved, Eagle Talon swallowed, walking the few steps to the lodge entry, bending slightly to enter. Straightening, he looked ahead to avoid the faces of the Council members, shuffling slightly to the side as the other braves entered, until all five of them stood in a nervous line near the small fire burning in the center of the lodge.

"The Council has discussed your situation and has come to a decision," pronounced Flying Arrow. There was a long silence. Eagle Talon used all his willpower not to seek out the source of the deep, authoritative voice.

"We have decided your period of shame is over with the rise of the next sun." Eagle Talon heard the exhale of tension from Brave Pony beside him. "We have further decided that your actions were brave, but reckless. Therefore, the coup each of you counted will be half recognized and half forsaken. Perhaps in the future you will remember the lack of feathers in your hair when it comes time to make a decision."

But I have five coup, how does one wear half a feather? Eagle Talon could feel his great chief's eyes on him. Flying Arrow, as if reading his mind, answered. "Those of you who counted coup in an odd number shall take the lesser number of feathers than one half." *An extra punishment because it was I who talked the other braves into attacking the Pawnee.*

"Brave Pony, Pointed Lance, Three Knives and Turtle Shield, you may return to your lodges. Eagle Talon, you will remain."

What is this?

The four warriors who had been dismissed circled the lodge fire sun-wise, keeping their eyes straight ahead and then quickly exited, their relief and desire to be away from the Council evident in their haste.

When the sound of their ponies could be heard no more, Eagle Talon lifted his eyes and, for the first time in over a moon, searched the faces of the Council. All were turned to him, firelight heightening the reddish-brown chasms of their aged skins. Tracks on Rock spoke, "Our advance scouts happened on the bodies of three Cheyenne warriors. They had been shot, stripped of their clothing and beads, and scalped. The tracks surrounding their bodies were shod hooves. Two of them were shot in the back."

The faces looking up at Eagle Talon were somber—worried. Flying Arrow shifted his cross legged position slightly. "The waste of our tatanka brothers we saw seven suns ago? And now the killing of the three Cheyenne? The scouts say they appeared to be watering their horses when they were attacked, nothing more. These are bad omens. We must know more about the hairy-faced-ones— what they plan, how many there are and how they think."

Tracks on Rock spoke in a low tone, "Do you know in what direction the white eyes you met, Roo-bin and his woman, went?"

Eagle Talon slowly shook his head. "I did not ask. I only knew from Spirit that we would meet again." Several of the Council members turned to one another. There was a murmur of low voices. Tracks on Rock threw several sticks on the lodge fire. The flames leapt higher, heightening the intensity of the shadows playing on the hides of the lodge.

"Turtle Dove has told me that the hairy-faced-one of many winters ago, the tall one to whom we taught the ways of Spirit and the land, Zeb-Riah, was with Roo-bin.

Eagle Talon nodded, surprised.

"We know Zeb-Riah traps in the lands of the Ute, where water turns rock red. The Council has not decided, but we wish to know if you would be willing to seek out this man you believe is your spirit brother and see if he will share his knowledge of the white eyes with you."

Eagle Talon thought quickly. *If they decide, it will be a directive couched as a request. If I refuse, I cannot maintain my honor. But, if Walks with Moon is right, she will give birth within two moons. That I will not miss.*

"I would be honored if that is the Council's decision." There were nods of approval and another murmur. "But..." a hush fell over the lodge, "my wife expects the birth of our son in the season of *hihpa ye*. It could be earlier. Once in the land where water turns rock red, my search for Roo-bin would be shadowed with the worry I would have for Walks with Moon."

Tracks on Rock and Flying Arrow leaned toward one another, speaking several words quietly. Tracks on Rock smiled at him. "Your son? How are you so sure Walks with Moon will bear a son?"

The image of Walks with Moon, her eyes-narrowed, serious, and believing, flashed through Eagle Talon's mind. "Walks with Moon assures me."

There were several chuckles from various members of the Council and Tracks on Rock's smile broadened. "All of us here have learned not to argue with the women. We understand, but if the child arrives later, your travels may meet with the first snows." Eagle Talon nodded. *I had not thought of that.*

Flying Arrow waved his hand signaling the end of the discussion. "We will make a decision by the next moon."

THE COALS GLOWED IN THE FIRE RING, THEIR LIGHT casting a dull glow over their sleeping robes. Lying on her side, Walks with Moon pressed her breasts against Eagle Talon's back, kissing his neck lightly. Her hand slipped under his arm and across his chest, her fingers playing softly on his skin. She knew his thoughts, as he knew hers.

"It is a great weight now gone," he chuckled. "I shall have to practice looking people in the eye again."

Walks with Moon brushed her lips to his neck again, letting them linger. Her hand traced downward across the muscled ridges of his belly to the hairy warmth between his legs. Closing her fingers around him, she whispered, "I have been missing you, husband. We should celebrate." She moved her hand in a slight rhythm, feeling him quicken, his body hardening, his girth filling her hand.

Eagle Talon turned over to face her, his tongue finding her breast. He began to slide one leg over hers.

"Husband, we are past the time for that. We must use our other ways." *The image of straddling him, looking down into eyes that once again shine brightly, already stirs my want.*

Yet another image fed Eagle Talon's desire. Raising his mouth from her skin and smiling, he turned her tenderly over to her belly, and in that gesture Walks with Moon sensed a deeper need. *His manhood has suffered ... let him fill you in this way...*

Eagle Talon rose to his knees pulling her up and backwards to him. She eased her upper body to the robe, supporting herself with her arms, as he positioned his outer thighs against her inner legs, spreading them. And as his fingers gently dipped into the wetness between her legs, his other hand warm and comforting over the roundness of their son, a heated tingling spread through her abdomen. His hips moved against her buttocks and slowly her body opened to his presence, a wave of intense pleasure, long missed, sweeping through them both.

June 25, 1855

LITTLE MEDICINE

"I AM RIDING," STATED JOHANNES FIRMLY, SITTING UP on Sarah's bedroll with a wince. "I am not driving the wagon." His eyes roved from Rebecca, to Sarah, to Reuben and then to Zeb with a determined look and an annoyed tone in his voice. "Besides, you need at least four hands with the cows."

But Rebecca was just as determined. "I can ride with Reuben today, Johannes," she said. "I've been aching to get on Red, and Lord knows she's getting unhappy trailing behind the wagon."

Reuben glanced quickly at her, his eyes straying to her abdomen. "But..."

Leaning over, she raised the brim of his hat and kissed him on the forehead. "I shall be fine, Mr. Frank. I am nowhere near that far along yet."

Reuben glanced at Zeb, seeking support but the tall mountain man merely shrugged his shoulders. "I've seen Indian women ride up to the day they give birth." His face was impassive, but his eyes were twinkling. "Doesn't do them no harm."

Johannes began to protest but Zeb interrupted him. "Tell you what, Johannes. Why don't you just stand up from that bedroll, walk on over to the tailgate, hop on down and take twenty steps?"

The Dane returned the mountain man's stare, his jaw tightening. Sliding his legs over the bunk, he rose, clenching his teeth as he did so, sweat immediately beading on his forehead.

"Go on, jump off and take a stroll." Zeb tipped his customary keg seat back, leaning his shoulders into the canvas, taking out cigarette paper and preparing to roll a smoke.

Johannes took a tentative step, then another. His leg buckled, but he caught himself on a trunk. He stood again, white faced, then backed slowly to the bedroll sinking back down. He bent his leg backward peering down over his shoulder to try to see his wounds. "Just how much meat did that son-of-a-bitch chew off my leg?"

Zeb sprinkled tobacco on the rolling paper and looked up. "A fair amount. And it's gonna be swollen something fierce for the next few days. I checked it last night when you was asleep. So far there's no infection and them stitches seem to be holding." He looked hard at Johannes, "And we still won't know about the hydrophobia for a spell. But that's then. This is now. Even if you was to make it to the horse and get in the saddle, them tooth holes might open up again. If you get dirt or horse sweat in 'em you may not stay so lucky."

Zeb finished rolling the cigarette, raising it to his lips and moistening the edge of the paper. "And that mare of yours is going to be a mite spooky for a few days. Horses don't forget bears all too quick. Nothing flaps Buck, but even he gets a might jumpy when one of them grizzlies is close." Without realizing it, he reached up two fingers running them down the two long purple scars on the side of his face.

"That settles it, Viking," said Reuben. "We'll give Sarah a break from driving that freight wagon. She can handle the schooner and you can take over her spot for today." Sarah smiled, obviously pleased with the idea.

Reuben rose, "And you, milady Marx, can get your first lesson in pushing beef." Rebecca grinned, her eyes dancing as she looked up into his.

Zeb struck the flint, lighting the cigarette. With one long arm, he parted the untied flap at the rear of the wagon and peered out. "We're jawboning. The sun's almost up. I'm not real sure we'll find out today or tomorrow if that shortcut is possible, but we surely won't if we don't get started."

Reuben grinned at the mountain man. "Then, let's get this outfit moving. Could you help Johannes over to the freight wagon? Rebecca and I will ride out and tell Philippe and the boy what the plans are. We'll come back up and see how the wagons are doing after the sun rises and we're on the move. Shouldn't be too long now."

REUBEN SLID HIS EYES TOWARD REBECCA. SHE SAT EASY and fluid in the saddle on Red, back straight, chin lifted, focused ahead in the semi-dark. *Feels like she belongs right there next to me.* "I have a confession to make," he offered.

Her head swiveled toward him, her silence the question.

"I wanted you last night." He laughed softly. "Matter of fact, I want you most every time I look at you but I couldn't figure a way or a place that wasn't freezing for us to be alone."

"Mr. Frank, I am flattered but now that we are betrothed, we should approach this properly. Your ardor will have to wait until we are married."

She must be teasing. "Little late for that, don't you think?" He waved his hand at her midsection. Besides, that could be months...or more."

Rebecca stared straight ahead. "Regardless of my condition and despite our having admittedly delightful carnal knowledge of one another, it is never too late to be proper." Her voice lightened, a passionate tease underlying her words. "However, I shall make your patience worthwhile on our wedding night."

Reuben looked glumly at Lahn's ears and sighed. *She's serious.*

The sky was lightening with the promise of the day as Reuben and Rebecca reined in Red and Lahn by the small fire Philippe had built in the lee of a giant spruce tree. His coffee pot chugged and vibrated as he sprinkled snow on the bubbling, dark colored brew. "*Señor* Reuben. *Buenas Dias*," he said, looking up from the brewing kafee. His eyes slipped past Reuben widening in surprise as he realized Rebecca was the other rider. He rose hastily, bowing and sweeping off his hat, "*Señorita* Rebecca. Again my congratulations." He grinned, "Soon I will have to call you *Señora*."

Rebecca laughed. "I'm sure that will be quite a while from now, Philippe. From what Zeb says, we're not even sure if we can find anyone to conduct the ceremony." Reuben was silent, hiding his frown by pretending to study his saddle horn.

Philippe poured a cup of kafee, offering it to Rebecca, "*Señorita...*"

"Why, thank you, Philippe." Rebecca leaned down, taking the steaming tin cup. She took a sip, closing her eyes tightly and wrinkling her nose, "Oh my. That might be the strongest coffee I have ever tasted." She leaned out from Red extending the cup to Reuben.

"Thanks, Rebecca." He took a long sip, then another, letting the warmth seep through his leather gloves. "Johannes is gonna drive the freight wagon today. Sarah will be in charge of the prairie schooner and Rebecca's gonna help us push cows," he grinned at the brunette, his eyes traveling slowly down her form, admiring the tailored fit of her heavy black wool jacket and thickly woven grey riding dress.

Philippe's eyes widened. "*¿La vaquera?*"

Rebecca chortled. "No, I'm not a cowgirl yet, Philippe, but I am sure that under the expert instruction of you men, I soon will be." The vaquero's eyes slid to the stock of her Sharps protruding from the scabbard and he nodded approvingly.

"We'll ride up through the cows and tell Michael to come and get some coffee with you."

Michael's reaction was similar to Philippe's. His eyes rounded and his mouth dropped open when he realized it was Rebecca riding alongside Reuben.

Rebecca smiled warmly, "Are you going to teach me all about cows, Michael?"

Michael's eyes darted to Reuben, and then back to Rebecca. He blushed. "Yes... Yes... Yes, ma'am."

"Philippe has some of that devil's brew for you," Reuben said. "Take a break. Rebecca and I will mind the cattle." The boy's face lit up.

They watched Michael trot toward the small distant glow of Philippe's fire. Reuben swept his arm toward the slowly milling herd. "The trick with these cows, maybe more so in these hills, is to achieve a fine balance between keeping them moving and not stirring them up. You can take that lariat, which one of these days one of us will show you how to use, and just kind of slap it against the side of your saddle or your leg, once in a while using your voice," he demonstrated. At the sound of his "Hehhh!" several of the near cows looked up, startled, taking a few quick trotting steps. "Every once in a while one of these cows will get into trouble. She'll slide down the embankment, or they want to go a different direction, or get enticed by an especially tasty looking patch of grass off the trail. Don't go after them alone 'til we show you how."

"Is that what happened when Johannes had his encounter with the grizzly?"

"Exactly."

Rebecca laughed nervously, looking around. "Don't worry Mr. Frank. I will not be straying into the timber after a cow."

Reuben chuckled, "Good." He looked east to the ridges of Wolf Creek Pass some miles behind them. A thin band of gold was beginning to permeate the pale blue of the sky through the tops of the trees silhouetted at the highest points of the ridgelines. "The sun will be up shortly. We'll help Philippe and Michael get these cows started and then ride down to see how Johannes is doing with the wagon."

WITH REBECCA CLOSE BEHIND, REUBEN RODE UP TO THE freight wagon. "How's it going, Viking?"

Johannes glanced sideways at him, then back ahead, his hands lightly tightening, then loosening one line, then the other as he guided the wagon between several trees that encroached on the trail and a large slab of rock.

He nodded down toward his leg. "Take a look. I'm black and blue up to my belt." He eased the wagon past the last tree as he turned to Reuben. "Zeb was right. It would have been foolish for me to ride this morning." There was a determined edge to his voice as he added, "But I will be in the saddle this afternoon."

Deciding not to argue, Reuben chuckled, "Zeb is usually right."

"Usually, but not always," called out a voice behind them.

Zeb eased Buck between the rear of the wagon and the trees crowding the narrow trail. He rose up in the saddle, squinting and sat back down. "Don't think we're going to make the cutoff today."

Reuben's eyes flickered to Rebecca. *Another day behind.* "Why not? Snow's almost gone except in the shade now that we've come down in elevation and we got an early start."

Zeb pointed, three or four miles beyond the narrow swath zigzagging below them in the trees, to where it disappeared into a rugged, narrow canyon. Beyond was glimpses of a greening, elongated and widening meadow. "Put your spyglass on that meadow, Reuben. I do believe there's smoke down there in Little Medicine."

Lifting the telescope to his eyes, Reuben confirmed Zeb's spotting.

The mountain man nodded. "It's likely that it is Chief Guera Murah's tribe. They like the hot springs down there. And if that is them, it would be good to stop, talk and pass the pipe." He looked hard at Reuben. "Those Utes are going to be your neighbors for quite a spell. Wherever you put the ranch, they will consider it to be their land. It would be best to get off to a good start, even if it means losing half a day or so of travel."

"Are they going to be happy to see us," Rebecca asked, her voice tinged with worry, "after we killed two of their warriors?"

Zeb shook his head. "Different tribe, Rebecca, and not likely they know. But we will have to keep them spotted horses out of plain sight."

Thirty yards ahead of them, Sarah was maneuvering the prairie schooner on the narrow trail. Reuben raised his hand to his mouth, amplifying his voice. "Hold up there, Sarah." Red hair and a pale face peered around the side of the canvas, then disappeared. The wagon rolled slowly to a stop.

Zeb stroked his mustache with a thoughtful look. "Some of the Ute believe the springs at Little Medicine have great powers. They call the place Spirit's Crossing and they can be dang territorial when it comes to them springs. Not much for sharing. Not too sure it's a good thing if we suddenly push three hundred cows through their camp without announcing the visit first, either. Let's you, me and Rebecca ease on down there, make sure it's Guera Murah's band, introduce the two of you and let them know, delicate like, about the cattle behind us."

Rebecca looked pleased, but nervous. "Rebecca, they'll be surprised and respect that a woman is with us and you should meet Ouray's wife, Black Mare, but take that Sharps out when I tell ya, and ride with it across your lap."

Reuben jerked his eyes to Zeb. "Thought you said this tribe has been friendly?"

"A drawn rifle helps 'em stay that way," said Zeb, quietly.

June 25, 1855

*T*HE NOOCHEW

LIFTING HIMSELF PARTIALLY FROM THE SADDLE, REUBEN craned his shoulders, looking back up the trail they had been descending. The wagons were long out of sight and even the bells of the lead cow could no longer be heard. *Probably dropped halfway between the wagons and Little Medicine.* There was no snow at this lower elevation, the forest changing from tall conifers and aspen to occasional aspen patches, willows and alders in areas of springs and greater moisture. On the south-facing slopes of the rocky, undulating ridges, grew scattered pinyon pine and juniper. In the partially visible meadow several miles below them rose tendril tips of grey smoke and other more mysterious vapor plumes.

They rode three abreast, Rebecca between Zeb and Reuben. The horses cast sideways glances at one another, softly whinnying and shaking their heads from time to time. Buck seemed especially alert, as if he knew their destination. The chill of higher altitude was gone. Twice they had stopped to shun clothing, tying their jackets and coats atop the bedrolls lashed to the rear of their saddles. Two large birds soared overhead in a cloudless sky, their flight path seeming to follow southern ridge lines, their great brown wings almost motionless, outspread, with irregular light circles on the undersides. Their high-pitched screech echoed from the skies, sifting through the trees around the trio of riders.

Rebecca's eyes were fixed on the circling birds. "Golden Eagles," said Zeb. "Them two is just young-uns; you can tell by the white spot on their wings." Shielding his eyes with one hand, he lifted his head. "Four, maybe five-foot wings. They get up around six or seven foot when they're full-grown. I've seen 'em take antelope fawn, even small yearling deer. Some say they can see a rabbit at five miles. If you watch 'em long enough, they'll fold their wings and drop out of the sky like a rock. Then you know they're after dinner."

"Magnificent," Rebecca murmured.

"Yep." Zeb spoke softly, not much above a whisper. "I figure we'll be down to that canyon in an hour or two give or take. We'll kind of ease into that meadow, make sure whoever is making that smoke is friendly." His eyes traveled from Rebecca to Reuben. "If I slide my long gun back into my scabbard, do the same."

"And if you don't?" asked Reuben.

Zeb's eyes clicked to him and then browsed back down the trail. "Then you'll know what to do. Likely won't have any choice." Rebecca cast an anxious glance at both men.

"I'm pretty sure it's Chief Guera Murah's bunch. Ute means 'land of the sun' in their language. They be quite different from them Sioux you met, Reuben—more colorful. Like lots of beads and baubles on their clothes and weapons, and they're big on paintin' themselves and their horses. Truth be known, most other tribes are their enemies. They only get along well with the Apache, particularly them Mouache and Capote, the Southern Utes, over in the San Luis Valley and stretchin' down south to north of Santa Fe, below where you picked up those cows, though Guera Murah is full-blood Jicarilla. Their biggest enemies is the Cheyenne, Crow, Shoshone, Blackfoot and Arapaho." Zeb reached into his shirt, pulling out his tobacco pouch, extracting his chew and biting off a piece. "But they've had fights with the Sioux and Pawnee. They got good at fighting since takin' on them Spaniards a couple hundred years back. That's when they first got horses. Got in some big scrapes with the Diné, too. Sometimes even teaming up with white men to fight them. Got every bit as good on horseback as any Indians, 'cept maybe less so than the Apache and Sioux, but not by much. Them Sioux call themselves 'The People.' Utes call themselves the 'Noochew.'"

"Diné?" Reuben glanced at Rebecca, not surprised that she wore a puzzled expression.

"Navajo." Leaning over Buck's side, Zeb spit a wad of chew at a twisted aspen by the trail, hitting the white trunk dead center. He grinned at Reuben. "I like to practice my aim." Falling silent for a moment, he ran his fingers down his mustache. "Best you know more about these people. Indians put a lot a store in ceremonies. Utes have their Bear Dance every spring. And they ain't above drying leaves from them manzanita bushes and smoking it mixed in with their tobacco sage. Sometimes make tea of it, too. Addles the brain a touch—gets them closer to Creator. Closer to Spirit, the Sioux would say."

Zeb swayed to the side and spit again, the brown gob flying in an arc, narrowly missing a thinly trunked alder. Reuben leaned in toward Rebecca to hear better. Zeb grimaced, then went on with his lesson.

"Ute chief once told me there's seventeen different bands. They all get along mostly but each has their own peculiar customs. Them southern tribes I was talking about like peyote. Comes from a cactus." He laughed. "Got talked into tryin' it once. Makes you feel like you're floating and colors get extra bright. Bluest sky I ever seen, rosiest prickly pear blossoms, too. My head wasn't right for three days."

He turned toward Reuben, his face serious as he held his gaze. "If it is Chief Guera Murah, it's likely his son, Ouray, will be a part of any talking, and they'll pull out a pipe. They have several. You'll know what he's thinking 'bout by which he chooses. If it's a black pipestone without much carving, he's just being polite. If it's made of that same clay but all carved up with some inset beads? That means he respects you. And he has one pipe made of salmon alabaster. Don't know how long it took to decorate it but it's quite something. If he uses that one, well, means he's a mite fond of you, and respects you too. Only seen him take it out twice. One time was when Kit

Carson and I visited their winter camp. Carson and Guera Murah are friends."

The mountain man shook his head. "Though mebbe Kit wouldn't get the same treatment now since he's leading them Army boys out of Fort Union and Fort Massachusetts against the Mouache and the Jicarilla, back in the San Luis. News travels fast between these Indians."

"How long have they been here, Zeb?" Rebecca asked quietly.

The mountain man peered down the trail, studying something and then turned to her, one eyebrow arched, "Damn near forever. Hundreds of years before them Spaniards from what I gather. According to Ute legend, they was all brought here from the south by a half wolf-half man god name of Sinauff. Carried 'em up here in a magic bag and then Coyote, their symbol of mischief, set 'em loose.

"Another thing, you may see some younger Indians that don't quite look like the rest of the village—flatter faces, slightly higher foreheads. Those would be slaves captured in raids, mostly from the Paiute, maybe some Navajo. Them tribes do the same to the Utes. Then they trade slaves for horses or whatever goods they want. It died down some, but when they opened up the Old Spanish Trail from Santa Fe to Los Angeles twenty, maybe thirty years ago, the fighting picked up again. Matter of fact, if we can't use that shortcut, we only got two choices. Either head north from here and join up with a branch of the Old Spanish Trail down on the Gunnison over to Fort Uncompahgre, or backtrack over Wolf

Creek, then down to the Animas River. One's the northern, the other the southern branch of the trail. I reckon the northern would be better."

He stared at Reuben, the weathered lines around his eyes tightening, the history lesson over. "Follow my lead, Reuben. These folks are gonna be your neighbors for a long time. Might be your only neighbors for years. I'll interpret best I can. Guera Murah was raised Apache. Ouray was raised in Taos. Speaks a mixture of English, Spanish and Ute. I'm half good at Sioux but less so with Ute."

Looking sharply at Rebecca, who was staring wide-eyed at him, Zeb warned, "Three more things and then we'll be getting close enough where we best hush up and move quiet. Since women can't smoke with the menfolk and Guera Murah's wife has passed, Ouray is likely to introduce you to his wife, Black Mare. Fine woman—quiet, but strong. She's half Kiowa Apache. 'Bout your same size. Matter of fact, you two look similar in more ways than shape. It's just as important you get along well with his wife as it is Reuben gets along with Guera Murah and Ouray. They already formed their opinion of me. I got their respect and vice versa, but I wouldn't call them friends. They are great hunters, chase buffalo like the Sioux, and maybe the most skilled hunters in the mountains—deer, elk, fish, rabbit. They consider me competition of sorts but I've always been fair, so we get along. Done some trading with them, too. The women pick all sorts of wild vegetables, wheatgrass, bentgrass, poa, stipa and sunflowers. Grind it all up into a sort of wheat. Add chokecherries and cook up dried round cakes. And gather pinyon nuts. Add it all to their larder for a nice break midwinter from elk or deer meat."

Zeb fell silent. Reuben waited, then prompted him. "What of the third thing, Zeb?"

"Been thinking about how we need to tell him what you plan—that ranch and the cattle."

"Do we have to tell them, Zeb?" Rebecca asked.

Zeb cast a quick look at her from narrowed eyes. "Yep. They'll know right off anyway. Probably already do. We gotta bring the cattle through one way or the other. They may have seen a cow or two from them Spaniards, but they never seen three hundred. Best to be up front with them unless the timing ain't right. One thing above all else, they got to trust you. Trust means a heap site more to Indians than most white men." He bent over the saddle and spit into the grass by Buck's front hooves. "And they ain't particularly keen on white men. They never liked the Spanish and back in 1843, Fremont brought a bunch through here, looking for a railroad path. Damn fool got hisself stranded midwinter. Lost half his men and had to backtrack to Taos. The Utes still talk about it. Now them Mormons is stirring up trouble with the Northern Band. But unlike white men, if you look 'em in the eye, they'll judge you on the person you be." He thought for a minute. "We'll just kind of ease into it. If nothing else, it wouldn't be bad for you to get the chief's nod of approval for that ranch."

"Approval?" Reuben felt a bristle flash up his spine. "The ranch will just be a tiny piece of land in this huge country," he said, sweeping his arm, "besides, I want to buy it."

Zeb laughed. "Reuben, they figure this is their land. It ain't for sale. They saw what happened when the Navajo and the United States signed the treaty of 1849." He snorted. "Treaty of Peace, they called it. The government liars and fools broke it in months." Zeb shook his head in disgust. "They ain't much on trusting white men agreements and you got nothing you could trade, even if they was inclined."

Should I say anything? Reuben rode quietly for a minute as they wound their way through a narrow gorge with broken rock walls that rose high enough to block the sun. A small creek, that had cut the canyon over eons, rushed alongside the tight turns of the trail, swollen with snowmelt. Carefully picking his words, Reuben said slowly, "What about diamonds?"

Zeb and Rebecca's heads jerked toward him in surprise. "Diamonds?" Rebecca gasped.

"My father gave me six large diamonds to use for buying the ranch. He was thinking in the European way."

Zeb gave a surprised chuckle. "I'll be go to hell. That's what you was talking about back in St. Louis." He wagged his head, "I ain't even sure they know what a diamond is, Reuben. The Spanish traded them beads and glass, which they set great store by. I doubt they'll think a diamond is more than just another piece of glass, but I don't rightly know. It's probably best you say nothing for now."

Reuben nodded. "I'd appreciate it if you didn't mention it to anyone. Just Johannes knows."

Staring straight ahead, Zeb agreed in a dry voice, "Yep, less people that know, the better."

Scanning the rocks above them, Zeb reined in Buck. "We'll ride single file from here. Rebecca, drag out that Sharps. Stay between me and Reuben. Any trouble, you take out the first that comes at you, then hightail it back to this canyon. There's some broken rocks at the mouth and a patch of cottonwoods. You can cover us with your long gun there," his mouth set grimly. "But if it gets real troublesome, you get on Red and skedaddle back up that mountain so that Johannes and that Mexican know what's going on."

A short time later, the jumble of stone cliffs fell away, mingling with cottonwoods. The raucous calls of magpies echoed in the trees. Zeb held up his hand for them to halt. Buck pawed the soft, sandy ground as the mountain man peered carefully through the stand of timber toward the open green that marked the beginnings of the meadow beyond the trees. He slowly swiveled his head upwards, his eyes suddenly widening, the muzzle of his Enfield beginning to rise. Then his facial muscles relaxed and the gun sank back down. He hitched his head slightly to the left. "Look up real slow. They been watching us."

Reuben lifted his eyes from the trees. Standing above them, partially hidden fifty feet up in the rocks and one hundred feet away, stood two braves, arrows nocked in their bows, the colorful lines that ran down the front of their tanned, fringed leather shirts clearly visible. Zeb raised his hand, palm out, toward them, whispering,

"Yep, it's Ouray's bunch." The two braves raised their hands in response, returning their arrows to the quivers behind their backs.

"Come on," said Zeb. He threw a sideways look at Reuben, adding, "Let that be a lesson to you. An Indian who doesn't want to be seen, usually ain't."

THEY RODE SLOWLY INTO THE UTE CAMP, STEAM FROM the hot springs rising surreal and selkie-like at various points in the extended meadow behind the lodges, a smell of sulfur in the air. Reuben stopped counting the tipis at fifty. *Must be better than a hundred.* They appeared to be clustered in three groups, one large and two smaller sets of lodges off to the side. Two tipis larger than the others occupied the center of the largest cluster of cone-shaped lodges. Four large fires burned with groups of Indians clustered around each, some standing, some sitting, all swaying back and forth. Several small children ran toward them shouting and squealing in loud voices and a number of Indians stood up at the nearby fires turning to face them, talking among themselves and gesturing excitedly. One man ran from one of the fires to one of the tipis in the center of the camp. From it emerged a man and a woman who walked slowly toward them, a small phalanx of braves forming to their sides and behind them, some carrying lances, others long black clubs with knobs on the ends. Two warriors cradled muskets and several had bows.

Keeping his eyes fixed on the gathering crowd advancing toward them, Zeb spoke from the side of his mouth. "The couple up there in front, that would be Ouray and Black Mare. Remember, he's got a lot of pull. I think they are having a powwow. That one small group of tipis yonder is Indians from the Northern Ute, the Uinta. And that other set of lodges? That's the Yamparika tribe from the Yampa River country." Leaning down, he slid the Enfield into the double belly scabbard above his Sharps.

Rebecca glanced at Reuben, her eyes blinking rapidly, her complexion pale. Reuben nodded and they both eased the Sharps into their scabbards. Ouray, his wife and their guard stopped when twenty feet away. Zeb raised his hand, palm toward them. "*Miaue Wush Tagooven*," said Ouray, raising his hand palm out in reply to Zeb's silent greeting.

REBECCA STUDIED OURAY. HE WAS STOCKY, RUGGEDLY handsome, about five foot, nine inches tall, with broad muscular shoulders. *Younger than I imagined. Perhaps four or five years older than me.* His leggings were of loose, dark leather, fringed heavily on the outer legs, intricate bead patterns approximately three inches wide running from the waist down to equally wide double bands of beads at the cuffs, which rested on heavily stitched moccasins with a squared off toe. His lighter leather shirt was likewise heavily fringed at the waist, shoulders and sleeves, an extra layer of leather sewn over each shoulder adorned with a dark-colored bead pattern. A white, red, turquoise and yellow beaded belt tied with leather fringe wrapped around the middle of his shirt. Below a long intricate beaded necklace was a triangular pendant of carved antler, also inlaid with beads. His face was round and eyes wide-set. His nose with well-defined nostrils and high cheekbones balanced well with his rounded chin and lips, his upper lip slightly thicker than his lower. His long, jet-black hair was parted low on one side and tied in tight braids that hung either side of his chest almost to his belt. *Very chief-like.*

Black Mare stood at his side but one step behind. She was shorter, perhaps five foot, two inches. She wore a one-piece, loose fitted, lightly tanned, leather dress. Its bottom and sleeves were as heavily fringed as her husband's garments. The long, irregular fringe above her square-toed moccasins ended just above a series of colorful, beaded, ornamental ankle bracelets that rose one after the other four or five inches above her ankles. Her belt was simple woven leather fastened with some type of cinch of antler or bone.

Her build was willowy but with distinctive womanly curves, Rebecca noticed, and handsome features. Her eyes were large, brown and set wide, her chin slightly more pronounced than his, as were her cheekbones. Her face, more angular than her husband's, was framed by long, smooth jet-black hair, carefully brushed and parted in the middle, braided on one side. *I see what Zeb meant about the resemblance.* Her hair tapered to the bodice of her leather dress, its embroidery descending from her shoulders in the shape of a "V." *That would have been her cleavage if her clothes were of European make.* Rebecca realized with some surprised anxiety that she was the object of study, too. Her eyes met and held Black Mare's for a long moment and then the lips of Ouray's wife parted, her teeth wide, white and expansive in a genuine smile.

Rebecca felt mesmerized. *Powerful woman. Like her husband.*

CHAPTER

40

June 25, 1855

$\mathscr{T}$HE BARTER

REALIZING ZEB HAD OBSERVED HER NONVERBAL exchange with Rebecca and her lack of reservation, the smile disappeared from Black Mare's face as quickly as it had emerged. *"Mique Wush Tagooven,"* Zeb said somberly to the Ouray, motioning to Reuben and Rebecca to stay.

Wrapping the reins around the saddle horn loosely with one turn, Zeb swung one lanky leg over Buck's ears and sprang lightly to the ground. He patted the mustang's neck as he walked toward Ouray and Buck blew softly. Black Mare cast her eyes downward, then lifted them looking past Zeb. *Sizing up Rebeca again. Good. Things will go a heck of a lot smoother if the women hit it off.*

Ouray and the mountain man extended their arm, each wrapping their hands behind the elbow of the other, and shook once.

"Soon, *mi amigo* you will no longer need campfires to warm your people. Summer already warms the valley," said Zeb, his words a mixture of English and Spanish, with a few Ute words thrown in. Ouray bobbed his head almost imperceptibly, responding in the same mix of languages. "*Si*, Zeb-Riah, *Tahchat* brings warmth to the earth. Our scouts tell me you have not been at your camps for many moons."

"Had to go over *las montañas*," Zeb gestured with his arm to the east, "and meet my friends," he waved his hands toward Rebecca and Reuben. "They have several others with them. *Dondé es* Chief Guera Murah?"

Ouray's expression darkened slightly. "My father meets with Kit Carson in Santa Fe." He paused. "How many?"

"*Tres hombres*. One will be leaving soon, *y una mujeres*."

"*Espanola?*"

Zeb held up one finger. "*Solamente uno.*" Ouray's lips pressed together tightly. "He is a vaquero," Zeb added.

Ouray's facial muscles twitched, relaxing slightly. "*Por que* they come?"

Better choose the right words. "They come to grow cattle."

The Indian's eyebrows raised. Black Mare's eyes shifted from Rebecca to Zeb, a questioning look on her face.

"Reuben Frank," Zeb pointed at Reuben, "has been entrusted by his family to raise cattle on the land. We have cattle on the trail several hours pony ride on the other side of the gap and two wagons, one with supplies to build the lodge."

Ouray studied Reuben, his stare unblinking, his features impassive.

"Where does he plan to grow these cattle?"

"Somewhere on the Uncompahgre, up toward La Montana de Roja. He has come to ask the permission of Chief Guera Murah, son, Ouray, and the Ute."

Ouray's eyes shifted from Reuben back to Zeb, the hint of a smile on his lips. *Thank you for the guidance, Spirit.* Zeb waved at Reuben to join them. The young Prussian dismounted and walked toward them; Zeb carefully watching Ouray and Black Mare's expressions. Ouray's eyes slowly scanned Reuben from his boots and spurs to his hat, lingering on the pearl-handled Colt slung low on his hip. Reuben stopped at Zeb's side, holding the young leader's gaze. His eyes shifted momentarily to Black Mare and he nodded his head.

There was a long pause. Misunderstanding the sub-chief's silence, Reuben offered in a level tone, "I would like to give you a cow when we come through today. Their hides are good and they have a great deal of meat." Ouray's brow wrinkled.

Zeb fought a wave of concern. *Should have warned him about offering a gift. Don't want to make a fuss. Need to buy some time to think.* Reaching into the open collar of his leather shirt, he pulled out his tobacco pouch, extracting a chunk of chew. He offered it to the chief who smiled, taking the molasses-laden tobacco and biting off a chunk.

Turning slightly away from Ouray, Zeb offered it to Reuben, his tone a mere whisper. *"You never want to offer a gift. They will expect to give you something of equal or greater value in return, even a wife."*

Reuben refused the offered tobacco, his face impassive. Zeb redirected his attention to Ouray, who smiled, his teeth brown from the chew.

"Ouray, my young friend here is very skilled in the ways of cattle. He has brought fine animals." Zeb pointed to Rebecca, "This is his woman. They have agreed..." he corrected himself, "...they have arranged to be married but there is no one with sufficient *puwa* to marry them. Reuben asks if you could assist. If he gave you one of his cows, which has a fine hide and much meat, could your *bowa'gant*, your medicine man, or your *puwarat* perform a wedding ceremony?"

Ouray's eyes widened in surprise, shifting back and forth from Reuben to Rebecca, before falling to Black Mare. A smile flitted across his wife's face and she nodded her head in approval. Zeb spat some chew off to the side and Ouray did the same, wiping his lips with the palm of his hand, then spoke to Reuben.

Zeb didn't catch all the words but got the gist. Struggling to suppress a smile, the mountain man winked at Reuben with the eye hidden from the chief by the bridge of his nose. "Ouray says you picked a good time to offer your trade." Reuben's eyebrows shot up. "This is the last day of the powwow. The tribe's *bowa'gant* and *puwarat* have great *puwa*, and the tribe is ready to eat and powwow with their friends, the Unita-at, and the Yamparika. It would be a good night for a wedding but finalizing the trade requires further talk. His father, the chief, has traveled to Santa Fe and the question of growing cows remains. We must smoke at Black Mare's lodge so that final decisions can be reached." Reuben's eyes widened and his jaw fell slightly open. Zeb added, his voice without inflection, but his eyes narrowed in caution, "and discuss the permission of the Noochew."

Gesturing at Rebecca, Ouray spoke quickly to Black Mare. Bobbing her head, she waved to Rebecca to dismount and come to her. Rebecca hesitated, looking confused. Reinforcing the invitation, Zeb called, "Black Mare would like to spend time with you." Zeb could not stifle the grin under his mustache as he added, "We are going to her lodge and smoke the pipe to finalize the trade Reuben has proposed." Rebecca threw a wondering look at him. "Black Mare will introduce you to some of the other women over by the fire."

Rebecca hesitated for a moment and then dismounted, Black Mare meeting her halfway. Rebecca curtsied and smiled at her young Indian counterpart, who clapped her outstretched palms together, taking Rebecca's hand and leading her toward the nearby fire where a number of women stood watching the scene with great curiosity. Ouray wheeled abruptly, issuing a quiet command with unmistakable authority. Two teenaged girls with flat features and dressed more plainly than the rest of the tribe ran forward, leading Buck, Red and Lahn away. The guard of warriors around him dispersed, walking in different directions back to their lodges or one of the fires.

The three men made their way to Black Mare's lodge. The lodge fire had diminished to a few dim, glowing coals, coddled by white ash. Ouray threw several sticks on the fire as he and Zeb seated themselves cross-legged, then watched approvingly as Reuben, still standing, scanned the walls of the lodge with fascinated interest.

The young Prussian's eyes lingered on the elk and buffalo robes on their bed, the lance, bow and heavy black-knobbed club huddled in one corner with the chief's war shield, and the several feathered, intricately beaded head-dresses, carefully hung on racks of mule deer antlers. Ouray smiled at Reuben's attention to the beaver hides stretched on rounded alder sticks, hanging on the lodge walls from rawhide strings, their hair cut and scraped in fine depictions of elk, deer and eagles. After a few minutes, the Indian gestured to him to sit.

Several handsome baskets, heavily woven with great care, some beaded and all colored with bright vegetable dyes were tucked against the hide walls of the lodge. Reaching behind him, Ouray picked up the shallowest of the baskets. It was thirty inches long, oval in shape, and six inches deep with a high, curved, woven handle, its contents covered by a folded deerskin colored and painted with images and forms in a circular pattern. *The diary of each winter past.* He carefully lifted the story skin from the contents of the basket and withdrew a leather pipe bag, wondrously embroidered with beads. Thick, light rawhide stitches bound its ends, part of it raised, and including a full beaded moccasin stitched into its lower third. Ouray laid the pipe bag carefully in front of him, and began to speak, watching Reuben intently. Zeb haltingly repeated his words in English, trying to be careful in his translation, "This bag contains the three pipes used by Chief Guera Murah and his son, Ouray. The designs made by the beads are the sacred symbols of the Noochew. The blue is water, the yellow fire and sun, the green is the earth." Zeb pointed. "The interspersed beads are the hail of the thunder beings, the turtle—a symbol of the land, and the moccasin means home to them."

His face solemn, Ouray pointed at the yellow beaded paw print with long claws on a field of red.

"And that is the sign of the bear, sacred animal of the Noochew."

Ouray slid three pipes from the bag, laying them on the beaded surface. One was long and black, beautiful but with minimal carving, a second, longer, also black and carefully carved and a third, its wood grains swirling in light and dark brown, intricately carved and artistically decorated with small beads and glass baubles. Zeb held his breath.

Without hesitation, the young leader picked up the salmon alabaster pipe. Reuben's eyes shifted quickly to Zeb's and then back to Ouray, who was loading the bowl with what Zeb knew was sage tobacco. Pulling a burning stick from the lodge fire, he lit the pipe, inhaling deeply twice. Leaning forward, he proudly displayed the pipe to them, then presented it to Reuben stem first. Reuben's eyes darted to Zeb, then back to the pipe. He lifted it, inhaled and coughed.

Ouray grinned, "Very good sage tobacco. The leaves are very young this time of year. Black Mare picked it only last week."

As Reuben exhaled, still coughing, Zeb commented, "Ouray says this is the finest sage tobacco you can find." Reuben's eyes flickered in understanding. The young man raised the pipe to his lips and inhaled again, but Zeb noticed he did not draw smoke into his chest, letting it linger instead in his mouth. Reuben passed the pipe to Zeb in the same manner it had been given to him.

Ouray looked intently at Reuben. "How long ago was your woman promised to you?"

Reuben blinked, as Zeb repeated the question, "Since yesterday," Reuben responded.

Zeb clarified, "*Uno sol.*"

Ouray grunted, obviously well satisfied with the response. "*Tuhaye.* Good. It is not wise to let these things linger." He chuckled, then stared at Reuben for a moment before his tone turned serious again. "On your marriage, I will accept your trade, but I wish for you to add a blanket with the cow. The Noochew have few wedding rites, but the *Puwarat* will perform a ceremony this evening as we powwow with our brother bands from the north. It will be a great cause for celebration." Smiling slyly, he added, "And the first time whites have ever been joined in our village."

Zeb repeated Ouray's words to Reuben. The young man's face indicated that he caught on immediately. "Tell Ouray that Rebecca and I would be honored to be married here among the Noochew..." At the mention of the word, Ouray smiled and nodded. "...and though he has offered a very fair trade, in return for the blanket, my woman has been traveling a great distance, and has no wedding dress."

Zeb watched the Indian's face carefully as he relayed the Prussian's counteroffer. Ouray's expression was stone-like, but his eyes flickered approvingly. *He likes to trade and he is impressed that Reuben did not agree so easily.*

The Indian raised the pipe to his lips, then handed it to Reuben, smoke curling from his mouth and nose as he spoke, "Black Mare is shaped much like your woman. She has fine, ceremonial, white doeskin dresses. One, she has worn only at two ceremonies, and I will have our braves put up a lodge by the hot springs closest to where the sun sets for your wedding night."

He and Zeb exchanged knowing glances and laughed. Reuben looked from one to the other, perplexed.

"There's no time to waste in making *noohdtoohwuhch*," said Ouray, still chuckling. "Children are the heart of the family."

Zeb repeated the words and Reuben joined in their laughter, his face reddening. He turned his gaze to Ouray. "That's a fair bargain. I accept. You are right on the children. One must not wait." Ouray nodded his head vigorously, chortling, not needing Zeb to interpret Reuben's tone or intent.

Without taking his eyes from Reuben, Ouray spoke, Zeb listening carefully, interpreting the few times it was necessary.

"You have many cattle? You are asking for much Ute land for these cattle?"

Reuben looked briefly at Zeb without blinking, replying without hesitation, "We have three hundred cows and twelve bulls. We hope to double that number over the next few years. We will need enough land to build our home and barns near a creek, for water and to irrigate fields where we can grow grass to cut and feed the cows in the winter."

"Irrigate?" Ouray asked, repeating the word.

"*Irrigar*," Zeb spoke the Spanish word. "To move the water over the fields." Ouray nodded his head, still looking puzzled and Reuben continued.

"In the summer, we will bring the cattle higher in the mountains and they will graze the grass there before the first snow."

The young leader listened intently, his gaze fixed on Reuben. As they passed the pipe again, Reuben's eyes watered.

"You will never interfere," Ouray questioned, "with the Tabequache crossing over, hunting or fishing the lands on which you grow cows and build your lodge?"

Reuben shook his head solemnly. "No."

"You will never take up arms against the Tabequache or any of the northern band of Noochew without first airing your grievance to me?"

"No."

Ouray stared into the fire, absently throwing another stick on the coals, then raised his head. "I will not stop you, nor can I give you permission. Each man must follow his path. I must speak to my father, the chief, when he returns from helping Carson parlay a treaty between the white horse soldiers, our Ute brothers, the Mouache, and my father's fathers and mothers, the Jicarilla." He was silent for a long moment, then added, "Roo-bin, the most sacred of the animals to the Noochew are the *kweeyahguht*, the bear, the wolf, and the coyote. One day, perhaps, I shall tell you of this."

Saying nothing more, Ouray carefully knocked the ashes from the bowl and placed the pipe gently back in the basket, covering it with the painted deer hide. Rising, he walked over to the tipi flap, opening it and calling out an order.

Zeb could hear the sound of running footsteps receding in the direction of the fire to which Rebecca and Black Mare had been headed. *I'd give five dollars to see the look on Rebecca's face.* Then a thought struck him and he chortled, drawing Rueben's attention as Ouray returned to the fire, "What's so funny this time, Zeb?"

Zeb grinned at him, mildly feeling the sage tobacco, "I was thinking to myself about what Rebecca's gonna think of all of this and then I remembered she can't understand Black Mare's language. She may not figure it out 'til the last minute."

Reuben swallowed, then chuckled weakly, "Good, she'll be less likely to change her mind."

"Zeb-Riah," Ouray said, "there is a creek that flows northeast toward where the sun rises on the opposite side of the river that turns rock red, one third sun's ride as the river flows from the Box Canyon and La Montana de Roja. We call it *El Dallas* Creek. As one rises above the river a quarter sun's ride along the creek, the land levels. Grass grows high there, sometimes this high..." he raised a hand to his chest. "The warmth blesses the meadow most of each sun, even in the winter. The fishing is better than in the river of water that turns rock red. It would be a good place for Roo-bin and his woman to grow cattle and children."

Zeb fought with himself over whether or not to say something about Rebecca's land on the Red Mountain. *This is not the time. The mention of the Spanish land grant will only anger him.*

Reuben weighed Ouray's words carefully and then nodded, smiling. "Thank you for your guidance. The Tabequache will always be welcome at our lodge."

Reuben began to stand but Ouray motioned him to stay seated. The leader rose and walking to a far wall of the lodge, bent over another larger basket for a moment with his back to them and then turned, a beautifully beaded, fringed leather shirt in his hands. He held it up by the shoulders looking critically at Reuben, then the shirt, nodding. "It will be a little big, but will be good for the celebration." Reuben opened his mouth to protest but Zeb caught his eye with a warning squint as Ouray laid the shirt carefully in Reuben's hands.

As they stepped from the tipi, Ouray pointed across the slightly rolling, open grassy area to one misty column of steam rising from a solitary spring to the west. Two braves on ponies and a third on a horse dragging a travois piled high with lodge skins and poles were already moving toward the rising steam.

Ouray walked away, issuing a directive in a loud voice. Turning to Reuben, Zeb said quietly, but quickly, "I'm not going to mention the locations in your father's scout's map, nor the land grant in the other map. There will be another, better time, and Chief Guera Murah should be present. But I do know this Dallas Creek. It is one of the prettiest and most productive creek bottoms in the upper half of the *Uncompahgre*. It lies below the mountains they call the *Snaefel*. Better sun, less snow, higher temperatures in the winter than Red Mountain. You understand, Reuben, he has made no specific promise?"

Reuben nodded absently, obviously not focused on what he had just been told. The young man looked at the shirt in his arms, the Indians on their way to build the tipi for their wedding night and then over at the fire a hundred yards away where Black Mare and Rebecca were surrounded by a number of other women who were laughing and clapping. Rebecca appeared bewildered.

"Did you hear me?"

The young Prussian turned to Zeb, his face blank. "Sure...sure, I did."

Zeb laughed. "And another thing. Don't be expecting no big ceremony. This ain't a wedding like you've seen. Might be all of a minute or two, just for you cause of the trade, and he likes you. Most times, the brave and his woman go off to her parent's tipi—share the sleeping robe. Doubt they get much sleep though. Then come morning, that's it. They're hitched." He fixed his gaze on Reuben. "And if the woman is pregnant, then the Ute consider her married already."

Reuben blinked rapidly. "But...but what if Rebecca objects? This is kinda sudden."

Zeb slapped him heavily on the back, forcing him forward a step. "Well son, either way, that dark haired English woman is finally going to be your bride." He chuckled, stroking his mustache and looking off in the distance. "I might just have to hang out a shingle as a matchmaker." Turning his gaze east back up to the pass, a pang pulsed through his heart. *Should've pondered this before. Now I know where to come for nuptials in these parts—maybe.*

Reuben looked over toward Rebecca again, returning his gaze to Zeb, still wide-eyed. "You'll be fine, Reuben. She ain't going to say no, and Ouray will take good care of you. He'll give you a lodge to get changed and spruced up in. Most likely a brave will bring you sage leaves. Rub yourself and your armpits down with them. No need to be smellin' like the trail tonight." He grinned at the dumbfounded look in the young man's face. *Like a hare under an eagle's shadow.* "I'm gonna head up the hill, let them know what's going on and move the cattle down here quick like. I don't think anyone will want to miss the shindig. I don't suspect those critters will wander far from that green grass on the north end."

Zeb briefly relayed his intentions to Ouray. The young Ute leader nodded his approval, beaming as he surveyed the village already beginning preparations for the final night of the powwow and the wedding of the white-eyes, a surprise to them all.

June 25, 1855

*W*HITE DOESKIN

REBECCA STOOD TRANSFIXED IN THE CENTER OF THE excited women. Unable to understand but little of their chatter, she caught only a few of Black Mare's scattered Spanish words...*ella...novia...fiesta.* Hoping for an inkling of understanding, she glanced at the youngest girl, barely a woman, standing close to Black Mare. *Perhaps a younger sister?*

Black Mare stoically but warmly introduced her to each of the other females. Rebecca could neither pronounce nor remember their names, except for Chipeta's. The young woman's eyes were fixed on Rebecca, a gentle, almost sad smile playing on her lips. Like Black Mare, she was short, not much over five feet. She too wore a one-piece, loose fitting leather dress, long fringe hanging from the sleeves and tapers on the lower portion. Her black hair, parted in the middle, swung about her shoulders as she laughed, shyly covering her mouth with her hands.

Black Mare tugged on the shoulder of Chipeta's dress, gesturing and glancing at Rebecca. Chipeta leaned close, whispering something to Black Mare. Chipeta's eyebrows arched and her mouth opened. She stared at Rebecca, and then toward Reuben standing with Zeb fifty yards away in front of the lodge Black Mare shared with Ouray. Reuben appeared to be holding something leather draped over his arm and Zeb was leaning close, talking to him. Black Mare's eyes flew back to Chipeta, then to Rebecca. She held up her hands, quieting the laughter and clapping. She spoke in a serious tone, nodding toward Rebecca just a foot away before lifting her chin toward Reuben. The heads of the women swiveled, their faces etched in surprise.

Rebecca watched as Reuben turned toward the group of women, Zeb still talking to him. *He looks a bit lost. What is going on?* Her attention snapped back at the words *matrimonio* and *boda*, repeated earnestly by Black Mare.

Rebecca felt suddenly lightheaded. Her heart jumped and her fingertips pulsed with a rush of adrenaline. "Do you mean there's a wedding? My wedding?" She raised one shaky hand, pressing her fingers into her chest as she spoke and though she tried to control it, she knew her expression was far from composed. Her eyes darted between Black Mare and Chipeta, the older woman nodding at Rebecca, pointing with her chin toward Reuben, then Rebecca again. Black Mare's straight white teeth flashed brilliant in the sunlight against her sun-tanned skin. Wrapping her arms around herself, she made hugging motions, her head bobbing assent. The women surrounding them began giggling, whispering behind raised hands, nodding obliquely, first at Reuben and then at Rebecca, with teasing but genuinely warm expressions on their faces. Looking around the circle, Rebecca grinned weakly, still unable to fully grasp the implications. Young Chipeta smiled, gesturing from Rebecca to Reuben, and then raised her hand toward the sun, arching her arm toward the west where the sun would sink.

"You mean... You mean..." *Rebecca Marx, stop your stuttering.* She drew in a deep breath. Speaking very slowly, her voice quivering, she gestured, "You mean, Reuben," she pointed at the Prussian who was now walking away, two men in conversation at his side, "and I," she again raised her hand, pressing her fingers to her chest between her breasts, "are going to be married today when the sun sets?" A vision of the twinkle in Zeb's eye a short time before and his words—*and smoke the pipe to finalize the trade Reuben has proposed* flashed through her mind. *So much for any long, proper wait for the touch of my betrothed on my body again.* Her skin tingled with the memory of Reuben's hands trailing down her skin, and her cheeks warmed. Seeing the look on her face, the other women laughed, bobbing their heads vigorously, exchanging sly, suggestive looks. Rebecca's eyes flickered from face to face around the circle, awed by the glowing sense of companionship. *I could be back in England, my girlfriends gathered around, teasing me about my wedding night. Truly, we're no different—the universal energy of females.*

Black Mare spoke again, then grabbed Rebecca's hand, walking her swiftly toward her lodge with Chipeta trotting alongside. The other Ute women, chattering happily, followed close behind. Stopping at the flap of the tipi, Black Mare turned and faced the group, uttering a few short, curt commands. Disappointed murmurings erupted from the women, then more chattering as they turned and walked back toward the fire.

Chipeta opened the flap to the tipi and stood back. Black Mare quickly entered, literally pulling Rebecca inside. Rebecca breathed deeply, savoring the smell of leather and faint wood smoke, taking in the details of the baskets, a single headdress, the bed of buffalo robes, Ouray's weapons and shield. *Remarkable. So this is where Reuben made his trade. I shall have to ask them exactly what that was all about.*

Chipeta put a few sticks on the ebbing lodge fire, prodding it back to life, then joined Black Mare, who knelt by a row of baskets. Muttering to one another, they pawed through the various articles in several of the woven containers. Then Black Mare stood. "*Ayh-eeh!*" she exclaimed, holding up a leather dress by the shoulders, appraising it. She turned the garment so that the front faced Rebecca, pressing the dress against her own body and smiling broadly.

Doe hide? Rebecca marveled at the dress's creamy whiteness. The leather was evenly tanned and meticulously, perhaps even lovingly, stitched. From its collar fell a pointed, triangular pattern of blue, yellow and green beads ending in the center of a semicircular design in turquoise, which rose to pointed ends just below the shoulders. Chipeta stood proudly next to Black Mare holding a wide-fringed, light brown leather sash, two

rows of blue and red beads on its edges and silver conchos stitched every few inches around its length.

Rebecca's legs trembled. "You *are* serious. I am going
to be married tonight?"

The two women spoke rapidly to one another smiling
and nodding, pointing at the dress then to Rebecca.

Black Mare stepped toward her, holding the dress out,
her thumbs pinning the leather to Rebecca's shoulders.
"*Aye-eeh*," said young Chipeta, cocking her head to the
side, her eyes sparkling with excitement. Another rapid
succession of comments flowed between the two women,
Black Mare still holding the dress up in front of Rebecca,
Chipeta's enthusiasm needing no interpretation.

Ouray's wife stepped back, motioning to Rebecca to
undress. Not quite believing Back Mare's request, Rebecca
stuttered, "You, you want me to take my clothes off?"
Black Mare nodded, moving her hands down her own
dress, imitating the movements of disrobing.

Rebecca was unable to control her shocked expression. The two women exchanged surprised glances.
Black Mare walked to Rebecca and gently but firmly
began slipping off her light jacket while Chipeta knelt
and fumbled with the buttons at the front of her riding
skirt. Rebecca was stunned, unsure whether to protest
or giggle. Her mind raced. *Reuben may have asked me to
marry him but he certainly didn't say anything about
tonight!* Down to her chemise, bloomers and undergarment now, she had to stop herself from stomping her
foot. The two puzzled women stood back, their hands
outstretched, thumbs and forefingers testing the texture

of the chemise, admiring the silk. *They have never seen what's under these European clothes.* Black Mare gestured to continue disrobing. Rebecca could feel the heat in her cheeks as she slid off the chemise, her breasts exposed and warm in the reflection of the lodge fire, its small fresh flames reaching toward the smoke hole. Rebecca hesitated. Again, the two young women looked at one another, Black Mare motioning somewhat impatiently with her hand. Rebecca could feel her cheeks grow hot. She sighed. *What was it that I said to Inga? We are all women.* Shyly, she slid off her undergarments, standing naked in front of the two Indian women, her hands clasped self-consciously below her abdomen.

Black Mare held the chemise, bringing it to her cheek, slowly stroking the silk across her face and her neck, respectfully turning her gaze away from Rebecca. Chipeta pointed to the crumpled bloomers and undergarments on the lodge floor. Giggling, she shook her head, then arced her arm again from east to west, shaking her head again. Rebecca felt another blush climb up her cheeks. *On this night, there will be nothing between you and your man but your wedding dress, and then, not even that....*

Laying the chemise gently down on the bed of hides that she shared with Ouray, Black Mare cast a last longing look at it, then turned, pulling out another basket, round and high, which she brought to Rebecca. Chipeta gently raised Rebecca's arms up and the two women took silvery leaves from the basket, rubbing them between their hands, the pungent scent rising between them. *Sage—Silver sage; Zeb called it woman's sage.* Slowly and delicately, they feathered their hands over the entirety of Rebecca's body, their soft touch and the earthy, sweet smell reminding her of Reuben's fingertips, making her skin tingle. *This is really happening. I am to be married, in an Indian village,* a tender feeling calmed her, *to the man who is the father of my child. Ah, Mother, I do hope you're watching. You were always concerned if your daughter would ever marry.* She chuckled and Black Mare nodded, casting her eyes down but not before Rebecca saw her mouth curl into an approving smile. Rebecca lifted her own gaze toward the smoke hole, the blue sky beyond seeming to waver as the heat and smoke rose from the lodge fire.

JOHANNES LIMPED SLOWLY TO BENTE, GRINNING AND carrying his saddle. His chuckle morphed to a wince as he threw the heavy leather over her back and adjusted the cinch. "That's some news from Zeb, isn't it, Bente? Now, how do you suppose that farm boy talked milady Rebecca Marx of London into a wedding in an Ute camp on half a days' notice?" *Maybe Reuben ought to be instructing me in the ways of women.* "I can't wait to see this."

Bente shook, adjusting the fit of the saddle on her withers and blew softly. "Not all that enthusiastic, eh girl?" Johannes laughed, patting the mare's rump. Leaning his elbows over the trough to give his leg a rest, Johannes looked up at the sky, cloudless and brilliant. *Going to be good to be back on the horse—always hated driving wagons.*

He chortled again, thoroughly amused. *Better check these saddlebags.* He tightened the rawhide ties to the twin leather pouches behind the saddle, rummaging in one, then the other, his fingers finding his tin cup, leather gloves, extra knife, ammunition and a folded piece of heavy paper. *What the hell is that?* Pulling it out, he unfolded the paper. MISSING—DOROTHY ANNE EBERLYN—Age 14. *Oh! That notice from the mercantile about that poor girl whose family was killed.* Shaking his head, he refolded the poster, turning to throw it in the coals of the fire yet to be extinguished by Michael, then hesitated. He opened it again, reading, then shrugging, and shoved it back half folded into the saddlebag. Lifting his left leg with hands clasped beneath his thigh, he positioned his toe in the stirrup, lifting himself painfully into the saddle. "Come on, Bente—we got a wedding in an Indian village between a Prussian farmer and an English aristocrat to go see!"

"How much longer do you think, Philippe?" A tinge of anxiety crept into Johannes' question.

"Maybe another hour." Pushing back the brim of his sombrero, Philippe looked up at the sun, not yet setting but threatening to soon touch the ridgelines in the western skyline. "We'll make it, *Señor* Johannes. When we get to this gap, I'll ride ahead. There's no place for these cows to go except the trail from what *Señor* Zeb told us. You and *Señor* Zeb stay behind and keep them moving.

I don't think either wagon will have any trouble. *El muchacho es un careterro muy fino.*"

"Yep, he does handle those lines well. Did you see the way he eased that wagon around those downed trees?" Johannes glanced nervously at the sun, then back down the trail toward the wagons in front of them.

"*Señor* Zeb had a good idea on the spotted ponies. When we get the cattle out of the canyon, I will take the two spotted horses west into the trees and tie them off for the night, hidden on a long tether line. *Mañana*, I will return and lead them through the trees on the north edge of the meadow to where the cows will be. Hopefully, the two *Indio* guards at the bottom of the canyon, with so many cows, riders and wagons passing before them, will not take close notice."

Behind them rang the ding and dong of the lead cow's bell and behind her, the cries of more cows, louder and more frequent as the narrowing of the trail pressed them together.

Philippe rose in the saddle looking ahead. "*Señorita* Sarah's wagon has just entered the canyon. I shall ride up there and make sure she has no problems."

Johannes reached out his arm, resting a hand briefly and lightly on Philippe's forearm. "You know there's kind of a promise between Zeb and Sarah?"

Cocking his head toward Johannes, he looked directly into the tall man's blue eyes. "*Señorita* Sarah has told me they are not betrothed. Is this incorrect?"

"No," Johannes said, Philippe pleased by the sound of admittance in his voice, "but there is a history between them going all the way back to St. Louis."

Philippe allowed a smile to play on his lips. "I see," he said, spurring Diablo into a trot without a further word, feeling Johannes' concerned eyes on his back as he rode to catch up with Sarah's wagon.

REUBEN FINISHED RUBBING HIS NECK WITH THE SAGE leaves from the basket the young Ute man had brought him, his eyes surveying the interior of the lodge he had been given to prepare for the wedding. *Fewer baskets and no headdress. Only one piece of beaver pelt art,* his eyes ranged the leather wall, *and slightly smaller, too.* He slipped on his trousers and then the ceremonial leather shirt Ouray had lent him, the heavy leather brushing across his back as it slid over his shoulders down to below his hips. Aside from some looseness in the shoulders, the shirt fit well.

His head snapped up at the sound of running feet and shouts outside the tipi. From a distance, the faint cries of cattle and the whoops and whistles of Johannes, Philippe and Zeb drifted in, muted by the lodge's hide walls. *The outfit!* A slow, rhythmic beating of drums began mingling with the sounds of the approaching herd and the hum of voices toward the fire rising as more Indians congregated. Smoothing his hands over the shirt's beadwork, Reuben swallowed, fighting a prolonged pang of anxiety. *I wonder what Rebecca's doing? And what she's thinking?*

The three women had poked their heads out of the tipi as the loud excitement erupted all around the lodge when the cattle first came through but now the commotion had died down, replaced by the buzz of many voices from the direction of the main fire. Rebecca listened as the muffled grunts of the cattle receded slowly to the north. Black Mare and Chipeta stood only a few steps from her, moving their heads from side-to-side, looking critically at the brown leather sash tied around her waist. Every few seconds, one or the other of the two women darted forward to straighten a piece of twisted fringe bent from long storage in the basket or to adjust the belt to a slightly different height. Finally, they circled around her, nodding approvingly, talking rapidly to one another, Black Mare pulling the collar line up at the back of Rebecca's neck. From outside, Rebecca heard the rattle of the wagons and Sarah's voice, muted by the tipi. "Whoa there." Suddenly struck with an idea, she turned, walking toward the tipi flap, waving for Chipeta and Black Mare to follow her.

Outside the lodge, the village was full of activity, people streaming toward the fire from all directions, talking and laughing. Sarah was tying off the lines of the prairie schooner, stopped a hundred yards away, and was preparing to climb down from the driver seat. Motioning to the two Ute women to follow her, Rebecca walked briskly toward the wagon, the redhead looking up as they approached, her jaw dropping.

June 25, 1855

TRADITIONS

"WHEN I FIRST LOOKED, I THOUGHT THERE WERE THREE Indian women coming up to the wagon," Sarah exclaimed, her eyes round and shifting nervously from Rebecca to Black Mare and Chipeta. "Is it true? You're really getting married tonight?"

Without breaking her stride, her gaze brushing past Sarah, Rebecca nodded curtly, "This is Chipeta and Black Mare." At the sound of their names, the two women nodded and smiled at Sarah, who tentatively raised her hand in a partial wave, her mouth still open.

Ignoring her, Rebecca opened the tailgate, pulling out the ladder. She climbed into the wagon and turned, motioning Black Mare and Chipeta to join her. Chipeta glanced at Black Mare for permission, who nodded, and then the two women clambered up to the wagon bed.

Rebecca made straight for the trunk at the head of Sarah's bedroll. Opening its large, domed and ornately scrolled top, she rummaged through the trunk quickly, casting articles of clothing haphazardly behind her over the bed, finally finding what she had been searching for. Straightening up, she turned with a white silk chemise in her hand, handing it to Black Mare with a smile. Ouray's wife gasped, taking the garment and smoothing it in her fingers, grinning broadly. Looking at the younger woman apologetically, Rebecca suddenly raised a finger in the air, "Wait, I do have something for you." She turned and bent over the trunk again, objects flying around the wagon, straightening up with a black tweed riding jacket, silver embroidery on its rounded edges and red buttons vertical in three lines across the breast under the shoulders. Holding it out toward Chipeta, she spread the shoulders of the garment between her hands. "Yes, this will definitely fit. It has always been a bit too small for me. Try it on." Chipeta looked at her, not comprehending until Rebecca made the motions of putting on the jacket. Understanding flashed across Chipeta's eyes. She donned the jacket, pulling on its lapels to position it over her shoulders, and then slowly twirled so that Black Mare and Rebecca could see. Black Mare nodded approvingly.

"*Muy bonita,*" Rebecca said, smiling at her awkward Spanish.

Hastily gathering the clothing strewn around the wagon, Rebecca shoved it in a jumbled bundle back into the trunk. She wheeled briskly to her bedroll, rolling it half back and removed the flour sack wedged between two trunks to level off the surface under the bedroll. Opening one of the trunks, she reached in an arm, groping carefully. "Ah, there they are," she exclaimed, gingerly withdrawing two rolled skirts, unwrapping and spreading them out on Sarah's bedroll. In each was an ornate wineglass etched with gold in a grape leaf design. She held them up and both women gasped. "I will need these for the *boda*." Smiling, she gazed at the goblets. *You surprised me, Mr. Frank. Now it is my turn to surprise you.* Pulling a small, heavy towel from the trunk, she carefully rolled the wine glasses securely cushioning the crystal stemware so that they did not touch one another.

SARAH PURSED HER LIPS AS SHE WATCHED REBECCA, Black Mare and Chipeta walk away, the fringe at the bottom of all three women's dresses swaying with the movement of their hips, Rebecca carefully cradling the rolled towel under her arms. The two Indian women looked back, smiling and waving, their figures silhouetted against the setting sun but Rebecca did not turn around. *Well, milady Marx, it appears even a wedding has not thawed your ill temper.*

Sarah turned at the sound of a horse coming in at a lope. Philippe reined in Diablo only feet from where she stood, the big black stallion snorting, reaching out his muzzle and roughly nuzzling her chin. Raising her hand, she stroked his nose. "He is a beautiful horse, Philippe."

Brushing the dust from his sleeves and hat, the vaquero nodded, a smile blazing across his olive-tanned face. "Like his master, *Señorita* Sarah," he said, his eyes burning into hers, "he does not usually take to people."

Sarah stared back, transfixed for a moment, then looked hastily away. *I hope Zeb is not watching.*

"The sun will be down in about half an hour. That's when the festivities will start," he paused, studying her face, "I thought... I thought maybe we could go over and watch together."

Sarah searched the meadow, looking out toward the distant dots of the cattle for Zeb. *I can't very well go alone.* "I'd like that, Philippe."

Philippe sprang from the saddle. "Diablo, you stay here and mind the wagon." The stallion snorted, his head shaking up and down. "Are you ready to go, *Señorita* Sarah?" Grinning, Philippe held out his elbow for her to put her arm through.

"Give me just five minutes, Philippe. Let me freshen up, put a little rouge on and change my skirt and jacket— oh, and brush my hair."

"*¿Cinco minutos?*" Philippe's eyebrows raised.

Sarah giggled. "Okay, cinco minutos...well, I promise not more than ten. This is Reuben's wedding. I can't very well attend looking like a dust ball."

Philippe smiled. "*Señor* Zeb," he watched her face closely, "said it will be very brief, so we should not be late."

Sarah, halfway to the back of the wagon by now, turned, "Surely a minute or two will not matter."

Philippe simply grinned. "Better to not take a chance, *Señorita*..." adding as Sarah turned again, "It is *Señorita* Rebecca's wedding, too."

Sarah fought against the tightening in her jaw. Whirling without saying a word, she took the few steps to the ladder.

MORE THAN ONE HUNDRED UTE CLANSMEN WERE already gathered around one of two large bonfires in a large circle, their numbers swelling steadily. On one side of the fire, two small earthen pots, twenty feet apart, glowed, tendrils of fragrant smoke rising from them. Behind the smudge pots, a man and a woman, dressed in colorful ceremonial leathers, beat a slow rhythm on drums set ten feet apart. Leaving the drums, they danced to either side of the smudge pots, singing in low guttural tones, shaking tortoise shell rattles in each hand, their rattling in seductive cadence with one another.

Sarah glanced nervously around for Zeb, then up at Philippe. *I do like the feel of my arm in his.* Philippe was intent on the drummers. Several in the gathering cast curious stares at them, their faces seeming to harden when their appraisal moved to Philippe's sombrero.

Her eye was caught by the activity at the second lower, but far wider, fire visible fifty yards from the crowd growing around the first. A number of women labored in its glow, several laying out food on two logs which had been split in half and set on stumps, the others slowly turning thick, sharpened sticks skewered through four hindquarters of elk, either side of the skewers resting in the crooked fork of branches that had been cut and stuck into the ground several feet from the edge of the fire ring, which glowed ever brighter in the growing darkness

"That'll be where the powwow ends," said Philippe leaning close and following her gaze. "Generally the visiting tribes leave the day after a powwow for their main villages. It seems these *Indios*," he swept his arm around the buzzing, ever-expanding circle of Indians, "they are staying to see the wedding." He chuckled. "If the gringo army had not stolen it, I would bet my *estancia* that none of them have ever seen white eyes married. I have heard Utes have no formal wedding. Many of these *Indios* have never seen a wedding ceremony of any sort."

"Then how do they get married?"

Philippe looked down her, his eyes smoldering with insinuated invitation, "They do what's natural between a man and a woman, *Señorita* Sarah, and that marries them."

STANDING IN THE SHADOWS AT THE EDGE OF THE GROUP of Utes on the opposite side of the fire, Zeb ran long fingers down his mustache watching Sarah and Philippe, a bile building in his chest, half anger, half hurt. *Seems our talk didn't mean much.*

From directly behind him boomed Johannes' voice. "Quite a crowd. Haven't they ever seen a wedding before?"

Zeb tried to laugh. "No, Johannes, they probably haven't." Zeb couldn't help grinning at the comically quizzical look on Johannes' face. The Dane turned to Michael, immediately behind him, shouting above the rising din, "See this, Michael. One day you'll meet a pretty girl and wind up in this type of commotion."

Michael looked up at Johannes, his eyes wide, a slight smile on his face, his hands nervously twisting together "I ain't... I ain't getting ma... ma... ma... married."

Johannes threw a lanky arm around the boy's shoulders and shook him gently, "All smart men find a good woman and settle down sometime." His face momentarily clouded, "It's the dumb ones that don't."

Focused on Sarah and Philippe again, Zeb said absently, "The *puwarat* ought to be jumpin' out any time now."

"The what?"

Zeb tore his eyes from Sarah. Glancing briefly at Johannes, he leaned forward slightly to see Michael who had voiced the question. "They call their shaman the *puwarat*, and their medicine man, the *boca'gant*. They have great *puwa*, son, great power." Michael drew his head back, the quizzical expression on his face unchanged.

Johannes' tone was sarcastic, "*Puwa*? And where does this magical power come from?"

Zeb frowned, "Careful, Johannes, some of these Utes know some English. You never want to joke about their medicine or their customs. They set great store in *puwa*. All the Indians believe in *puwa* one way or the other. It is the energy that binds all things, the energy stored in all things. And anyone, but especially the *puwarat* and *boca'gant*, can direct the energy for good or evil. All Indians believe it to some extent. Call it by different names, of course." Zeb stared hard at Johannes. "And they'd be right, Johannes. God don't reside just in some church."

Johannes opened his mouth to retort but the murmur of the crowd suddenly changed, its tone intensifying.

The shaman burst into the ring of the firelight, his intricate ceremonial regalia beaded in a variety of dazzling colors that sparkled with different hues in the firelight, a bear's head, mouth open, fangs showing, resting on his own, the sleek brown pelt shimmering in folds over his shoulders. He held two large leather gourds in his hands high above his head. As he shook them, lights flashed around the leather.

Johannes stared, "My God, Zeb, how do they create those lights?"

"Inside them rattles is quartz. Not many other tribes have figured it out, but when you put them rocks in the gourd and shake 'em hard and quick, them rubbing together somehow creates white flashes of lights around the outside of the rattle. The Noochew believe it to be one of the symbols of power of the *puwarat*."

Impatient, Zeb turned back toward where Sarah and Philippe had been standing, but lost sight of them as the crowd gathered closer. Out in the circle of flickering orange-red light, the shaman shook his rattles, first at one smudge pot, and then the other, the white cracks of light around the leather mysteriously mingling with the sage smoke. The watchers grew silent, an air of expectancy settling over them.

"What are those smoking pots?" Johannes whispered, leaning toward Zeb.

Zeb turned toward Johannes, replying quickly, "Them would be smudge pots filled with sage and cedar. Smoke cleanses the air and drives away bad spirits. Reckon they'll be bringing Rebecca and Reuben out shortly." Zeb fell silent as either side of the circle began to part, braves and Indian women shuffling backward forming corridors with their bodies. *But no sign of Sarah.*

Then, out from the shadows, came Ouray leading Reuben. Zeb had never seen the Indian leader so magnificently dressed, a breastplate of double-sided antler over ceremonial leathers decorated with quillwork and embroidered with hundreds of beads that sparkled in the firelight, his feathered headdress flowing down almost to the back of his knees. Following him was Reuben, wearing a ceremonial reddish brown leather shirt, ornately fringed and cross-stitched with patterns of beads. Zeb made a mental note that he was not wearing his holster. Instead, he had tucked the Colt into a wide, cream-colored beaded belt tied on the side with strands of rawhide. His cowboy hat, pulled low over his forehead, accentuated the shadows cast by the flames.

They reached the center of the space between the smudge pots, Reuben standing facing the fire, his back to the slow beat of the drums. Ouray stepped backward several steps, leaving the young Prussian out alone under the dissecting gaze of hundreds of pairs of eyes.

Another murmur arose. Black Mare walked slowly through the opposite corridor of bodies, swaying gently to the drums and into the circle of firelight followed by Rebecca, then Chipeta. There were excited murmurs from the women in the crowd and guttural grunts of praise from many of the men. Rebecca's long dark hair fell across her shoulders, accentuating the creamy white leather of her dress, which—Zeb couldn't help but notice—snugged to the curve of her hips, the V-shape of its embroidered yoke falling from the neckline to just above her bosom, and its fringed hem swishing hypnotically side to side with her every step.

Rebecca wore beaded moccasins, and above them colorful beaded ankle bracelets rose to the fringe hanging from her dress. The soft leather mounds of Rebecca's breasts, accentuated by the crescent-shaped embroidery sweeping across her midsection, were enough to rouse any man. Watching, Zeb thought again of Sarah and fought down a few urges that seemed none too gentlemanly. In contrast, Rebecca's expression seemed stunned. Under one arm, she carried a tightly rolled towel.

Black Mare led her into the space between the smudge pots, then stopped, and smiled gently toward the Prussian, guiding Rebecca with a hand on the brunette's arm to within a foot of Reuben, positioning their bodies back-to-back, sides to the fire, the couple centered in the rising smoke of the smoldering sage.

Like her husband, Black Mare retreated backward several steps, standing next to the Ouray—*in attendance but not on display*. The shaman leapt from between the drums again, his rapidly moving rattles sparking white. He was chanting and moving rhythmically to the increasing tempo of the drums. Dancing between the couple and the fire, he turned suddenly, facing Rebecca and Reuben from the side, white lights bursting from the rattles as he shook them down the outsides of each of their bodies, from shoulders to ankles. He reversed the direction of the rattles, still chanting, repeating the process, but this time beginning at their feet. Handing off the rattles through the darkness to Ouray, he danced, swaying back and forth in front of Rebecca and Reuben, slowly drawing from the inside of his shirt a type of brush with long heavy, reed ends pouring from its bone handle. The beat of the drums quickened as did the movements of the *puwarat*, undulating first to one smudge pot brushing the smoke toward Reuben, then toward Rebecca, backhanded, then forehanded, three times each way. Then swaying, the bear skull on his head appearing almost alive, to the other smudge where he repeated the brushing procedure moving the smoke toward the couple. Moving catlike toward them, he reached out his hands to either of their far shoulders, slowly turning their bodies until they faced one another. He held the brush in the air, uttered a piercing cry and took two quick steps backward out of the direct light of the fire.

The drums stopped. There were shouts and many of the women began to clap their hands again. Zeb scanned the crowd around the fire.

"That's all?" Johannes asked, his voice incredulous.

Zeb turned back toward him, "That's it. That's the whole shebang."

The crowd grew suddenly silent. Looking back into the firelight, Zeb watched, engrossed, as Rebecca unwrapped the towel she had been carrying, letting it drop to her feet. She stretched her arms skyward, each hand holding a wine goblet. There was an excited gasp from the circle, some of the crowd stepping forward to see better. Twirling the goblets in her fingers above her head, the flames caught on the gold inlay, glittering and shining a yellow-orange as she turned back to Reuben, her face looking up at his, the crowd murmuring.

Zeb's gaze shifted from Rebecca and Reuben, once again searching the gathering. His body tensed as he found the outline of Philippe's sombrero in the shadows, Sarah's small figure standing next to him. A sick feeling lanced through him as he watched the vaquero lift her chin with his finger and bend his head down toward hers, his sombrero obscuring both their faces.

Zeb didn't need to see their lips meet. *She's gonna kiss him back.* He pivoted on his heels, blood rising, anger replacing whatever thoughts he might have had. He gave a quick nod toward Johannes, not trusting himself to meet the Dane's eyes. He broke from the circle, his gut twisted and his heart racing, his mind numb. *Gotta find Buck. Leave a note. Can't be around folks. Need to go home.*

Now, where the hell is he going? Not wanting to miss any part of the ceremony, Johannes looked quickly over his shoulder at Zeb's tall, retreating form. When he looked back, he realized how engrossed he'd been— he hadn't even noticed Michael had stepped forward and was standing next to him. The teenager's lips formed a circle, his eyes wide, and his eyebrows had disappeared under his hat brim as he stared fixated at the activity by the fire, the spellbound crowd and Rebecca.

REUBEN'S EYES WERE FILLED WITH LOVING ADMIRATION, a hint of a smile playing on his face as he looked down at her. *He is so handsome.* The circle had grown completely silent, the Utes looking at one another impressed by the wine glasses and wondering what strange custom the white eyes were engaged in. Rebecca turned her head toward Black Mare who smiled, reaching behind her and picking up a bladder bag, then stepping forward, filling both wine glasses with tobacco sage tea. Rebecca handed one filled glass to Reuben, who took it from her hand with an amazed look on his face. "Where in the world...? I'll be go to hell."

Rebecca giggled, her face radiant. "No, Mr. Frank, you are not going to hell; you are going to be married and if we are to be wed Ute style, we should at least throw in a few Jewish traditions." Her tone grew soft. Looking into his eyes she said, "Had I had more warning, I would have insisted on you doing the *Tish*." The pleased twinkle in the young Prussian's eyes made her smile.

"Where did you...?"

A coy, mischievous smile played on Rebecca's lips. "I smuggled them from the trunks you so brutally forced me to leave behind in St. Louis." *What were Inga's words?* "A girl has to do what a girl has to do."

Reuben grinned down at her. "Are these for what I think they're for?"

"That's right, Reuben" she said quietly, "Our marriage is also the marriage of two traditions, the first, of these wonderful people who have blessed us with their hospitality and customs." She swept her arm at the circle of Indians who murmured, transfixed by the white eye's ritual but understanding the gratitude in Rebecca's tone. "And now we are about to share with them the ancient Jewish custom of the breaking of the glasses."

They raised their stemware toward one another, extending and interlocking their arms, each drinking over the elbow of the other, their eyes fixed on one another. Unlocking their arms, Rebecca took the glass from Reuben and kneeling, placed both glasses side-by-side on the towel, which she had spread on the ground. The sun-lit warmth still rising from the earth wafted evocatively up her leather dress, caressing her bare skin. Wrapping the ends of the cloth over the goblets, she stood, holding out her hand to Reuben. Looking at one another, they raised their right feet in unison and with a smashing motion, brought their heels down on the towel, shattering the covered wine glasses. The crowd gasped, many of them whispering to one another and pointing.

Taking her other hand in his, Reuben faced her, "I love you Rebecca Marx. Would you accept the honor of marrying me this night?"

Reuben's face was blurry and she felt the cool trail of tears streaking her cheeks. She blinked. *For the first time, I know.* The noise of the crowd faded and the circle of Utes became but a blur, her entire being focused on the man in front of her. *The man whose baby grows inside me; the man whose touch brings feelings I never knew existed; the man who has risked his life to protect mine.* She could feel the tremble in her lips as she smiled up at him. "I do accept, Reuben Frank, and I, Rebecca Marx..." her voice broke and she took a deep breath, "... am not only proud to be marrying you this night..." she paused, biting on her lip to still the quiver, trying to will away her tears, "but I do love you, Reuben—very much. I am *in love* with you."

A wide astonished grin spread across Reuben's face, a soft tenderness in his eyes. He cleared his throat, "I think, Mistress Marx, we are now married."

Rebecca blinked several times, trying to focus his misty image. "And I think Mr. Frank, this is where you kiss me." Reuben leaned forward, his lips meeting hers. She molded her body to him, their flesh seeking one another through the leather that separated them.

There were shouts and claps and the drums began to beat again as their lips parted.

Ouray and Black Mare moved toward them, standing close, Chipeta slightly behind, all three bobbing their heads and smiling, Black Mare's and Chipeta's eyes dropping to the towel that covered the shattered goblets.

Though her voice was low and throaty, Johannes had caught most of Rebecca's words as she gazed teary eyed up into Reuben's face. "...I love you Reuben...I am in love with you." *Congratulations my friend; live long and happy with your bride.*

Johannes' delight in the moment and the unusual scene was briefly darkened by a nagging sense of loss, and a tinge of jealousy. *Could've been a double wedding, maybe. Inga, I do miss you so—I hope you heard my whisper in your ear there at the end.*

The shadowy image of the sketch of the missing young girl in the poster flashed across his mind, combining with the memory of Inga's pleading, frightened eyes looking up into his from the crook of his arm at Two Otters Creek. *Tragedy and life—inseparable.* He cleared his throat, glancing quickly left and right to see if anyone had been watching or sensing his thoughts, then forced his attention back to the fire. Reuben and Rebecca were locked in a passionate kiss, their bodies molded together, the crowd around him whispering, smiling and nodding approval. *I'll congratulate them in private tomorrow. Their minds will be elsewhere tonight.*

BLACK MARE REACHED OUT A HAND SQUEEZING REBECCA'S arm, while Ouray looked at Rebecca and Reuben, nodding approval, his eyes shining. Many in the crowd moved toward the second fire from which wafted the enticing aroma of grilling elk. Reuben glanced for a moment out into the darkness in the direction of the faint sounds of galloping hooves, then over Rebecca's head toward the food, but Ouray tapped him on the shoulder, shaking his head and pointing in the opposite direction toward the dark cone shape of the wedding tipi one hundred fifty yards away.

Reuben turned to her. "I think," he gulped, mouthing the word once before he could speak it, "wife...Ouray insists we go down to the tipi and investigate the *puwa* of that hot spring." Reuben's smile turned inviting and seductive. "If I remember correctly, milady Marx, you made certain promises that the wait for our wedding night would be worthwhile."

Rebecca felt the moist and languid warmth of desire begin to spread through her. Gazing up into his eyes, she ran her fingertips down his cheek, whispering in response, "And Rebecca Marx always keeps her promises, husband. Take your *Eesha* to our honeymoon cottage," she smiled, "and you can decide which holds the most heat—the water from the spring, or your wife." Reuben's cheeks darkened. She saw a primal hunger steal into his stare and without a word, he turned, holding her hand, leading her toward the wedding lodge, the steam rising silver in the moonlight just beginning to spill over the eastern ridges.

June 25, 1855

*U*NCOMPAHGRE

WITH A REPROACHFUL SNORT, BUCK CRANED HIS NECK back at Zeb as the mountain man gave the cinch a final angry tug.

"Sorry, Buck," Zeb said, patting the tobiano's rump, "ain't right to be taking it out on you."

The reins and lead rope to the mules in one hand, his other on the saddle horn, and one moccasin toe suspended in a stirrup, Zeb looked back over his shoulder at the glow of the fires and the milling throng. *Must be over; most of the crowd is headin' toward the food.*

Mounting, in one fluid movement, he wheeled Buck and dug his heels into the mustang's side, the horse accelerating under him even as they turned. At a gallop, they raced northwest across the meadow into the darkness, the headwaters of the Rio Grande shining silver in the rising moon, the hum of the wedding and the sounds of the feast fading rapidly behind them. Zeb didn't look back, concentrating instead on the memory of towering conifers, ledges, the rich rusty earth of Red Mountain and the cabin he called home. He thought of the warm glow of the cabin's oil lamp shining dully on the interior logs, the solitude drawing him like a magnet. *Gotta get back to the mountain. Be alone.*

Behind them, the mules wheezed in protest, not used to much more than a fast walk over the previous months. Leaning low over Buck's front shoulders, Zeb looked back at the three dark shapes behind the mustang, giving a sharp tug to the lead rope in his left hand. "Stop your bellyachin'. We'll slow down a mite in a couple of miles."

They galloped through the cattle, cows clumsily lurching from their path, moaning in low-throated objections. By the time they reached the tree line, the moon had cleared the eastern ridgeline, its silver debut transforming to a dull reddish-orange. *Like her hair.* Zeb's jaw muscles tightened as he slowed Buck's pace to a trot giving the tobiano his head through the trees. The mules, relieved at being out of a gallop, fell single file into a silent, grey line behind the mustang.

June 27, 1855

AFTER TWO DAYS OF SOLID RIDING, THE MULES GRAZED contentedly, shifting their weight from one rear haunch to another and from shoulder to shoulder, resting their weary muscles.

Four hundred feet lower and several miles out from them, three fires silhouetted the sunset-softened outline of Fort Uncompahgre. Zeb waited one hundred feet inside the tree line, studying the broad delta of the confluence of the Uncompahgre and Gunnison rivers. Buck stood slightly behind him. "Wish I had Mac's spyglass," he said in a low tone to the horse, the mental picture of the spyglass in Reuben's coat evoking a pang of guilt, which Buck punctuated with a snort and a stiff, simultaneous push of his nose into the small of Zeb's back.

Zeb turned to the tobiano, running his hand twice down the mustang's cheek. "What are you trying to tell me, Buck? I shouldn't have left? I'd made it clear which trail to take. Johannes will find that note. They're all trail wise, and Reuben's got a head on his shoulders. They'll know the way."

Buck cocked his head, rolling his eyes. One big brown eye stared directly into Zeb's through the murk of dusk, one ear flicked forward. "You ain't helping, horse. We'll feel better when we get back home." *And not so unsettled.*

Leaning one shoulder against a tree, he gauged the last pale band of yellow-pink light where the sun had set. Buck nuzzled his head, knocking off the coonskin cap. "Hold your hooves, Buck. We ain't going nowhere 'til it's dark and we can't be seen from the fort. We'll skirt around this timberline and hope we beat the rise of that damn moon." He nestled his shoulder against the tree again, reaching into his shirt, pulling out his tobacco and biting off a hunk.

Chewing slowly, he watched the far distant fires brighten with the descent of the dark. He fought a feeling of unease mixed with loss, tinged with another pang of guilt. Gathering up the lead ropes of the mules, he joined the animals in a straight line behind the mustang, knotting the end of the lead rope to Buck's saddle. Mounting the tobiano, he immediately leaned over, sliding the Sharps from its belly scabbard. He checked the load, placing the rifle across his thighs, and pulled both pistols from his belt, checking to make sure each of the Colt's cylinders held a round, and then the ball and cap weapon, holding it close to his eye, critically examining the primer. He shoved both pistols back in his belt and then, sitting motionless, fixed his eyes on the remnants of the trading post miles out. *They ought to be pushing them cows over this ridge four or five days from now.*

A nagging voice spoke from another corner of his mind, *Go back. Settle things with the redhead once and for all.* He looked west to the high, mostly flat silhouette that marked the edge of the Grand Mesa, the last trace of pink and crimson almost drowned by the steel grey indigo of the rapidly descending night. *Ain't good to be confused in this country. It'll get you killed,* he reprimanded the second voice in his brain.

"It's about time, Buck," he said to the impatient mustang, an air of purposeful finality in his voice, "We're going home." Urging Buck gently forward with a squeeze of his knees and a soft "click, click" from his tongue, the tobiano began to ease through the trees, zig-zagging, leading the string of mules, Zeb checking every so often to make sure they were not skylined to eyes anywhere below.

June 30, 1855

ZEB LOOKED AROUND CAREFULLY, HIS EYES INVESTIGATing every contour, small patch of brush or cluster of willows. Satisfied, he lifted his scan to the broken tree line a half-mile out in either direction. Towering, rugged faces and spines of rock rose above the conifers and aspen patches on the south and east sides of the valley. A wide break in the rugged contours directly across from them to the west marked Dallas Creek where the muddy waters of early summer tumbled out, mingling turbulently with the rushing, reddish flow of the Uncompahgre boiling toward its marriage with the Gunnison. *Dang, can't get that wedding off my mind.* Then high overhead, a bald eagle screeched. *Good omen. Guess I made the right decision.*

Sure that no one could be concealed within rifle shot range, Zeb reined in Buck, curled a lanky leg over the horse's withers in front of the saddle horn and rolled a smoke, his eyes continuing to search the terrain. Lifting his face from time to time, he enjoyed the warmth of the midmorning sun, smiling at the looming jumble of peaks ten miles up valley where he knew the flanks of the mountains narrowed into a box canyon, marking the beginning of Red Mountain Pass. The red rocks and soils of *La Montana Roja* shimmered between dense, dark green lines of the conifer swaths that reached, like groping fingers, up toward the barren red alpine crags of the mountain and lingering snow cornices.

Dismissing another tug of conscience, he took a deep breath. "Almost home. Feels good, don't it, Buck?" The tobiano shook his head, craning his neck back, then looked forward and blew. "If you ain't pleased, I can't help it." Zeb raised the cigarette to his lips, wetting it, then lit the smoke with his flint, dragging deeply, his eyes shifting from the faint trail ahead weaving upriver past Uncompahgre Peak and toward the Red, *El Diente*, and Wetterhorn mountains at the head of the narrowing valley, then to the less rugged terrain that marked the sloping and meandering plain of Dallas Creek, which spilled in from the direction of the Snaefel. Wrestling with himself, he took another puff on the cigarette, then absently flicked it with his middle finger and thumb into a patch of soggy snow.

The cigarette landed, its smoke quickly extinguished. Zeb shook his head. *Wasn't too smart, throwing away half a cigarette. Gotta get myself undistracted.* Straightening his leg, he picked up the reins, then sighed, setting them down again, his hand on the saddle horn, his gaze shifting from Dallas Creek to upstream along the Uncompahgre. Buck bent his neck back at him again, then, hackamore jiggling, wagged his muzzle three times up toward Dallas Creek, and whinnied.

Zeb sighed again. "Well, hell, Buck, you got a point. We got plenty of time to get to the cabin before dark. While we're here, we could mosey up Dallas Creek and see if it looks like what I told Reuben. Imagine he's thinking about it also. Want to make sure I told him right. Might be some beaver sign, too."

They wound their way slowly up alongside the creek, taking the southwest fork a bit more than a mile above the Uncompahgre, skirting wide where the willows thickened, detouring often to avoid deep, lingering snowdrifts in hollows or on the north side of swales, Zeb's eyes roving the landscape. The paint's head was high, ears pricked, a slight prance in his climbing step, alert but relaxed, seeming to be in better spirits than he had been for days.

Jagged saw tooth peaks, shimmering white with snow yet to melt, cradled the valley, their power and protection like a grand hand, fingertips dusted in flour curled upright around the palm of the plateaus. Jagged pinnacles kissed the cloudless sky, the long imposing line of the Snaefel anchored by their highest point, Snaefel Mountain, rising abruptly four miles to the southwest, their grey faces and avalanche chutes guardians of the plateaus, lending power and ancient energy to the meadows.

Zeb and Buck, mules trailing behind, broke out on a bench, its widest expanses a mile across. The gently rolling surface was lush with early grass; its slope ending to the west and north at the toe of a narrow, treed ridge. The creek disappeared over a short rise to yet another plateau above them to the southwest. Pockets of aspen trees, some interspersed with conifers, dotted every contour of the spiny ridge. Staggered willows, alders and aspens lined the creek as it snaked across the bench from above.

The air was thick with the smells and sounds of early summer growth. The cries of hawks and shrill of birds serenaded the meadows. Colored patches of wildflowers popped from the green of the grass and the grey-blue of occasional sage. *Yep. As pretty as I remembered it.* He looked southeast toward the sharp tops of Wetterhorn, Uncompahgre, *El Diente* and Red Mountain Pass, *and my cabin,* then back at the Snaefel. "Well, hell, Buck. We're here, and the sun ain't hardly moved. Let's gander up at that next little rise around this ridge and see that top meadow."

They made their way across the moist ground, squishy from recent melt under the four sets of hooves, the grass already shin high and deep green. The splashes of wildflowers quivered in the slight wind.

Riding slowly up the shallow rise, they skirted the edge of the massive stand of mature aspens and young quakies that marked the southwest beginning of the ridge. The upper bench had slightly less grass, and a bit more lingering snow. Conifers dotted its upper reaches, jostling with aspens for position. Zeb reined, looking behind them at the green of the lower meadow dissected by the serpentine sliver of Dallas Creek squeezed between its phalanx of willows and alder.

Lifting himself in the saddle, he twisted backward to the north, his eyes following the course of the Uncompahgre downriver, the current visible here and there through the low broken ridgeline below them, its rushing thread disappearing in the distance toward the delta. *Wonder where they are now? Maybe two days from coming down on Fort Uncompahgre?*

Settling back down in the saddle, he took up the fixings to roll another smoke, studying the higher of the two bench meadows. *Could grow a passel of hay here. And a direct shot for movin' them cows up into that high coun-*

try below them peaks each year when the snow clears. That ridge would break the west wind. His eyes slowly returned to the bench below them. The creek reflected brown-blue from this angle as it cut a crooked course across the rolling green. "Waddaya think, Buck? Back up there in them aspens where the slope falls off, they'll be able to see the Snaefel behind them, and maybe upriver toward Red Mountain, the pass and them other mountains, too. Yep, it's a fine spot for a ranch."

He picked out several likely building sites, his mind painting a picture—a modest, one and a half-story log home, hand-hewn, smoke curling from a rough stone chimney. He imagined jackleg fences, and a two-wheeled track of a road winding up from the Uncompahgre, past the house, to further down the meadow where a barn and loafing shed joined a series of square and rectangular corrals. He saw the shapes of mottled colored cows, so real he could almost hear them bawling, saw their great twisted horns glistening in the sun, dotting the meadow. His mind painted horses tied to the hitching post in front of the home, swishing their tails lazily at flies, the small forms of three children playing. Laundry fluttered in the breeze, hung over a rope strung between tall posts driven in the ground. He saw two women coming from the house, stepping from the covered veranda along its front, lifting their hands above their eyes to shield their view from the sun, their gaze seemingly fixed in his direction. One of the women was short and heavy, her features dark-skinned, the other petite, a red auburn sheen around her face where the sun reflected from her hair.

Zeb took a pull on the cigarette, shaking his head to clear the unexpected vision. *Must still have some of that sage tobacco in my blood.* Taking a deep breath, he looked up toward the box canyon and the three peaks of the Red Mountain, where his main cabin sat, his mind's eye recalling the comforting familiarity of the stock pen and the warm, welcome texture and whispers of the logs. He studied the half cigarette still remaining, grey smoke curling in spirals from its glowing end until caught by the wind. He sighed, "I guess I ain't gonna finish this one neither."

Flicking the half-smoked butt into nearby snow, he straightened in the saddle, looking once at the scene of his vision, and once toward his home on Red Mountain.

"Damn!" he shouted, digging his heels into Buck's flanks. The startled mustang leapt forward in a gallop, saddlebags flapping on his haunches, mules braying in surprise behind them, the grass a blur beneath their pounding hooves.

TO BE CONTINUED...

Coming next, Book Four of the
Threads West, An American Saga Series,
Moccasin Tracks ©2014

THE HOMESTEAD

REUBEN REINED IN LAHN HALF WAY UP THE TIMBERED ridge. To the southwest, the Snaefel poked its line of sharp white peaks into the brilliant, blue belly of the sky. Behind him he could hear the plaintive, muted bawl of the cattle, still a mile distant. Occasionally, a faint hoot and holler of the drivers echoed eerily between the smooth bark of the aspens.

The subdued roar of a creek, guarded by willows and alders, rushed with the last of the melt through the broad meadow tucked under the ridge. Wild irises poked lavender blossoms above the emerald green expanse, while nearly hidden in the almost knee-high grass, the yellow, red and white blossoms of other early wildflowers unfurled. Further below him, the silver serpentine thread of the Uncompahgre River coursed its way north through an ever widening fertile valley framed on all sides by yet more rugged, jagged peaks of the San Juans and the Uncompahgre.

To the south, the valley tapered to a narrow end at the toe of three stately peaks clearly red in color, their flanks embracing the steep faces of El Diente and the Wetterhorn, and another looming cone-shaped peak behind them.

The leaves of the aspens around Reuben fluttered imperceptibly, stirred by a touch of wind, the whisper of their movement bending branches supple with new growth imparting a welcome. The palomino shook his head, whinnying, and Reuben leaned forward, patting the horse's neck. "I feel it too, Lahn. We're home."

CHOICE OF TRAILS

SHE FELT THE WARM PRESS OF HIS CHEST AGAINST HER back, the perfect fit and pressure of his thigh draped over the flare of her hip. The smell of sage and sulfur, of tanned leather and soft smoke, mingled with the scent of their bodies, and of their loving.

A foot scraped the grass just outside the flap of the lodge. Taking his hand from the gentle capture of her breast, he tensed, reaching for his pistol, then relaxed as someone cleared their throat outside the tipi, and a familiar voice filtered through the hide wall. "Don't want to interrupt, but we need to talk. I have a note that was shoved in the flap of my saddle. You need to read it."

SACRIFICE

"THEY SEEN US," HE SHOUTED AT HER. "RIDE HARD FOR them rocks. Follow me!" The ground was a blur, the screams of the Yamparika growing louder behind him, the black stallion and the mustang racing for the cover of the rocks, mountain mahogany and juniper still several hundred yards away.

He glanced quickly back over his left shoulder. She was just steps behind, her mustang's eyes wide and white, its neck stretched out like the stallion's, her small frame low over the pony's withers, the mustang's wild mane brushing her chest, her chalk-white face and wide eyes fixed on the protection toward which they galloped.

Several shots rang out behind them, the bullets kicking up small explosions of dust ahead of their horses. *They'll get a better bead with the next rounds.* He drew the Colt from his belt and extending his right arm rearwards, fired twice. More shots rang out. The mustang screamed and stumbled, trying to keep its footing, then pitched forward, throwing her young rider onto the sandy soil of the creek bottom. *Bad luck.*

Hauling back on the reins, he wheeled the stallion in a spray of sand and dirt. The girl was on her hands and knees, shaking her head, stunned. Leaping from the saddle, he gathered her from the waist, holding her folded in his arm like a rolled blanket.

There was a hiss in the air and his leg buckled. Searing, numbing pain shot up his thigh to his hip, the shaft of the arrow quivering as he tried to keep his feet, its tip protruding from the other side of his leg. "Sono-fabitch!" He cursed in pain and rage, panicking the stallion, which wrenched its head and reared, ripping the reins from his hands.

LEGACY

Eagle Talon tested the blade of the knife with his thumb, then held the weapon at arm's length, cutting edge facing him, centered in front of his eyes, carefully comparing the angle of each honed side of the steel. *A few more draws across the sharpening stone.* His gaze drifted to the tree line of the Little Laramie River, the green leaves tinged with a yellow cast, and here and there a burst of bright yellow in the cottonwoods where a tree limb was dying, its leaves preparing to fall ahead of the rest.

Beyond the tree line to the northwest rose abrupt buttes, and ever higher rolling, grassy hills, gold-brown and dry with the ending of summer stretching endlessly upwards toward the headwaters of the South Fork of the Powder River and the tribe's winter camp. He bent forward, his elbows resting on his knees, the sharpening stone held in one hand above his crossed ankles, the knife in the other.

The pleasant warmth of sun after the morning frost playing on his bare shoulders was intercepted by Walk with Moon's shadow as she walked slowly toward him, her feet oddly spaced, her step slow, her hand on the great roundness of her belly which stretched the leather tight across her hips.

She smiled at him. "It is time, husband. Your son wishes to not miss the season of *canwapegi wi* and to meet his father." The corners of her mouth twitched suddenly, her cheek muscles tightening. She pressed her eyes closed, her body swaying slightly.

Eagle Talon hurriedly cast the knife and sharpening stone to the side, scrambling to his feet, stepping toward her and placing his hands gently but firmly on her shoulders "Walks with Moon? Do you mean, now? Now is the time?"

She smiled up at him, one small hand rising, her palm resting on his cheek. "I wanted to be sure, Eagle Talon. This is my first..."

"Of many," Eagle Talon smiled down at her.

She bit her lip. "That, Eagle Talon, will be decided by *Wankan Tanka*. Now, please go to tell Turtle Dove."

NURSING A GRUDGE

THE THIN, SWARTHY FACED MAN LEERED AT REUBEN, HIS eyes mere slits beneath a filthy, beaded headband, "Ahh...*muchacho con la perla pistola*. We meet again." At his feet the bloody, battered boy raised himself to his hands and knees, blood streaming from his nose and split lips, his face pale, craning his head sideways to look at Reuben and Philippe, one eye swollen shut, his one good eye beseeching.

The outlaw raised a leggin' clad leg, his thigh lifting his leather loincloth and viciously heeled Michael in the back driving his chest back into the dirt. The seven men behind the outlaw, slowly spreading out from one another, laughed.. One was very tall, with a musket. Another had a round face with wild eyes and unruly tow-headed hair spilling from beneath a battered hat. Curling back his lips, he stuck the tip of his tongue, pink and disgusting, in a bulge through the gap in his front teeth.

Reuben felt a seething anger rising in his chest. *Think.* He could sense Philippe's slow side step away from him spacing out their adversary's targets, and without looking knew the vaquero's hands were hovering around the grips of the twin Onyx-handled Colts snugged crosswise in his belt. *Eight to two. Unless they get lucky, we can take them.*

As if reading his mind, the leer on the outlaw's face tormenting Michael twisted with a mocking, vicious curl of his lips. Shadowed by the remnants of the log structures in front of them, more men drifted out. A barrel glinted in a roofless window aperture to their left and above the gathering group of desperados. *Nine, ten... eleven...twelve, thirteen, fourteen. It's a trap!*

"So, you *men*," the desperado leader spat the word contemptuously, "gonna let this poor boy suffer?" He viciously kicked Michael's prostrate form in the side, the young man groaning and coughing, doubled up. Reuben could feel the lethal energy radiating from Philippe twenty feet to his right. *Easy, vaquero, easy...Make a mistake now and all three of us will be dead.* Never fully diverting his attention from their leader, Reuben's eyes swept the band, picking targets, prioritizing the most dangerous first.

"That's right, pistolero," the thin man's voice was sarcastic and taunting, "Fourteen to two." *He doesn't think I've seen the man with the rifle, above.*

"Three." Johannes' calm voice rang out sharply from slightly behind him, twenty feet to his left. Willing his gaze to not slide from the ragged line of killers sixty feet in front of them, from the corner of his eyes Reuben saw the broad muzzle of a weapon swing up and into position. *Mac's shotgun! That'll equalize things a bit.*

"Three?" The bandits shared a menacing chuckle. "A tall blond gimp will make little difference." The swarthy man, never taking his eyes off Reuben, leaned to the side and spit, grinning malevolently. "So your women in the wagons are now alone?"

ZION

RESTING ONE HAND ON THE SHOULDER OF HIS FOUR-year-old son Paul, Joseph wrapped his other arm around his wife's ample shoulders and squeezed. "Roberta, we are truly blessed by the Lord."

His wife beamed up at him from the crook of his arm, her dowdy round face split with a smile, eyes shining, her arms bouncing their two-year-old daughter.

John the Elder walked to them through the group of men, his eyes surveying their first day's work with pride. "We made significant progress. If we could have rounded up more men, I think it would be done," he said, gesturing toward the skeletal structure of a large barn one hundred feet from them, two and one half stories high, its rafters and eaves framed in the traditional Dutch design. *A hawk's wings in a downward curl.*

Through the open studs and behind the fresh, light-colored rough sawed lumber forming the structure, sage and grass covered hills, with pockets of brush turned gold and red, rose from the wide meadow. The toes of the rises dipped in the slow current of the Bear River before escaping their contours and wandering in shallow curves through a wide meadow to the west. Forty miles to the south, the rugged ridges of Porcupine Pass rose abruptly from the floor of Cache Valley, and still further loomed the sharp white peaks of the Wasatch Front.

John stood, his medium build a full foot shorter than Joseph's lanky height, his drooping salt and pepper mustache lifting in a smile. "I'm sorry, brother Joseph. We should have been done today. You're far to the north of Salt Lake, it's a good ways to travel and the men of a number of the outlying farms didn't want to leave their families alone on account of the Ute. We will have the roof and siding up tomorrow, and the loft and doors also."

Smiling, Joseph glanced toward the feast laid out on the long table behind them, "I think everyone's fixated on the food after a long day. We are honored to have you all as our guests." He turned toward the four stocky women who stood behind the table, their hands folded demurely in front of their white aprons, light colored sun bonnets shading their wide smiles. "And thank you, too, ladies, for helping Roberta prepare such a fine supper."

John smiled. "This is your farm, Joseph. Would you lead us in prayer?" The men removed their hats and everyone bowed their heads as Joseph gave thanks to God.

As dictated by tradition, the hosts and their children hung back. They would eat last. Joseph squeezed Roberta to him again, a surreal satisfaction stealing through him as he studied the super structure of the barn. *Before the sun rose today, that was but a patch of grass.* "It's quite something," he whispered, "and makes the place...well...official. Do you ever think about those people from that other wagon train headed to Cherry Creek we met on the trail, right before Fort Kearny?"

She looked up at him, her blue eyes blinking in surprise, her short dark hair bobbing up and down. "How odd you should mention that. Yes, I do, Joseph. Frequently, though I don't know why they made such an impression on me. That very tall blond man with a thick accent that we spoke with seemed to be truly impressed by the reading of the Elders that day. There was something going on between he and that equally tall, pretty young blonde woman. They kept exchanging looks, and he walked away with her, though they were on opposite ends of the congregation during the service. Very strange. And that beautiful, dark-haired slim woman who was with that rugged looking young man with the big brown hat over by the wagon. I don't think they ever stopped talking."

Joseph chuckled. "I watched them, too. I couldn't help but wonder if they were brother and sister, deeply in love, or if they didn't like one another at all."

Roberta giggled. "I looked closely. None of them wore wedding rings. I wonder what has become of them?" she asked, looking up into his face.

EMANCIPATION

THE HOWL OF STRONG GUSTS SWEEPING DOWN VALLEY from the west drowned out the intermittent gurgle of the river. Mountain peaks towered sharp and dark, silhouetted against a star-studded sky that had lost its day glow. The luminescence of the coming moon, silver above the ridge lines, brightened the drifted patches of snow, remnants of the early storm from two days ago.

The medium-height, thin figure of a man, his short curly, salt-and-pepper hair dully reflecting the sheen from the emerging lunar light, turned to the small, heavy set, slightly hunched and shivering female figure on the mule. "Lucy, keep Sally quiet. We didn't walk all this way as freemen to have no trouble now."

He peered intently back upriver to the dim, beckoning glow of oil lamps from a building's windows. Near it glowed a sister light in the shape of an elongated dome. *Looks like the canvas top of a wagon.*

"I'll sure enough keep her quiet, Israel. What do you think we should do? I'm hungry and cold. Do you think it's safe?"

Israel spoke slowly, thinking. "Well, this is the edge of the country. We sure are a long way from Oklahoma. This ain't no plantation and I'm betting all that grows here is hay. You can hear them cattle. It's going to be getting colder soon, and these thin clothes of ours ain't going to be much help with winter coming on. We're about out of food, I lost my last fishhook yesterday and I only got three shells left in that pistol. I don't see as we have much choice. We have to take our chances."

Lucy laid one hand lightly on Israel's forearm. *Her fingers are trembling.* "You're my man, Israel. I'll do what you think."

Looking at the halo of lights a mile or so out, she spoke in a low voice through chattering teeth, a tinge of doubt edged in the hope of her tone, "Maybe folks this far out will be happy to have company."

"Well, let me do the talking, woman. And if there's any sign of trouble, we'll just back our way out of there somehow. Let's tic off the mule before we git too close. They don't have to know we have a critter just yet." He squeezed her arm and smiled grimly at her through the darkness. "One thing I'll tell you, we'll freeze to death and starve before we are slaves again."

The gripping, sizzling reads of the *Threads West, An American Saga* series unfold over the course of five eras:

1854 to 1875—The Maps of Fate Era
Book One, *Threads West, An American Saga*
Book Two, *Maps of Fate*
Book Three, *Uncompaghre—where water turns rocks red*
Book Four, *Moccasin Tracks*
Book Five, *Footsteps*
Book Six, *Blood at Glorieta Pass*
Book Seven, *The Bond*
Book Eight, *Cache Valley*

1875 to 1900—The North to Wyoming Era
This era includes eight other novels

1900 to 1937—The Canyons Era
This era includes seven other novels

1937 to 1980—The Coming Thunder Era
This era includes six other novels

1980 to present—The Summits Era
This era includes six other novels

An American Saga

The _Threads West,_ _An American Saga_ series now Honored with Twenty Five National Awards!

A Sweep of the Major Categories!

THE THREADS WEST SERIES IS THE PROUD RECIPIENT of twenty five national awards as of the date of this printing, including Best Book of the Year award or finalist (runner-up) designations in the categories of Western, Historical Fiction, Romance, West/Mountain Regional Fiction and Design! Thank you readers, and USA Book Review Awards, Next Generation Indies Awards, Independent Book Publishers Association-IBPA, Forward National Literature Awards, International Book Awards, and Independent Publisher Book Awards (IPPYs).

Winner

- (BEST) Western 2014 and 2015 (International Book Awards)
- (BEST) Historical Fiction 2014 (eLite Awards)
- (BEST) Western 2010 and 2012 (USA Book News Awards)
- (BEST) Romance 2011 (Next Generation Indies Awards)
- (BEST) Historical Fiction 2011 (IBPA- Ben Franklin Awards)
- (BEST) Design 2011 (IBPA- Ben Franklin Awards)

Silver Medalist

- (BEST) Historical Fiction 2013 (IBPA-Ben Franklin Awards)
- (BEST) Regional Fiction 2012 West/Mountains (IPPYs)

Finalist

- Multicultural 2015 (Next Generation Indies Book Awards)
- Western 2014 (International Book Awards)
- Multicultural 2014 (USA Book News Awards) (Uncompahgre)
- Multicultural 2014 (USA Book News Awards) (Maps of Fate)
- Romance 2014 and 2010 (USA Book News Awards)
- Historical 2014, 2013, 2012 (USA Book News Awards)
- Historical Fiction 2013 (IBPA- Ben Franklin Awards)
- Romance 2011 (Forward National Literature Awards)
- Romance 2014 and 2011 (International Book Awards)
- Best Overall Design 2013 (Next Generation Indies Awards)
- Best Cover Design 2011 (Next Generation Indies Awards)

Be part of the Threads West Stampede!

Hop on board the Threads West Express! The adventure and romance of America, her people, her spirit and the West is comin' down the tracks at ya! Keep your ear to the rail for upcoming specials, excerpts, videos and announcements *only* for Threads West Express members!

Sign up to receive insider information, updates and contests at:

www.ThreadsWestSeries.com

Follow the conversation and participate
in the games and promotions at:

www.facebook.com/ThreadsWest

Have questions or comments about the series? Contact us at:

ThreadsWest.Media@gmail.com

Shop the Threads West Express!
www.ThreadsWestExpress.com

As a thank you for buying this book and being a part of the Threads West Stampede, we invite you to join the Threads West Express team. Send us your comments/feedback and receive discount coupons that can be used at the Threads West Express store!

Canvas Tote Bag

Limited Edition Prints

**Photos of
Threads West Country**